THE
ΛSTONISHING

the Northern Highlands

the Cave N

Withered Hills

Perpetual • View

the North River

Silver Head Mountains

North Division Road

Fort Truth

• Stone Bridge Hollow

the Black Plains

Little Eagle Way

YORKELAND

Common Highway

Golden Hill Place

Empress Alley

• Flat Rock

Crooked Lake

• Sandy Creek

• Bullhead Corners

BORDERLAND

• Totenville

Lower Yorke Bay

North Point

Widow's
Peak

Lake of the Clouds

The Grand Highway

Majestic
Falls

Horseshoe Break

ANGLYA

Eastgate

Wick's
Grove

The Great
Valley

Idlehaven

The Great Road

Mons Hotax River

The Green Road

Great Northern Sound

The North Light

Fountain
Brooke

Ravenskill

The Barrens

Whisper
Point

The Vast North Sea

ENDLESS ISLELAND

Heaven's Gate

Pig's Hollow

Gravesend Hole

The South
Light

VICTORY
ISLELAND

Hell's
Gateway

Yorke Bay

A New Map of

G.N.E.A.

The Great Northern

Empire of the

Americas

PUBLISHED BY
J.E. STANHOPE & CO.

NEW PAVONYA

ALSO BY PETER ORULLIAN

The Unremembered
Trial of Intentions
The Sound of Broken Absolutes
The Vault of Heaven – Story Volume One
Beats of Seven
At the Manger

(Forthcoming collaboration with Brandon Sanderson)
(Forthcoming – *Wired for Madness* with Jordan Rudess)

THE ASTONISHING

PETER ORULLIAN

BASED ON THE ORIGINAL STORY BY
JOHN PETRUCCI

dp

descant publishing

ISBN: 978-1-7338105-1-7

Printed in the United States of America

Dust jacket illustration by Aurélien Rantet.

Dust jacket design by STK·Kreations.

Map by Sean Mosher-Smith.

Published by Descant Publishing
PO Box 13017
Mill Creek, WA 98082
www.Orullian.com

CONTENTS

NOTE

—◦—

JOHN PETRUCCI

I n the months before the release of our self-titled album, I was in London doing some press engagements for the record. In my hotel room, I got hit with this idea that would later become, "A Life Left Behind." I came up with the verse, chords, and melody, and sang it into my iPhone. I remember thinking, *This has the vibe of a concept album.* And that was the spark.

I realized the first thing I needed to do was write a story that we could base everything on. I didn't want it to be haphazard. I didn't want it to be loose. I wanted to have a specific foundation of a story.

We were headed out on tour soon, so I began framing the story in a mobile way, making notes as to what I wanted the story to be about. I'd jot something down on paper, or capture thoughts on my phone. Sometimes it was bullet points answering questions like: What's the focus? What's the main theme of the story? I began jotting down character names and other details that came to me in stream-of-consciousness sessions that occurred in the lounge of the tour bus or in the dressing room or at home on a break while I was driving somewhere. It was on my mind now. Things I was hearing and seeing in my life were informing it all.

Finally, I realized I needed to sit down and write the story. So, I sat at my laptop and wrote the title, and then started typing. I did dozens of revisions until I got it to a point that I felt like it was presentable to the guys. I bounced a lot of things off my wife Rena, who's creative and a great sounding board. I tried to be disciplined about it, which meant I did the writing anywhere I could: airplanes, buses, you name it.

As I was putting the proposal together to show the band, I knew it was ambitious and would ask a lot of them, as well as of the fans and record label. It would be expensive and involved. But I had a certain fire to see it all through. Because of that, most of the critical decisions were made up front. I wanted it to be a show with two acts in presentation. I wanted it to be a double CD of two hours of music. I wanted to use a real orchestra, real choir, real piano, etc. I wanted to do a novel, a game, a Broadway show, and more. All of this was part of a fairly comprehensive outline I showed the guys once I had it all laid out.

There were question marks like, "Should we have guest vocalists?" That came later once we started having real discussions about the record. But a lot of the plan was laid out well in advance, even down to Jordan and me getting together in the privacy of our houses, just piano and guitar, to really hash out the themes, etc. I'd tried to think it all through ahead of time.

And while it presented a challenge to bring it all together, it's been a satisfying journey to see it through.

That journey began in earnest right after the tour of the self-titled album. We knew *The Astonishing* was going to take a long time to create. So, rather than taking any real down time, Jordan and I began getting together almost immediately. We spent a few days a week in each other's homes, developing iPhone recordings and song-seeds into more fleshed out musical ideas, recording them into software for a few months.

But at some point, working out of our homes wasn't conducive to the process. So, we continued writing the score to the story in the studio with our engineer, Rich. And we did that for a few months more. But while we were writing it, we were actually doing pre-production with a click-track and mapping out all the sections. So, by the time we were done, and as we sent it to the guys, they had mature guides and demos to work with as they approached their parts. Then, one at a time, the guys came in to record the drums, and bass, etc.

The whole time we were sending these recordings to David Campbell, who was in California, so he could come up with the arrangements, which he then recorded in Prague and L.A. We recorded real piano, a Steinway Grand, and Hammond B3 at a separate studio. It was a huge project to manage. And the mix process was involved.

So, procedurally, it was different from most of our other albums, since the whole band didn't move into the studio and record together all at once. And it took months and months to accomplish.

Obviously, now the album is done and we've toured extensively to support it. We released a game. And the novel has become a reality. Longer term, I'm still hopeful of seeing it as a live production, whether on Broadway or off-Broadway or as a one-off. I look at it as an evolving thing. And I'd love to see the various characters presented in that way.

As much as the characters, though—and maybe more—what I'm passionate about with *The Astonishing* from a story perspective is the theme, which for me has two parts. With music as a center-point, there's this idea that not only music itself, but the act of creating music is so essential to who we are as people, and that the absence of music or the ability to create music would create chaos in the world, dystopia on a mass level. That was a powerful concept that I was writing and creating the story and characters around.

The second piece is the whole technology idea, which is where the scifi comes in. But it's really based on what's happening now, where so many things and jobs and actions that people used to do are being replaced by machines and automation. It makes you wonder how far is that going to go? Are we going to get to the point that even the creative arts are no longer done by people. I've seen these insane videos of machines playing guitars and drums, etc. Does it get to a point that they do it so much better than a person ever could that people just throw their hands up and say, "Screw it, I'll do something else?" Is it like self-driving cars, where people ask why would I do it myself? Can creative arts be put into that same box?

My contention is that even if machines can do it better, humans need not just to hear music but create it. Creating is essential. It not only helps us express our humanity, it's part of how we *are* human.

So, I'd say the concept of the story and those two ideas were maybe bigger at the onset than writing around the characters. But the characters grew and helped me land the themes of the story, and do so that much more here in the novel.

The Astonishing has been a meaningful journey for me. Everything from the process of such a large project, to the story themes, to the music, to the unique performance approach we took, it's been a rewarding experience. I'm grateful to everyone who's been a part of it.

And I'm excited to be able to share part of that initial vision with you in this novel. It's going to take what you know and like about *The Astonishing* a little bit further. I couldn't be happier with how it's turned out. I hope you love what Peter's done with the story as much as I do.

Enjoy!

John Petrucci
Winter 2017

NOTE

———◉———

PETER ORULLIAN

T elling stories about music isn't new to me. It's the perfect meld of my two greatest passions: stories and music. In fact, my fantasy series—The Vault of Heaven from Tor Books—is precisely that, with a music magic system centered on music principles. So, when it turned out that Dream Theater's concept album, *The Astonishing*, was about music, it seemed a natural fit for me as a writer.

But perhaps some deeper context is important. I'd moved to Seattle to study with famed vocal instructor David Kyle, who trained the likes of Geoff Tate, Ann Wilson, and Layne Staley. During that time, I worked for Xbox, which provided an important touch-point for me with DT. I was doing some promotional work, and flew to NY to conduct an event with the band. I'd met them once or twice at after-parties when they were on tour. But this was a whole day hanging out, and then a whole evening at dinner. Good times.

It formed enough of a relationship that when *The Astonishing* was announced, I was able to shoot some of the guys a note suggesting a novelization. Turns out John already had that in mind. And truth be told, he had his pick of authors to write it. In fact, I know several who wanted the gig. But because I had an email address I was likely among the first to send a proposal.

Not long after, John and I had an extended phone conversation in which he shared deeply about the record. I, in turn, shared with him my writing and music background. Once I'd understood more about the core concept, I felt it was important for John to know that I had working knowledge not just of narrative structure, but voice and vocal performance, as I'd trained and been on tour with metal bands. My belief was that it would help me write with an authenticity that would be hard to find elsewhere.

John, though, is a smart and patient cat. He essentially had me audition. He wanted a sample chapter. I asked him which song or scene, since he'd forwarded me the album in advance of its release. He chose "A Savior in the Square." So, I took a bit of time, wrote it up, and sent it to him.

The short story is: He liked it.

The longer story is that, meanwhile, James Labrie had dug into all my other books and short fiction and was delivering John the "book reports." Turns out James loved my work, and gave it the thumbs up to John.

It's probably also important to note that I'm a DT fan. I care about this project. Some writers dream of getting to novelize Star Wars or Star Trek. Both would be awesome, for sure. But getting to collaborate with DT, for me, beat all other collaborative scenarios.

It eventuated in eight or ten very long phone calls with John while he was on tour. We crawled through all his notes. I asked a thousand questions. I pitched new ideas on the fly. And we both got those goose bumps you get when something feels right and excites your imagination.

After that, I set to helping shepherd the book to the right publisher for this edition—a beautiful, comprehensive artifact that core DT fans could collect and treasure. I wanted there to be something that carried a bit of import to it.

Once we landed the publisher, I started to write in earnest. John had given me complete creative license to expand on the core narrative. And I did just that. New characters. Subplots. Backstory. World expansion and world building. In the process, I borrowed some of the more appropriate ideas from my other novels where music plays a role of magical influence. They were perfectly suited to how I envisioned Gabriel's gift working. And then I took that further in this more post-apocalyptic, dystopian setting. I won't lie: It was fun as hell!

There were also elements of the album I recognized where John—with a limited number of words and a more audio-visual depiction—had used some shorthand in his storytelling, and had, of necessity, left things out. My advantage with the novel is that I had more room to grow and explain and get inside the characters' heads. And that's what I've done.

Having worked for Microsoft, I'm a technology fan—an early adopter in many regards. But I'm also painfully aware of the degree to which it can place distance between us and humanity. And when you couple that with a conceit that suggests technology replace music and music creation…let's just say the theme struck a chord with me. Corporations work hard to try and leverage music in their campaigns, because they know there are few if any passion points stronger than music. And they mostly fail, because music is so intensely personal. That's part of its beauty. It's why I personally dislike music distribution models that use gatekeepers or tastemakers to influence what music we should get to hear and enjoy. I'll step down off my soapbox now.

Suffice it to say that I enjoyed exploring the theme John had set forth. I think it's an important topic, as well as one that, hopefully, set the groundwork for a ripping good yarn.

I was honored to be a part of this project. I thank John for trusting me with something he cares so much about. And to Jordan and James and John and Mike, who gave me their time, too, with thoughtful conversation and responses to my inquiries. It's a unique group of musicians, as I'm sure you'd agree.

With that, have at it! I very humbly hope you enjoy the book.

Peter Orullian
Winter 2017

FOREWORD

—○—

DAVID CAMPBELL

First, it was an exciting and then, a daunting invitation. Dream Theater had just reached out to me to help them arrange the music for their momentous album, *The Astonishing*. It was exciting to think about working with a band with the awesome artistry and virtuosity of Dream Theater, but it was daunting, due to the magnitude of the project and the amount of work it would require to pull it off. We would produce more than two hours of seriously substantial music, in great quantities, employing big forces: a symphony orchestra, a large choir, various folk-related ensembles, etc. It would become the most extensive band project on my resume.

Once I dug into the project, I found it interesting to compare it with earlier masterworks and artistic styles of past eras.

The Astonishing follows the tradition of grand opera, particularly Wagner's dramatic stories, like *Götterdämmerung*, a dark, cataclysmic tale. These works from the 19th century utilized a large orchestra, a robust opera chorus and some new specialty instruments that were invented at the time, in order to make a louder impact, lower lows, more heroic fanfares. Wagner was trying to overwhelm the audience with sonic power, before the arrival of contemporary rock technology like electric guitar, deep bass, and elaborate rock drum kits. Some musicians would say that Wagner's operatic spectacles were the precursors of metal music, progressive rock and dense electronica.

In that same 19th century era, composers wrote "Tone Poems"—music based on literary works. It was large orchestral music that inspired the listener to imagine scenes, stories and characters, using the orchestra to tell the story without narration. A notable example: Richard Strauss wrote *Thus Spoke Zarathustra*, based on a novel by Nietzche, again taking place in a dark world of philosophic struggle, involving an Übermensch—a super-human character. This piece of music is one you will surely recognize if you watch the "Dawn of Man" opening of Kubrick's *2001: A Space Odyssey*.

A little earlier, Franz Liszt wrote numerous big orchestral pieces inspired by literary work written by Dante, or based on dark dramas like *Faust* or *Hamlet*.

The music of *The Astonishing* developed from John Petrucci's fully conceived story idea, in similar fashion to those 19th century works. The story of *The Astonishing*, set in a totalitarian society that made humanly created music a relic of the past, is right in line with those earlier tales of epic consequences and philosophic struggles. While one might think that a society without humans making music is unlikely, we've had examples in fairly recent history of music being forcibly removed from daily life. For instance, earlier this century, the Taliban in Afghanistan banned the use of music except for ceremonial drum dirges. And in the 20th century, China endured the "Cultural Revolution", which viewed the act of listening to Western music or owning instruments such as the classical violin as a criminal activity. Ironically, now that the "Cultural Revolution" is long gone, where do you find the greatest number of classical music students? In China. (Reportedly, at least one million Chinese children are learning classical violin, and playing Mozart, Beethoven, and other Western composers.)

Clearly, the concepts of banning music in society, and then the redemption and re-embracing of music after governmental policy is changed, are not as fictional as one might assume.

Today, one could argue that there is a variation developing on this theme. Music is more prevalent and accessible than ever, but fewer people are willing to pay for it, or even understand that it is a product of hard working professionals. Something so constant in people's lives—music—has lowered in monetary value to the point where some musicians, just like Gabriel, the hero of *The Astonishing*, might find no viable profession in music while living in such a cultural climate. Theoretically, the music making and composing in our current culture could die out if the musicians can no longer feed themselves via creating music. It's an ironic twist that could foreshadow a future along the lines of *The Astonishing*.

The idea of elaborate, allegoric tales re-imagined on rock albums has a substantial tradition as well. For instance, Rush envisioned a future society on *2112,* and years later released a novelized version of their 2012 album *Clockwork Angels.*

Some might call *The Astonishing* a musical, but due to its big philosophic concepts, fabled story line, and hefty orchestral/choral backdrop, it rides confidently on the road paved by Wagner, Liszt, Rush and other epic musical storytellers.

It was an unforgettable experience to be part of the production of *The Astonishing.* Some days, while racing with time to pull off this elaborate and challenging project, I humorously thought about how much drive and speed was mustered by the heroes in those other literary works, and how that heroism inspired composers to create the thrilling music that followed. Dream Theater was certainly inspired in a similar way, by their own original storyline.

— David Campbell, Los Angeles, Fall 2017

THE
ΛSTONISHING

BY
PETER ORULLIAN

BASED ON THE ORIGINAL STORY BY
JOHN PETRUCCI

PROLOGUE

---○---

YEAR 2277

The sun came down heavy. The air smelled of dry grass. Most days, there'd be a southeast wind brushing the blades together to form whispers only the wind and grass could understand. But along this long road that traveled out of the Borderland, the very edge of the Great Northern Empire, Gabriel waited in silence. A rare silence. Not because of heavy sun or dry grass or vacant winds. The silence was rare because neither his own songs nor those of the Empire's noise machines—the people called them NOMACS—disturbed the stillness. Beside him on the migrant road his brother, Arhys, waited, staring down the highway with a furrowed brow. A contingent of Arhys' militia watched with him. An escort of sorts. And in the moments after dawn, the sound of slumping steps rose in the distance.

The slow footfalls were music of a kind. A tired drone. Traveling field workers returning from spring harvests in the South Republic, where they slaved as loaned labor from the emperor. It pricked his conscience that the people of Ravenskill, people like these walking home again, paid him, and Arhys, and all the militia fighters for their service. What little they could keep for their work didn't go far, but they portioned out some to keep the Ravenskill militia going.

"Do you see her?" Arhys asked soft as a whisper. Though his voice wasn't good at it.

Someone else might not have heard the deep strain in his brother's voice. Gabriel did. Maybe because it was his brother. Maybe because he had a sense of people. The sound of them.

"She'll be here," Gabriel assured. "Evangeline is stubborn. She married you, didn't she?"

An old joke. But still good for half a smile.

The first of the Empire's field laborers stopped at a rusted gate, where transport soldiers from the South Republic handed readmission documents to G.N.E. border guards. Routine exchange. But the enemy fighters still eyed each other with suspicion as each laborer was examined for damage and counted.

"They treat them like cattle," Arhys spoke low and through his teeth. "But not much longer."

"This isn't the time." Gabriel placed a hand on his brother's shoulder. "They're threshers and pickers. Machine drivers. Too weak to fight. The South will have walked them miles to bring them back just strong enough to pass—"

Gabriel stopped, knowing his brother's wife should be among the hundreds being checked back into the Empire's populace logs.

"And they'll undercount by one," Arhys said cryptically.

But Gabriel understood. "Evangeline is strong," he said. "Your child will be fine."

"She shouldn't have gone. I shouldn't have let her go." Arhys started toward the gate.

Soldiers on each side of the entry raised pulse rifles toward Arhys, who'd worn field clothes today. His militia uniform would have gotten him shot on sight.

Gabriel grabbed his brother's arm, pulling him to an abrupt stop. "Just where do you think Evangeline is in that line? Think about it."

Arhys looked down the impossibly long queue of field-hands. "She'll be last. She'll make sure the rest pass through before her."

"So relax." Gabriel gave his brother's arm a shake, then let go. "Let's not get shot before she even gets here."

"You afraid of getting shot, little brother?"

Another old joke. Good for a full smile, though. "You're God damn right."

So, they stood as the sun strengthened behind them. A mild breeze finally did kick up, sweeping the knee-high grasses along the road. It was the kind of day that would otherwise make you forget about human tariffs. Forget about the collapse of what they once called a constitutional government. People voting. What, two hundred years gone by? Now there were a dozen smaller Americas. Each with visions of their own. All fighting one another. Except when they had to share essentials.

Like human labor. Things machines couldn't do for them.

"Oh God," Arhys whispered.

Gabriel looked around fast. Evangeline was indeed last, and being helped by an older woman. She was emaciated. Frail. Sweat stood out on her dark skin. And she was gripping her belly down low. *Where the baby would be.*

And still, when she caught Arhys' eyes, her face brightened a touch. She waved.

Arhys started forward fast, moving to intercept her at the gate.

"Stand back!" a border guard commanded.

Arhys didn't seem to hear him. Or ignored the command.

A half second later, the guard focused his aim on Arhys and fired. A deep pulse pushed fast through the space between them, dropping Arhys to the ground. His body folded, his muscles flexing, constricting. His face pulled into a rictus of pain.

Gabriel got fast to his brother's side. "Breathe through it. Relax your back."

The pulse shivered across Arhys' skin, raising it in painful-looking bumps.

Mutters erupted from the line of field workers. They all knew Arhys. He'd stood to defend many of them. And a few began to mill nervously, angrily.

Gabriel held up a hand toward them. "We're fine. Let's just finish the transfer." He shared a look with Evangeline. *He's all right.*

But she didn't look good, herself. How long had she been walking in such obvious pain. The child wasn't due for six weeks.

Arhys grabbed Gabriel's shirt, twisting it in his fist. "Sooner or later you're going to have to do it."

This was old, too. More argument than amusement, though. Arhys meant Gabriel's sense of people. Their sound. He had an understanding of music as a *human* expression. So different from than machines of the Empire. And he'd seen it move people. Change them. Arhys thought it a gift. A weapon. Something the Empire couldn't control. Gabriel wasn't so sure. Sometimes it felt just like another yolk. Not too different from the kind the slave laborers wore—an expectation you couldn't escape or understand.

Evangeline had just passed through the gate, when a new droning filled the air. Far away at first, but approaching fast. Moments later, three NOMACs appeared over the eastern hills. They were spherical, fitted with multiple lenses, armed with discharge arrays, and possessed of acoustic amplifiers that could throw sound in broad patterns or tightly focused bursts. They also acted as a communication net—roving signal transponders that connected to the Empire's data space—perhaps the Empire's greatest asset and weapon.

The machines swept down toward the crowd, one briefly blocking the sun as it came to hover directly over them.

Another NOMAC disappeared to the south—precautionary surveil-lance—sometimes the Southern Republic took back labor after it was checked in. The census accounts would appear correct, but field hands would be diverted back to Southern Republic tobacco and corn crops.

The third NOMAC began a broad loop around the entire valley—a video feed for the Empire's remote combat team. Mostly a waste. The Empire would sacrifice field hands before deploying a fully trained contingent. Resource management was a science of precarious balances.

The southern soldiers started to withdraw.

"Hold tight," said an imperial guard. "Just until we scan 'em through."

A shrill pitch erupted in the valley. It came almost inaudibly high. But it bit at the back of Gabriel's head, like an ice pick pushing up into his cranium.

The others didn't seem to hear it. Not in the same way, anyhow. Gabriel tried to block it out, shoving his palms against his ears. But it was no use. The sound moved along a spectrum beyond simple audio. Or in addition to it.

And he sensed what it was for. It sought the *signatures* inside them all. Validating them as surely as a fingerprint would. Only more *authentically*. It resonated down inside them, identifying them uniquely, making the accounting complete in a way paper and road tattoo permits never could.

This was new.

And it hurt like every last hell. Like a scouring sand wind-whipped against the skin. Only inside.

Then it was gone. The note abruptly ceased, echoing down the road in thin receding waves. And behind it, a smaller sound. A weak cry as knees met the road, and Evangeline collapsed.

Arhys forced himself to his feet, fighting the convulsions still wracking his body. The NOMACS took no interest, coming to form a line fifty feet above them at the borderline, slowly rotating.

The old woman who'd been supporting Evangeline was at her side, propping her head with a rolled up woolen jacket. "The child's coming."

"It's too soon!" Arhys argued, taking Gabriel's hand for support.

Gabriel helped his brother to Evangeline's side. She stared up at them over gaunt cheeks. "Not how I pictured it," she said with a weak smile.

"It'll make a good story," Arhys replied. "Now, save your strength."

She nodded, while the people of Ravenskill—laborer and militia—formed a broad circle around her, turning their backs to give them privacy.

Gabriel noted the soft hum of the NOMACs above. When they weren't issuing their dissonant songs or blaring notes, the soft hum was almost musical. Almost.

Over the next four hours, Evangeline struggled. Her body was weak. And there wasn't much comfort or refreshment for her labor.

Arhys held her hand throughout, speaking softly to her. Encouraging her. Loving her the only way a man can when he's mostly useless and worried and proud. And finally the child came. Its feeble cry fell flat against the whir of the NOMACs. The flying machines, as though completing a witness of the birth, then flew off to the northeast again, leaving the road in a heavy silence.

One of Arhys' men removed his shirt and handed it to the old woman, who wrapped the child and gently placed him in his mother's arms.

"Xander," she said softly, giving the child a name. Her eyelids dropped, closed, and she sighed with exhaustion.

"Evangeline?" Arhys stroked her cheek with his rough fingertips.

She tried a smile to answer. It trembled on her lips.

Gabriel had seen this too many times. How in God's name could this happen? With the technology to make machines fly, and communicate over long distances, and look into the body of a man to know him. How did childbirth put a woman in such mortal danger?

The simple answer was that some had access to the keys of the kingdom. Others did not.

Arhys locked Evangeline with his serious gaze. "Xander won't live like us. He'll be safe. And he'll have opportunities ... he'll be free."

She might have smiled. It was such a slight thing, it was hard to tell. Then her breathing slowed. Her arms fell loose around the child. She never did look up again at Arhys before breathing her last.

The old woman retrieved the child as Arhys looked down at his dead wife. "No, Evangeline." He shook his head. "No."

There was dogged determination in his voice. He was willing her back to life. Defying her death. The anger of grief and desperation of loneliness filled his words. Arhys would battle this thing. He'd fight her death for her. And God be damned!

But she was gone.

And none of his determination or love could change it.

Men and women alike wept as they stood in the circle. It wasn't the first time one among them had died giving life. And their cries suggested it wouldn't be the last.

Gabriel listened to it all, hanging his own head at the loss of one who'd always made him feel welcome. Evangeline. She'd never asked anything of him. She'd always set a place for him at supper, insisting on his presence. She'd listened to his songs and found meanings in them he hadn't been able to see for himself. She'd had that special kind of sight.

"Take it back," Arhys said, hard and low.

Gabriel looked up. "Arhys?"

"Take back her life, Gabriel." Arhys' eyes were uncompromising and imploring. "With your song. I've seen you move people. Stir them. There's something in your music. You can change this." He paused a long moment. "I'm begging you."

Gabriel shook his head, not to deny his brother, but at the incredible request. "It doesn't work like that," he said. "I'm not—"

"Will you try?" Arhys pressed.

Gabriel stared into his brother's grief-stricken face. There was a hollowness opening up in the man. A loss.

Yes, Gabriel had stirred a thing or two. He'd been studying deep history and apocryphal writings of music theory. But giving life back to one who's passed? That was a God's power. He was just …

He looked again into his brother's eyes. "I'll try."

Gabriel could never have anticipated the faith and trust Arhys had in Gabriel's song, but the relief that filled his brother's eyes told it clearly enough. He gently took his child from Evangeline's arms and sat back to give Gabriel room.

Turning his attention to Evangeline, Gabriel took her hand, and began to feel for the sound of her. It had always been an easy thing with Evangeline. Hope lived inside her as natural and necessary as breathing. Where others had given into despair, Evangeline didn't even need to think about fighting hopelessness. It had no hooks in her.

But like the early morning grass, her sound had gone dry. Still.

He'd thought he could take hold of that hope and brighten it, as you do when fanning an ember to make it bright and hot again.

But he had nothing to latch on to.

So, he came at it differently. He invoked memory after memory of Evangeline: The day she teased Arhys from his serious face to full-out laughter—there were many of those; her quiet feet on the floor as she left early, before any were awake, to tend to the sick and dying at the makeshift hospice at Gravesend Hole; the simple encouragement he'd heard her whisper to a ten-year-old James Kelvin, when the boy was rejected by his first love.

She had a way of helping people to their best self. To see the finest they had to offer.

And Gabriel had read in an old book once that memory had energy. So, maybe if he could capture the sound of her through her countless acts of kindness, he could give it a voice and somehow sing life back inside her.

It was an outlandish thought. But the way his songs often worked was ... outlandish. It didn't make sense, really. He couldn't explain it. There was a gentle power in it. Arhys thought it could be more than gentle. And Gabriel had tried to understand how. Read anything he could find in a time when so much information had been lost to wars that often focused on destroying data and technology and infrastructure. Books were like precious metal. Education and understanding were hard won. If available at all.

Gathering everything he could summon of who she had been, he sang a long quiet tone. He voiced it in a deeper register, like a bow drawn over an unfingered cello string. It had an inviting quality, patient. And he did what he could to have it touch some inside part of her.

But he could feel nothing resonating. Nothing that *heard* his note, responded to it.

Gabriel began oscillations. Moving slowly up in pitch, following a melodic instinct that kept Evangeline at the center of his song. He sang no half-tones. He avoided sharp turns and staccato stops and barking rhythms. If hope still resided inside her mortal frame, he meant to call it forth with a similar long-suffering beauty.

He sang for several minutes. Or that's what it felt like. No one spoke. No shuffling feet. Only the occasional gust of warm morning wind lifting the smell of fallow dirt and dry grass.

It was Arhys who broke the silence. "You can't conquer death with supplication."

Gabriel shot his brother a hot look. He had no idea what he was doing, and he damn sure knew Arhys hadn't a clue about it.

But Arhys' eyes never wavered. He might not have a gift of song, but he'd stared down death more times than any man should ever have to. His Ravenskill militia had always been badly outfitted. Men and women died defending an ideal. And they died often.

He was not a gentle man. Not by nature. But his hard stare might be right this time.

Gabriel thought he could feel Evangeline's skin cooling beneath his fingers. If time were a factor, he needed to hurry. He squeezed her lifeless hand, and sat forward, his face now above hers. So peaceful. And was she wearing a slight smile, even now?

He let the question go, and took a lungful of air. Then he changed the images in his mind. He imagined all the dead Evangeline so thoughtfully prepared for burial in the aftermath of a militia battle. She'd always done so with reverence. With an unspoken belief that their stillness wasn't final, but a transition to the next part of life. But there was still loss in these images. Children left fatherless, motherless. And it was this that gave Gabriel's song its bite.

The initial deep sonorant note rose fast and full, both in pitch and volume. The song landed in violent stabs, commands to live. It still bore a melody, but now the vehicle for the song was a loud galloping insistence.

And none of it was planned. No part inspired by other songs.

There was power in it, too. Gabriel could feel it. It surged inside him. Made his skin run hot and chill. He didn't know to what end the power worked, but it was there. Unbridled. Important. Filled with grief and hope and worry.

It struck him indelicate, even as he sang it. So loud and so close to her face, and yet the entire valley filled with the sound of it. Did grass shiver at its touch? Did he feel that? Or imagine it?

And still, Evangeline did not stir.

Gabriel resisted the urge to look at his brother. Instead, he redoubled his efforts, weaving Evangeline's name into the raw sound, since names have their own kind of power. Old stories told of clay brought to life by the introduction of a name.

In the end, he was unleashing a barely controlled barrage of her name, willing her to live.

Sweat dripped from his nose and cheeks onto her face. There was a pressure building inside him from the expense of singing this way. Though he knew not exactly what he was doing, or what that cost might be.

Sometime later, her cheeks wet but still cool, he stopped.

The silence that followed was more deafening by far than mere death. Death has its own silent song. Gabriel had heard it all too often. But this was different. This was the silence that followed a storm of noise that carried hope for the escape of death. The weight of it was crushing since the sudden stillness and absence of sound were a kind of final epitaph. Failure.

Gabriel's attempt to revive Evangeline with his song had failed.

He'd failed his brother.

He'd failed all those who had, like Arhys, harbored hope that one day Gabriel's song would show a new kind of power. One that would help them end the tyranny of the emperor.

He'd certainly failed himself. It was his song. He should better understand it. Better know how to apply it.

But most of all, he'd failed Evangeline, and the child that now came into the world motherless.

Involuntarily shaking his head no, he whispered, "I'm so sorry, Eva. I ..."

No one spoke or moved for another long while. Then some slowly moved toward Ravenskill and home. One woman came and took Xander from his father's arms, knowing he'd need them for other uses.

Alone now with Arhys and his dead wife, Gabriel finally met his brother's eyes again. Not hard anger anymore. Disappointment. The start of long heartache. And bitterness. Gabriel wasn't sure how he saw that, but it was there. It was the kind of inevitability that leads men to lives of quiet desperation.

Arhys then tenderly picked up his wife's body and began the long walk home, leaving Gabriel alone in the midst of the vast clearing at the edge of the Borderlands.

His brother was nearly out of sight when another sound came up from inside Gabriel, unbidden. There are few things worse to see in the face of someone you love than disappointment. It may be worst of all.

Save for the special sadness reserved for those who disappoint themselves. That was this sound.

It erupted from Gabriel into the bright hot morning. It laid the dry grass down. It cracked the earth as if parched by seasons in the sun.

The sound echoed up and out in long reverberating waves. The throb of it traveled the road and valley like a wall of sobbing sound. In the wake of it, more silence came. More stillness.

When Gabriel was himself enough again to see anything more than the blind grief inside him, through watery eyes he thought he saw Arhys at the farthest point in the road before it turned east, taking note of Gabriel and his shivering song.

Then his brother turned, and carried his dead wife away, leaving Gabriel alone.

CHAPTER 1

—◉—

YEAR 2285

C hill morning air hung like a shroud in the hills below Window's Peak. The mountains behind Arhys and his militia—good men and women from Ravenskill—still held snow. The rising rock and cold made it a good defensive position from which to stage an attack on the convoy. A sizeable shipment of food and other goods were being transported overland from Eastgate to the Emperor's Palace by way of the Grand Highway. Arhys planned to intercept it.

The mission had two objectives. First, it would provide for the fundamental needs of most of Endless Isleland. Such was the opulence of Emperor Nafaryus, that a convoy destined for one man and his palace could sustain a handful of cities. The second objective was a happy consequence. Seizing the goods meant the emperor wouldn't have them. The idea of depriving Nafaryus of anything got Arhys as close to a smile as he was bound to get these days.

A runner sped into camp, his feet light on the cold ground. "Commander, the convoy is thirty minutes away."

Arhys nodded grimly—which often served as enough of a salute for him. Then he stood. He'd been awake, fully dressed and armed, for hours, though the sun wouldn't touch the sky for a while yet. But these were good hours. His hours. He liked to sit in the dark cold before leading his militia to fight. He would remember old promises, and he'd rehearse words he'd speak to the families of men and women who would die before the day was through.

The price of freedom.

Not something he said or took lightly. And it came with a weight, like a yolk formed of heavy stone. Still, he'd grown used to bearing it. Harder to do without Evangeline to lighten the load. But he'd spent enough time with ghosts this morning. He had to get his people ready to fight.

He started as he always did, he went to wake Gabriel. He found his brother already awake, sitting in front of a cold fire. Orders had been to eat a cold breakfast—no risk of signaling the convoy of militia presence.

But Gabriel wasn't eating. He simply stared into the ashes.

"If I was a man of letters, I'd have a metaphor about ashes to share," Arhys said. "But you're the reader, not me."

Gabriel didn't reply. He didn't even look up. A tense silence stretched between them. Finally, his brother spoke, his voice low and even, with maybe a hint of shame. "I can't do it, Arhys. Not yet, anyway. You ask every time. And I try … I'm closer to understanding how the music works. But I'm not sure, even then, how I'll make a weapon of it."

Arhys sat opposite Gabriel. "It'll come. Just keep trying." He paused, thinking how to inspire his brother. "We'll keep fighting, Gabriel. With or without you. But eventually, for us to win? For us to put down the emperor? We need you. We need your song, like the way you cracked the ground when Evangeline …"

Gabriel finally looked up at him, searching his face. "That's what I'm telling you. I don't know what happened there. I was just … grieving."

Grief was something Arhys understood. So, he let that lie a moment before pushing. He slid around closer to his brother, put a hand on his shoulder. "Maybe the power in your song comes from intense emotions. Next time you take it to battle, try to harness what makes you sad or angry or just plain irritable."

Gabriel smiled wanly. "Because I'm irritating."

"Glad *you* said it."

The old brotherly exchange eased the tension between them.

Arhys clapped Gabriel's back twice. "You'll figure it out. And when you do, we'll free every citizen of the Great Northern Empire. But right now, I've got to get the others moving. Be ready to go."

Arhys made a hand signal, and his two lieutenants slid out of hiding—they were always close, watching out for him. Together the three walked briskly through camp. The measured sound of their boots over hard soil brought others out of their sleep and scrambling to dress and prepare. Some were up, and simply took hold of their weapons and followed.

Less than three minutes later, two hundred men and women had formed a semicircle around Arhys in a natural clearing hemmed in by blue spruce and aspen trees.

As he always did, Arhys surveyed his militia with deliberate focus, locking eyes with as many of them as he was able. He wanted them to feel counted, known, that they mattered.

"There's no glory in war," he began. "And seizing a number of transports isn't the kind of hero's moment that's likely to be written about by storytellers."

Arhys let that much settle in on his militia before going on.

"But every man and woman here has family back home that are hungry. It's your mother or father. It's a spouse. For many of you it's children." He started to pace slowly back and forth. "Most of these people work the crop fields, don't they? They do it in the G.N.E., and then they follow the weather south and do it as traded slave labor. Our emperor—the one who's supposed to lead us, take care of us—sends them to work for his enemies, keeping most of the wages and food that are part of those contracts.

"And those that don't hunch over crops are running small shops in Ravenskill, Fountain Brooke, Whisper Point, Gravesend Hole and a dozen other towns, where they pay a seventy percent tax to Nafaryus, and from what remains have to buy goods and supplies and all the rest."

The soldiers began to grumble.

"It *should* make you angry," Arhys agreed.

"Hard to imagine getting any worse," one man said.

Arhys stare at the man who'd made the comment silenced the muttering. He turned and walked toward him. The man smiled sheepishly as Arhys came to stand with him face-to-face.

"If we don't stop it," he said, speaking as much for the entire militia as this one man, "you can bet your life it will get worse. You have a daughter, John. What are her prospects?" He kept the man locked in an intense gaze as John's eyes lit with internal revelations about his little girl's future. Arhys nodded. "Help me stop it from getting worse, so she has options."

He returned to where he'd been standing. "But here's the good news: We can win. We can be free." He spoke it softly, then again, forcing them to near silence in order to hear him.

Perhaps it was the cold air, or because they stood moments from possible death, but hearing these words whispered in the shadows of Widow's Peak, spoken low and firm … it sent shivers down Arhys spine. He saw it do the same to the others. And strangely, above their shivering flesh the idea of it burned in their eyes. It was that sensation of hearing something that is right and true and making the choice to follow it with conviction, damned be the costs.

They were ready to go to war.

A few did shoot looks at Gabriel. Arhys wasn't the only one who hoped his brother's talent would prove useful to them in a fight.

Gabriel returned every look. "I'll be there with you," he said firmly.

Arhys nodded. But his mind shifted to thoughts of Xander, home in Ravenskill. That was his first and best motivation for everything. That and the vow he'd made Evangeline. He had only to invoke the thought of them to steel his blood.

His eyes focused again on his waiting army. "Let's go."

They fell into the four formations he'd outlined the night before. Two would wait in the scrub oak on the other side of the Grand Highway, and two would wait in the trees that lined the north side. Not an elaborate plan, but a good one.

An old piece of machinery—an elongated rusting tractor—was dragged over the highway to impede the convoy's progress. One of the men believed that ages ago, the machine would do the work of a hundred field hands.

The morning drew out, and before long, the transports came into view. The Empire had vehicles with propulsion systems that allowed for low-level flight. But from what Arhys understood, they were costly to make and the fuel wasn't easy to come by. They were used for war, for show, for demonstrations, not for mundane tasks like goods transportation.

So, these transports came along on heavy tracks and wheels. They could handle poor roads and fallen trees and the like. But a twenty-foot high, sixty-foot long hulk of a tractor? They'd have to stop to move it.

The smell of fumes boiled out of the transports as they came to an idle between Arhys' four ready brigades.

Once hemmed in, the transport deployed a few armed guards. Standard procedure. Perfect. Arhys wended his way through the trees with a woman from his faction. They were dressed like country field hands.

"Need some help?" he asked. "My wife is good with a set of tools. Get you going again."

The first guard pointed the barrel of his pulse rifle at them both, scanning them for weapons up and down with his scope. Finding none, he lowered the gun, and cocked a skeptical eye at them.

"Just happened to be close by?" he questioned.

"We live in the hills." Arhys pointed back toward Widow's Peak. "We walk the highway in the morning looking for roadkill we can use."

The guard snarled with disgust and condescension. "That your rig?" he asked, looking toward the tractor.

Arhys followed the man's eyes, playing dumb. "Not ours," he replied after a long pause. "But if I don't miss my guess, it looks suspiciously like a trap."

With a hand signal from Arhys, close-combat teams stepped from concealment on each side of the convoy. In the space of moments two hundred men and women clad in soiled makeshift uniforms surrounded the seven transports. They wielded a broad mix of weapons—handguns, knives, fightsticks. They came in staggered formations, giving room for the specialties of rear teams who remained hidden. Of these range-fighters, a few dozen had pulse rifles, taken from G.N.E. soldiers over the years. Roughly half carried carbine weapons, old things newly oiled and loaded with self-packed shells. Those shells misfired as often as they worked—brass and powder were generations old. A few dozen more carried bows; the engineering on these was quite good, and more than a few had explosive tips. Among the most important were snipers at longer distances still, in strategic firing positions. They'd learned to attack in a choreographed order and from different angles. This allowed each the benefits of his or her weapon without endangering the others.

((O))

They did have rockets. But they'd learned from experience that using them on a goods convoy defeated the purpose, since invariably the rockets damaged the goods.

When the shuffle of militia feet ended, the returning silence highlighted the laughter the guard blared at Arhys.

"You just keep trying," said the guard, composing himself for the moment. "We keep killing you and you keep trying. What will you do, you rebel mongrel? Steal forever? Sacrifice fifty to feed your little town for what ... a week? You are all anger and bad planning. It's good the emperor puts you under his boot or you might die in your own cesspools."

None of it ruffled Arhys. Men with clean uniforms and new guns like to brag. But he'd put one of his militia up against any G.N.E. soldier in any contest.

"Drop your gun," Arhys commanded in an even tone.

"I'll do you one better," said the guard.

The man waved a hand, and the transports at the front and back of the convoy opened on each side, spilling soldiers onto the highway. Maybe a hundred of them. Arhys' battalions outnumbered them, but these G.N.E. goons were all armed with the latest pulse weapons. And this was twice the number a convoy usually came with. They weren't prepared for this. Arhys would lose many if he went through with the heist.

That was the struggle.

Was leadership staying committed to something, regardless of the odds and sacrifice? Or was it looking after the best interests of those you led, even when that meant showing weakness to the enemy? Weakness that could later be exploited?

"Scylla and Charybdis," Arhys muttered—something Gabriel had taught him.

"The bandit can obviously read," the guard said, and rammed the end of his gun into Arhys' chest, trying to provoke him. Killing healthy workers wouldn't go down well with the emperor, not when subduing them might work. But if attacked, G.N.E. men had the order to put down insurrection with prejudice.

Arhys spared a look at Gabriel, waiting to see if his brother would do something. Maybe now he'd find what he needed to weaponize his song.

Gabriel ever so slightly shook his head. Disappointment rolled through Arhys. He'd be glad he'd rehearsed his words of condolence.

The soldier never saw the hand signal. But a small movement in his wrist, and a crew of archers who'd been ordered to stay back, launched a volley of explosive-tipped arrows into the troop transports.

In a second, the transports' metal sheeting erupted into shrapnel that tore outward into the backs of the G.N.E. troops. Maybe half the bastards dropped.

Some dead. Some screaming in pain. The other half began firing their pulse rifles indiscriminately toward the sides of the road. Towards Arhys' militia.

The sound of a body slumping to old asphalt or packed soil was one Arhys would never get used to, no matter how often he heard it. A chorus of bodies falling to the ground was maddening. It haunted his dreams. Such a helpless, final sound. Like that of a sigh.

But this wasn't Ravenskill's first fight. Those of his fighters with pulse rifles dropped to kneeling positions and returned fire. Arhys had trained them to go slow when shooting to kill. Get into a stance where you can stabilize your aim. Take a full breath.

The air blurred again. This time energy pushing the other direction, back toward the transports. G.N.E. troops fell, their bodies clattering to the road-top more noisily for all the gear they wore.

Arhys drove forward, pulling a concealed knife, and pushing the length of steel into the lead guard's chest. Not the safest attack, but maybe the most gratifying. He then gave a quick overhead wave, drawing his carbine wave of fire.

The crisp late August air erupted with gunfire, the reports echoing up and down the road. The disruption of flesh by pulse fire was replaced by mists of blood kicked up by iron rounds tearing into the bodies of G.N.E. troops. Most of these uttered guttural noises and stumbled backward with hands over bleeding wounds. The luckiest fell where they stood. Being gutshot was a horrible way to die.

Arhys snatched the pulse rifle of the man he'd just put down and searched for Gabriel, making sure he was safe. Still no kind of song from him. But his brother had begun dragging wounded Ravenskill soldiers to safety.

Then he saw her.

Alemdra.

The woman who'd approached the convoy with him, pretending to be his wife.

She lay sprawled across the highway.

Arhys rushed to her side and knelt. "Alemdra?" He felt for a pulse. Silence.

He'd seen hundreds die in the past few years. Men. Women. Children … friends. The nature of their fight almost never left them time to see to proper burials. There was hardly time to grieve. Hesitation made you a target. And yet, this time, Arhys paused.

Months ago, when they'd devised the ruse of the scavenger family, he'd asked for volunteers to approach road transport and assault crafts with him. He had scores of brave followers. And any one of them would have said yes. But he'd scarcely finished asking before she'd shouted, "Me!" She'd come forward with a devious grin on her face. "I'll play the wife. And if it comes to it, I shoot first."

It was one of the rare memories of laughter Arhys could recount, and a favorite story when nights drew out.

Now she lay dead. Sadness and anger swelled in him at the sight of her.

"I'll take down ten for you," he said. Vengeance was all he could offer.

Without standing, he whirled and began firing the pulse rifle into the remaining G.N.E. soldiers. Bitterness had a way of steadying Arhys' aim. And only one energy burst sailed high. The others compressed the chests of their marks and put down ten bootslicks—his name for G.N.E. men, whose leather footwear always gleamed too brightly for him.

A lull came. His militia awaited his next command. The G.N.E. reeled, scrambling for cover from which to shoot. Gunpowder, the scent of coppery blood, the fresh smell of seared ozone from the pulse weapons, it all lingered on suddenly still air.

Then the world erupted again. This time from above. Arhys shot a look skyward and saw six NOMACS descending with impossible speed. The sound they emitted grew louder and more cacophonous with each second. It burrowed inside his head, blurring his vision, clouding his thinking.

Arhys looked back at the fray. His own people were cupping their ears, trying to stave off the sheer oppressive volume and disorienting bray of the noise machines. G.N.E. soldiers were quickly inserting into their ears something they called "silencers"—form-fitted armament plastique that blocked all sound. He'd seen this before. His own fighters used cotton or wax when they had it.

But the reduced effect of the NOMACS blaring sounds still left his militia as target practice for G.N.E. pulse weapons.

He shot a last look at Gabriel, feeling like this might be the first or best way for his gift to answer the weaponry of the NOMACS. But Gabriel never saw him. He was trying to revive an unresponsive woman. Glenda. A mother of two.

Arhys issued his last command. A retreat gesture. His people leapt back into the scrub oak and spruce as quickly as they'd emerged. They'd count later, but he'd gotten good at casualty estimates. They'd lost a third. And they had nothing to show for it.

He'd thought this far north that they'd have a longer window of time before the NOMACS could trace them and arrive. Either they'd had especially bad luck—NOMACS patrolling the nearby region—or there were more NOMACS than just a month ago, enough to now accompany convoys. That changed everything.

Or maybe the technology was evolving. Maybe the disparity between the G.N.E. forces and Arhys' militia was widening. And he had few resources to address the gap.

"Cover fire!" he shouted.

Immediately those still standing who held pulse weapons began sending bursts into the sky toward the NOMACS. It was one of the few things that hindered them, could disrupt their circuitry, he reasoned. And the rest sprinted for the density of the trees on the north side of the highway, where the flying machines weren't able to follow.

Racing for safety, Arhys allowed himself only a moment's despair, silently thinking of Evangeline—before he grew another shade harder. Darker.

They'd learn from this. And next time, they'd be ready.

Those of us that are left…

CHAPTER 2

O n this night, they ran a warm camp. Small fires glowed here and there in the wooded foothills of Widow's Peak. Gabriel had pleaded with his brother to let them have this much. Thaw themselves. Hot food. The safety most feel sitting around a campfire. The propensity to remember and share. Because they'd lost so many.

"The fire doesn't seem to be helping." Arhys was consulting a set of maps. "And it's a risk."

"The convoy moved on," Gabriel told him. "And fire always helps. Has its own kind of music."

Arhys paused. "Did you feel anything? Have any idea of how to—"

"No," Gabriel said, cutting him short. "Weaponizing a song isn't going to come naturally to me. It's not how I think about it. It's more like the sound of fire—"

"Sooner or later, we'll be out of options," Arhys pressed, an edge in his voice. "I wouldn't ask otherwise."

Gabriel nodded, still watching his friends hunkered around a dozen fires beneath the sprawl of spruce and aspen. He knew his brother's intent was right, despite his impatience. And he wanted to do it. For all the others as much as for Arhys. He couldn't think of a single one of them who hadn't lost someone at some point in this insane war.

"We should go back," Gabriel suggested. "Get those that fell. Bury them." He turned to look at his brother.

Arhys opened his mouth to argue, then stopped. He seemed to be seeing someone in his mind. "Maybe we should, at that."

"They're grieving," Gabriel added. "On top of the work camps, and rations, and taxing, and lack of medicine and education … they're fighting a losing war. People they know are dying. And we haven't even given them the chance to say goodbye, the way we do back home."

"There's something of humanity in a funeral," Arhys said, seeming to quote from something he'd heard.

Gabriel looked back at the silhouetted forms of men and women ages fifteen to seventy, each bearing a mourner's silence in the company of low fires. He promptly left his brother's tent, and made his way to the closest flame.

He didn't rush in. He didn't break the quiet solemnity with words or greetings. Instead he hunkered down, rubbed his hands in the heat of the nearest coals, and bore them company for several long moments.

Then he began to sing.

Something quiet and slow.

There were other songs. Fight songs. Rousing melodies to stir the heart. And maybe someday a kind of song to battle the Empire. Just now, he sang a slow burning tune that felt of memory and gratitude and hope. He let words find him this time. Not worrying over rhyme or cadence. It was a story-song. Their story. The people of Ravenskill. It spoke for them. Declared their permanence. Their strength. Because they were willing to sacrifice for the right things. For freedom and dignity. It gave a voice and value to their losses. It made them unafraid to face another day of the fight. It stirred them gently, then firmly, warming them inside the way the fire did their clothes and skin.

And as he sang, he watched their faces change. Somber expressions softened. Bitterness fled. Weariness became the good tired of bearing another's burden versus the kind of despair which taxes the soul.

Those who'd been huddling around the other fires began making their way toward Gabriel, to hear his song. He kept on. But somehow it hurt him to do so. He became aware that there might not be so much anguish to alleviate if he could just find a way to live up to the promise his brother carried of Gabriel's gift.

But Gabriel hadn't asked for this. None of it. Not his love of music. Not the unique way it moved people. And certainly not the expectation to use it to liberate anyone.

None of that stopped them from crowding into the small clearing to hear to him sing. Odd thing to be in the company of so many and feel so alone. He would like to have said something, maybe sung something, that could put an end to their suffering. But he didn't know how to sing such a thing. And even if he had, would it have been honest to do so?

But he did feel something. When he looked around and thought about the people surrounding him. He found some strength in that. Maybe they'd find the same in each other. So he wove his song onward and began to name them, telling the things about them that he found unique and comforting.

It was just a song. Not a great one. Not a shabby one. But the flicker of firelight in their eyes seemed changed again. There was more faith in it than before.

Then, he saw one who hadn't joined them. Through the trees, two fires over, sat a man still leaned into the blaze, his back to them.

One kind of song had moved most of his brothers and sisters of Ravenskill. He knew it would take something more for Don.

When he finished, those nearby began to speak with one another, sometimes to recount memories for friends who'd fallen that day, sometimes to talk about how they'd win out the next time they faced the G.N.E. Some remained quiet, with contemplative, if not smiling, faces. Arhys joined them, and began to talk about Alemdra.

Normally, Gabriel would have stayed. These were important stories to tell. But not while Don sat alone.

He made his way through the trees to the man, and sat without speaking at his side. They observed the fire for a long while together in silence.

"I don't need one of your songs, Gabriel," said Don. "No offense."

"Not why I came," Gabriel answered. He let that sit for a long moment. "Your son was brave. Honest. Everyone liked him."

Don's wide reminiscing eyes remained so, and he nodded. "I know."

"It's right to be heartsick," Gabriel said, and threw a stick on the fire.

"I know," Don repeated.

It was hard to say how long they sat in companionable silence, listening only to the crackle of spruce wood burning. But somewhere in that night, Don did whisper. "Maybe a line or two."

Gabriel didn't editorialize Don's change of heart, but only began to sing a soft *sotto voce* kind of song. Like talk-singing. It might have sounded to others like a eulogy of sorts, or an epitaph read by a knowing friend. But it wasn't the words this time. Or the sentiment. This song, Gabriel gave something of himself to. This song he sang to move Don *inside*. Not emotionally. Any song might do that.

On this rare occasion, Gabriel did his best to tap into that other kind of power his song could have. And for this purpose—helping someone bear a burden—he had a better idea how to sing that gift.

He kept it low, not drawing others to them. And he spoke-sang a music truth for Don to mend something inside the man that had broken. He couldn't take it away. He didn't think he'd want to, even if he could. But he could draw together the fragments left behind when a father loses a son, and give him a better place to mourn from. More strength to do it.

Sometime later he stopped. No fanfare. No big last note or lyric. And he kept on sitting at the father's side, keeping filled a place his son would have occupied if he hadn't fallen that day in the convoy battle.

Don's shoulders relaxed a bit. His eyes weren't so tight. He was still in pain. But it was sufferable.

And Gabriel kept him company, suffered with him.

Sometime later, in barely a whisper, Don said, "You're ... well, what you do, Gabriel ... it's astonishing." He nodded his head at some internal thought. "I see why some call you that."

Astonishing. Gabriel wasn't comfortable with the euphemism. It expected too much. "Nevermind all that."

Deeper into the night, they swapped stories of James, Don's son, when it wasn't too painful to speak his name. Some they sniffled at, some they laughed.

And all through it, they never once saw—anymore than Gabriel did when he'd sang at the crowded campfire—the small NOMAC, no more than the size of a large orange, capturing the exchange, the changes, and the songs.

CHAPTER 3

————◉————

Faythe quietly closed the door behind her as she entered the unnamed hall at the furthest south wing of the palace. No one came here. It was locked for one thing. But it was also far. There were three empty wings between this and those used regularly by the staff and family. An entire floor of empty bedrooms, too. And three more vast halls of old artifacts—items from before the End Wars. In fact all these end halls were known collectively as the Hall of Artifacts. But this immense chamber stood at the end of them all. This was a last place. A forgotten place.

She'd flown all night to be here for the eastern sun. It cascaded down through three-story windows on the right, falling in slanting patterns. Motes lazed in subtle indoor winds, caught like fireflies in the shafts of sun.

Slowly, she walked, taking in the quiet and stillness. One by one she thought their names—all the instruments that lay cloaked in dust or fastened inside their cases: trumpets, violins, clarinets, drums, cellos, pianos, a harpsichord, tubas. On one stand a viola d'amore. So many. And she knew them all.

The dry scent of dust and tarnished brass did have a sadness in it though. Disuse. No one really knew how to use these anymore. Some believed law prohibited it. Truth was, people weren't interested. Easier and faster to have the machines do it. More precise, too. These tools required time and practice to reduce error. And in the end, there'd always be wrong notes, rushed phrases. Because they were used by humans.

Faythe hunkered down and picked up a small curved horn. After wiping the mouthpiece, she gave it a firm blow. The single clarion note echoed up into the vaults of the hall like a call to war. Still sounded regal, despite years of blackening and neglect.

"You think that's such a good idea," came a voice to her right.

Faythe wheeled in the direction of the stranger. "What? Who?"

"Settle yerself, little miss," said an older man. "I won't be sharing your secrets."

The stranger appeared roughly her father's age. He had thick hands, fingers like short steel cords. And lively eyes. He wasn't the worrying sort, she could tell by his easy smile.

"You know I've been here before?" she asked.

In response, he reached up and pulled down a hand-sized bit of black metal with several charcoal-colored reflecting panels on it. "You'll be wanting this," he said, and removed a rectangular component from the side of the device.

Faythe shook her head. "What is it?"

"Your little music player," he pointed toward her pocket. "It ran out of juice, didn't it? Stopped playing those songs you like so much."

Faythe hadn't told anyone about the music player. She'd kept that much for herself. She served her office dutifully, avoided anything that subverted her father's authority. But this. It was the first thing that had made sense in a long while.

"How would you know?" she followed.

"That's what happens." He ambled half way between them, extending the component. "Anything that needs power winds down eventually. You're just lucky I happened to have a solar battery for that thing."

"So, you *have* been watching me." Faythe made no move to take the power source, though she desperately wanted it.

"Don't make it something it's not," said the man. "I put the damned thing in here to begin with, expecting you'd happen on it eventually. Glad you finally did. Took you long enough."

"You put it here?" she said, incredulous.

"Where are my manners?" said the man, "I'm Jack. And yes, I put it here. Do you see any other electronics around? This is where your grandfathers gathered all the old hand-instruments. I think originally it was to be a museum of sorts. But they lost interest even in that much of it. Left it to rot, they did."

Faythe stayed focused. "This all still means you'd have to have known I came to this place secretly. That's suspicious, right? Or do you have an answer for that one, too?"

Jack laughed. "Yes, it's suspicious. But I don't have a mean bone in my body. To be honest, I was looking for a hand organ. I'd gotten the notion I could learn to play one."

"And?" Faythe asked.

Jack raised his hands and wiggled his fingers. Turns out these are too thick, stubby, and clumsy for music. Gave up."

Faythe looked around. "I have a feeling *giving up* is a familiar story to most of these." She swept a hand out, pointing to the array of instruments.

"You talk about them as if they could hear you." Jack's smile widened as he said it.

She liked that idea.

"Just back from the North Western Realm, eh?" The man took two steps back and plopped into a seat as if it were one he occupied often.

"Goods Accord," she said, not bothering to question him on his information sources anymore. "Brokered a truce with the Lakes Territories for safe passage of Pacific lumber and other materials."

"Sounds boring," Jack said.

"There's an art to negotiation." Faythe removed her music player and replaced the power component, noting again the cryptic word "bug" scored into the back. "Mostly it's patience and understanding what's important to the one you're speaking with."

A joke seemed to tremble on Jack's lips, but he never offered it. And, eventually, a silence fell between them.

After many long moments, he said with a reverent tone, "Not all silence is awkward. Just like not all silence is heavy and sad. Some silences are beautiful. They're filled with the ghosts of memory. They hold up a backdrop against which a whisper means everything."

Faythe nodded to that.

"Take this silence, for example." Jack looked her square in the eyes. "On the one hand it's filled with echoes of notes played long ago. You can hear them, can't you?" He paused, putting his hand to his ear, but wore a serious face. "On the other hand, it's just a damn shame to see so many possible notes left unearned." His eyes swept around the graveyard of instruments.

With the man's shoulder turned, she noted the patch on his shoulder. "You're a NOMAC engineer," she observed. "Foundry level."

"Guilty," he replied, and saluted. "I'm systems maintenance and new chassis design. Not sound development … those guys are strange. Keep trying to make the perfect music, they do. Hells, one went so far as to just play all the damn notes at once and said it was the most complete composition possible."

Faythe looked past Jack to the high sunlit windows. Out in the sky she could see more than one NOMAC. "They're more than music machines now. They're our early defense warning, aerial combat, communications grid—"

An urgent message flashed in the display of her eye contacts. Her father requested her presence immediately.

"You go on," said Jack. "I can see you've been summoned. We'll catch up another time."

She found his grin both disconcerting and charming, before she stepped quickly from the Hall of Lost Things.

CHAPTER 4

E mperor Nafaryus sat behind a broad terminal, looking across more than ten video monitors. Every screen showed the same scene from different moments and vantage points—the Ravenskill militia's most recent attack on one of his supply convoys. This had to stop. Not the attempts to steal. Most of what was taken was eventually taken back or replaced by the thieves themselves once they were caught. No, what would stop was the insurgence. The disrespect. The attempt to undermine his authority.

His son, Daryus, arrived first, rushing into the command room and quickly checking to see if he was, indeed, first.

"Where are the others?" he asked, barely hiding his gloat.

"Your sister just returned from the NorthWest Territories, where she brokered a truce." Nafaryus reclined, appraising his over-eager son. "Flew all night to return."

Daryus grimaced at the unspoken praise awarded his sister.

"Your mother," Nafaryus continued, "will come as she pleases. She's the queen."

Daryus began to pace, which meant he had a request he was working up to. "Did you see my report on the increased drone capabilities in our military program?"

Nafaryus shook his head, as he glanced down at the monitors and back up at his son. "Because you think you're ready for your moniker, I take it," Nafaryus said.

"The Strength Program has yielded an eight percent increase in production across all categories," Daryus argued. "And we see three percent fewer losses of trade labor to other nations." He paused. "Yes, I think I've earned it."

The family name was Delain. But it was seldom used. And given names in the palace family were largely replaced by ritual when a child had shown exceptional value to the realm. By tradition, these second names were types. They spoke to a value or attribute or capability. They were also meant to influence the people to some extent. So, for him, Nafaryus had been a way of warning a population that had begun to grow seditious that they'd best be cautious. And nearly two years ago now, he'd given his daughter her second name, Faythe, because she had a way of inspiring confidence, making peace.

Nafaryus shook his head. "You're not ready for a second name." And what he was about to show him was proof of that. "Leadership isn't all an exercise of strength. I want you to leak a rumor to the rebels that we've developed a cloaking technology to mask our fleet movements."

"We have no such tech," Daryus said matter-of-factly.

Nafaryus sighed with deliberateness. "Yes, but they don't know that. The threat of it is something we can use to our advantage. It's a leverage maneuver. You need to start thinking further ahead. How to compromise your enemy, not simply how to bowl them under."

Shortly his wife, Arabelle, the queen arrived. Arabelle's name, given her by her father, a historian, derived from the Latin *orabilis*, which meant to petition or make an earnest request for help. This was because Arabelle could see all sides of an argument, and so could be appealed to without her showing bias.

And just behind her came Faythe. His daughter looked tired.

"Before I show you why I've asked you here," Nafaryus said, "I want to take a moment to congratulate and thank Faythe for her work with the North Western Realm. She's struck a peace accord with them to allow the transport of goods from the far realms across their borders. I could not have succeeded, myself. Well done, Faythe."

Arabelle put a hand on Faythe's arm and gave it a congratulatory squeeze. Daryus shot her a tight glance, and returned his attention to Nafaryus without a word.

Faythe could have seized the moment to gloat a bit. But she only smiled in return. *Sparing her brother the agony of having to listen to more of her success.* That was her nature, and Nafaryus loved her for it.

He then keyed the panel in front of him, projecting one by one the video captures of the convoy attack.

"There was another raid by the Ravenskill militia," Nafaryus began. "Goods transport coming from Eastgate. Some of it imported from across the North Sea. Not irreplaceable, had they succeeded, but it would have delayed several efforts, including Daryus' Strength Program."

There was new technology - thought technology - being developed in some of the European City States, and Nafaryus had funded the purchase of prototypes.

"But they *didn't* succeed," Daryus emphasized. "It looks to me like the drones took care of it. Used some of the acoustic tech, the readout says."

"Yes, the goods are safe," Nafaryus agreed. "But we lost over a hundred G.N.E. troops in the attack."

"Which, with all due respect," Daryus argued, "are replaceable. Conscription efforts are up by half in the last two months. By the end of the year, the standing army will have doubled."

Nafaryus leaned forward over the panel. "This is why you're not ready for your second name. We are not here to discuss resources. Or the strength of our military."

"Daryus may have been coming to it," Arabelle gently interjected, suing for peace.

Nafaryus left off, waiting to see if his son understood. Daryus stood silent, his face pinched with anger and embarrassment.

"You've put him on the spot," Faythe said. "Daryus has talked to me often about the need to address the leadership of these rebel factions. I think the Strength Program is part of that initiative, isn't it, Daryus?"

All the assistance seemed only to make him angrier. After a long moment, he said, "I will take a battalion and fly to Ravenskill tomorrow. I will end this. I've been tracking Arhys and his rebel fighters for years now. I've been in the field more than once to try and subdue him. It's time to stop trying to *subdue*. We need to put him and his rebellion down for good."

Nafaryus eyed his son, then also his wife and daughter. "There has always been unrest. Disobedience. Even attacks. But this," he stood straight again, pointing to the projections, "this is more organized, larger, than we've ever seen. It speaks of confidence and planning. Something has changed with the Ravenskill faction in recent years."

"All the communities on Endless Isleland take a false sense of security at being across the Great Northern Sound." Daryus crossed to the console and tapped a sequence to bring up the military map.

Beside the projections of the attack rose a large projected facsimile of New Anglya. Daryus circled Endless Isleland with his finger.

"Our coastal defenses are relatively weak." He tapped the map at several spots. "We have a small navy, but it's spread incredibly thin. Really just the drones, with an extended sea range."

Nafaryus held up his hands. "It's not the security of being at the edge of the realm. Increased presence isn't the answer."

Daryus stood like a statue, his arm still pointing. His mouth still open to some unspoken word. But Nafaryus didn't have time for posturing. He keyed off the transport attack.

"Arhys is the leader of the Ravenskill militia." Nafaryus pulled up a new projection of just the man focused on him during the convoy attack. "He mocks us, mocks the royal family and tradition, having taken a second name himself."

"God of War," Faythe supplied.

Nafaryus nodded. "And he's smart. Worse. He's driven."

Daryus stepped forward. "I'll take care of it—"

"But it's not only that," Nafaryus interjected. "I think we've found why he's so confident."

Nafaryus ended the projection of Arhys, and played the last bit of video capture from the new stealth drone.

In their midst, the scene played out where the brother of Arhys, this Gabriel, found a way to heal and inspire a broken company of ragtag fighters back to their cause, back to opposing Nafaryus and the empire.

"This," he pointed at Gabriel, "this man. They see him as some kind of savior."

"He believes in God?" Arabelle asked.

Nafaryus considered the question. Not of God. But of belief. That was a dangerous idea. It gave people hope. And every empire Nafaryus had studied, if overthrown, was toppled by people with hope. The suppressive effects of the machine music weren't taking hold in Ravenskill the way they used to. This *savior* was the reason.

"I don't know what he believes," Nafaryus finally answered, "but it's not in the empire. And his songs are encouraging dissent. This is the real threat. If we eliminate Gabriel, we cripple the Ravenskill rebels."

"Then I'll—" Daryus began.

"We're all going," Nafaryus interrupted. "Yes, I want you to mobilize the first battalion. They should be ready for military operations, but I suspect this will be more for show. Have the parade detail attend us."

Daryus appeared happy to have a part to play, but disappointed he wasn't entrusted to take care of this on his own.

"Arabelle, you and Faythe will attend, as well. I want it recorded that we've made every effort to find a peaceful resolution here."

"Then we are seeking peace?" Faythe asked.

Nafaryus heard the concern in his daughter's voice. He left the console and came up in front of her, taking her hands in his own. Father's do things for their children. Objectionable things, sometimes. They answer to responsibilities the child shouldn't have to worry about. And it changes them from what they were. But they do it anyway, because they don't care about themselves the way they do their children. His father had done it for him, even when Nafaryus continued to put distance between them.

This all ran through his mind before he said simply, "I just want to meet this Gabriel. We need to take precautions. But what kind of leader would I be if I ignored a man who can inspire the people the way this one does. Or, maybe I'm wrong altogether. That's why we're going."

Lying is something fathers sometimes do for their children.

Faythe nodded.

"Be ready at dawn," Nafaryus told them, and strode from the control room, ready to meet this Ravenskill messiah.

CHAPTER 5

⎯⎯⎯⎯◯⎯⎯⎯⎯

The acoustics lab could feel more like a foundry at times. The engineers here created and tested new drone designs, in addition to maintaining the systems the G.N.E. military used to control the machines. Audio design took place in another location—special sound proofing was required for that. Nafaryus liked it here, though. This was the nerve center of his power. It felt good being close to it. That, and Jack worked here.

"Condescending to visit us again down here in the pit," Jack said. He could get away with talk like that when he was the only one here, and they both knew it.

"If you weren't so good at your job ..." Nafaryus offered a distracted smile.

"That's all it would take then?" Jack asked with mock surprise. "Fail a bit more and you'll reassign me?"

"The new designs—the small ones," Nafaryus said, moving past the greetings, "They're working. I picked up some useful information from one of them about a rebel movement."

Jack's eyes told the story: He wasn't entirely on Nafaryus' side in these things. But he kept it mostly to himself.

"Well, sooner or later something we create down here will get us to peace, huh?" he offered as a middle ground. "Trying to find a perfect music certainly didn't do it."

"The drones do more than sound submission," Nafaryus countered.

"Ayeah, but that's where it started, isn't it? Machines to replace the creation of music, trying to find some kind of ideal. And along the way, we gave something up." Jack held up his hands, calling for a truce before they tangled on this again. "And yes, I know you only allow my debate because we shared a misspent youth."

Nafaryus had put his old friend to work in the sound lab for two reasons: he was the best innovator in sound delivery, and he'd known Nafaryus since they were maybe six-years-old, long enough that he didn't curb his tongue when he had an opinion to share.

"That's actually what I came to talk about," Nafaryus said.

"Our misspent youth?" Jack laughed from his belly.

Nafaryus shook his head, and collected his thoughts. "What we gave up with the automation of song."

Jack's face turned serious fast. "You really want to talk about that?"

"This rebel movement in Ravenskill." He began to pace, feeling unsettled. "Your reconnaissance drone captured some footage of its spiritual leader."

Jack remained silent, waiting.

"We haven't seen this in generations, Jack," he paused, the words he meant to share seeming suddenly strange, dangerous, "he sings. He makes music."

The grin on Jack's face started as a smirk, but blossomed like a flower in the morning sun. "You're shitting me."

"There are even rumors that his music has some kind of power or influence," Nafaryus added, impatient already with the whole affair.

"More than just inspiring some jerkwaters to rise up and fight?" Jack was shaking his head in amused disbelief. "You know, music has long been used to incite rebellion and oppose authority. Shostakovich and Stravinsky did it for the Russians centuries ago. Music hath charms, they say. But I wouldn't put too much stock in supernatural claims. That's what folks do when they need a messiah."

Nafaryus eyed his old friend. "Some call him 'savior.'"

"Of course they do," Jack put back. "He's giving them hope. You know," he went on with a bit more care in his words, "you could play that same part for them. Kind of like emperors used to do ages ago. But you'd have to change your approach."

Nafaryus slammed his fist down on the table to his side. "I did not create the system! But I manage it better than any before me ever did."

Jack didn't immediately reply. He let the anger dissipate for a time. "I'm no counselor, Edward—Jack only used his real name when it got cold and serious like this—"but I think you're talking about your dad here. Not some rebel militia or its unlikely singer."

Nafaryus glared at his friend for mentioning his father. Jack remained silent but unflinching under the scrutiny for several long moments.

"I've never said this," Jack began, low but firm, "and you won't like hearing it. Could be you'll end our friendship, throw me in prison, have birds peck at my flesh because of it. But you realize that while music had gone out of society long before you rose to the throne, it was you who pushed the audio designers to convert sound to a weapon. People weren't interested in music before you. But now they're afraid of it. Hell, it's not even music, really."

"That's enough, Jack," said Nafaryus.

Jack hunched his shoulders. "You said you wanted to talk about it."

Nafaryus let that go, deciding how to frame his question and decided Jack's own words came closest. "It's about hope. Whatever else music can do, it can give hope. And hope isn't something we can afford to let these people have."

Jack's eyes may as well have gone red, the anger was so intense. "You're going to have to explain that one, my lord."

Nafaryus continued to pace. "I'll be frank. I'm the emperor. I wanted to be emperor. I take it seriously. I like the authority of it. I like to lead. And I don't need the trouble and confusion created when some kid decides he has it rough in the fields."

"I'll give you credit for honesty," Jack interjected.

"Under my command, we've grown our borders, increased our national output, and made life relatively safe for G.N.E. citizens." He paused there.

"That all sounds very adequate," Jack said.

"And that's my point." Nafaryus stopped his pacing and stared at his old friend. "Adequate is damned hard to deliver. No one is ever fully satisfied. And yet I wake and sleep this office because I wanted to hold the power. Do well with it. It's all I think about." He held a moment to be sure Jack was listening. "I can't give them more hope right now. I can't afford it. I'm not a prophet or seer. I don't know what's coming. When the world broke, no one knew what was coming then, either."

Jack was nodding. "I see. Hope is dangerous, you're saying. It's not the fighting and dying in rebel encounters. Or even losing those fights. You think you're protecting them from disappointment."

This was why Nafaryus came to talk with Jack. He cut to the heart of matters. But it wasn't the all of it.

"And I was the one chosen to lead. I trained for it. Sought it to the detriment of …"

Jack offered a conciliatory, warm chuckle—a friendly kind. "You drove a wedge between you and your father. You were ambitious, while he was trying to mend fences. Bad combination."

Nafaryus saw his father in his mind, and felt suddenly distant from everything, everyone. "He loved music. People had given up the pursuit of it by then. Left it to the machines mostly. But not dad. He used to play for me in the Hall of Lost Things. He started that collection, you know."

"I know," Jack said.

"We even wrote a song together once." Nafaryus could vaguely recall its melody. "It was one of the last things we ever did together."

"I know. He lived a long time," Jack submitted.

"But I moved on from music," Nafaryus explained. "At least the art of it. The creation."

Jack shared a thoughtful look with him. "And the enjoyment, it sounds like."

Nafaryus couldn't talk about this anymore. Not today. "I'm going to Ravenskill tomorrow. Full battalion, parade dress."

"That'll make an impression," said Jack. "I'm sure no one will feel intimidated."

Nafaryus ignored that. "I want a few of the new prototypes to attend us. They'll lend themselves to the pageantry. And I may test the new sound designs they carry."

"I don't think they're ready for mass use," Jack argued, then quickly added, "but I'll have them set to go."

"Thank you." Nafaryus prepared to leave.

"How long has it been?" Jack asked, giving him his intense look again.

"Since what?"

Jack stepped up close to Nafaryus, proximity being a disarming tactic in conversation. "Since you heard anything besides what comes programmed for the drones."

Nafaryus stared back a good long time before exiting the sound lab in silence.

CHAPTER 6

—◉—

oft predawn light lay across the town square. A quiet time. Peaceful. Gabriel took a long breath in the stillness. He loved the people of Ravenskill, and he was glad to be back home from their failed raid, but he rose every day to enjoy these moments alone. Moments without complication. Moments without expectation. Just the slow way of things before the world awoke and the rough edges of life came rushing back in.

But it wasn't only the soft light, or quiet, or calm that brought him here. He came because, when the square sat vacant, it offered beautiful acoustics for his music. He never played or sang loudly—he didn't want to wake anyone—but he wouldn't have been loud anyway. The right accompaniment for these moments was gentleness. From his corner in the square, he softly ran his fingers across the strings of his worn guitar. The sound quietly rang out, reaching every far surface as mild as a thought.

When all had come again to silence, he realized there was a third reason he came to the square. In these moments, nothing was required of his songs. There was no greater intention or plan for him or his music. The music itself was the thing. For its own sake. Not a tool for revolution. Not an object of concern. Maybe it was selfish. But he'd heard the way people talked about him, about what they called his *gift*. Yes, there was power in his music. But power to lead men in war? Topple a government? How could he make them understand?

The power of music wasn't a destructive thing.

It was the power of an early morning, when quiet light lent a man strength.

Gabriel played another chord and let his mind wander, slowly adding words to his song. He sang them just above a whisper. Had the wind come, his song might have been swept away. But the stillness remained. And he sat in his corner of the square, giving air to a slow song that needed no urgency or audience.

Until a door across from him opened.

A woman emerged, wearing the tattered garments of a field picker. She started toward him. A child in her arms. A look of worry in her face.

Gabriel's song died in his throat.

It seemed a long time as she crossed the cobbled stones. The stillness changed. It became the long silence of a cemetery, the peace that followed the end of all struggles. As she drew closer, her look of anguish mixed with an unspoken plea.

Before he could stand, the woman dropped to her knees in front of him. She'd been crying, her lashes wet. She looked down at her child as if for some strength to speak.

"She can't breathe" the woman finally said, her voice hitching with emotion. "Her lungs are weak. And I can't afford to take her to the city for help."

The child drew a wheezing breath.

"She's getting weaker," the woman added. "She doesn't sleep. She's not eating ..."

The woman didn't need to say it. She'd come because of Gabriel's music. Because of the rumors. Rumors that said there was something inside his songs.

Gabriel stared down at the babe. It wasn't the unfairness of a world where some had so much and others had so little that he saw. It wasn't even the helplessness of a mother unable to afford her child's medical care. He saw only what he took for granted. He saw that he could fill his lungs to sing a song, where this little one struggled to find every breath.

The child wheezed again. This time more slowly. She was dying. In the quiet peace of this early morning, she was dying. Maybe she'd last the day. Or a week. But not long.

And the child wasn't alone. Many from Ravenskill—hell, from villages all across the northern empire—were going early to their graves. Some from lack of medical care. Some from a life of hard labor. Some few ended their own suffering, unable to face another day.

But a child…

And in that moment, there was no feeling of conflict or expectation. No indecision.

He placed a reassuring hand on the woman's arm. "What's your name?"

She looked up at him, puzzlement on her face. "Rena."

"And the child?" he asked.

"Audra," Rena said. After a long moment she added, "I believe it means nobility. Strength." The irony of it brought a small weeping laugh from the woman.

Gabriel smiled. "It's a good name for her."

He set his old guitar aside, placed one arm around Rena—so that she could feel part of whatever song he could find—and began to sing a melody. He sang what men once called *sotto voce*. Like he'd sung for Don when his son was taken from him. A song like his morning music. Quiet. About quiet truths. About the strength in gentle things. Like a child's struggle to breathe. And just like the song he'd been singing for an empty courtyard, this one fell softly against the stones, reaching every surface gentle as a thought.

But this song was for Audra. And for Rena.

He didn't notice as a man and young boy came up beside them. Watching. Listening. He was focused on the babe, lending what he knew of strength and deep breaths and tomorrows to his choice of notes and words. He didn't rush.

And sometime later, the child gave a long sigh—the kind one can only make with healthy lungs.

Rena looked up at Gabriel, an expression of momentary disbelief passing to gratitude. Her lashes were more beautifully wet now. He'd remember that a long time.

A strong hand found Gabriel's own, and he was suddenly aware of the others—a man squeezing Gabriel's fingers with thankful vigor.

"I'm Michael. And that's my little girl,"—he gestured toward Audra—"Thank you." Michael squeezed Gabriel's fingers again with the rough hand of a field picker.

Then beside Rena was a younger woman. She wore a delicate circlet with a single depended jewel the color of sapphire—the mark of a crop follower, a woman who moved from harvest to harvest trading physical pleasures for coin or goods. There was a wound in her. He could see it in the way she was careful not to catch Gabriel's eye, as she gently took the child from Rena's arms.

"You need to rest," the younger woman said. "I'll watch after Audra."

Gabriel saw it then, the likeness between them. Sisters. Which made a kind of sense. Only family would tolerate a crop follower.

Another door opened. This one Gabriel knew. Himney's bakery. Himney made breakfast bread. Hot and buttered. The old man was always first in the square to open his shop, filling the air with the good smell of it.

"Himney," Michael called, startling the old man, "come see this."

Himney squinted through the morning shadows as he shuffled over. "You're all up early for a roll," he quipped with a smile, easing his large belly into their midst. "You're always first in line, Michael. But you're putting me behind—"

"Listen." Michael gestured toward the babe.

All stood quiet. And Himney's good-natured smile fell in realization that the child was no longer wheezing. His eyes rose to Gabriel. "That's a beautiful silence, my boy. I'm guessing you lent the child a song. That about right?"

Gabriel only looked back at Audra, who had already found sleep now that breathing was no longer a fight.

"I think this earns you a free roll. But I still charge for butter." Himney's warm rolling laugh gave the morning a new tone.

"What's this?" came a rough voice; a voice that wasn't used to being contradicted. Arhys strode toward them, his son Xander at his side.

Arhys always expected trouble. Always wore a serious expression. Ever since Evangeline had died, Arhys couldn't seem to find laughter. Hearing Himney laugh had no doubt made him suspicious. His brother pushed into their growing circle, dark rings around his eyes. The militia leader hardly slept. He worried and planned and worried and fought. His life was a fight. Every hour of it.

Like struggling to breathe, Gabriel thought.

Himney, who simply wasn't afraid of anybody, said, "Have a look, captain. Your brother sang the child to sleep. How's that for sedition?"

The others laughed. Arhys did not. He stared long at Audra, then into the eyes of her mother. Of course he knew them. He made it his business to know all the families in need. He did it so that when his militia fought, he could make a point of letting them know who they fought for.

Then Arhys' eyes lifted to Gabriel. There was a deep ache in his brother's face. Old wounds. Evangeline, his wife. Gabriel hadn't found a song to help her. The remembrance of it burned inside him. But Arhys' eyes didn't show condemnation, unless it was of himself. If only his brother could move on. His zeal for his militia was making him miss the good days he might spend with Xander.

Finally, Arhys nodded. A slight thing. Acknowledgment. Gratitude.

"Well this all turned a bit somber fast," Himney joked, looking askance at Arhys. "Young Gabriel, since my bread is likely now to burn, what say you favor us with a song? I can hardly think of a more fitting way to celebrate Audra's rosy cheeks."

Himney was right. Audra's cheeks now held a flush glow. "Damn fine idea," Gabriel agreed.

He swept up his guitar and stepped onto the stone portico in his corner of the square. The light of day was strengthening in the east, which was also part of why he came here each morning. To watch the slow gathering of sun. It prompted many a song.

Today, though, none of those songs seemed right. Not a hundred of them. Sharing looks with those around him, he did find it. Audra's song. The one he'd created minutes ago. *But with a little more volume,* he decided.

He struck a strong chord, and behind its echo he ran an arpeggiated melody, making the two harmonize like a set of fast pipes. Then he settled into the song, lifting his voice through the silences of morning and the square. Himney tapped a foot in a rocking motion that had his belly swaying a beat behind. Rena and Michael's smiles almost felt like counterpoint. Rena's sister wouldn't look up at Gabriel. Arhys watched with stoic eyes, still, unable to fully embrace any distraction from the principles that moved him.

And slowly, Ravenskill awoke.

It was always this way. The town rising. Field workers filed into the street, some to Himney's for a roll, others with their own thin meats or boiled eggs, as they walked to the fields. Other shop owners set out stands of goods for passersby. Many of Arhys' militia found their way into the square, too. The town priests started their rounds—walking daily in oversized boots to homes where sickness or hardship had laid a claim—today, they crossed toward Gabriel.

In half an hour, the square was full. The day's work was put aside for a short while as they listened to Gabriel sing—something he didn't often do for crowds. Once, there'd been spiritual revivals. Once, concerts and performances. Even further back, traveling troupes had played musical dramas for pennies. This wasn't like any of those things. This was Gabriel's way of speaking. He did it now so others could hear. They stood still and listened, transported for a few moments from their cares. But it also quickened the blood. And he liked the way of that. It was how music *moved* inside his chest. It could take you places with a simple belief and desire.

It was precisely what the music of the machines lacked. Their resonance worked only on acoustical law. It had a certain power. It could shake a man. But it couldn't *move* him.

Gabriel sang with more energy, giving more of himself to Audra's Lullaby. He turned into new modes, leading from the key of D. He sang the feeling of victory. But not necessarily of battle. He wanted everyone to feel and understand the triumph of a long, healthy breath.

While he sang, the sun broke in the east.

Light flooded the square.

A moment later came a deep sonic blast that filled up all sound and space. It seemed to rise up from the earth beneath them, like thirty bass horns sounding at once. It reverberated in Gabriel's bones. Almost painful. He stopped his song. People turned towards the east road.

A brief pause. Then the blast repeated, holding longer this time, as if daring a response.

Into the silence that followed, hooves sounded on the road stones. The distant sound of boots rose, marching in time. Then above it all, another blast of horns. Tenor trumpets this time. A different declaration. An arrival.

Shortly, twin lines of G.N.E. soldiers marched down each side of the road and into the square. They were led by mounted captains in broad-shouldered uniforms, their horses chuffing as they came. Bright flashes of sun glinted off ceremonial swords hanging from each G.N.E. man's hip. And every one of them held a black rifle that could discharge bursts of energy to tear a man's flesh.

The horns continued the announcement until a large hovercraft, three decks high, moved into the square behind the G.N.E. regiments. Cannons stood trained on the Ravenskill people, as though their operators expected—*wanted*—trouble.

The silence stretched.

Then a man stood up on the bridge of the craft and slowly surveyed the crowd. He appeared like a judge ready to cast judgment, his mouth a grim line. His own uniform was draped with golden cords over the shoulders and a double row of buttons down the front. It was an affectation from the long dead military traditions of the Parisians.

After several long moments, he inclined his chin with a hint of arrogance and looked down at Arhys with challenge in his eyes. He pointed at Gabriel. "We've come to hear you sing. To hear this gift of yours."

"Emperor Nafaryus," Gabriel whispered to no one.

From several tributary roads, more of Arhys militia flooded into the square. Fighting odds were better now. But they didn't have the firepower. Nafaryus' hovercraft alone could reduce the square to rubble. Not to mention the burst rifles his troops carried.

Arhys said nothing, his stare sharp and accusing.

Gabriel also remained quiet, but felt the weight of the emperor's glare as he turned toward him and his worn guitar.

"So, you're Gabriel, whom some call *astonishing*. Well, astonishing, please don't stop on *my* account. Let's have a song." He uttered a mocking laugh.

That broke Arhys' silence, and he shouted with open defiance. "We're gathered in peace, my Lord."

Another man stood up on the bridge of the hovercraft. It was Prince Daryus, the emperor's son. He slowly descended a set of stairs through all three levels of the open-air landship cruiser. A reticulated set of steps unfolded to the stones of the square. Daryus walked down into the midst of the crowd, and came face-to-face with Gabriel.

"My father has made his desire known. Do not test his patience ... or mine." Daryus' words were more than threat. They were hateful desire. He wanted an excuse to lay waste to the people of Ravenskill.

When Daryus sneered, Gabriel saw his brother begin to lose his composure. He dropped his guitar and rushed between them. "It's all right, Arhys.

I'll sing. Might do them some good. All they know is the noise machines."
He tried a smile to ease the tension.

"They're here to mock you," Arhys said, unmoved. "To mock us all."

"You're probably right," Gabriel admitted, "but they'll also see they
don't need to feel threatened by a song. Not mine, anyway. Then they'll
leave us be."

Arhys looked down at his son, just a step away. Too many of his soldiers
left children fatherless when they fell beneath the empire's war machines.
Without turning away from Xander, he nodded. Gabriel knew it was bitter
for Arhys to submit to such an order. But for his son's sake …

"I'll sing—" Gabriel began.

But before he could finish, immense loudspeakers set atop the hovercraft
blasted a stab of cacophonous music—an eerie confluence of minor notes.
The music of the noise machines. It was like the blast of the deep horns from
before, but filled with more notes—like voices, but false things, inhuman.

It blasted twice more in quick succession, followed by a tinkling run of
sounds. An approximation of music. But again false.

Finally, it blasted another long moment. And three more times in quick
succession.

It was all a reminder that the *empire* told them what music was. Nafaryus
might listen to Gabriel sing, but there'd be no mistaking who was in control
of something as simple as musical expression.

In the silence that returned after the blasts had echoed out, a third
figure emerged from the upper deck of the landship, as if awakened—*and
irritated*—by the dissonance of the noise machines.

It was Faythe, the emperor's daughter. He saw her face every time he
held an imperial coin, her countenance pressed into the metal as a token of
her father's esteem. He'd always thought the image a pleasing one. At the
sight of her in person, Gabriel forgot to breathe. It wasn't that she was the
emperor's daughter. Though that was true enough. Or that she was lovely.
Which was also true. Or even that she seemed irritated by the empire's

form of music. Because such seemed clear. What caught his attention was the look of compassion that rose in her face as she looked over the people of Ravenskill.

When he followed her eyes, like seeing for the first time himself, he realized how thin their clothes actually were. How thin and frail their bodies—sunken cheeks, hollow eyes, bent backs. Even the militia's uniforms were ragtag things. Truth was, they were often being worn by a fourth or fifth soldier, who'd removed them from the body of his former brother, cut down in war.

Dear God.

And yet …

The look of Faythe's concern for his people made his heart trip in his chest. He could love a woman with compassion that honest and immediate. And it didn't hurt that she didn't seem to care for the NOMACS. He had to work to keep a grin off his face.

Maybe there's an agitator in me, after all. He almost did grin then.

Emperor Nafaryus gestured grandly, inviting Gabriel rather sarcastically and impatiently to honor him with a song.

But what do I sing?

Looking still at Faythe, the seed of an idea came. He thought about the beauty of a long life lived with someone you care about. He thought about that moment when all the love and hardship came to an end, and you sent your loved one on their way. Without regret. He wanted the beauty of a life like that. It's what he thought love might mean.

Then he looked out at his own people with their thin clothes and thin shoulders and thin hope. And he knew they would all soon stare down a dark path. The path Audra had nearly taken today. It wasn't hard labor or taxes that beat them down. It was uncertainty that hurt them. It was not knowing if it was all worth it when that moment came, if their seconds in the sun had been for nothing, despite the difficulty and pain.

It was the idea of facing that dark path alone.

A few steps away stood a mother who'd woken this morning believing she'd bury her child. A mother who'd sought someone to stand in the way of that cruelty. Someone to stand beside her if it had to be.

And then there was Arhys, and all his soldiers. *My dearest God.* Poorly armed men and women who dared to stand in the way of that dividing path—the path between another day in the fields and the cold earth. Men and women who went to that earth early, never knowing if they'd made a difference, uncertain of their own choice to defend Ravenskill, especially because they left families behind.

And for his brother, it meant more. He'd lost Evangeline. He'd watched her die in the moments after Xander came into the world. That scar had changed him.

In that moment, Gabriel knew what he must sing. The feeling of it, anyway.

This time, he didn't pick up his guitar. He wanted those who heard him to only hear his voice. Hear what he had to say. The people began to clap, defying the emperor's tight hold on them, encouraging Gabriel to show the bastard his music.

Gabriel gave his brother a long look, searching for the words. *Evangeline.* Such remarkable strength she'd had, even to the end. And finally, he found a way in:

When your time has come
And you're looking toward the light
All that really matters

He gestured toward Xander. And as Arhys looked at his son, Gabriel ruffled the boy's hair—the way an uncle will—and sang:

Is what you leave behind

Arhys nodded understanding to Gabriel's words, and pulled his son close.

Gabriel then looked around at the men and women of the Ravenskill militia. There was a desire to believe in their eyes. A desire to latch onto something that made their choices worthwhile:

So, let your hearts be free
Keep your spirit burning bright
Set down the stones you carry
Take the weight off your mind

He then stepped back up onto the portico, so all could see him. All the town. The field pickers and shopkeeps and visiting priests:

When you're facing the path that divides
Know that I will be there by your side
Find your strength in the sound of my voice
And you'll know
Which choice is right

Because he'd chosen. Chosen in a way he hadn't before. He'd done so the moment Rena had brought her child to him. Whatever good he could do with his voice—even if it meant finding the weapon inside it—he would. He'd stand by them. Right to the Goddamn bitter end. Which might have to do with revolution, and absolutely had to do with his willingness to go gently with them into the dark, and reassure them that they were on the right path. Give them certainty in their hard choices.

And that was no small thing.

Then he caught sight of Rena's sister. What did his song do for her? He found that, too:

In this fleeting life
We can sometimes lose our way
But night is always darkest
Just before the new day

She raised her chin toward him, thanking him by way of a grin. She might be stronger than any of them, and by damn it did him good to see her smile.

Then he let the rest loose. Loud and strong. He gave it the same large feeling he did when he stood at the canyon of the great divide and sang to bridge the gap of all he could see:

When you're facing the path that divides

Know that I will be there by your side

Find your strength in the sound of my voice

His gaze shifted to Faythe then, who stared back at him, her eyes soft and grateful and touched by a hint of wonder. His song resonated with her. He could feel it, like a twinning of their spirits. In that moment they were connected by his song in a way he couldn't put words to. Nor did he feel a need to. Rather, he finished his tune the best way he could think to do it.

And you'll know

Which choice is right

His final note seemed to sustain a full minute. It resonated every bit as much as the machines' bass horns. More. Because it got inside them. Not just to their bones. But someplace deeper. He could see it in the way the lines at the corners of their mouths and eyes relaxed.

They'd face Nafaryus if they had to. And if need be, they'd walk into the dark. Together. But there'd be no uncertainty. Not anymore.

When he turned to face Nafaryus, he thought he caught a brief look of understanding in the emperor's eyes. But the man's face quickly pinched with impatience and anger.

"Very moving," Nafaryus said with thick sarcasm. "It's no wonder people are convinced of your providence. You make them believe utter foolishness." He paused for effect. "You give them false hope."

Gabriel looked around at his townspeople, at Arhys, their expressions expectant. He didn't have eloquent words. He wasn't trained in argument. But he wouldn't let the emperor's words go unchallenged.

He looked back at Nafaryus, taking care not to appear arrogant or defiant, and said simply, "No hope is false."

The emperor's son, Daryus, grabbed a rifle from a nearby G.N.E. soldier with hasty intent. But his father put a hand up, silently commanding all to stop. Daryus froze. Even the horse company stilled.

Nafaryus leaned forward, his eyes locked on Gabriel. "First, step down from your portico there. It puts you too much above the rest of your kind."

Gabriel complied, sensing that they were dangerously close to a massacre right here in the town square.

"Good," said Nafaryus, "At least we know you can listen. Which will help you with two more … requests, your emperor will have of you."

Gabriel knew enough not to speak, but only waited on his lord's command.

Nafaryus glanced at Faythe, then locked Gabriel in with another harsh stare. "Second, don't ever look at my daughter that way again. I won't have it. Don't test me on this."

The emperor waited until Gabriel nodded ascent.

"And lastly, I feel like I should remind you who leads the Great Northern Empire." Nafaryus used an incredulous tone. "You've got these admirers practically swearing allegiance to you. In fact, I suspect if I tried to place you under arrest, this crowd would turn hostile. We'd have a riot. And then my men would have to use weapons on innocent people who made a bad choice simply because they were touched by song. That sound about right to you, Gabriel?"

Gabriel refused to be baited, even though he knew Nafaryus was right. He stood silent.

"Fact is," the emperor went on unabashed, "I *am* calling for your arrest."

The crowd erupted. Angry shouts filled the air. Weapons were brandished, whether Ravenskill militia with actual guns or townsfolks with any implement they had at hand.

Almost as fast, imperial guards responded. "Kneel!" they commanded—it was the first response to sedition.

None knelt, and the mob grew louder, more frantic.

Nafaryus kept looking only at Gabriel. And grinned. He picked up what looked like a communication handset, and spoke into it. His voice blared from the sky, filling up the air and echoing off every surface. The NOMACS. They were transmitting his voice at a volume and pitch that rumbled and touched everyone and everything.

"He'll surrender on his own," Nafaryus said. "If he doesn't, I'll return and raze Ravenskill to the ground." He pointed at Gabriel. "You have until midnight at week's end. Saturday we celebrate two-hundred and fifty years since the close of the End Wars. A commemoration is planned. We'll now also use it to mark the end of the empire's internal strife, when you turn yourself in. This gives you nearly three days to see to your affairs."

The imperial guards seemed to feel vindicated for not being obeyed, their faces smug.

The landship fired up, thrusters pushing a hot wind that blew against his face and all the crowds. It served as a reminder of the technological power the emperor had at his disposal. And the fire that he'd rain down if Gabriel didn't comply.

The same pomp he'd arrived with attended Nafaryus's exit. Horse hooves clattering, horns blaring, NOMACS sluicing through the air. When it all had gone far enough down the road to no longer be heard, Arhys turned questioning eyes on Gabriel, *Where do you stand?*

CHAPTER 7

D aryus strode directly to his offices when they arrived back at the palace. Part of it was the humiliation, but more of it was to check if the new drone capabilities had captured what he'd set them to capture. His father may not think much of his Strength Program, but he'd show him he was wrong. Nafaryus would be forced to recognize Daryus's achievements. Succession wouldn't be a simple matter of bloodline. Daryus intended for his father to *mean* it.

He'd no sooner reached his desk, when Arabelle followed him in. "Your father isn't in the business of embarrassing you. You know better."

"Really?" He whirled to face his mother. "He wouldn't even let me defend his honor. That entire town was mocking him."

"I think that's a little strong—"

"Or at least they didn't show him the proper respect." Daryus slammed his fist down on the oaken table. "He's setting dangerous precedents with these games. Three days? Imagine what that militia can prepare in three days. Do you think they're just going to hand Gabriel over?"

"Then you think your father made an empty threat about razing the town?" Arabelle questioned.

Daryus threw his hands up. "That's not the point. Defiance needs to be met swiftly. Decisively. These rebels will decide to protect their own. And now they have three days to fortify themselves."

"Against our army," she said with patience. "Are you really concerned?"

He paused, regaining his composure. "Of course not. But why risk a conflict where we might lose valuable resources. With one shot I could have put an end to their spiritual leader and ended this uprising."

"Maybe," Arabelle replied with a gently skeptical tone. "But these Ravenskill people might also decide not to risk losing their homes and loved ones in a battle for one man. This Gabriel, if he's so attuned to their needs, may give himself up. Your father's a better politician than you're giving him credit for. If his idea works, nothing is lost and we take this Gabriel. Alive, even."

"They won't do it," was all he said. She just didn't know the feelings of the people the way he did; she'd not been to battle across the empire the way he had.

But then she surprised him. "What's this really about, Daryus? It's not Ravenskill? Or even their singer? Tell me."

They'd skirted this discussion more times than he could count. He grimaced thinking about the moments when he or she had failed to say it out loud. But he was done with that.

"He chose her presentation," he said, tension in his voice.

"You're talking about Faythe." It wasn't a question.

"Not a formal thing. Just something she created on her own one day, playing in the garden." He stared into the lights reflecting off the surface of his desk. "She said it was a geological survey. She wore a lab coat. And he chose to attend her pretend presentation rather than my graduation from cadet school. I earned top honors." He paused a long moment. "He'd have been proud."

"He was," Arabelle assured him.

"A military career isn't even what I wanted," he said. "I did that for him."

"I know. He just gets distracted—"

"No," Daryus said with force. "Don't make excuses for him. He prefers Faythe. He always has. I've accepted that." He looked up, feeling heat in his eyes. "But that doesn't mean he can't respect me, too."

Arabelle gave him a motherly look. "He does, Daryus. He wouldn't have you in line to replace him otherwise."

That was hard to argue with. But it didn't change the family dynamic one damned jot. A lifetime of geological presentations.

"I suppose I'll just have to be sure his faith in me is justified," Daryus concluded, and gave his mother a smile so she'd think they'd found some peace.

"He only stopped you because killing Gabriel or Arhys might have caused a riot." Arabelle used a factual tone. "And this way, he can test Ravenskill resolve and resources."

Daryus didn't want to debate it, and kept his mild smile.

"Are you going to be all right?" she asked with a mother's instinct.

"I'm fine." He lied. "Maybe a little tired is all."

"Well, get some rest," she said. "There's a dinner in honor—" She left off.

What his mother didn't say was that Faythe was being honored tonight for her diplomatic work abroad the last few weeks. He bit back his anger as his mother quietly took her leave.

Daryus quickly sat and pulled up the data download from the drone scans conducted at the Ravenskill square. There'd been some good fortune in their visit. The music man had been holding some kind of concert, bringing most of the people into one place. The emperor's procession had been announced and designed to do some of this, too. But the crowd must have comprised fifty percent of Ravenskill by the time Nafaryus addressed the crowd.

And the drones had scanned every last one of them.

Daryus didn't need to understand the numbers and data associated with the tens of thousands of profiles. What was important is that the new technology appeared to have worked. He now had a complete acoustical signature of almost every man, woman, and child in Ravenskill. That was dangerous information if you knew how to use it.

And in addition to the new imaging capability, one of the other features of the Strength Program was the knowledge of how to use that information. Abuse it, some might say.

Daryus smiled.

He'd prove himself, put down this rebellion, and win support for his program all with one simple act. He only needed the opportunity.

CHAPTER 8

─○─

Nafaryus' convoy hadn't completely cleared Ravenskill before Arhys signaled his four best men to help him escort Gabriel south out of the city in a small convoy of their strongest landcraft. Just beyond the Passage route, which bisected the island, his militia operated a training compound centralized around an old military bunker that ran several stories underground. Gabriel would be safe there, while they prepared.

The lights down in the bunker were old, and often flickered. What light they did shine came weak and uninspiring. Metal and concrete and porcelain. Everything dull and hard. And somehow smelling like chilled earth.

But these many dimly lit rooms that smelled of the earth housed captured pieces of Empire technology—pulse rifles, audio dishes, and more. One entire floor housed the efforts of Ravenskill efforts at weapons design—not as sophisticated as the Empire's, but sometimes effective—gun turret frames, heavy artillery, carbine refinement techniques for ammunition manufacturing.

They were more than the rumpled militia they let on to keep Nafaryus at bay, while they grew.

Gabriel sat opposite him, shaking his head. "Knowing where I stand means giving myself up."

"You're a fool," Arhys said, biting back his anger.

Gabriel sighed with patience. "I'm no martyr, Arhys. But one life for tens of thousands. You know I'm right."

Arhys stood, tired of the debate. "Every member of my army would rather die than surrender you to the emperor." He paused, glaring down at his brother. "You're the one hope we have in this whole thing."

"We've tried that," Gabriel argued. "I don't know how to do what you want me to do." He grew quiet. "I never have."

Evangeline's name needn't be spoken for them each to understand.

Arhys began to walk the stone-tiled floor. Back-and-forth. His eyes cast down, lost in thought. "Perhaps the demands of this timeframe will pull it out of you. Three days. Maybe the pressure ..."

"Do you really think the emperor will burn Ravenskill?" Gabriel asked, disbelief in his tone. "He'd be crippling our production, which means a deficit on taxes and our town goods. It hurts him to do it."

Arhys considered it. "Maybe. But he's said it now. If he doesn't follow through, every precinct with a resistance will press that advantage. Nafaryus can't afford to fight a civil war on every front."

"Then I should turn myself in." Gabriel stood now, too. "It buys you time to continue building our defenses. If he marches on Ravenskill in three days, what chance do we honestly have?"

"And what does it say to every person in Ravenskill whose already fought and bled with the hope you'd one day help us win ... if you give up." Arhys words came in tight succession, his voice straining. "It tells them they don't matter. That their sacrifice didn't matter. You don't have the right to make that decision, Gabriel."

"Do you think we can win?" his brother questioned. "I'm asking for the truth here."

Arhys leaned forward, placing fists on the table between them. "We're as strong as we're ever going to be. And his mistake is telling us when he's going to come. Instead of giving yourself up, you should be helping me plan our defense."

Gabriel stared into his brother's eyes. Arhys returned the stare, never wavering. "I'm with you."

"Goddamn right you are," Arhys said with some relief.

"And if we lose, we'll say it's your fault," Gabriel joked.

Arhys wasn't the joking kind. But he smiled this time. A genuine smile, and not the forced variety. "I can live with that," he finally replied.

Gabriel then tapped the small control console at the table's edge. Across its surface a relief map of New Anglya lit up. With a voice command, they expanded Endless Isleland. "How will they come at us?" he asked.

Arhys hadn't yet looked at the map. "The first question remains: Do you think you can find a way to use your voice for this?"

His brother shook his head. "I don't know, Arhys. There's no trigger for this. No manual. Most of it's instinctive."

"Maybe we should have you practice focusing on destructive thoughts and tones," Arhys suggested.

"And if that's how it works, what are the chances I'll master it in a few days?" Gabriel asked rhetorically. "And who gets hurt in the process."

Arhys gave him a dead look. "That's part of war, Gabriel. All my people understand that."

"You want me to practice on them?" Gabriel said, incredulous. "Maybe you *are* insane."

Arhys held up his hands. "All right. You decide how to find a way. But I'm convinced that's how we win."

"And if I don't ..."

Arhys always had a contingency plan. "We overwhelm them with numbers."

"Ravenskill?" Gabriel made no attempt to disguise his confusion.

Arhys fingered the map controls, zooming much further out, to show not only New Anglya, but all of Yorkeland, and even the northern reaches of New Pavonya.

"I've already sent word to every resistance command across the Empire of what we're up against." He eyed the terrain like a man possessed. "I've put it to them. We make a united stand now."

Gabriel did some quick calculations. "There's no way they'll all be here in time."

Arhys looked up at him. The cold indifference had returned. "They're not all coming *here*."

CHAPTER 9

——o——

F aythe stood leaning against the balustrade of her personal balcony. The view had always inspired her before. Lush gardens, statuary commemorating prior family leaders, water fountains. The trees brought birds. Other animals made the gardens their home. It had always suggested a simple kind of peace and tranquility to her before. Civility, maybe. Now, it highlighted an ugly lie, a secret that had been kept from her.

The door to her private chamber opened. She didn't need to turn to know her mother had come to talk.

"Did you know?" she asked Arabelle, without turning. "About the people? How they live?"

"I did," her mother affirmed. "From reports mostly. I'd never been there."

"And the other cities and villages across Yorkeland and New Anglya, they're the same?" Faythe braced for the answer.

"To one degree or another," Arabelle said. "We're rebuilding a world, Faythe. That's going to take time. The End Wars were devastating. You know this."

She finally turned to face her mother. "You know what I find remarkable. That despite the living conditions, those people," she pointed southward, "seem to live with hope."

"Your father—"

"Not in us," she interjected. "Those people weren't living on the promise of imperial assistance. And you know it." She changed the discussion. "Why did you keep this from me?"

Arabelle strolled to the balcony's edge, looking out. "Oh, Faythe, there was no conspiracy of silence. If it was to remain a secret, you wouldn't have been asked to go to Ravenskill today. Besides, you're young. And your talents aren't in resource management. Your father and I knew you'd do well in negotiation proceedings with other nation states. Eventually, you'll see and witness every consequence we're still suffering from the End Wars, not just the condition of our agriculture."

Faythe initiated a file sequence and gave her mother access. She watched as Arabelle saw information stream across her own personal lens monitors.

"I pulled that up on the way back to the palace." Faythe waited for her mother to return her stare. "Migrant slavery? We rent out our own people?"

Arabelle sighed heavily. "Not something I'm proud of. But our own economy is tenuously balanced. I don't think it will be a permanent practice."

Faythe looked out from her balcony again. "I grew up with a lot of privileges. I always knew that. But I didn't understand the sacrifices others were making so I could wake up to this." She nodded toward the gardens.

"Places more importance on the truce work you're doing, doesn't it?" Arabelle observed.

That got Faythe thinking. "Why did father ask me to come?" She didn't wait for an answer. "Part of him must have thought I could help establish some peace between the government and Ravenskill. But things got out of control."

"Your father doesn't like to feel threatened," her mother said, "that much I'll say."

Faythe's mind raced with excitement. "It's not too late. I'll go back and establish a dialogue with them. I'll find this Gabriel. He seems to be the one they look to."

Arabelle gave a small smile. "This wouldn't have to do with anything more than the good of the empire, would it?"

Faythe didn't demure. "I'd go, even if I didn't admire Gabriel."

Her mother's brows rose with an unspoken question.

"You heard the same song I did," Faythe said, remembering the sound of it. "It managed to inspire hope and confidence in a people who have little to hope for. You can tell me if I'm wrong, but that sounds like a rare quality for a man."

Arabelle reached out. Faythe thought her mother intended to pull her into an embrace. Instead, she fished into the pocket of her overcloak and held up Faythe's music player.

"I suspect a music man might hold a particular place in your heart." Arabelle waved the device.

Faythe had no idea anyone knew, other than Jack. "Does father know?" she asked, worried.

"Of course not." Her mother handed the music player back. "I keep my confidences. I just want you to be cautious of where you place your loyalties."

Faythe took the device, holding her mother's stare. "I love father. But he's a hard man to be close to, isn't he?"

Arabelle smiled again, a more motherly smile. "He loves you. Make no mistake about that. I'd just say he's made of equal parts of love and ambition. But he tries. In his own way, he tries."

"He's going to level that town if Gabriel doesn't give himself up," Faythe said. "Is that the ambition you're talking about?"

"I guess that only happens if you don't prevent it." Arabelle's words sounded now more like an empress. "And I wouldn't walk in as you are. You're recognizable now. Some of the Ravenskill folk won't pause long enough to know your intentions before doing you harm."

Faythe began to plan. "I'll figure out a disguise, and leave first thing in the morning."

Arabelle did then pull her into a firm hug. "Be careful. This won't be like the conversations you've had with other nation states. Much of Ravenskill considers themselves at war with us."

"I will," Faythe said, eager to make the arrangements.

A kind of calm settled into her as her mother left her chambers. She'd be doing the thing she was best at, brokering peace, with a man who tried to help his friends and family, and did so with music. It was hard to ignore her feelings. This Gabriel was unique. And she wanted to get closer to him.

((O))

Arabelle closed Faythe's door and proceeded down a number of corridors, back to her son's offices. She found him there, still huddled over his work station, reading, making notes, a wild kind of light in his eyes. He looked up as she came in.

"I have a task for you," she said matter-of-factly.

"Of course," he said.

"Faythe is going back to Ravenskill in the morning—"

He stood up fast. "What!"

"It sounds ill-conceived, but I think she may be right." Arabelle came close to Daryus, giving him a serious look. "She believes she can broker peace between us and Ravenskill. And before anyone's killed or anything's destroyed, I think we owe it to everyone to give her a chance."

"With all due respect, mother, neither you or Faythe knows these rebels like I do." He came around his desk. "This is foolish."

"Maybe," Arabelle conceded. "Which is why I'd like you to shadow her. Don't impede her work. But be near in case things go badly. Keep her safe. She's going unescorted."

"Unbelievable." Daryus returned to his monitors.

"Can I count on you?" Arabelle asked.

Something then shifted in her son's eyes. It wasn't a look she knew in him.

"Yes, of course," he said. "Thanks for trusting me to do this. I'll make sure everything goes as planned."

Something in his final words bothered her. But Arabelle left it alone, she'd meant to speak with her husband since returning, and the hour was growing late.

CHAPTER 10

———◉———

Drones filled the sky over Perpetual View, most of them concentrated to the North where the Withered Hills began. Some emitted deep resonant blasts of suppressive sound, meant to break the courage of the enemy, quell them into submission. Others were laying out broad swaths of energy bursts, pushing rebel attackers back by brute force. Nafaryus observed from the bridge of his battle cruiser for only a few moments, before taking command of his counter-offensive.

"Send landing troops up the North River," he directed. "Bring two hundred in men at them directly from the east."

A lieutenant rushed off to see it done.

"Do the forward drones have incendiary capabilities?" he asked his field marshal, Moore.

"At least a handful do, yes," said Moore.

Nafaryus nodded. "Send them wide. Around the rebels. Set fire to the trees behind them. And to the west of them, too. Push them toward us."

"Shouldn't we try to push them *out* of the city?" Moore asked.

"The rebels won't harm innocent citizens." A drone exploded in the sky just ahead of them. Nafaryus didn't flinch. "Fighting near the city will hinder effectiveness."

Moore found a control console and made the adjustments to drone commands himself—several moved quickly west to execute the flank maneuver.

"Take us closer," Nafaryus pointed, indicating where he wanted to be.

His pilot looked ready to argue. The rebels were launching airborne artillery against the drones, and having some success. The battle cruiser was a much easier target. But the pilot did as he was told. Drones parted as the cruiser moved to the northern edge of the city. Below, rebel fighters on the ground conducted their field operations with an uncanny precision, especially beneath the onslaught of drone sound barrages.

"Who are they?" he asked.

Moore came up beside him. "They call themselves Prayer Fighters. Their hold is in the ridges beyond the Withered Hills."

Nafaryus's battle cruiser had been heavily soundproofed, and still the faint rumble of drone blasts could be heard on deck.

"I've seen no reports from you about new tolerances to drone suppressive audio." He gestured at the continuing attack. "How do you explain this?"

Moore had no answer.

"Other than the stuff they jam in their ears, we don't know. They've penetrated to the city center," a relay tech announced.

"Cardinal missiles," Nafaryus commanded. "All of them. Disperse pattern. Now!"

The battle cruiser arms commander responded immediately, and the world below them went up in a wave of fire and smoke.

A long moment later, his lead tactician spoke into the silence. "Estimate forty-three percent of their force taken out, my lord."

Nafaryus barely heard him. Something about the timing of this attack bothered him. It was too coincidental with his morning rendezvous in

Ravenskill. What worried him more was that the Prayer Fighters seemed unaffected by his drones' normal means of subduing them.

The bridge then heaved violently. Tremors shook the deck-plates.

Nafaryus steadied himself against the console in front of him. "What's happened?"

"Direct hit to the hull by a rebel rocket propelled explosive." The pilot's hands danced to compensate. "Anti-gravity engine is failing. We're going down!"

"Brace yourselves!" Nafaryus cried. "And arm yourselves!"

Another question rose sharply in his mind: How did they come by such powerful weapons?

The battle cruiser listed and began to fall. Slowly at first. Then a sharp report echoed around them, something supersonic, and they were in freefall. They crashed hard into the smoking remains of the foothills just behind Perpetual View.

"Don't wait for them to board," Nafaryus commanded. "Take your weapons and meet them at the doors. Get outside to safety." The battle cruiser might well explode, if other engine systems had been compromised.

Nafaryus pulled his own pulse pistol and rushed to the rear of the cruiser. He wasn't prepared for the stench.

Behind the back hatch, scorched earth still smoked. As did huddled forms, that had curled into fetal positions, either to protect themselves or as their muscles constricted in the heat. The flesh of them, burned and burning, was gut-wrenching.

Nafaryus pulled his handset and called his ground captain. "We're down. Rally to my signal." He then took direct control of the drones sent west. Instead of fire to drive the rebels toward them, he directed them to simply set them on fire. He called for the river squads to land immediately and come west into the lower hills rather than try and flank those who would now burn.

He had only to worry about the rebels to his rear, those in the city itself.

Fighting broke out all around the downed cruiser. He heard some of his bridge command cry out. But he had no time to try and help them. And the cruiser might still blow. He took off at a dead run toward the city. He'd meet his forces half way, and hope he didn't run into any rebels.

Running steps came up behind him. Moore. The marshal was keeping his back free of being an easy target. Good training.

Far distant, he thought he began to hear screams as of men afire. His two hundred men came in from the North River, surrounding him, as they pressed to the city's edge. They were still outnumbered by the rebels, but they had better weapons. He called every drone to descend on the city, and bludgeon every Prayer Fighter they could find. His men he sent into the buildings to chase the rebels into the streets.

"My lord?" It was Moore. "They've got one of the Prayer Fighters alive. I thought you'd want to question him."

Indeed he did. Nafaryus followed Moore to a squat building on the edge of the city. The inside still smelled like the ozone of pulse rifles. In the far corner sat a badly wounded rebel.

Nafaryus holstered his gun, and pulled a chair up to sit in front of the man, who'd been bound to a similar seat.

"The empire has won," Nafaryus began. "We will always win. We simply have better technology. You know this."

The man's head continued to hang down. Was he still alive?

Nafaryus reached forward and yanked the man's head up by the hair. "You will show me some respect!"

The man looked through one good eye—the other swollen shut. "You probably think you've won," the man said, his lips covered with blood.

Odd remark, Nafaryus thought. *Is he mocking me?* "You might be the last Prayer Fighter. How is that for losing?"

The man's good eye tracked Nafaryus's mouth closely as he spoke.

That's when he knew. Nafaryus raised a hand to shield his mouth, and issued an insult on the man's family name. The man didn't blink or make a sound. Nafaryus lowered his hand.

"You're deaf," he said. "You were all deaf. That's how you withstood the audio assault."

"NOMAC noise lost its edge," the rebel said, turning an ear toward Nafaryus.

"You gave up your hearing to fight?" Nafaryus stared at the man with new wonder. "But you know the drones can do more than this."

"Ayeah, but we understand how to fight force." He grinned knowingly. "Pulse weapons and explosives. We get that. Up here, we don't have a weapon-answer for sound."

Nafaryus heard something in the man's reply. "Up here?"

"Will you play at being naïve, too?" The man laughed. Not a bitter sound, more like real laughter. "Everyone under your heel knows about Gabriel. Hells, his brother put out the call for disruption."

It all locked into place. Arhys would try and prevent Nafaryus from consolidating enough force to make good on his threat, maybe even discourage him from going through with it. Divide Nafaryus' attention. Spread himself too thin.

"Seems you failed at your attempt," Nafaryus remarked, wanting to tease more information out of the man.

"Heaven's no," said the rebel. "Do you think this is all the Prayer Fighters? Not to mention that we got a look at some of your new drones. Useful information will get back to the right people."

"But not from you," Nafaryus said with menace.

"Oh, that don't matter none." The man's expression got serious with his one good eye. "You, sir, have galvanized an empire, all right. It's just not the one you think it is."

"Oh?"

"War is coming." The man leaned forward, his chair squeaking in the sudden silence. "All across the Great Northern Empire folks like me are standing together. And Gabriel will lead us. Put down your bad music. Set us free, he will."

Nafaryus clenched his fists, controlling his anger. "Is that so? Well, I met your savior this morning. He didn't seem very intent on leading a rebellion. And in a few days time, he'll be so far down in the prison bank that no earthly thing will hear a word he sings."

The man shrugged nonchalantly. "I doubt you'll take him so easily. Good luck trying." He grinned at his own defiance.

Nafaryus leaned in, making sure the man's one eye was watching him speak. "You see, my friend, every rebel from every faction can deafen himself. And you can give this war you want as many fronts as you like, to divide my resources as you think." He came so close the man would be able to feel his breath. "But that assumes that I've remained idle with my own war preparations, doesn't it? Do you think, maybe, if I'm pushed to it, that I'll unleash experimental technology that you need no ears to hear? Or feel?"

The man said nothing. There was new fear in his eyes. But new defiance also.

Nafaryus got up and strode from the concrete room. There was truth in what he'd said. But that didn't negate the rebel's truth. What he knew for sure was that the influence of this Ravenskill singer had reached too far. And resistance fighters were adapting to the drones, even when it meant sacrificing their hearing. He admired their commitment. But he wouldn't cede power without a fight.

CHAPTER 11

———◉———

The roads of Ravenskill hummed with activity. Field workers were moving through the streets on their way to another day of crop-work. Merchants were already in their shops, doors propped open to allow the scent of fresh-baked goods to fill the air. Day-trade had begun, haggling over small items sold out of hand-carts or rusted vehicles. And children too small to work ran and played with the kind of abandon reserved for those who hold no fear of the adult world, or need it. A day after her father had come here and issued his ultimatum, it looked like life here had returned to normal.

It had a different feeling. All of it. And it didn't take her long to give it a name: community. The Palace, all of Capital City, even the other governments she'd done diplomatic work with, none of them had given her the same familial sense as Ravenskill.

She had to be careful. A stranger asking about Gabriel at any time would likely evoke suspicion. In light of her father's ultimatum yesterday, Ravenskill caution would have doubled. More than that, they might be downright hostile with her if they found out who she was.

Faythe kept her hood pulled forward, to avoid detection, and began to inquire about Gabriel. She found an older man squatting in the alley-shadows of the morning sun. "Do you know where I can find Gabriel?"

"Sorry, miss," he said, his mouth missing half its teeth, "Can't spare a minute. I'm late on something."

"Of course," she replied, having chosen the man because he hadn't moved all morning, and might have seen Gabriel pass this way. Nor did the man move after she left him standing in the shadows.

Another half dozen men and women she asked, keeping the question down-beat, as though she and Gabriel were acquainted, and maybe he was expecting to meet her. But she caught the looks of suspicion all the same. She finally decided that hood or not, she wasn't likely to simply show up and be given the location of Ravenskill's favorite son.

The afternoon had begun to wane, when a gentle tapping came on her shoulder. "You still looking for Gabriel?"

Faythe whirled to see the kind face of a tall, portly man wearing a baker's apron. "Name's Himney," he said, taking her hand in his and pumping it twice with vigor.

"How did—"

"We're a close-knit bunch, we Ravenskill folk, miss." He rocked back on his heels the way a man does when he's expressing pride or happiness. Or both. "We sort of have to be, don't we? And well, folks tell me things. I'm something of a hub, if I can say it that way. And I don't mind a bit." He paused, giving her a somewhat exaggerated expression of suspicion.

"You want to know who I am," she said, anticipating his next words.

"I'm not going to tell you where Gabriel is anymore than the others did," he said, chuckling warmly. "Arhys is bit tightly wound, but he'd be right to take me to task for doing such a thick-headed thing, don't you agree, Lady Faythe?"

"I do," she said, not surprised he knew her. "But that doesn't help me at all."

Himney produced a warm buttered roll. "Take a bite. Friendship always begins with food."

Faythe did so, her mouth exploding with the rich flavors and textures of butter-crème and flaky dough. She hadn't expected this in Ravenskill.

"I'll take your expression as approval, and as a surprise. We don't have the palace cutlery, but we're not the simpletons your father believes us to be," Himney said. "Now, the bald fact of it is I can't whisper a word. But, there's a young lad who can, and will, if he judges you to be right."

"Right?"

"Stand up," he clarified. "Of good moral fiber. Not. A. Threat." Then Himney pointed toward some children playing near the water fountain. "Ask for Xander. You can use my name if it's of any help to you."

Faythe nodded. "You're very kind, thank you."

He waved that away. "I tend to get a good read on people." He tugged gently at the hem of her hood. "That's Georgia Twill, my lady. Dead giveaway to a man like me, who, before he wore his apron, tailored for the first family of the Southern Republic. And I saw the look you gave our Gabriel. Wasn't mean. I wouldn't point you to Xander otherwise. But I'll still let the lad decide about introductions. To his father, that is. I've pushed Arhys a bit too much lately. Free rolls or none." He smiled wide and ambled back to his shop, handing out more bite-sized rolls as he went.

Faythe shook her head and grinned. The baker seemed to collect intelligence as well as the drones did. She then hurried, without rushing, to the children. But when she got there, she either didn't see Xander, or she'd forgotten what he looked like.

"Excuse me," she said, addressing the tallest girl. "Can you tell me where Xander is?"

All the children stopped. A ball they'd been kicking bounced impertinently in the sudden stillness. Each gave her a long look, then sulked a way, a few holding hands as they went.

The square had practically emptied now. Townsfolk off to work, children scattered from their play, Himney's booming voice having retreated, too. Only the sound of the fountain seemed to fill the air.

So, when she turned, she started and fell back a step. Xander stood two paces behind her.

"You surprised me," she said.

Xander said nothing.

"You're Xander?"

The boy nodded.

Faythe smiled to reassure him. "I'm looking for your father. I'm a friend. You can trust me."

The boy cocked his head with skepticism she thought a child his age shouldn't yet know. "You want to see Gabriel."

She didn't see any point in lying. "Yes. But I'll ask your father's permission for that."

"What can you do?" he asked. Then his eyes widened, as if he realized who she was.

"I promise I can help," she told him. "And if it's far, we should hurry."

Xander stood still for several long moments, his boyish face appearing to consider the prudence of taking her to his father. He finally nodded to himself, as if concluding some interior logic, and took her by the hand.

They walked south along a main road for a short while before Xander took them onto a series of footpaths. They wound through brush and over hummocks to arrive at a compound well hidden inside a dense grown of elms and walnut trees. The fencing had been painted shades of brown and green to blend with the environment.

As they approached a gate, a man appeared, dressed in makeshift camouflage. He carried a rifle. Faythe recognized it as the pre-war carbine type.

Before the man could issue a warning or inquire of them, Xander spoke. "Will you please go get my father? We need to talk to him."

The man hadn't stopped looking at Faythe. "Xander, your father—"

"Trust me," Xander interrupted. "He won't want us to have waited."

The boy didn't speak with insolence or assumed privilege, but rather as if doing the man a favor.

Faythe got the impression this wasn't the first time, as the man ducked quickly through the gate and disappeared.

They waited quietly, birds singing in the trees above them. One might almost forget the ugliness of the fight this place represented. A fight necessitated by her father. But that's why she was here, to try and broker peace.

Strident footsteps rose from inside the installation. Their cadence suggested anger, or impatience maybe.

Arhys appeared, flanked by two men, the gate guard in tow. "Xander, you can't interrupt—"

"Father, I wouldn't come if it weren't important," the boy said, holding up his hands in a calming gesture.

Arhys came to the opposite side of the gate. "What is it? Who is this?"

Xander looked up at Faythe, then back at his father. "Be patient while she speaks." Then he nodded to her.

Without hesitation, she drew down her hood.

Faythe had come this far, and she had no intention of turning back, though, if she had, the look on Arhys' face right now could have inspired it. She thought she could see all his thoughts, distaste, reprisal, how he could leverage her against the emperor.

"I can imagine what you're thinking," she began, "and I don't blame you. But I'm not here on my father's business."

Arhys threw the gate open and stepped threateningly close to her.

Xander got between them, though he stood only to their midriffs. "Why would she come alone, and reveal herself, if she were against us."

"The emperor is cunning," Arhys answered, keeping his glare locked on Faythe.

"The emperor," she countered, "doesn't know I'm here. If you have any intelligence of his court, you know I am Faythe, his daughter, and a political ambassador. Not a spy."

"Come to convince us to surrender my brother, no doubt." Arhys positioned his men on each side of her.

She gave both soldiers a long look, to be sure they knew who they'd be taking into custody, if it came to that. Returning her focus to Arhys, she said calmly, "No. And I believe I have a way to avert the ultimatum my father gave Gabriel, and perhaps even restore some peace between the empire and Ravenskill."

Arhys laughed. "A solution for all our woes. And at such an opportune moment." His smile faded to a grim pinched line of mouth. He glared, his hatred, fueled, she knew, by the deaths of so many of his friends, friends who'd fought for a better life for their people. "You can understand my mistrust."

"I do," she said. "It's why I came alone, unarmed, and without telling my father."

Arhys softened a bit. "What is this plan of yours?"

"That's something I'll only discuss with Gabriel." Faythe could see the anger mounting in Arhys again, and quickly added, "That's my only condition. And if he refuses, then do with me what you will."

She never dropped his hard stare. He was a formidable man, tall and rough at the edges. The kind of man needed to fight an empire. But she sensed that he trusted Gabriel. And after a long moment, he nodded.

"Xander, you get back to town. I'm sure there's something useful you could be doing." The boy saluted and raced back down the footpath. "Follow me," Arhys said, and led her through the gate into the compound.

They crossed between several well camouflaged buildings, netting and branches overlaid everything to make it all seem like forest growth. At the center of the facility, a broad concrete circle had been painted in striated patterns of brown, green and black—more disguise. A set of stairs descended into it from the perimeter.

The two guards were ordered to wait at the top, while Arhys led Faythe down out of the light and into heavy shadow. He keyed a dead-bolted steel door, and locked it behind them, once they'd passed through.

Then into the bowels of the earth they descended. Multiple staircases, long hallways, countless doors. A survival bunker. Her father had such a place beneath the palace, meant for dire times like there'd been during the End Wars.

The style of décor was antiquated down here. The whole place smelled of neglect and rusting steel. Certain places had been cleaned and refurbished, a medical bay, a broad set of weapons lockers, a few meeting rooms, and even some living quarters. But most of it sat in disrepair. It gave her the impression of living decay. In some places, water dripped and pooled in stale pools on vinyl flooring that had curled up at the edges.

Their footsteps echoed ominously ahead of them as they passed deeper into the bowels of the bunker. Then, at the deepest point they descended, the light got a bit brighter, the floors and walls refashioned with tile and fresh paint. It still felt somewhat antiseptic, but that beat decrepitude.

Arhys paused at a door with a long steel handle. "If you attempt to betray my brother, or play me for the fool, I'll know. And I won't care who your father is when that happens."

He didn't wait for a reply, and slid the door back. Gabriel looked up from a table where he sat reading.

Faythe had visited heads of state, rulers, even despots, but she couldn't remember being quite so nervous. She admired Gabriel for his concern for his people, and she was intrigued by the fact that he made music, real music, which hadn't been done in centuries. But this was more than that. She felt drawn to him by more than mere appreciation.

And from the look in his eyes, she guessed he felt the same.

"Lady Faythe," he said, standing. "Nafaryus's daughter. And his leading diplomat."

"Gabriel," she replied. "The soul of the Ravenskill rebellion."

Arhys voice boomed in the small Spartan room. "We're freedom fighters." Then he slammed the door shut, his boot-heels clacking as he retreated down the exterior hall.

"I didn't mean—"

"I know," Gabriel cut in. "And so does Arhys. But he's lost more than anyone in the fight. He's entitled to his bristles."

She smiled at that, then pointed to the open book on the table. "What are you reading?"

"Ah, this." He hefted the book. "Apocryphal music theory. Arhys believes there's something more to my music than I've uncovered. I'm trying to determine if he's right."

"To fight my father," she surmised.

"To save my people," he answered.

"And what have you discovered so far?" she asked, genuinely interested.

Gabriel's eyes focused on the book again. "There seems to be evidence that we all have a fundamental ... sound. Something about us that is integral to *who* we are that can be given a voice."

She eyed him carefully. "To destroy?"

He looked up. "Potentially," he said. "Though I suspect it could be used in any number of ways."

She felt like she did the first time she held her music player. "Can you show me?"

Gabriel seemed to consider the wisdom of doing so, but not for long. He turned his focus back to another book on the table, and soon uttered a string of quiet sounding words. They had a hum-like quality. The book began to shimmy, pages ruffling as if caught in a mild wind.

Faythe stared in wonder. Music alone had been a small miracle in her life. A secret she kept with difficulty—it was hard not sharing something that seemed so important and wonderful. But this? Music that could stir a page? Could move physical objects? It went beyond her imagination.

"Inanimate things can be moved," Gabriel said, still watching the book. "I think the same will be true of people. But a person ... they've got emotions and memories. I believe they can probably be touched in other ways, too."

"Good to hear," she said with renewed enthusiasm. "Because I think my father can be turned."

Gabriel set his music book down. "About me surrendering?"

"And the ongoing unrest with Ravenskill," she added. "There's another side of my father. You'd expect me to say something like that, but it's true. He may be drawn to power, but he's not a warmonger. There's a gentler part of him that I think we can appeal to."

"If he walks back from his order, he'll look weak," Gabriel reasoned. "Men drawn to power don't like to look weak."

"We'll have to reframe it somehow," she argued. "We have to try. Otherwise either you turn yourself in, or he will bring a sizeable force to tear Ravenskill down."

He came around the table, leaning back against it. "When he came to hear me sing, I thought I saw him … I don't know, enjoying it for a moment. Moved by the song in some way."

"That's what I was going to suggest." Faythe stepped closer, glad to be nearer Gabriel. "Maudlin as it may sound, I think you prepare what you'd say to him in a song. I'll return and ask him for a private audience, away from the palace. We'll meet him together."

She reached a hand out to him. He took it, and the feel of it was more than just conspirators with a dangerous plot. The small smile on his face suggested he felt the same.

"We're an unlikely pair," he said. "But maybe that's precisely why this will work."

She offered a deliberately conspiratorial smile. "I don't think we're so unlikely a pair."

He laughed, but his face quickly stiffened in thought, and he glanced back at the music apocrypha book. "The other half of theoretical personal music signatures is that if music can enliven a soul, affect physical things … it can deaden them, too."

She drew back to study his face. "Which means what?"

"I think the music of the NOMACS is more than just abrasive to listen to." He never dropped her gaze. "I think it takes something away. I think your sound engineers have found a way to use music to alter us somehow. Remove the urge to even know real music. Or pursue anything with passion. I'm convinced it's a form of control."

She shook her head. "I'd have heard—"

"Do me one more favor," he jumped in. "When you request the audience with your father, ask him to meet us at Heaven's Cove. There's an old amphitheater there with great acoustics, completely abandoned. But most importantly, ask him to keep the NOMACS far from Endless Isleland all together. This won't work if the NOMACS interrupt us. In fact, it would be good if he didn't listen to them at all tomorrow."

She agreed it made sense, even if she wasn't convinced the NOMACS were everything Gabriel thought they were. "I'll do my best."

Then, she did something slightly impetuous. She leaned in and kissed him. Not deep or long. Though not as a friend does with a light peck. Part of it was admiration, she couldn't deny that. But the larger part came from an attraction that was equally hard to deny. Not infatuation. She understood those feelings. This had a weight about it, a sense of being in the right place, with the right companion.

The best part about the kiss, though, was that he kissed her back. It seemed to place a kind of seal on their relationship. A promise of a future. And with that, the urgency to get this work underway swelled inside her.

"I'm going back to the palace now," she said, squeezing his hand once before letting go and moving purposefully do the door. "I'll request the audience. We'll plan on tomorrow night. I'll come back early so we can prepare." She picked up a pen and wrote a code on a piece of note paper. "Use this to pull down the encrypted message I'll send you."

She gave him an encouraging look, and set to go. He raised a hand to stop her.

"Hold on." He squinted, as if puzzling over something. "You're not as indifferent as your father or his soldiers, or even other citizens across the empire." Gabriel glanced at the book beside him, then back to her. "You've come across real music somewhere, haven't you?"

Faythe admired the bit of reasoning. She might even be able to use it with her father. She pulled the music player from her inner pocket and showed it to Gabriel, earbuds and all. "It's an old music player. Found it in a musical artifact archive."

He shook his head with good humor. "What's on it?"

"More than I have time to tell you." She waved it in the air. "Thousands and thousands of songs. All types. Right now, I'm listening to something called Christmas songs from a group of musicians once known as the Trans-Siberian Orchestra. Hundreds of years old. But beautiful, powerful music. Makes me sad for the traditions we've lost."

"Sounds like they're not lost," Gabriel offered.

Damn but she liked the way this man thought. "I'll be back," she said, and hurried with a Ravenskill escort through the labyrinthine bunker toward the surface, and her father.

CHAPTER 12

———◦———

Daryus crouched behind a thicket of ivy, watching his sister and Arhys' son, Xander, at the gate to the hidden rebel compound. Such good fortune. Now, he'd not only be able to deliver Gabriel to his father, but he could crush the Ravenskill militia, or most of it, with one fell blow, now that he knew where to strike. He smiled in the cool shadows.

The conversation didn't quite carry though. He had no doubt Faythe was asking for the chance to negotiate something between the Empire and Ravenskill. Their mother had maybe even colluded with Faythe in this. But Daryus knew his father; he'd never have sanctioned this. *Yet another chance to earn his respect. And my second name.*

He quietly sent coordinates with one of the new fist-sized com drones back to the broader network. His command: full release of Strength Program protocols, even those still in testing. He demanded they be ready by tomorrow for invasive maneuvers.

Then Arhys' voice did reach him—there wasn't anything subtle about the man. "Xander, you get back to town. I'm sure there's something useful you could be doing."

Before the little group disbanded, Daryus disappeared back through the trees. He followed a series of simple skiff marks he'd made on the series of trails he'd followed, to retrace his steps to Ravenskill—a chance to test non-tech training. There, he pulled up census records on his tech lenses and found Arhys home, and let himself in with a master key he'd had created—a simple energy rod, that altered to match the mechanism into which it was inserted.

Inside the home, his plans took further shape with a simple examination of the family décor. People tend to place things they prize the most in conspicuous locations. They dress their living space as monuments to their priorities in life. And with few exceptions, these weren't drastically different from one person to the next. Something that made manipulating them so much easier.

Of course, children would prove powerful leverage against their parents. But the delicious truth that hung everywhere in Arhys' home was his un-diminished love for his woman. Her picture hang everywhere. Some of just her. Some of she and Arhys together. Close examination of the art revealed a signature common to most—whether charcoal sketch, oil painting, or needlework. That signature belonging to Arhys' wife.

Daryus's delight was sweetened by the fact that she was dead. Not because he took any pleasure in her death. That mattered not at all to him. But it meant the only thing Arhys had left of this woman he so idealized, besides her picture and some bits of art … was Xander.

Whatever value the boy had to his father would have grown exponentially, now that it was just the two of them. That was how the townspeople were. Their priorities rested on family, not the empire. A simple fact that would now be even easier to exploit.

Daryus walked the first floor, cataloging each means of entry. The front door stood locked, and the paths through the front yard leading to the door rarely trod. It gave him an even deeper picture of who Arhys was, both as a father and as a leader. People entered his home through a door near the kitchen. Familiarity. Weak leadership, Daryus believed.

But it also made likely where young Xander would enter. Daryus' good fortune held, as behind that door sat a chair deep in shadow.

So, he sat. And waited.

While he did, he called up the latest results on the drone modifications, and the Strength Program. In reality, he could just send a two-wave fleet of drones here tomorrow. The first, a blunt force attack, to discourage and scatter the Ravenskill resistance. Real time video would be piped to every news agency in the empire, to set a firm and final example of the empire's view of rebellion. Then, what of Ravenskill remained—because he'd learned not to underestimate Arhys—would feel the effects of what he liked to call "detuning."

One of the new technology protocols mapped the sound frequencies that shifted through living organisms. Those frequencies could be *disrupted*. "Detuned." Catastrophic organism failure resulted. It was experimental, but even if it didn't work perfectly, whatever damage resulted would likely achieve the same effect.

Ground troops would be ready as a third wave, if they were needed. But that would probably just be mop-up work by that point.

Daryus thought through each maneuver meticulously calculating approaches, drone volumes, timing, propaganda broadcasts, official statements by the Emperor. All of it.

Then, when he'd satisfied himself with what he could do in the first place, he allowed himself to consider his actual plan. The military solution would still have a place. But that would only confirm for his father the value of the Strength Program, and his readiness for his court name.

The opportunity he had before him was to deliver the Ravenskill messiah ahead of crushing the rebellion. And do it before Faythe could broker any kind of peace accord.

She'd, no doubt, assume it petty competitiveness. His parents might view it the same way. But he'd help them understand the dangerous precedent she would have been setting by negotiating with rebels. It would be the first step to the end of the empire Daryus would one day inherit and lead. He couldn't have that.

Of course, if Arhys had the courage to turn his back on his son, the military solution would still deliver a broken Gabriel, dead and silent. But a simple game of leverage could have Daryus delivering this singing man to his father alive, before wiping Ravenskill clean. It would show finesse and strategic thinking.

And on the heels of that victory, he could share how he'd been able to target only the rebel fighters with the new drone technology, keeping the complicit laborers alive to continue working the fields and producing other empire goods.

Footsteps came from beyond the door. Not heavy footsteps.

Daryus smiled in the shadows behind the door. There was beauty in his plan. His father would see it. And he'd have to acknowledge it wasn't something Faythe could do. It required a dark kind of initiative.

The door opened. Xander stepped in. Bright sunlight flooded the kitchen, then receded.

Daryus eased a foot up against the entry, to prevent it being opened again. "Hello Xander."

The boy whirled, his little fists coming up in a defensive posture.

Daryus shook his head. "Wiser for us not to fight. We're going to be here a while. Or at least until your father gets home."

The boy stared Daryus in the face, his brow pinched with fear, but also maybe determination. "You can't beat him."

That soured Daryus's mood. "Do you know who I am?"

Xander stared, trembling but defiant.

"You're shivering," he said with mock concern. "Have a seat, my boy. Relax. The truth is I'm here to offer you the opportunity of a lifetime." He smiled, relishing each moment of this. "Let's hope your father's smart enough to see it the same way."

CHAPTER 13

———————————◦O◦———————————

Arhys watched horrified as video relays of the decimation at Perpetual View streamed across his command monitors. Some were propaganda disseminated by the empire. Some were from the Prayer Fighters, letting Arhys know they'd begun disruption maneuvers, and their levels of success and loss.

And Perpetual View wasn't the only disruption. Wick's Grove, Flat Rock, Frigid Springs. Fighting was taking place in them all. Reports were showing a new empire tech was crushing dense matter. NOMACS were evolving as weapons.

The images told one clear story. The emperor's patience had ended. They weren't trying to discourage resistance anymore. They were unleashing the full weight of their artillery. He had just a little more than a day to be ready for an invasion force landing in Ravenskill.

Behind him, the door opened, and Gabriel came in, his guitar hung loosely in one hand. By the look in his eyes, he'd seen the videos himself.

"I know it's hard to watch—"

"All these people don't have to die." Gabriel let the door close fully behind him before continuing. "I have a better way."

Arhys shut the monitors off and swiveled to face his brother. "The emperor's daughter has offered peace."

"It's hard to believe, but she thinks her father may listen to us." Gabriel raised his guitar to indicate his music.

A hard wave of excitement lit Arhys chest. "You've discovered a way to—"

"Not yet." Gabriel came in and leaned back against the wall. "But Faythe and I both saw something in Nafaryus yesterday when I sang."

"Disgust," Arhys offered curtly.

Gabriel shook his head. "He had the look of a man remembering something. Faythe thinks he can be reasoned with."

"And you? What do you think?" Arhys pushed. He trusted his brother, but he had many lives to think about.

Gabriel considered it for a long moment. "I think he can be reminded of something other than the pursuit of dominion. I think he fears losing what he has. I think, if he's not listening to the drone of the NOMACS, we can get him to hear something else."

Arhys snickered. "The emperor doesn't go anywhere unescorted by the NOMACS."

"He will tomorrow night," Gabriel countered. "Faythe is going to convince him to meet us at Heaven's Cove, without the NOMACS."

"And you think he'll actually do this?" Arhys didn't believe it.

"I do," Gabriel said with confidence, looking in the direction of the hallway Faythe had departed from. "She has a unique ability to convince. And we know her father favors her. He may come thinking he'll convince me to turn myself in before his army arrives. But if it's just him, I think I can sing something that will get inside him."

Arhys narrowed his focus. "But not to kill him. To change him."

"Yeah," Gabriel said. "Or at least soften him. Isn't the whole idea of our resistance to find peace? That's all I'm trying to do."

Arhys glanced at the black monitors. "I think that time has passed." Then something Gabriel had said circled back to him. "You said 'not yet' when I asked about your song. Do you think you're on to something?"

Gabriel sighed, but nodded. "There are old ideas about vibration theory. And if you break it down, that's all music is."

"Have you tried to use it?" Arhys felt the excitement creeping in again. He'd been waiting ten years for his brother to find a way to harness the power in his voice as a weapon against the empire.

"No, but I'm convinced it's not just a theory." Gabriel gave Arhys a steady look.

"Come here." Arhys keyed the monitors back to life, and dialed in a separate set of telemetry. "When the NOMACS were here yesterday, we picked up some scanner waves we haven't seen before. The machines were taking some kind of inventory of us."

"They already have names and location," Gabriel said, his voice uncertain.

"The nature of the scans suggest their cataloging something more *individual* about us." Arhys sat back. "The point is that they'd only do that if they thought they could use it in some way against us. I think the rumors about drone advancements are true."

"Then what's coming tomorrow may be different than what we've heard before." Gabriel shifted his guitar to his other hand. "Makes the idea of a song seem smaller, doesn't it?"

"Or bigger," Arhys said.

His brother showed him a confused look.

"Come with me."

Arhys grabbed at Gabriel's shirt and tugged him out the room. He led him from the bunker, and drove them both to the Ravenskill port. There the swift-boat he'd ordered to be ready raced them across the Great Northern Sound to Idelhaven. The craft had a long arcing hull for slicing sea waves, and three outboard engines. The wind ripped past them, as their driver pushed the boat at full speed.

Once, the sun in a cloudless sky over a dark blue sea would have been a welcome distraction. Wide-open spaces felt good. The certainty of sun and wind and water felt good, too. But Arhys couldn't remember enjoying wide-open places since Evangeline died. He'd tried. He'd taken Xander once or twice on fishing excursions off of Whisper Point. He felt like an ass for not being able to fully give in to the simple joy of fishing with his son, instead feeling the heavy absence of his wife every moment they were together.

But maybe it keeps me sharp. And angry.

Someone needed to be those things, if Nafaryus was to be stopped.

They disembarked on a beach near Idlehaven, out of sight from any port. A land officer pulled onto a near-shore dirt road and whisked them away in a landcruiser to a prairie depot west of Idelhaven. The corrugated metal had been well preserved, painted variants of green to make it hard to see from any real distance.

"None of this is like it was ten years ago,"

"What" Gabriel asked.

"Our fight against the Empire." Arhys watched the depot grow larger as they approached. "We've captured Empire tech. We've built our own. We're an army now, not just a ragtag group of disgruntled slaves. We keep it quiet, but we've grown."

Gabriel nodded without any real surprise. "Nafaryus seems to have discovered your secrets."

"Not all of them," Aryhs said cryptically.

"The charade," Gabriel replied, "making Nafaryus think you were little better than pitchfork wielding malcontents … you were waiting for the right time. The right moment."

"And the right song," Arhys added, "But I couldn't sit idle until that came. I had to plan. Build."

Two men appeared from snatches of high-standing grass, rifles held up, barrels down. Arhys issued a hand signal, and the door clicked as if electronically released.

Inside, a spacious warehouse had a dozen practical engineering stations. "A technology mill," Gabriel whispered behind him.

"We call it the Foundry." Arhys started toward the interior. "Any tech we harvest from the empire comes to the Foundry. In addition to our own research."

"Who funds this?" Gabriel came abreast of him. "And how do you keep it a secret from the empire?"

"We hold back a percentage of the crops and sell them on black markets." Arhys pointed toward a weapons development bench. "We sell a portion of what we make in oversea trade, too. The rest comes from a few merchants who've found disfavor with the emperor." He surveyed the whole of it. "It's still woefully inadequate. But we're making progress. And the whole operation moves frequently. Never the same place twice."

"So, you've got some kind of new weapon, I'm assuming." Gabriel looked closely at the handful of innovation modules they passed, where engineers hardly noticed them.

"No great epiphany there." Arhys brought him up beside a hulking man with dark skin. Jeffer. Solid muscle. Looked like a hired dock hand. But he had the finest weapons mind Arhys had ever known. "I put Jeffer here on a special project the day Evangeline died."

Jeffer turned toward Gabriel. His eyes widened in surprise. "Gabriel? Damn, Gabriel? Sometimes I think you a myth. What's a song gonna do, they say? Magic, some say." He blew air through his lips, causing a wet raspberry. "Everything's got science in it somewhere. Even God. He's the ultimate scientist, you know?"

Arhys tried to focus his friend. "Jeffer, we want to see Project Jane."

"And sometimes, God has got to use science to bring his people low," Jeffer said, ignoring Arhys. "Right now, that's us. Mostly because we don't have the tools to do the building for all our ideas. But some we do."

"Is it ready?" Arhys asked.

Jeffer reached into a drawer of his workbench and pulled out a band of thick fabric. "It's not been tested. Only way to do that is against real NOMACS. Ours blew up." He handed the band to Gabriel.

"What is it?" Gabriel asked.

Jeffer smiled wide and proud, and a little deviously. "You know how sound works, yeah?"

"Well, I—"

"This is the evolution of what the old ones called active noise control," Jeffer explained in a rush. "See, sound is just a pressure wave. Folks used to reduce noise with the tech. But we've taken it three steps further. We're gonna cancel it all out."

Gabriel nodded. "So, I put this around my throat, and it will amplify what I sing and convert it to an antiphase wave of the same amplitude as the NOMACS."

Arhys smiled, and felt some confidence for the first time since Nafaryus had come to Ravenskill.

Jeffer looked pleased. "That's right. Where'd you pick that up?"

"I read a lot." Gabriel smiled now, too.

We've recovered a few NOMACS over the years, although recently they've had a tendency to self-destruct. But we've managed to squeeze a few sounds out of them. We've even logged enough to engineer the inverted phase of their most common suppression audio."

"This could work for anyone, then," Gabriel suggested.

"Nah," Jeffer shook his head emphatically. "To convert the wave, we had to model on a particular voice. Each voice is like a fingerprint, you know. Unique down to the smallest part. Arhys here got us some recordings of you. We deconstructed those until we had your voice print exactly. Most of the sound resonates up from the throat, which is why the band," he finished.

Arhys took the band in hand. "What about reach?"

"Not indefinite, a'course," Jeffer admitted with a bit of regret. "But it throws maybe three mile, I'd say. Sounds like the voice of God it does." He smiled at the call back. "See, God's in the science. All the damn time!"

Arhys handed the weapon back to Gabriel. "Add that to whatever you can do with the signature discoveries you've made. And the emperor has one hell of a surprise awaiting him tomorrow."

"If it works the way we engineered it," Jeffer qualified. "Got to use it against real NOMACS, and it's got to be used by Gabriel here, to boot."

Gabriel shook Jeffer's immense hand. "You're a genius."

"I kind of am, aren't I?" the big man said, and fell into a fit of giggles you wouldn't have imagined a man his size could generate.

Gabriel joined him. And Arhys was helpless from joining them both. It was the first laugh Arhys remembered having for a very long time.

CHAPTER 14

F aythe entered her father's private medical room, where he sat being examined by his personal physician. Arabelle stood nearby, observing the examination intently. Every ache and illness Faythe had ever experienced was treated in this very room, by this very man. Doctor Browning. The man had a kind face and patient eyes. His slow way of talking and few words somehow inspired confidence in his healing abilities. Nafaryus, though, was a bad patient.

"I'm fine," he complained. "This is a waste of time."

"It's protocol," said Browning. "You aren't permitted to be reckless *and* imprudent. Sit still."

Arabelle defended the family physician by clearing her throat.

Faythe hurried over to them. "I heard what happened, father. Are you all right?"

Nafaryus caught Browning's eyes as he stated in exaggerated fashion, "I'm fine," to which Browning took his leave

Arabelle looked a question at Faythe, which was precisely why she'd come directly here—to appeal to her father about Gabriel and the ultimatum, ask for the meeting at Heaven's Cove.

But she began by establishing the logic of it. "These attacks are going to continue, father. All across the Northern Empire. Some small. Some like Perpetual View."

Without looking at her, he asked, "And how do you know this?"

She glanced at her mother, knowing her next words would upset him. "I went to Ravenskill to meet with Gabriel today."

Nafaryus head turned slowly toward her, as if he were actively controlling his anger. "To what purpose?" he asked in a low, latent tone.

She needed to establish more logic. "How many of your military died today in Perpetual View? Were there any citizen casualties? What about infrastructure? What was destroyed? What will need to be rebuilt, and how much will it cost?"

He frowned at her. "You aren't asking questions you want answers to. You're establishing a base for argument to convince me of something."

Of course he'd know. She could have predicted that. But she needed him thinking about it. "Historically civil wars are the most costly and least effective way to unite people. Or even subdue them."

"You think this is civil war?" Nafaryus asked, returning his attention to Dr. Browning, who was taking several readings with a hand monitor.

"It's not just Ravenskill anymore," she said, stating the obvious. "And all these bands and militias have one unifying thread."

"Gabriel," her father said, sounding like the word soured in his mouth.

"Gabriel," she echoed. "I'd be derelict in my duties, and irresponsible as an ambassador of the empire, if I didn't try to find a peaceful resolution to this."

Nafaryus gave an ironic smile. "I thought I'd already done that."

She steeled herself, and replied, "Threats make bad politics, father. And martyrs breed civil war."

"And what you fail to understand is that leadership sometimes means making unpopular decisions." He gave her a long look. "Mortal decisions."

Faythe wouldn't back down. "And you've entrusted me with the task of seeking solutions that prevent direct conflict. Wasn't it you who taught me that military action was an expensive proposition, one better used as a last resort?"

Nafaryus sat silent a good while, before uttering to her, and to himself, it seemed: "If we weren't in a last resort position when we met Gabriel yesterday, we are today after Perpetual View. Drone feeds report rebels gathering at Stone Bridge Hollow, Flatrock, Frigid Springs, Majestic Falls, Wicks Grove, Sandy Creek, and that list doesn't include their suspected training facilities, which are swelling with green ranks fresh from the corn fields."

Faythe knew all this, having read the alerts on her return from Ravenskill. "If you have to put down every insurgent, father, you're going to cripple your own economy, not to mention the repair costs we'll incur once it's all over."

His cheeks flushed red, his eyes narrowed. "What would you have me do, then? Retract my decree on Gabriel? Let the rebels know they can intimidate and manipulate the empire? How do I rule then, Faythe, tell me?"

She let everything remain quiet, hoping her father's temper would abate. She could understand his perspective. In a way, it made sense. But she had to get him to Heaven's Cove. This was escalating too far, too fast. And she couldn't let Gabriel be killed or taken. At least not without trying to prevent it. He'd come to mean something to her in a very short time.

"Meet with him," she said in a measured tone.

"What?" Her father's incredulousness came loud and sharp.

"He's the reason people all across the empire have hope of—"

"Of what?" Nafaryus cut in. "Of freedom? Am I a ruler of slaves? Is that what you think?"

She had to be careful here, if she was going to convince him. "We may view their relationship to the realm differently than they do, but that doesn't change their feelings. And they're going to make decisions based on those feelings. Decisions like fighting you anywhere and everywhere. And the man who makes them think they can win is Gabriel. The smartest course is to try and leverage his influence. Not make him a martyr."

"You're stepping outside your area of expertise," Nafaryus said dismissively.

She touched his shoulder, as only a daughter can. "No, father, I'm not. This is precisely what I'm good at, and you know it. Meet with Gabriel tomorrow night. Someplace neutral. There doesn't need to be a crowd. No drones. Let him propose a solution that meets your approval. I have his word that if you can't find common ground, he'll submit to you as you demanded."

"And if I don't," Nafaryus asked, the question sounding both defensive and genuine somehow.

"Then I suspect Arhys will be ready to issue in an age of civil war with the empire." Faythe didn't need to dissemble about that. "That's a fight you'll ultimately win. But not before great cost. And it would define your legacy. You'd be the embattled emperor who had to destroy half of his realm to preserve it. And even if you do win, the historians aren't likely to be kind to you."

Nafaryus humphed a laugh. "Men are usually misunderstood. Leaders hated by half of those they rule. I'm not unfamiliar with these things."

Faythe kept on. "But you have another opportunity in front of you. What if Gabriel and I could find a way to preserve peace without you losing face? Isn't it worth at least hearing a proposal? Especially if you have the option of turning it down and having Gabriel give himself up? There's nothing for you to lose."

Arabelle held up her hands like a judge calling an end to argument. "She's as stubborn as you are. The difference is that you're failing to see how important this is to her. And while it's your right as emperor to say no, as her father, you'd be damaging a relationship of trust that I know matters to you. Don't alienate her out of pride. You may even be able to turn this into good public relations, if needed." She adopted a formal tone, as if reading a royal communication. "Emperor Nafaryus shows exceptional understanding of his people's needs, meets with leaders to find new solutions."

"I hadn't thought of that," Faythe said. "It's a good idea."

Nafaryus didn't yet look moved.

Arabelle caught his eye. "You and Faythe really are quite a lot alike. The same unbridled ambition. The same passion. The same inquisitive nature." She squeezed his arm. "You know I'm right, Bug."

Faythe reeled. Bug was the word inscribed on the back of her music device. "You've heard it, too!"

Nafaryus looked up at her in surprise and concern. "You have the music player?"

"For years," she admitted. "Finally lost power. But the music is … it's overwhelming."

His eyes grew distant. "My father gave it to me when I was a boy. Bug is what he called me when I got under his feet too much."

"Music was the one thing you and your father shared," Arabelle put in. "Then he got too busy, the way you're busy now. But you and he had that secret pleasure. Made things easier when he couldn't find time for you."

Still appearing lost in the past, Nafaryus asked, "Where did you get it?"

"I found it in the Hall of Lost Things." Faythe then turned the conversation back to the matter at hand. "If you've known real music, doesn't it make hearing Gabriel out worth the meeting."

"Let me see it," her father said, extending his hand.

She handed him the device. He punched in a number: two-thirty-seven. The song flashed on the readout display.

"It's still here," he muttered.

"The song you and your father wrote together," her mother said softly.

Nafaryus shoved the player back at her. Doubt still showed in his eyes. If he thought it through, it would lead to the drones, which stood at the center of his power.

So she said again, "No drones. You need to hear him. You have my word its safe. The meeting will be at Heaven's Cove."

Nafaryus stared at her a long, long time. Finally, he showed her the barest of smiles. "I'm not entirely heartless. I'll meet with Gabriel. I'll listen. But if his proposal doesn't impress, we'll see if he's a man of his word, and turns himself over. If he doesn't, only he'll be to blame for what follows."

Faythe hugged her father. "I knew you would," she whispered in his ear, and left to send word to Gabriel that she'd succeeded in arranging the meeting.

CHAPTER 15

—◦—

Daryus sat quietly on an oak bench in the shadows of Arhys' home, Xander beside him. He had firm hold of a long knife whose flat edge he rested on the boy's closest leg. Evening shadows had begun to play across the wood floors, as light from the windows fell into the darkened room. Xander had settled down quickly, no doubt overconfident in his rescue when his father returned home. The possibilities delighted Daryus. He hadn't been this eager for anything in a very long time.

The back door opened, as it had before. In came the man, his feet announcing him with a heavy rhythm.

"Keep the lights turned off," Daryus said evenly, before Arhys had even come into the room proper.

"Prince Daryus." Arhys stepped fully into the room. "I had a report you'd skulked into town. But you've made a mistake coming into my home."

"Your son thought so, too." He tapped the knife twice on the boy's leg. "But he saw reason soon enough."

By the light of the windows, Daryus saw Arhys' eyes widen, then quickly narrow. "There are five men close enough to hear my voice. There always are. You'll be dead before you can harm him."

"I somehow doubt that," Daryus replied casually, as though having inane dinner conversation. "And I'd be surprised if you wanted to test that assumption, given all you've lost already. Poor Evangeline."

Arhys took two threatening steps forward, his hand pulling his revolver—an S&W 500 he liked to keep handy and a safer weapon for him to discharge at this range. "Don't you use my wife's name again."

Daryus watched, unconcerned. "So, as you've noticed, the lights are off. This is because I've rigged them to a pulse sensor I'm holding." He raised a hand to show him his device. "If I let go of this, sharp-shooters positioned to see you through these lovely windows will kill you. For my part, I'll do my best to be sure you die watching your son curl around the knife I'll stick inside him."

"What's wrong with you?" Arhys said, still holding his weapon aimed at Daryus. "He's a boy. He's got nothing to do with any of this."

"Of course he does," Daryus said with a deliberate hint of glee, "He's a pawn. Leverage." He raised the knife up near Xander's throat.

Arhys lifted his other hand in a calming motion. "Where's your honor?"

"I see." Daryus chuckled in a bemused fashion. "So, the raids you conduct on supply transports that aren't meant to feed people in the metropolitan areas, those are honorable? The way you hide in the bushes and attack like bandits?"

Arhys glared defiantly. "If we had equal weaponry, our approach would be different. And we'd win."

Daryus nodded with exaggerated sarcasm. "Of course you would. Of course you would. But now let's get to the crux of this, shall we?"

"Not until you let my son go." Arhys' voice filled with the tone of command he no doubt used with his militia.

Daryus shook his head. "If I have to ask again, I'll just do it. I'm trying to be magnanimous first."

Arhys looked at Xander. "Are you all right?"

The boy nodded. "Yes, sir."

Arhys lowered his weapon, but didn't put it away. "I have routines. If I don't check in soon, my men will come in uninvited. And security sweeps will be initiated even before that. You don't have much time to make your bargain."

"Bargain?" Daryus's dark humor faded. "An ugly term, but apropos." He pointed the device at Daryus. "Your very next decision, will decide whether your son lives or dies. So, consider it carefully."

Arhys never dropped his gaze. Daryus respected his mettle, if not his methods. "Give up your brother. Turn him over to me, and you'll get Xander back unharmed."

Arhys said nothing, staring, his eyes alight with anger and calculation.

"And more," Daryus continued. "Tuition, board, and a stipend for his next dozen years at any educational institution you name. Then, a guaranteed yearly sum for the rest of his life, at a rate double your wealthiest Ravenskill citizen. How does that strike you?"

A long quiet followed, giving Daryus the impression he'd struck a chord with the man. Arhys' eyes darted to Xander, then to one of the photos of his wife. *Oh, lovely, some old debt he feels to her for the boy.*

Then the Ravenskill Militia leader began slowly to shake his head. But before he could voice his dissent, Daryus layered on. "You understand this means more than just education and wealth, don't you. Our boy Xander here would be *free*. I'm promising that he will no longer be counted as an asset of the empire. He'll be able to pursue any line of work he chooses. Or to not work at all, if that suits him." He laughed. "For all I care, he could stay here and do charity work in Ravenskill, giving his money away to crop followers."

Arhys had stopped shaking his head. "You're asking me to kill my brother to save my son. What kind of choice is that?"

"I said nothing of killing your brother," Daryus argued with, he thought, a convincing tone. "I won't lie, we want Gabriel so we can remove the heart of your rebellion. But we're not in the business of outright murder if we can avoid it."

"Why would I believe you?" Arhys pointed at the knife in Daryus's hand. "You're a hypocrite right now."

"Nonsense," he rejoined as if they were debating a morning cribbage game. "The situations are not the same."

Now Arhys laughed. The sound harsh and dry. "You're trying to cripple us by taking something that matters to us. How is it not the same?"

Daryus was beginning to lose his patience. "I don't have time for this. You're obviously conflicted, which should make your son feel wonderful. I'm going to leave now. Give you the evening to think about my proposition. If I'm stopped ... I'll kill your son."

Arhys gave Xander a courageous look. "Don't worry," he said.

"Dad..."

Daryus placed a small communicator on the table beside him. "Let me know what you decide," he said, tapping the device. He then poked the boy ever so slightly with the tip of the knife. "Let's go."

He stood Xander up, and used him as a shield to negotiate his way past Arhys to the back door, pausing there to share a final thought. "You realize, you can continue your ridiculous rebellion without Gabriel. I'm not asking you to disband. I just want the singer. And for that, your son returns safe, and he'll have the life you could never have given him, even if you want to continue to wage your *war* on the empire. You'll just do it without Gabriel."

"Why does he matter that much to you?" Arhys asked.

Daryus grinned. "It's this business of fathers and sons." He didn't bother to explain that. Didn't matter. He knew Arhys would come around, and give Gabriel up. Perhaps with the idea that he'd mount a rescue for his brother. But Daryus knew down to his bones that the Ravenskill militia leader would never let this boy be taken and killed.

Just outside, he transferred the boy to an Empire guard, who secreted him away. Then he moved through the mild Ravenskill evening, a deep sense of accomplishment flooded him. It felt good to make things happen. He might not even care about receiving his second name anymore. In some ways, he was already leading the empire. It was a simple matter of being willing to do what was necessary.

It made him wonder if his father had been deliberately aloof in order to teach him this lesson. He was the kind of man who would never have negotiated for Daryus' return, if he'd ever been taken and held for ransom.

But he *was* the kind of man who would recognize the shrewdness of this game to get Gabriel without conceding in any way to the rebels.

Passing one of the fist-sized stealth drones, he whispered. "First wave at dusk tomorrow. Go."

CHAPTER 16

———◉———

The stealth cruiser set down at a private landing pad five miles west of Forth Truth. There were no lights to guide it in, and no receiving party. Nafaryus kept these visits secret. The cruiser shut down, scarcely more quiet than when it was airborne, and sat ready for his return to the palace. He descended the craft's stairs beneath a dark sky, even the stars were absent, trapped behind a low ceiling of clouds. A small detail got him to the overland vehicle, and rushed him toward Truth.

At the far side of the Black Plains, the "fort" was a low profile installation at the habitable edge of the empire. Beyond it was vast forestlands. And to find Truth, one would have to either know its location or search the dangerous plains that stretched east and south: treacherous terrain seeded with genetically engineered vipers and other predators, loose soil that gave way to hot pots, and rovers who skulked in raid parties along the Common Highway and North Division Road.

Natural defenses for Nafaryus' most clandestine operations.

"Uneventful ride in?" Captain Rawls asked, as Nafaryus entered the station.

"I wasn't seen," he replied, answering the real question. Rawls was paranoid, which made him perfect for this command.

"Good, good," Rawls said, turning and leading Nafaryus deeper inside. "We're monitoring the attacks all across the empire. They suggest only nibbles right now."

Nafaryus shook his head. "Perpetual View was not a nibble."

"I mean to say that today's attacks are meant to get your attention," Rawls clarified. "We know Arhys put the word out to every rebel faction. They owe him no allegiance, but then again they're all aligned in their hatred for the empire."

"They have my attention." Nafaryus turned into a production facility, where communication and video development took place. "And my son is organizing a counter-offensive. I trust you've seen all this in the command reports." Nafaryus had read them himself on the flight here.

Rawls nodded and kept on feeding the information with a fanatic excitement. "You gave Gabriel three days. That ends tomorrow. The rebels are telling us that tomorrow is going to escalate. Everywhere at once. They're baiting you to deploy forces to answer every contention, which, if you do, will give you a drastically reduced force to send to Ravenskill."

"I know all this," Nafaryus said sharply.

"So—" Rawls seemed unruffled "—since Arhys alerted his brothers-in-arms, so to speak, about the—what are they calling it, "the ultimatum?", yes, that's it, "the ultimatum,"—well, since Arhys let all rebel fighters know, we've poured gas on that information."

"Poured gas?" Nafaryus questioned. "Are you reading from the old libraries again?"

"It means we've fueled the story," Rawls explained. "We've colored the details to make you appear quite reasonable, but disseminated the story to average citizens, who, like the fighters, have also heard about Gabriel. Some covert polling shows that this average citizen either believes or hopes Gabriel will topple your government."

Nafaryus smiled at the tactic. "So, you've struck a little doubt and fear into the minds of all those waiting on a miracle. Good."

Rawls nodded with more enthusiasm than was necessary. "Exactly! Most of the empire now knows that Gabriel will either turn himself over to you or be destroyed by this time tomorrow. Regardless, there's been a commensurate rise in the access to certain indicators of hopelessness and despair."

That got Nafaryus' attention.

Rawls keyed a nearby display. "Since we disseminated the updated story across all communication vehicles, there's been a dramatic increase in the access to what we call dirge poetry, guys like T.S. Eliot; people are looking up dead ancestors, ruminating on the past and those who've died; those reporting for work is down markedly, because, we believe, that they don't see much of a future worth working for, and—"

"I understand," Nafaryus interjected.

"There's so much more," Rawls said. "Indicators across those with access to health and mental care show prescriptions for suppressant drugs, elevated vital signs and activity, especially in the neocortex."

Nafaryus summed it up, so they could move on to his main purpose. "People are afraid."

Rawls seemed deflated to have it so tidily expressed, but finally nodded in agreement. "Yes."

"Good" was all Nafaryus gave the man. Over-congratulating Rawls could cause the man to get careless in his exuberance.

"And how are we fairing on the comparative work?"

Rawls's slightly crestfallen expression slipped into a wry grin. "Ah, glad you asked. We were able to harvest video samples from every established government across the mainland to the Western Rim. With some careful editing, we've been telling the story of how much better G.N.E. citizens have it relative to other city states and federate monarchies. Illegal emigration is down fourteen percent. And opinion of your leadership is up 4%."

"Double the communication strategy on this," Nafaryus commanded. "Start it tonight. I want dissenters carefully considering their options when calls for insurrection come."

"Done," Rawls agreed. "What else? You certainly didn't come here for a personal report on comparative progress."

Nafaryus looked past Rawls to the maze of production equipment he'd outfitted Truth with years ago—to render images he could use to influence public opinion. He laughed to himself, Fort Truth, what else could he have called his propaganda mill.

"I want a new video created tonight," he said. "I want it ready for my review when I arrive back at the palace."

Rawls shrugged, as if that wouldn't be a problem. "Of course. What's this new video?"

"It has multiple parts, actually." Nafaryus began to pace in front of the production stations. "I want every known rebel stronghold, and every place they've attacked today to receive a clip showing a large G.N.E. force deployed to engage them."

Rawls's brow furrowed. "They'll have intel on the size of our army. If they communicate with each other, they'll soon realize it's all a fabrication."

Nafaryus held up a finger. "Part of each video will tell the story of covert weapons manufacturing and new alliances with the Eastern Confederacy, and the Penn States Nation, as well as the MidWest Confederation. You'll convince them of the massive upsizing of our forces, and that we've sent an insurmountable segment to crush them … unless they cease their maneuvers."

Rawls began to nod. "We can do it. It'll look like broad-scale police state mobilization."

"Obviously, at some point, they'll realize the ruse, but that should suppress at least some of their operations tomorrow." Nafaryus continued to pace.

"Maybe," Rawls replied with some skepticism. "I think we should factor resistance fanaticism and loyalty. But we'll get it produced and disseminated tonight. The empire will wake to the threat of complete military occupation."

Nafaryus had already moved into the more important part of the news he needed to create. "Then, I want you to develop a compelling video that shows a defiant Ravenskill in full-scale conflict with G.N.E. forces. I want Gabriel seen trying to sing in the midst of the confusion and taking a wound."

Rawls had begun to nod again, when Nafaryus finished. "Show Gabriel's wound in the neck and mouth. Make it clear that he'll live, but that he'll never sing again, that he'll live out his days begin fed through a tube, unable even to speak. ."

His propaganda commander came to a pose of complete stillness, a large grin spreading on his face. "That's genius."

"I'll signal the time for you to send the video." Nafaryus made sure his commander was looking at him when he added, "I want every available resource dampening communication and transmission between Endless Isleland and the rest of the mainland as soon as the video goes out."

"Even the drone network?" Rawls asked.

"Yes. I doubt they've been able to layer in hidden communications through the drones, but let's not take the chance. Frequency silence for an hour once the video is sent. And active band disruption to coincide with that."

"They'll piece it together eventually," Rawls argued. "One way or another. You know they will."

Nafaryus waved a dismissive hand. "Well, there's one scenario where the boy does die. That'd serve the purpose of suppression as well as validating state video feeds. But if not, no matter, we're buying some time by dispiriting the rabble."

Rawls raised a hand as a cautious objector. "Don't we run the risk of making Gabriel a martyr? Maybe it creates conviction in those who've been unable or unwilling to join the resistance."

Nafaryus thought about that for several long moments. He could see that happening. He'd considered it, too. Most of the way here, he'd considered it. "It's a risk," he finally admitted. "But then, you don't know what real music means or feels like. No one does until they've experienced it for themselves.

Gabriel's been out with his brother on visits to the mainland. They've spread their seeds of dissent. And those they've not met have heard the first-hand accounts of those who do."

"I'm sorry, sir," Rawls said, blinking several times. "What does any of that mean for our video? It'll help me in thinking through the details we add."

Nafaryus stared coldly at the man. Not from hate, but to inhabit the feeling he wanted everyone who saw this video to feel. "When we confirm Gabriel has been killed, those who've heard him and those who've listened to the accounts of those who've heard him ... will despair. They'll lose hope. And then we can get on with the business of the empire, and see if we can't improve their lives with practical programs and planning instead of myths and dreams."

The light in Rawls eyes gave Nafaryus some confidence in his own plan.

"Keep my direct channel open with your ops lead," Nafaryus directed. "If everything goes to hell, and the rebels stage an attack on the palace city, this is where we'll come."

Rawls acknowledged Nafaryus with a distracted "yep," as he had already begun to chart out plans for the misinformation he was about to manufacturer.

CHAPTER 17

—◦—

The town square lay empty, awash in the shadows of evening. Except for Himney's place. From his bakery door and windows spilled bright squares of yellow light. They stretched across the stones like an invitation. Gabriel sat in his usual spot, turning melodies and lyrics over in his head, searching for the sounds and words that might touch the emperor. Nothing seemed right. Tomorrow at midnight his time would be up.

He tried playing a few things on his guitar to build some momentum. But most of what came out turned melancholy and even then the words were clumsy. On one level, it was preposterous to think a song would change the heart of a man. Especially Nafaryus.

Maybe even more ridiculous was thinking that these theories of individual sound held any credibility. If science could prove it, which it might one day, it hadn't happened yet. Not that Gabriel had been able to find, anyway. And even if he thought he could reach that part of the man, he'd need to know something about him. He'd need data of some kind. And then he'd have to figure out how to translate that into a musical expression.

Sounds like something the NOMACS would do, he thought.

Finally, he let it go for now. He never made progress on songs when he pushed too hard. Not to mention that a handful of Ravenskill fighters had trailed him and positioned themselves just out sight around the square—keeping an eye on him. It all made him feel tentative. And besides that, Himney's windows had been calling him all evening. He slung his guitar over his head, crossed to the bakery, and ducked inside.

A small bell tinkled as he entered. "Who's com a'knockin'?" Himney called from the back, then promptly entered the front of the shop.

The place had the heady smells of fresh bread and cooking rum, chocolate and cinnamon. Around the rather modest-sized counter-area burned at least seven lamps, in addition to multiple lights in the ceiling above. And from a small speaker in the corner, came the sound of spoken poetry.

"Good to see you, my boy." Himney's voice boomed in the small shop. "I don't get many customers at this hour."

Gabriel had, in fact, thought it strange that he was open. "I guess I never realized you were open this late."

"Every day," he answered. "Right up until I go home to bed."

Gabriel gave him a puzzled look.

Himney showed him his patient smile—one he seemed to use often. "Well, how shall I put it? Nothing so helps the tortured soul as a warm roll."

"Tortured soul?" Gabriel thought it both funny and apropos.

"People who come through my door at this hour aren't looking for pastries. They need comfort. I haven't met a problem yet that a warm roll didn't help." He reached down, grabbed one, and tossed it to Gabriel.

It took him by surprise, but Gabriel managed to catch the bread, which was, in fact, still warm. "Can't be good business to run your shop all these hours and sell nothing."

This brought deep laughter from Himney, who actually doubled over, bracing himself on the knees. When he stood upright again, he shook his head. "Oh, my boy, no one goes into baked goods for the money. And for my part, I did it so there'd be a place a young lad could come when he's run out of options. Always open. Always warm rolls."

Gabriel looked around the bakery again. "It's certainly bright."

"Makes me happy," Himney said. "Don't you feel that way about bright places? Low light is for intimacy and bad business. Bright light is for good spirits and honesty. Nothing so pleases me as a well lit room."

Gabriel had to admit that the room felt comfortable. Safe. "I think I agree."

"So, then," Himney pushed on, "I'm guessing you're here because our great Lord Nafaryus gave you a few days to think on a rather one-sided proposal. Tried to put the fear of hell in you. And by my count, you're a day from its deadline. That about the long and short of it?"

"Yeah, that's about the long and short of it." Gabriel took a bite of the roll, chewed. "Arhys won't let me turn myself over—"

"I should hope not!" Himney interrupted with as much boom in his voice as Gabriel remembered ever hearing. "I'd sooner cook with all salt and molasses than see you do such a damned fool thing."

Gabriel shook his head. "But it could mean the whole town—"

"We'll stand up just fine," he cut in. "And most would rather take their grave than lose what bit of hope you give them. You know this."

Gabriel let out a long breath. "What if I can't give them what they expect?"

Himney eyed him a good long time. "Son, in a very real way, you're going one better. And doing it already." He paused, a smile spreading. "Because you're giving them what they *need*."

He stared back at the big man with his big apron and big grin. "You're talking about hope."

Himney leaned slowly across the counter, bringing their faces nearer. "You're damn right I am."

For the first time, Gabriel smiled, too. "Nafaryus' daughter—"

"The one who took a bit of shine to you?" Himney interjected.

Gabriel hadn't thought it was that obvious. Maybe Himney just had that sense. "Yes, Faythe," he said. "She came to see me today. She wants to help broker peace. With some luck, we'll meet Nafaryus tomorrow at Heaven's Cove and try to convince him we're not the enemy."

Himney pointed at Gabriel. "That *you're* not the enemy, more like. He knows where Arhys stands. But it's you he's afraid of. Because you make people believe we can win against insane odds and all the emperor's technology. That's got to have Nafaryus up nights." He laughed deep and long at that.

But Gabriel found that problematic. "Nafaryus knows where my loyalties lie. And he's surely captured video of my part in planned raids. So, I guess I'm wrong there too, since I couldn't convince anyone I don't oppose Nafaryus."

Himney took up a rag and commenced wiping his hands of powdered sugar and other baker's bits. "You're going to sing him something, I'm guessing."

Gabriel nodded. "For a moment, I thought I saw him … I don't know, soften, respond, when I sang yesterday. Maybe I can find a song that will convince him to let us be. Remind him we're not so different from him."

Himney remained silent, but his eyes were alive with thought. Finally, he held up a finger. "Hear that?"

Gabriel listened. "No, what are we trying to hear?"

"The poetry, my boy." He picked up a roll of his own and took a mouthful. Around the gob, he explained. "I can't find music recordings, else I'd defy everyone and put them on for my customers to eat to. But poetry. Don't you think it's musical? Its got ebb and flow and rhyme and meter. And meaning. Closest thing to music I can get."

Gabriel knew Himney too well to think the comment was random. "You think I should sing a poem?"

Himney have him a mock look of irritation. "Heavens, no. I mean, I'm not saying it couldn't work." He stopped, composed himself. "How long did you linger in the dark before coming in for a roll?"

"How did you—"

"They all do," he answered. "Even when they don't know this is where they'll wind up, they foot around, worrying, skulking, giving themselves headaches and such." He pointed a stubby finger at Gabriel. "You, though, you were out there in the dark trying to dream up this song you need to sing. And it won't come. You're trying to conceive perfection in sound and narrative. Something to move the immovable. A great work. Finish it tonight. Sitting on your porch in the square."

Gabriel put a hand on his guitar. "I need to get it right."

"Which is why I mention my poetry." Himney jabbed a thumb at his little speaker. "See, there's this old saw that goes something like this: The short story writer does what the novelist can't; the poet does what the short story writer can't."

"By that logic," Gabriel suggested, "silence is best of all."

Himney shook his head. "The point is that you're trying too hard. You're overcomplicating it. Strip it all down. You don't need a song with a thousand parts. You don't need clever words. You can tell me if I'm wrong, but it seems to me that the power of your music is that it comes from someplace inside you. Trust that." He paused a long moment. "We do."

Gabriel recalled the brief look on the emperor's face when he'd sang at his request.

"The only music he really knows is the NOMACS. All created by machine. That's not what music is. I think, maybe, he just needs to be reminded of that."

"Assuming he knew it in the first place," Himney added.

"*You* didn't," Gabriel said, starting to feel the seeds of a more specific plan. "*No* one here did until I started sharing songs I'd created. But ... hearing a song is often like remembering. Because music is a human expression."

Himney clapped his hands. "There you go. All stripped down. No unnecessary words. Just humanity."

"It sounds a little sentimental when you say it out loud like that, doesn't it," Gabriel admitted.

Himney eyed him close. "Show me a man who doesn't like a bit of sentimentality, and I'll show you a robot. Worst part of technology is that it seems to put distance between people. Distance is cold."

"Still sounds a bit crazy to think just hearing a song can change a man's heart," Gabriel said.

"Oh, I don't know," Himney said, folding his hands atop his ponderous belly. "If my history's any good, music is about the only thing that ever really has."

Gabriel gave him a look of good-natured skepticism.

Himney's face broke into a shining smile of guilt. "Well, besides all that, you can lend it a bit of your secret ingredient. Start with his humanity, then add that part of you that makes us *feel* the song just a bit deeper. If that don't do it, nothing will."

A smile of confidence grew on Gabriel's lips. Maybe it was Himney's words. Or the bright lights. Maybe he just needed to talk to a friend. In the end, he held up his bread, Himney bumped it with his own in the fashion of a toast.

"To warm rolls," Gabriel said.

"God damn right," Himney added.

CHAPTER 18

―◯―

A few moments after Daryus left, Arhys slipped into the shadows behind his home. Snipers. Daryus had either been bluffing, or there were dangerous G.N.E. men in Ravenskill. Snipers belonged to the empire's Silent Operations team. Assassins was what they were.

If these men really had really been line-of-sight to take Arhys down, there were only a handful of places they could be. Arhys moved fast, taking a route that kept him out of the vantage of the likely shooting perches.

The air had turned chill. A thin mist hung in the air, turning the light from the few streetlamps into cones of murky glow. He skirted these, mentally running down the priority and strategy as he went.

The silent operators avoided contact. So, at least one of these shooters would be on the Fairfield Building rooftop. Access there was easy by way of a steel staircase in a rear narrow alley. But Arhys had interrogated one of these fighters before. He'd learned that in field operations they always took sufficient risk to get their lead man into the best possible position to achieve the objective. For Arhys, that meant one of the shooters had gotten into the Glenn's home directly across the street.

Darles Avenue, where he lived, was old. And homes there were set back from the road a good piece. But it would still be the highest percentage shot a sniper could get.

It would also mean the sniper would have to eliminate anyone occupying the place.

Please, God, no.

Arhys dropped into a shallow ravine, and ran hunched over. He reached the culvert, and had to go through on his hands and knees, sloshing through pools of stagnant water. On the other side, he crept out carefully, listened for a moment, then rushed on twenty yards before climbing up into the back of the Glenn's place. He stepped over a rusted chicken-wire fence, and crouched a moment more, surveying the back of the home. Everything was dark. But the window shades were all open.

Arhys kept close to the fence, using the darkness behind him to cloak his own dark shape, and got to the rear door. He reached for the handle, when he thought better of it—the door jamb had swelled in recent years. It would be a noisy proposition opening it, even it were unlocked. But the Glenn's had a root cellar with stair access into the home from beneath—a throwback Daryl Glenn was proud of, citing his deep Midwest ancestry.

Arhys crept around to the cellar door, slipped through, and felt his way in the total darkness to stairs in the middle of the earthen room. Gingerly testing the wood steps for noise, he found them sturdy. That had to be more of Daryl's obsessive maintenance and preparation routine.

Arhys went up slowly. At the door, he pulled two knives, and quietly entered the Glenn's kitchen.

Shadows fell from the dim light beyond the windows. Perfect surveillance situation: someone here could see out, but seeing in would present real challenges.

Stepping carefully toward the front of the house, Arhys' boot met soft resistance. Looking down, he saw Mrs. Glenn laying face up. No visible wounds. But her eyes stared lifelessly at the ceiling above.

I'm so sorry, Mary.

Arhys gave himself a single moment to grieve, then stepped over the dear woman and into the middle hall. Pictures of family lined the walls like accusations. But Arhys remained focused. There was no room for error.

He hunkered down, and leaned forward to peer into the darkened room that fronted the home—a place he'd sat for more than one idle conversation with the Glenns.

A single wooden chair, empty, behind a tripod with a soft brace. A sniper's barrel-rest. But no sign of the assassin.

Then a small tick. Just the faintest sound.

Arhys shot forward in a roll and spun. He hurled the knife back toward the sound, hardly aiming. But the knife plunged home, and a lithe figure dressed in tight-fitting black clothes slumped to his knees, still holding his weapon.

Before the shooter could recover, Arhys rushed him, and slit his throat—a death blow, and a silencing tactic. He couldn't be sure there wasn't a second person here.

Quickly, he took back his knife, wiped it clean on the dead man's shirt, and resumed his search of the home. Upstairs, he found another sniper perch—apparently belonging to the same man—and Daryl.

Arhys knelt at the man's side. Daryl had served in the Ravenskill Militia for a lot of years before Arhys had even joined. He'd led raids against forces six times the size of his own. Men and women still talked about Glenn-type courage. But the assassin had shot him in the back, and Daryl had fallen face-first into the pinewood flooring.

"You deserved a better end," Arhys whispered.

But he didn't have time to linger and mourn. This was the forward point shooter. There'd be at least one more. He got moving, silently calculating the risks now. He knew Daryus wouldn't worry himself over a couple of dead silent operators. All he cared about was getting Gabriel, and he was betting Arhys would trade Gabriel for Xander.

The real risk was the assassins themselves. They'd take a death personally. And they'd also be on the move quickly, to reduce risk of discovery. If there were more than two, he'd never get them all. He had to hope his instinct on vantage was accurate.

Out the back door he raced to the far corner of the Glenn's backyard. Over the opposite fence, and through the Olsen's high dead grass—they'd perished two seasons ago in the fields, victims of a NOMAC attack.

He went up the far side of their home, and checked the street in both directions. No one. All was quiet. He paused long enough to scan the windows of the Fairfeild building, saw no movement, and rushed across.

He ducked into the rear alley, and climbed as quietly as he could. At the top, he peeked over the edge. This time, he saw the man clearly, seated with his back against the retaining wall, a cigarette winking amber in the dark.

It would be a difficult throw, but he wouldn't be able to climb up and plant his feet first. So, Arhys drew one of the knives, thought through the motion, then stepped up, reared, and hurled the blade.

The man heard him make his final step, and turned his head in his direction, leaning forward as one does to try and peer through the dark. It put the knife's rotation off, and the butt of the weapon struck the man in the side of the neck and bounded down to the gravel rooftop.

The assassin's eyes grew wide in the night, seeming big and white. He reached for a weapon at his side. Arhys leapt down and sprinted for the man, diving and tackling him in a spray of pebbles and sand.

The man vaulted Arhys over his head, and rolled to a kneeling position, drawing a knife of his own. Arhys came up with his own blade in hand.

"I should have just shot you," the man said.

"You'll certainly wish you had in a moment," Arhys replied.

The assassin crouched into a fighter's stance. "This won't get your son back."

"No, it won't," Arhys admitted, walking forward as if he held no regard for the man's skill. "But what will it do for you if you kill *me*? Your prince's planned exchange fails, doesn't it? Because I won't be around to see it done."

Doubt rose on the sniper's face. Then he smiled. "I'll just wound you."

"So, I'm fighting to kill you, and you're going to try and just incapacitate me?" He uttered a low mocking laugh. "I think I like those odds."

A different kind of doubt crossed the man's face, and he took a few steps backward. Arhys came on, then crouched to recover his thrown knife. As casually as he could, in a single motion, he raised and threw the knife again.

He'd put the man off his game. Just enough to gain him a moment or two from the man's indecisiveness. And that's when the knife hit home, burying itself in his right shoulder—his throwing shoulder.

The sniper shifted his knife to his other hand, and came forward, anger boiling in his eyes. Arhys would have had it no other way. He took two long fast strides, faked a reckless stab, and when the man moved to block, he caught his arm and flipped him.

The assassin went with his body's momentum, using it to bring his own counter-strike up at Arhys' groin. But Arhys sidestepped the attack, and kicked the man soundly in the chin, like a wicked uppercut.

The sniper sprawled back on the roof, more pebbles skittering away as he skidded to a stop. Arhys pounced, driving his knife into the man's other shoulder, rendering both the assassin's arms useless. Then he pulled the blade up against the skin of his neck, prepared to silence this one, too.

A pained expression crossed the man's worried eyes. "Don't. I ask you. Don't."

Arhys glared down in disbelief. "What?"

"I'm like you," the man said, swallowing hard. "Just a soldier. Doing his job." He paused, looking both defiant and penitent. "I've got kids of my own."

Before Arhys could respond, a low hum emitted from the man's pocket. Arhys reached in and pulled out a communication device. If he didn't miss his guess, this would be Daryus checking in.

He grabbed the man by the hair, and yanked his head close. "You ask for mercy because you are a solider doing your job, and have a family. Yet you were hiding here ready to kill me in front of my son."

The assassin had no reply.

"Make this convincing," Arhys said, then he keyed on the device and remained silent.

"Phillips, you there?" Daryus' voice wasn't concerned or urgent. "Someone has taken out Jameson. Wanted to check on you."

Arhys shook his head for the man to remain silent. After several long moments, Daryus spoke again, "So, you got to them, did you?"

"One so far," Arhys answered, his tone promising it wasn't over.

"Then Phillips is there, and you maybe think you have some new leverage." Daryus chuckled through the comms device. "You're smarter than that."

Arhys didn't bandy more words. He simply pulled the flat edge of knife across the front of the assassin's shirt, to cause the whisking sound of steel against fabric, and nodded for Martin to do his bit.

The man gurgled, spit, gasped, and fell sideways with a loud thump. His eyes remained open and searching, as Arhys kept the knife at his throat.

"Very dramatic," Daryus said evenly, his voice sounding indifferent and distant. "As though I haven't heard men die before, or would find it tragic this time because I'm personally responsible."

Arhys kept the device close to the man's ear, but said nothing.

"I didn't care about Phillips or Jameson," he said. "You know that. So did they. Military men can't afford emotional investment can they? Makes them weak. Makes them … vulnerable."

Arhys glanced at Phillips. "He begged for life. Said he had a family."

"Mongrels," Daryus said. "A single step up from a Ravenskill whore. They serve the crown like everyone else. They'll be lucky to make the rank and file. And you clearly didn't care that he had a family any more than I did."

Phillips' eyes shifted to Arhys' own. They shared a silent message. Not that this information was a surprise, but that hearing it was different than assuming it to be true.

"How is my son?" Arhys asked.

"Alive," Daryus replied matter-of-factly. "I hope you're done with the heroics, otherwise I'll have to—"

"You won't hurt him," Arhys cut in. "Not until I've given you an answer. You want Gabriel. And I understand why now. *You* want to be the hero. You want to march him back to your father and earn his praise. Prove you're a worthy heir to his poison throne." Then something occurred to Arhys. "What assurance would I have that you'd do for my son what you promise?"

A quiet moment passed. "I don't hate you Arhys. Not you, in particular. I represent the empire. And if you need more than that, I'll have funds transferred to your account, and letters of acceptance anywhere Xander here would go to school. To be frank, once he sets down that path, I won't have anything to fear from him. He won't want to return to Ravenskill."

"You're an ass," Arhys said.

"I'm going to go now," Daryus replied. "Don't want your men tracking me. I'll be in touch." The commlink went silent.

Arhys stared at the device in his hand.

"You could kill me," Phillips said. "And I'd stand up for it. But for what it's worth, I'm not a threat to you anymore. Not you or your son."

"Change of heart?" Arhys asked, not believing, and not really caring, either.

"Does something to a man when his kids are ill used." Phillips' face had the look of granite. It was a look Arhys knew well; it stared back at him all too often.

Arhys let go the man's hair and sat in front of him, with his back against the retaining wall. He kept the knife in hand. But he was thinking of his promise to Evangeline to love and protect their son. His promise to give Xander a better life. He'd failed at every part of that promise.

"What will you do?" Phillips asked.

"I lose either way," Arhys replied. "I let people down who count on me if I give Gabriel up. And my son …"

"Since you've got to kill me, I'll tell you what a dead man values most." He looked up, as if gathering strength from the night sky. "I don't give a damn about the honor of the empire right now. Or my own soldier's pride. Or the unfairness of the slave-labor system. It's not rational to dismiss all the rest, but I'd give it all up to go home and just be with my family. I can't think of a cause big enough to sacrifice one more dredging hour away from them. How's that for a silent operator's confession?" The man made a darkly ironic grin in the dark.

Arhys listened, acknowledging the sentiment, and seeing in his mind Evangeline as she struggled to give Xander life before her own life had fled her body.

He let out a long breath, glancing skyward himself. "Maybe the only way to beat the empire is to get out of the fields. Get a better education. Can't do those things in Ravenskill."

And I made a promise.

"Come on," Arhys said, standing.

The man knelt and bent his head, ready to be dispatched.

Arhys nudged him with his boot. "I'm taking you to a holding cell. If the emperor doesn't demolish us tomorrow, you'll live, and I'll see you get home to your son."

The man frowned with confusion.

"I'll make a trade for a prisoner the G.N.E. is holding. They've got several." He helped the man to his feet. "And you won't be shooting for a while. Hold up your hands."

The assassin did so, seeming to know what came next.

Arhys severed several tendons in the man's fingers and thumbs. His hands would be long in healing, and never quite the same. His days of silent operations were over. Arhys wrapped the man's hands with two long strips from his own shirt, and walked him down the Fairfeild stairs toward the bunker prison.

CHAPTER 19

---◯---

The Palace City flight decks buzzed with activity as Faythe made her way to the royal family docks. It wasn't the late hour that made it strange. She'd never seen the military installation on full alert before. But she guessed this was what it looked like. Hundreds of drones hovered a few feet off the ground, receiving frenetically paced updates from ground technicians and software engineers. Battle cruisers were being loaded with forward operating troops and enough gear for sustained engagement.

This looked like the old video footage she'd seen of End War preparations.

She hurried to her own cruiser, where she found her pilot and attendant standing beyond the gate, where military personnel blocked their access.

"Let's get underway," she said as she got close. "We're running late."

Before her pilot could answer, a woman in military dress spoke up. "All non-military flights have been grounded."

Faythe came to stand close to the woman, towering several inches above her. It was an old tactic of intimidation, but an easy one to begin with. "By whose order?" she asked.

"Prince Daryus," the woman said flatly. "And before you ask, his initiative has been endorsed by the emperor."

A flutter of panic hit her. "What initiative?"

"I'm not at liberty to disclose that information," said the soldier. "Not even to a member of the royal family."

Faythe smiled, part genuine and part predatory. "You can tell me, or I can go all the way back to the palace and ask my father. He'll share it with me, since I oversee all palace relationships, especially when there'll be fallout in the wake of military action." She paused for emphasis. "Or, you can tell me now, and save yourself the demotion, lieutenant."

"Name is Ruthers, ma'am." The woman shook her head as if she'd expected the threat. "Always with the demotion. Most royals don't seem to understand that'd be doing a gal like me a favor." She sighed. "Here's the thing. Look at the loading bays. Think about the emperor's latest engagement with the local people. Is it really that hard to figure out where the prince is sending crown resources?"

It confirmed Faythe's suspicions. "When?" That would tell her if her father was playing her false.

"I don't have that information," Ruthers replied. "And that's the hot iron truth." She raised her wrist to show the familiar military brand that survivors of the Border Wars had taken as an emblem.

Authority wasn't going to work with this woman. Faythe needed another tack. "You've been in the G.N.E. brigade since the Border Wars, then."

Ruthers nodded with some pride and suspicion.

"You've watched friends die." Faythe knew directness was the only way.

The woman went still, but her eyes told Faythe that this solider was no stranger to death.

"I can't guarantee it," Faythe said, looking out the bank of windows to her left at the field of drones and cruisers preparing for war. "But I'm trying to stop this before any more G.N.E. soldiers are killed. My flight here is to get ahead of this whole thing and try to broker peace. My father knows this, too."

Ruthers stared back, intelligent eyes thinking through the information she'd been given. "The emperor's command team filed a flight plan to Endless Isleland not long ago. Perhaps you should go with him."

Faythe shook her head. "That will be too late. I have preparations to make."

Ruthers glanced at the brand on her wrist. The Border Wars had been bloody. Not like the End Wars, but the worst of their lifetime. "I can't just let you leave," the solider said. "I have to find a flight window, and prep to hide the fact. I can get you out tomorrow, ahead of your father. Not by much, but some."

Faythe could have argued, but she could see it would be a losing affair. "That'll do," she agreed, "for a start."

At that the woman barked a laugh. It had a musical quality Faythe hadn't heard before in a laugh. "You may be overestimating my abilities," the soldier said.

Faythe ignored that. "I can make a flight tomorrow work, but I need a secure and private communication channel now."

This time, Ruthers laughter was more caustic. "All comms are locked down. You'll need to walk the emperor or prince Daryus in here themselves to rescind that one."

"Again," Faythe said, pushing the point back to the bone, "You can either hold onto protocol, or you can help me try and save tens of thousands of lives."

The woman's smile disappeared. "What makes you think I can—"

Faythe touched a rare badge on the woman's uniform—an archaic scaffold tower—that indicated contribution to the military's drone tech labs. It was clearly why she was placed in command of the royal family's docks in times of military maneuvers. This woman was battle hardened, and a senior tech engineer.

The soldier looked over at her partner, a more junior officer whose face was unreadable. No help there. When she looked back at Faythe, she said, "Can you be sure I get drummed out of the corps for this?"

"I'll do you one better," Faythe said with her own wry grin, "I'll have you attached to my personal detail. Permanently."

Ruthers pivoted fast and led Faythe to a flight room down the hall. She ordered it cleared of eight programmers working through updates to drone software and engagement logistics. She shut the door hard, suggesting anger in her need for a private moment with Faythe—a signal to mislead those she'd ordered out.

"It's going to be tricky," Ruthers said, taking a seat at one of the terminals. "The drone network is thin, due to the massive recall for battle preparation."

"A secure line," Faythe said again. "First, I need to send an encoded message to Ravenskill. Something they can pull down with a password, but that won't be subject to audit or discover by other systems."

The woman's fingers were practically a blur, as she navigated the systems to prep the message. "Face the screen in front of you," she told Faythe. "Start now."

Faythe looked into the monitor. "Gabriel, I was successful. My father will meet you where we'd planned. Let us say, 11:00 pm. I can't get to you tonight. But I'll try to be at that spot an hour ahead my father, so we can talk it all through before he arrives. I have a good feeling about this. And I have confidence in you and your music. Be safe. I look forward to seeing you again." She nodded that she was done, then held up a hand to keep the line open. "Also, in the event we aren't successful, you should know that a massive offensive is being prepared. I don't have logistics or strategy, but it's hard to imagine most of this isn't aimed at Ravenskill, if we aren't successful. I thought you should know, as I'm sure it will inform preparations there." Then she motioned for the signal to drop.

"You're a very different person from your brother," Ruthers commented. "What next?"

Daryus's strongest political support came from New Pavonya, Victory Island, New Maineland, and the Mid Southern Peninsula. She guessed, knowing his methodical brain, that he was deliberately currying favor in a south to north motion. It wasn't enough for him to simply inherit the throne. He wanted *approval*.

"Governor of New Pavonya," Faythe said.

"Now? She'll be in bed," the soldier said, even as she set up the link.

A moment later, a recently awoken woman appeared on the monitor. "My lady, what's the escalation?"

"Governor Reesh, I've called an emergency peace summit in the town of Ravenskill for tomorrow. All southern provinces will be in attendance. I'd like you there."

"Your timing is rather transparent," Reesh replied. "Drop a summit where your father intends to raze a town."

"I don't believe that's going to happen in any case," Faythe said. "But of course it's a possibility. So yes, that's why. Having his southern political infrastructure at risk will stay his hand."

Reesh stared through the monitor for a good long while. "You're asking me to risk my life for your political maneuver. Why? What is Ravenskill to me?"

Faythe had anticipated this question. "New Pavonya is no different than Endless Isleland or any other province. Some important percentage of the people there fight in the resistance. As Governor, your oath is to the crown, but you don't send regional forces to cleanse this element do you? Because without them, the rest would lose hope and stop being productive. It's a balance you're managing. And until we have a better systemic solution, you've got to maintain that balance."

"My question was—"

"If the Ravenskill Militia is obliterated, and tens of thousands of civilians killed in the process," Faythe stopped there, to allow that idea to settle in, "then how long before New Pavonya falls in my brother's sights."

"We're on rather good terms with Prince Daryus," Reesh answered. "I'm sure you know this."

"I do." Faythe stepped closer to the monitor, simulating closeness to the governor, for intimacy, confidence, import. "And I've known him all my life.

A victory at Ravenskill in my father's name will become a campaign across the Great Northern Empire to cleanse it of rebel sentiment. He'll expect your support, given your relationship, and you'll be left with a people who've lost their will."

The governor now seemed fully awake. "I'm not sure what you're describing is such a bad thing, Faythe. People die in these rebel attacks."

"Yes, they do," Faythe agreed. "And the casualty reports show that many of them are citizens. So, the way I see it, it goes one of two ways: A broader campaign comes to New Pavonya, killing innocents, which militarizes even larger numbers of citizens to take up the rebel cause; or you simply sustain unprecedented casualties, which impacts your productivity both in the number of laborers and the willingness of those left to work."

Reesh was visibly thinking. "What do you propose?"

"Get to Ravenskill tomorrow by noon," she said. "There's an inn just off the main square. Take a room, and wait for me. I may be in late tomorrow, but your presence is all I need until I arrive. Then, we'll begin to draft a peace accord. Something to reduce the fighting and provide better services to the people. I know it sounds high-minded when I summarize that way, but it's all I have time for. Will you join us?"

"And in the meantime, I may die in a military action targeted at Ravenskill," Reesh said dryly.

"I won't lie that it's not a possibility." Faythe thought a moment. "But isn't your responsibility to be put ahead of your welfare."

Reesh smiled at the coercion. "And what does the emperor think about this peace summit? Will he be there, as well? Is his welfare first or last when there's risk involved?"

"I'm not going to play verbal games with you, governor." Faythe stepped back. "I'm giving you the chance to be a part of the peace process, of bringing safety and security to your people. Will you join us?"

"And if I don't?" Reesh asked, her face heavy. "Because I'm not sure I want to be a pawn in your private war."

Faythe gave a political laugh. "My war?" Then she thought about that. "Fine, my war. Then, just know that the names of those who come and participate in finding a peaceful more prosperous way forward will be published and celebrated, which will lead to future offices in the realm. Similarly, the names of those invited but who chose not to participate will be published. I suspect those names will find new lines of work."

"Ah, blackmail," said Reesh. "Quite beneath you, Faythe."

"You may call me by my title, Governor. And it's not blackmail at all. The rules of procedure call for the disclosure of official invitations to matter of state and reports by the attendees. You'd know this if—"

Reesh held up her hands. "I'm just being obstinate, Lady Faythe. Of course, I'll be there. I hate the fighting. If there's a chance in hell we can stop it, I'll come ahead and join. I wanted to push a bit, you understand, because I've been impressed with Daryus, and you'd better be thinking through your responses to this on every level."

Faythe thanked Reesh for her acceptance, and triggered off the monitor.

The rest of the calls went somewhat the same. She very nearly didn't get New Mainland. Endless Isleland went much easier. But in the end, all would attend. Whatever Daryus was planning, she would have a reason for him to stand down. The harder part would be convincing her father to do the same, if Gabriel didn't persuade him tomorrow to call off the offensive against Ravenskill. But she'd cross that bridge when she came to it. If her father had ever felt about music the way she did, she believed deep down that he could be softened enough to find another solution to the conflict. That would give her time to iron out a peace accord, and she'd start with Daryus' own best allies.

CHAPTER 20

―――――――◯―――――――

Nafaryus sat on a wooden bench in his private park on the south shore of Lake Halcyon. There wasn't anything left to do before tomorrow, but there'd be no sleep tonight. In lieu of sleep, he'd seek the peace he'd always found in this spot. The moon shone a mild path of light across the surface of the lake. Somewhere in the dark, a pair of loons called to each other. And it was quiet. No hum of machinery. No one asking for his orders or advice. Just the quiet.

"Care if I join you?" It was Jack.

"This is a restricted area," Nafaryus said. "How did you get past the security gates?"

With a smile in his voice, his old friend answered, "I'm a software engineer."

"So, you reprogrammed my security systems so you could disrupt my one moment of peace? I'll have to change your clearances."

Jack sat beside him. "Arabelle lent me her access key. I figured this is where you'd be, and I asked. But feel free to demote me. I could use the time off."

Nafaryus stared into the tranquil dark across the lake. "We used to swim here."

"That was before you put up the private gate," Jack prodded. "I think you also fell in love here."

Nafaryus nodded, then changed the subject. "Are we ready?"

"We? I'm not going *anywhere*." He picked up a stone and tossed into the lake. "But if you mean your drone army, yes. It will be. The Engineer Corps is working through the night and on through tomorrow. It should be a spectacular show."

"You're going. And this one's not for show." Nafaryus sat back, rubbing his weary eyes.

"Is that why you're out here? Heavy heart and all that?"

Nafaryus didn't immediately reply, thinking through the conversation he guessed Jack had come to have. "I won't change my mind."

"That's why you think I came?" Jack laughed warmly. "I've known you too long to believe I can sway you. And I don't play at politics or war. Not my game."

"So, you came for nostalgia's sake. To talk about swimming and falling in love." Nafaryus gave his old friend a skeptical stare.

"I suspect I came for the same reason you did." He paused, seeming to look for the right words. "To mark the moment. Something irrevocable is going to happen tomorrow. You set it in motion. And you asked for my help to succeed. So, our fates are joined. And it's the kind of thing a thoughtful man thinks about, even if he can't or won't change it."

"You think I'm making a mistake," Nafaryus said.

Jack looked out at the lake, where the loons called again. "I don't know. The endless fighting between the empire and the rebels isn't good for anyone. But then, I suppose you have to consider that they're not animals. They're fighting for a reason." He paused, sighing heavily. "It reminds me of the stories of how the End Wars began."

Nafaryus frowned at the analogy. "That would make me the President of Civic Unions & Federations. Histories mostly blame the CUF for the wars. Pushing technology ahead of humanity."

"Don't be offended," Jack's voice was easy and slow. "It's the natural correlation, and I happen to be sitting on your side of it. So, I'm not throwing stones. But they *were* zealous, weren't they?"

"Historians sometimes forget that they sought to keep men out of war. Fight it all with machines and no one dies." Nafaryus knew it was a thin argument, but not an indefensible one.

"Ayeah," Jack agreed. "Except that it got away from them, didn't it? The technology became aware, and proceeded to strategically try and eliminate anything that made us unique. The things that made us human."

Nafaryus looked up, where he could see the lights of a few drones out over the lake. "You realize the irony of you saying all this, since you're one of my lead drone designers."

"Don't think I'm not painfully aware," Jack said with a laugh. "I walk that line every day. Creative advancement balanced with tragic hubris. Ah, hell, Edward, I'm up three times a night worried I'm going to bring about the next apocalypse."

"Not your responsibility," Nafaryus said, and he meant it. "You do as I ask you. I'm accountable for any fallout."

Jack shook his head. "Maybe in the history books. But maybe not even there. It'll be the pair of us that gets written about. You gave the order. But I created the technology. 'Weapons maker guilt,' they call it. Bomb makers have suffered it for centuries."

"I know," Nafaryus replied. "Music has the same story. Drone audio suppression began as a desire to make perfect music. But the tech became self-aware, and one of its first initiatives was the eradication of natural music and the evolution of audio as a suppressive. We wrestled back control of the tech, but we'd already seen how it could help us manage populations."

Jack stood and walked to the water's edge. "Government changed. They held so much power, it ceased to be democratic. Became a monarchy. Here. Everywhere. Making unilateral decisions without the will of the people. Sometimes against it." He turned to Nafaryus. "That's why I came, Edward.

You're on the cusp of putting into use the most historically significant and devastating war technology since the advancement of the drone sound library. I knew you'd be thinking on it. I knew I wouldn't be getting any sleep. So, I thought I'd join you." He smiled, though the look of it was forced.

Nafaryus mentally cataloged the rebel factions, there were several, loosely associated. He thought through the raids that frustrated the supply chain to citizens and military alike. He considered the countless dead soldiers who'd died protecting the empire. He then thought of Gabriel, who threatened to reintroduce music and deliver false hope to the people, Nafaryus' daughter among them.

The litany of provocation burned inside him. He knew the danger of music. But he now also knew the realities of the wider world. The mantle of leadership meant he had to make decisions based on a greater need.

"I was wrong," Nafaryus finally said.

Jack looked back at him in surprise. "What?"

"About being the CUF President," he clarified. "If we're going to use the analogy, then this time we're the Republic of the Americas."

"How's that?" Jack questioned, cocking his head to one side.

"We're prudent with our weaponry. Seek to minimize casualties." He held his friends gaze. "But we'll suffer the losses for a better end state. The CUF wanted clean war. No human loss. And they gave the technology its head. You and I, we aren't doing that, are we?"

Jack offered a faltering smile. "Solid logic. But somehow it doesn't make me feel any better."

Nafaryus stood, and joined his friend at the edge of the water. "I'm not going to apologize for rising to power. Or for wanting to do so. Or even for how I exercise that power—"

"I'm not asking you to," Jack said.

"I know. But I want to be clear." Nafaryus chose his words carefully. "Leaders are sometimes wrong, but they're only really bad leaders if they're not thoughtful in their choices."

Jack put a hand on Nafaryus's shoulder. "You're a hard man, Edward. Pretty much immovable."

Nafaryus considered that for a long moment, then nodded. "Yes, but not thoughtless. Another man might do it differently. But I won't stand by while others try and undermine me—"

"Like the singer in Ravenskill?" Jack pressed. "With some songs."

"Nice try, old friend. But you and I both know nothing will inspire civil disobedience like a good fight song. Don't think I'm not aware of you skulking down there in the Hall of Lost Things, harvesting ideas for your engineering program."

Jack laughed. "You should have joined me. Your father would have. His love of music was the worst kept secret in the palace. I think he was hoping it would stay with you. Music seems to temper a man."

Nafaryus smiled at that thought. "You're right. He would have joined you. But I am not my father."

"No," Jack said. "You're not … you're *untempered*. And you're smarter. More in love with the throne, for sure, but not one to take us into the next full-blown war."

Nafaryus shook his head. "You should have been a politician, Jack. As for tomorrow, I'm not sure it can be avoided. But I've agreed to meet the singer to hear him out."

"That sounds like Faythe's doing." Jack smiled with a look of reflection in his face. "There's a lot to admire in that young lady. And you two are more alike than you know."

"You knew about the music player," Nafaryus said. "And didn't tell me."

"Any more than I told others when you had it," Jack shot back. "Not my place."

Nafaryus eyed his friend a long while. "Why do I feel like you're the one who helped her find the device?"

Jack just smiled back. "So, you've agreed to meet this Gabriel, then."

Nafaryus let out a breath. "If he's willing to comply, this all deescalates."

"You return them to their hopelessness, in other words," Jack said sourly.

"Anyone else would be put in prison for talking to me that way," Nafaryus replied with an edge in his voice.

"Someone has to," Jack shot back. "Unbridled ambition is the fastest way to damnation."

Nafaryus patted his friend on the back, and stared out at the night where the loons were talking again. "Like I said, I'm not going to apologize. But neither am I thoughtless."

The two men held a companionable silence there for some time.

CHAPTER 21

T he command room held a grave silence when Gabriel entered. Arhys
sat at the center terminal, his eyes distant. Gabriel had come as quickly
as he could, but sensed he was still too late. The entire compound had
a nervous energy about it, like the still heavy feeling of air before summer
storms.

Arhys stared into nothingness.

"The message said it was urgent," Gabriel said, speaking so not to startle.

Arhys' eyes cleared, focused. "An encrypted message has come in. It's
not from any of our allies."

"Faythe," Gabriel said immediately. He went to the terminal, keyed up
the communications network, and found the message. He typed in the code
they'd agreed on, and the video message Faythe had prepared began to play.

Gabriel and Arhys listened together. Then did so again before discuss-
ing it.

"She's convincing," Arhys commented, then turned hard eyes on Gabriel.
"Do you think you can do the same with the emperor?"

PETER ORULLIAN

"Yeah," Gabriel answered, thinking about his conversation earlier that evening with Himney. "I'm not saying we shouldn't be ready, just in case. But I'm convinced that something changes inside a person when they have no exposure to music, or maybe any art for that matter. They grow numb. Not entirely. But it's like having a blind spot. A place you can't see or understand. It affects the way you do things. The choices you make. We've become more enamored of data than daylight. More reliant on information than feelings."

"You sound like a pundit," Arhys quipped.

"I know how it sounds. It sounds … irrational." Gabriel searched for the right way to say it. "But it's like proving something insubstantial. Like the way you felt about Evangeline. You either feel it or you don't. It's beyond data and information."

Arhys raised a finger, a sign he intended to argue.

"Of course, they can measure its effects," Gabriel said, anticipating his brother's rebuttal. "But science can't explain how love begins, or what it consists of. The same is true of hope and just about any other human value we cling to. Hell, Arhys, they're the very things that make us human. Pare them away, and it's easy to understand how a man gets as cold as Nafaryus."

Arhys sat silent for several moments. "Fair enough. But I somehow don't think a song alone is going to be enough when you meet him at Heaven's Cove. Even if there are no NOMACS pressing down on you with their noise."

"I've been working through some techniques for focusing the sound. Getting it inside mass." Gabriel tapped his chest, then tapped the console next to them.

"Let's test it," Arhys said, and stood up fast, leading Gabriel down three levels to the holding cells. He stopped in front of a non-descript door in a long dim hallway. "I caught a G.N.E. silent operator earlier this evening. He's wounded, but not fatally. Test your song on him."

It wasn't the first time Arhys had put him on the spot to use his gift. *Evangeline.* He did need to test his knowledge. But the thought of actually using it on someone to cause harm … the idea twisted in his gut. He didn't want to do it this way. But there weren't a lot of options, and they were running out of time. He finally nodded. He'd test the knowledge he'd acquired over the last eight years.

Arhys ran his hand over the palm-lock, and the door clicked open. Gabriel drew the door wide and went straight in. The assassin sat with his back in the corner. His eyes fluttered open when Gabriel entered, but he didn't move. His wounds had clotted with blood, but he looked faint as if he'd lost a fair amount before the bleeding stopped.

"Going to finish what your brother started," the man said, a lopsided smile pulling at one side of his face.

"Not exactly," Gabriel replied. He considered what to sing, the notes, words, how to focus the sound. He wondered if the man's frame could handle it, given his condition.

Restore him a bit first.

Gabriel had long wanted to try and use his song to mend. *Since Evangeline.* But it wasn't the kind of thing you test on people. Except maybe on an enemy. He surveyed the man's cut fingers, a mess of coagulated blood. Those would have been deliberate, to keep the man from his craft. But his shoulders, where more blood had spilled out, seemed a good option.

Slowly, Gabriel began a kind of recitation song. Almost more of a chant. Low words, just above a whisper. He didn't attempt to understand the healing arts. Instead, he concentrated on the idea of healthy flesh, wholeness, and focused it on the assassin's shoulder wounds. If he could affect matter in one way, he believed he could affect it in another.

The man's face changed, not in pain, but surprise, his mouth dropping slightly agape.

A few moments later, he began to roll his shoulders, then lift his arms, a look of amazement spreading across his features. "My dearest God," the man said. "The rumors are true."

Arhys came to stand beside the prisoner, and gave Gabriel a hard look. "That's not what I had in mind."

"I wanted him strong enough to survive any attempt to affect something deeper," Gabriel explained. "But it seems to have worked."

The look in Arhys eyes was a mix of excitement and regret.

Some things we learn too late.

The assassin shot a dark look at Arhys. "Having your brother test some bad notes on me are you?" He paused, a threat in his eyes. "I read you wrong."

Arhys returned the man's glare. "War changes us all." Then he nodded for Gabriel to continue.

Gabriel looked back at the assassin, preparing a new set of thoughts and low words to try and touch that part inside the man.

Just as he set to sing, the assassin leapt to his feet, sending Arhys back hard against the rear concrete wall of the cell. With calculating eyes, he kicked Arhys in the head, knocking him unconscious. Turning, the man bolted toward Gabriel.

With standard training in close combat, Gabriel would be overmatched against a silent operator, even one with bad hands. But he crouched, ready to grapple the man to the ground, just long enough for help to arrive.

But, at the last moment, the assassin side-stepped, pushing Gabriel down as he rushed past and into the hall. Gabriel scrambled to his feet and took chase. By the time he got to the hallway himself, the man had gotten to the end of the hall, but turned in the opposite direction of the lifts.

He's trapped, Gabriel thought with some eagerness. He wanted to sing this man down.

Several running strides, and Gabriel turned in pursuit, finding a door shutting halfway down the short corridor. A stairwell *Oh, God!*

Gabriel slammed through the door and climbed. He was a flight behind the man, their fast, heavy steps pounding on the concrete in flat echoes. It smelled of dry cement and old dirt, and soon the entire vertical chamber was a chorus of heavy breathing and pounding boots.

"Stop!" Gabriel shouted. "You'll never clear the compound!"

The man pushed upward, and that's when Gabriel saw it. The man's right hand clenching the stair-rail, pulling, using it to pivot at each landing. *The song healed his hands, too.*

Whatever the odds of this man actually escaping, Gabriel couldn't risk it. Not just because of what he now knew. But because of the dark talents he used to kill. Gabriel had to do something now.

In a rush, he summoned a new set of words and sounds and gave them voice up the concrete column of stairs. They came in shouted bursts, rough and angry. The harsh song jounced along the cement walls and jangled down the man's nerves. The sensation of feeling the song touch the assassin rippled along Gabriel's skin, returning a dizzying spin of images. Cold faces. Still faces. The unblinking faces of the dead. The people this assassin had murdered in the name of the Empire.

The marks this assassin had put down. His kills.

The man up ahead of Gabriel cried out, as if seeing these faces for the first time, the people behind them. The holes their losses created around them. These were no longer simple marks stripped of their humanity, but people. People he had killed.

Gabriel tightened his song, giving all the space in his mind to the deaths of those he could now see. He let the loss accumulate inside him, the mourning that followed from loved ones, parents … children. And to all this he gave a new voice.

Again it came in angry shouting bursts. Rough and almost unmusical. But they had a hard beauty about them. A dire kind. Names of the dead. Names of orphans. Suffering in ways he'd never imagined. All of it shot from his mouth in a litany of accusation and indictment. And he could feel the song penetrating the man. Getting past skin and bone to whatever makes us move and feel and live.

A few moments later, the man screamed, a long unending, dying wail that kept on until the man had no breath. Then he heaved a shuddering lungful and screamed again. And again.

Gabriel couldn't stop the song. It continued to erupt from somewhere deep inside. Then he was practically tripping over the assassin, who'd fallen on the stairs. The man was crying out in pain, an anguish that seemed to creep up from somewhere beneath the surface.

Then he stopped. The man's eyes went blank. His arms went still. But he did look finally at peace.

Gabriel collapsed next to the corpse, heaving, his body wracked in alternating waves of cold and heat. His sweat poured from him. He lay that way a long time, hearing the echoes in his mind of the terrible song he'd found.

CHAPTER 22

—◯—

Arhys woke to cool shadows and quiet. And grey. Everything appeared grey, a continuum from charcoal to faded white. A moment later the ache in his head came on full. He squeezed his eyes shut against the pain, which didn't help at all. He'd been kicked. That was the last thing he remembered. He opened his eyes and surveyed the room. The infirmary. And almost every bed full.

With soldiers.

He'd visited this place before, but always to thanks his troops. Encourage them. Never as a patient. The wounded looked different from this side of things. Less heroic. More human.

"You awake, commander," came a hushed voice to Arhys' right.

He turned his head, bringing new heights of pain behind his eyes. It was Ensign James, Jimmy to his friends. "Yeah," Arhys answered as softly as he could. Even then the word felt like an ice pick puncturing his temples.

"Gabriel brought you in a couple of hours ago," Jimmy said. "Said you got kicked in the face."

Arhys started to nod, but thought better of it. "Yeah," he repeated.

"Well, don't worry none about it." Jimmy leaned further out over the edge of his bed. "Gabriel took him down. Did it with a song, too."

Arhys snapped his head to the side to look Jimmy straight, and immediately regretted it. "He said that?"

"No, not Gabriel. But a couple of the boys heard 'em in the stairwell. Gabriel was chasing him, and did something with his music to stop the guy."

Despite the pain it caused him, Arhys gave a small laugh. *Finally.*

"You, though," Jimmy kept on. "The guy got the drop on you. Coward move. But they say you just have a concussion. They didn't put nothing in your drip. Wanted you to be conscious first."

Arhys finally noticed the IV in his arm, and the bank of monitors on the right wall behind his bed. "I lost focus. I should have known better, especially with a silent operator."

Jimmy nodded noncommittally to that. "It's war. People get hurt."

That's when Arhys noticed something he'd failed to see before. The lower half of Jimmy's bed lay flat, almost as if still made. He stared a while, being sure of what he was seeing with his throbbing eyes, then caught Jimmy's unassuming stare. "God, Jimmy, what happened?"

"I was in Wick's Grove to aid with disruption. Got hit with new G.N.E. pulse tech," he said, slapping the bed where his legs were missing. "Rumor is it's just pre-production models the goons are testing. But it .. what did they tell me … it passes through skin. Something like that. It pounds at dense matter best, I guess. I got hit in the legs. Crushed my bones into so many pieces, they couldn't save them. I get to roll from now on." He pointed to a wheelchair beside his bed.

Arhys had seen the reports. He gave the man a salute. "I'm sorry, Jimmy. You're a hell of a soldier."

"That's debatable," Jimmy replied, and laughed at his own joke. "Mostly I'm going to hate staying back when the others are moving forward."

Arhys gave him a sharp look. "We'll find work for a roller." He offered a firm smile to go with that.

"To be honest, Commander, I got off easy." Jimmy looked around the infirmary, his own good humor faltering as he did so.

Arhys followed his gaze. Others had lost arms. A few had heads completely bandaged with gauze. More than one had tubes connected to machines that breathed for them. And except for those whose faces he couldn't see, he knew every one of them. Men and women who'd answered the militia's call. His call. And now fought a very different battle.

"So did you," Jimmy said, startling Arhys a bit. "If Gabriel hadn't been there, that assassin would have done you in before trying to escape."

No doubt about that. But Arhys had always known the risk. He'd gladly accepted it. Both for Ravenskill, and for his family, especially now for Xander. But had these people calculated the risk? The cost? Was it worth it to them? Could Arhys continue to ask them to face the only kind of odds he could give them?

Even with Gabriel, will it ever be enough?

Did he want to risk coming to visit his son here some day? Or worse, outliving the boy. He'd made Evangeline a promise. And he'd always assumed the path to keeping that promise was defeating the empire. But he couldn't ignore the fact that G.N.E. tech was outpacing their own, not to mention the imbalance of resources. Was he selling false hope?

"You get some rest," he said to Jimmy. "We'll talk more once I get something for my head." He pressed the button to call the attendant, and took from his pocket the communicator Daryus had given him. What had the prince said:

You realize, you can continue your ridiculous rebellion without Gabriel. I'm not asking you to disband. I just want the singer. And for that, your son returns safe, and he'll have the life you never could have given him, even if you want to continue to wage war on the empire.

Daryus had said something else, too:

It's this business of fathers and sons.

Arhys owed Xander a better life. The way things were going, he couldn't guarantee that. And Gabriel had been ready to turn himself in, anyway. Arhys would resent himself for betraying his brother, but Gabriel would understand, and Arhys could mount an offensive to take Gabriel back, escalate the fight against the empire, build a broader stronger coalition of resistance.

And Xander would be free. And safe.

He couldn't ignore that possibility that Nafaryus might kill Gabriel. If that happened, Arhys would hate himself. But he had to make a choice. Even were he not Xander's father, he always defaulted to protecting a child.

He keyed the communicator on, and sent Daryus a typed message. He'd make the trade. He gave the prince the time and place and plan. He didn't share the meeting Faythe had set up between Gabriel and Nafaryus, just that he and Gabriel were meeting there to discuss a counter-offensive.

Later, he'd have to have some story for how he fought to save Gabriel. He hated that part. The lies to cover lies. But it was a necessity this time.

He sent the note, turned off the device, and buried it back in his pocket.

"You'll forgive me saying, Commander—" it was Jimmy again, "—but you look even worse. You better get something in your drip fast. You okay?"

"It's war," Arhys replied. "People get hurt."

Jimmy's eyebrows rose to that truism. "Ayeah."

A moment later, footsteps interrupted the quiet. The attendant, Arhys thought with relief. Instead, Gabriel came into view.

"Just press this," his brother told him, handing him another small control that had lain just out of eyesight. It had exactly two red buttons. "Left one is for pain. Right one for sleep. Nurse says no more than three pain doses every four hours."

Arhys pressed the button four times, and settled back to outlast the pain. "I hear you did something remarkable."

Gabriel didn't flinch or smile or nod. "I killed a man."

"You know what I mean." Arhys swallowed hard. Concentrating hurt like hell. "You've taken your music to a new level. A fighting level. This is what we've been hoping for."

"What *you've* been hoping for," Gabriel clarified. "I still think we can avoid this whole mess."

"Maybe," Arhys said without conviction. "But their battle staging suggests they're coming against us whether you convince Nafaryus or not. Either way, I think we may have need of your song tomorrow before your meeting with the emperor."

"Jeffer's device," Gabriel said.

The medication began to make Arhys feel warm. "Yes. And whatever you've learned that helps you take down a silent operator."

Arhys found it hard to meet Gabriel's eyes, realizing what he was asking.

"If I'm wrong," Arhys pushed on, "then it's just preparation. If I'm right, maybe we'll do enough damage in open combat that we create some leverage for you in your meeting with Nafaryus."

Gabriel stood silent a long moment. "I don't like killing." He looked up the row of beds in the infirmary. "But I'm done letting them work their will on us. If we end up in full-scale war, I won't hold back."

Arhys still found it hard to meet his brother's eyes. "I'll get to Heaven's Cove ahead of you tomorrow. Secure the area before your meeting with Faythe."

The medication seeped deeper inside him, beginning to erase the pain. But somehow, it opened him to more fully feel the betrayal he was putting into place. He'd save Xander. And maybe they'd put up a good and long fight against the empire, in any case. But he was selling his brother out, regardless of how good a reason he had. And it made him feel like hell.

Gabriel then sat at his bedside, letting out a tired sigh. "Do you ever wonder how we got here?"

"Every day," Arhys said without any real regret.

"It's strange to me." Gabriel got that look of memory in his eyes. "I don't recall it being so bad when we were kids. Maybe I was just oblivious."

Arhys thought of Xander. "That's the way it should be for kids."

Gabriel nodded agreement. "There was still fighting, wasn't there. I remember seeing militia men in town. But it always made me feel safe, not worried. Like you."

"Me?" Arhys couldn't help but chuckle at that. "I seem to remember mostly beating on you. You were annoying."

Gabriel now seemed to be looking at something specific. Something in the past. "That day. Behind the Granderson's back field. Geoffry Windsor and his friends ambushed me. Beat the hell out of me. Broke my arm."

"Cowards," Arhys said. "Seven eleven-year-olds kicking and punching an eight-year-old. You're probably lucky it was just your arm."

"You tracked them down over the next week," Gabriel said, a shine now in his eyes. "Found them each when they were alone. Called them on their cowardice. Kicked the hell out of them all."

"I was good at fighting," Arhys said, with no particular pride.

Gabriel's eyes came back to now. "Made me feel safe. Like the militia men. Never worried about Geoff and his friends again."

Arhys put a hand over his brother's own. "I'm not in a life-threatening situation here. You don't have to—"

"That's not it," Gabriel said. "I'm not clearing my conscience or letting out pent up worry."

"Then what?"

Gabriel appeared to consider a moment. "I just wanted to say thank you, I guess. Even that time I hooked the last few dollars from dad's dresser to buy some archive access. I think I was researching archaic instruments. You took the blame. Remember?"

"I worked double shifts after school at the ironworks for three months as punishment." Arhys smiled at the memory of it. "Iron work is good training if you're going to wind up in fights."

Gabriel gave Arhys a firm grip. "I won't let you down."

There was an old saying about salt being poured in wounds. Arhys had a strong sense of that just now. It proved harder than he thought to bear Gabriel's intense gaze. "Good to hear," he managed.

"You look like you could use a little sleep." Gabriel squeezed Arhys' hand one last time, and gave him a resolute look. It was the fierceness he'd always sought in his brother.

A growing part of Arhys didn't hate the idea that before this was all done, he might join Evangeline in the path beyond life.

CHAPTER 23

———◉———

Daryus reread the message from Arhys. It wasn't a surprise, but it still gave him a feeling of deep satisfaction to have his plans coming together. This delicate statesmanship was precisely what his father needed to see from him. Particularly as this business was beyond Faythe. She didn't have the stomach to do what must be done to exert the empire's will.

Xander sat in the corner of the warehouse, tied to a metal joist. The child didn't look particularly worried. That irked Daryus. He could renege on his part of the exchange easily enough. But that would show weakness. Instead, he'd see the boy raised in the empire. Indoctrinated. That would twist in Arhys for a lifetime. And Nafaryus would love the irony.

He removed himself to the far side of the warehouse behind a bulk of twisted metal. There he opened his secure comm link, and hailed his father.

Morning light was just showing through the dirty ceiling windows. His father would already have eaten, taken his morning briefing, and be in his office for military report-in.

The screen flickered to life. "You're not here. You really should be—"

"I have news," Daryus cut in. "I'm in Ravenskill."

Nafaryus's eyebrows went up. "A day early? Why?"

"Turns out the rebels had no intention of surrendering Gabriel," Arhys explained. "Obviously we're prepared to send a battalion in. But we need Gabriel for two reasons."

His father listened with an interest Daryus rarely saw on his face.

"First," he continued, "we can't have defiance seen from any rebel faction. Not of this magnitude. You issued an ultimatum. The people need to know that the only right response to that is to comply."

Nafaryus nodded agreement. "I see your point."

"Second, if the rumors are true about this singer, we should study him." This was the strategic, forward-looking thinking he hoped his father would appreciate. "We can deconstruct his music, analyze how it's made and its effects. Then, we can replicate it and add it to our sound library."

His father's face showed genuine excitement now.

Daryus rushed ahead. "This would have the dual benefit of increasing our ability to manage the population of the empire, but also accelerate our plans for border expansion. It's not economically viable to continue sending field crews with the harvest seasons. We lose too many. But if, say, we grew our borders to extend to the southern coast, we'd expand commerce and influence exponentially. I have a cost analysis I can take you through when I return."

The smile on Nafaryus' face was like a good many late payments. But then a subtle change. A furrow in his brow. Some new thought.

"It's good thinking, Daryus," his father said. "I assume, then, you've some plan for capturing Gabriel?"

"I do," Daryus said, deliberately minimizing this piece of it, as though such a thing were a simple matter.

"I see," Nafaryus said. "Well, we should discuss the timing of all this. Your sister has negotiated a meeting between me and the singer for this evening."

Daryus clenched his teeth against a litany of curses. "What?"

"She thinks there's a peaceful resolution to all this," Nafaryus added. "I'm doubtful Arhys is going to just let Gabriel deal directly with me without exerting some kind of control. But I've given Faythe my word I'd take the meeting. It's to be at Heaven's Cove tomorrow. No escort."

Arhys held his tongue until he could speak with a rational tone. "Faythe should leave military matters to me. We're dealing with the empire's most dangerous faction. Not to mention the risk you're taking by coming here alone."

"I'm in no danger from a singer," Nafaryus argued, his voice sharp. "And whatever else the boy is, he's not a murderer."

"Maybe, but did you consider that he could be bait." Daryus resisted the mounting desire to shout.

Nafaryus shook his head, losing patience. "Faythe's assured me it's safe. I'm sure Gabriel thinks he can sway me. If taking him into custody is a mere matter of listening to him try, that's nothing." His father paused a moment, his eyes with a familiar look—he was concocting some plan. "Daryus, you should prepare some kind of military presence. We'll parade the boy through his own town to make a show of him under our control. That should have the right effect on the people of Ravenskill."

More parades, Daryus thought.

He wouldn't have Faythe ruining his plans, delivering Gabriel when Daryus had put in place a full solution to Gabriel and Ravenskill. But he'd need to navigate carefully. He was under no delusion of his father's preference for her.

"The meeting is a ruse," he began. "You're being made a fool of, father. If there's not already an assassination plot in it to remove you, it will occur to them soon enough that they have you in a compromised situation."

Nafaryus seemed to consider it.

"And if none of that," Daryus added, "then a stall tactic. Which begs the question of what they're preparing to oppose us."

His father's face had pinched tight in thought. "I've prepared materials to disseminate to defuse a broader call to revolution."

Daryus nodded to that as a necessary component of a larger offensive. "Don't change your plans," he told his father. "It doesn't frustrate any of my preparations. I will deliver Gabriel. I secured that piece of the plan last evening."

His father nodded with something Daryus hadn't often seen. Appreciation.

"But you're presence here unattended is unacceptable." Daryus began to see a way through.

"I've promised no guard. And no drones," Nafaryus said. "But as I told you, I'm not concerned for my own safety."

Daryus showed a patient smile. "That's my job. The first battalion and the droid fleet are mobilizing. I'm sure you're getting the latest this morning."

"But if you secure Gabriel," Nafaryus said, "there's no need of a full offensive."

Yes there is. And there will be.

"I'll bring them in off the shores of Endless Isleland as a precaution," Daryus said with the ease of a practiced liar. "A show of strength to punctuate the capture of Gabriel. And a safety net in the event Arhys and his militia try something foolish. You can't be too careful. Seizing their *savior* could turn them fanatic."

"Then you'll be there?" Nafaryus asked. "When I meet with the boy?"

Daryus wasn't going to let Faythe's plan unfold that far. "Don't worry about any of that. Do as you'd planned. If things go the way they should, you won't even need to release the propaganda reels."

Nafaryus didn't bother to say goodbye. The monitor simply went blank.

For several long moments, Daryus breathed, calming the burn of anger that had bloomed in his chest. *Not this time, Faythe. Not this time.*

He then pulled up a command screen, signaling his generals. "Advance the timeline to noon. You should be in flight within the hour. Formations ready and coming in from the northeast and south." He fell silent, considering, then added, "eradication."

That helped. And now he had intelligence on Arhys and Gabriel's little plots. His mood had begun to turn before he left the tangle of metal to return and keep watch over the boy.

Hearing him approach, Xander looked up. "Private conversation?"

Daryus thought about that for a moment. "Talking to my father." He sat on an old wood crate in front of the boy. "It's not easy being a son, is it?"

Xander gave him a flat look. "You mean like living in a palace, or like being tied up?"

The kid was more clever than Daryus had given him credit for. "I mean when fathers are too busy to take notice of their sons. Caring about other things more than their families."

An expression of understanding crept into Xander's face. "You don't hate us. You just want your dad's approval."

"I think it would be fair to say I hate you *and* I want my dad's approval." Daryus chuckled at his own joke. "Maybe hate isn't right, though. Maybe I'm just irritated with all the disruption your father creates."

"In trying to free us," Xander said.

Daryus crossed his legs and folded his hands around his knee. "Well, now, that's an interesting development. Turns out you, Xander, are going to be free."

The boy gave him a puzzled look, but said nothing.

"That's right," Daryus went on with a bit of magnanimity. "Your father and I have struck a bargain. You're going to have a nice life. Good schools. Plenty of money. No fieldwork in *your* future. I suppose in one way, your father succeeded, for you, anyway."

Xander's expression turned suspicious. "I'd rather your dad love you the way mine loves me. Then you wouldn't need to do any of this."

Sharp tongue, too.

"Some things need to be earned," Daryus replied. "And for all your tough talk, I know you've spent plenty of nights alone wishing he were home. Praying he *comes* home. Wondering how and why you aren't his first concern."

Xander's features softened. "Your father doesn't love you, does he?" Daryus hadn't ever heard it said out loud like that. It got inside him. He stared back at the boy, wondering about the truth to that question.

Long moments later, he offered a weak smile. "I think he does. But love isn't offercd in equal measures. And sometimes you're on the short end."

Xander nodded as if he understood, but didn't quite agree. "The empire killed my mother. How is your mother today?"

Daryus hardly heard him. "Today might have been the first time something I did actually pleased my father."

CHAPTER 24

—◦—

Faythe stood at the top of the old cathedral bell tower looking east out over the Great Valley. The sun lit the horizon in a spray of yellow, orange, and russet. Above her, the sky still held a bit of violet. A mild morning wind moved through the tower, blowing west across Lake Halcyon. It carried a clean scent. Water and willow. The great bell had fallen long ago, and sat deeply tarnished by time and weather, its call silenced.

She'd come to this place almost as often as the Hall of Lost Things. A once grand cathedral, now half in ruin, though the tower still ascended heavenward like a monument to the days before the End Wars.

And war was why she was here.

"My ancestors worshiped here." Commander Donovan said, stepping into view. He'd arrived like a ghost. The leader of the elusive Valley Men. They kept the great roads across New Anglya largely safe for civilians. Faythe had guessed he'd be first, being closest to the tower.

"It holds a certain solace," she said. "Shame it was damaged."

Donovan crossed the tower and looked down with her through the destroyed roof at the nave and transept of the place. "Yes, but she's still standing, wounds and all. That says something, too."

The stairs echoed with more arrivals, not nearly so stealthy an approach. Captains Markell, Peters, and Sondem stepped into the tower one after the other, each nodding a greeting.

That wouldn't do. Faythe went to each captain individually.

Judith Markell led the Eastgate Militia that operated from that city all the way to North Point. Victor Peters led the underground tech group that moved operations constantly. And Darnell Sondem commanded a sizeable force west of the Mirror Neck—roving bands from Flat Rock to Stone Bridge Hollow. She introduced herself to each of them personally.

"I have to say," Sondem said. "Your invitation was a surprise. We've had the tower under surveillance for several hours. Figured this was the old ploy. You know, gather the resistance leaders together and take them out in one tactical strike."

Donovan shook his head. "We've been monitoring all access across the Broad Plain as a matter of routine for years. Unless Faythe herself is a silent operator, the invitation is legitimate. No imperial presence."

"Thank you for coming." Faythe stepped back, so she could see them all at once. "I didn't want to risk a communication, for obvious reasons."

A few leaders made indistinct noises in their throats.

"I know you're aware of the situation in Ravenskill," she began. "The emperor's ultimatum comes due at midnight."

"We're aware," Markell said with some disgust. "Arhys has asked for help. No one has turned him down. No one will."

Faythe held up her hands. "I'm not here to negotiate peace with you."

Donovan eyed her closely. "The emperor's daughter and best diplomat doesn't want peace."

"I didn't say that," she replied with firmness. "I am working with Gabriel to try and resolve this before it escalates too far."

A few of the commanders looked surprised. All looked suspicious.

"That so?" Peters questioned. "What's in it for you? Or your father?"

"Look," Faythe said, losing patience, but maintaining a flat expression. "I've seen the preparations being made by the G.N.E. fleet. It's … overwhelming. As a precaution, in case diplomacy fails, I think each of you needs to move as much of your force as you can spare to Ravenskill. There's no doubt our military will make an extreme example of it, if we can't negotiate some kind of treaty."

Sondem scrubbed his chin. "Or, could be that you want as many of us in one place at one time to decimate our ranks."

"Check with Gabriel if you doubt my allegiance," she countered. "And the point is to have a presence sufficient to either deter an attack or meet it with success."

"Why?" Peters again questioned. "Why is the daughter of the man we all fight against trying to undermine his military? You realize it's treason. You realize if you're caught, you'll be executed."

"I'm doing my part to try and find peace. Prevent unnecessary deaths. My request is that you send what soldiers you can spare to Ravenskill to help defend that city. It will either turn out to be unnecessary, or you'll prevent what would surely be the single most catastrophic loss of life in G.N.E. history."

"Sounds like life is still going to be lost," Donovan observed. "You're asking it to be *our* lives, rather than those of Ravenskill."

"And once Ravenskill falls, who is next? Will you wait for my father to come for each of you in turn? One by one you will fall, and you will ask yourselves, 'why is no one standing with me?'" Faythe paused, as each of them considered her words. Then she added, "And fighters take an oath, don't they? To defend the innocent. I'm hoping you're not the kind of leaders that only protects their own. More than that. It will send a message to the emperor if you're all fighting together, organized. He'll have to consider whether he really wants civil war on that scale. Maybe we convince him to talk. If not, you've established a united front against him, which is something you're going to want and need, because Ravenskill will only be the first example."

Markell pointed at her. "The reason he's razing Ravenskill is Gabriel. Don't try to sow fear in us for our own people to manipulate our assistance."

Faythe stepped closer to the man, returning the accusing gesture. "Gabriel is the best reason for you to go. The thing the emperor fears most is Gabriel. If my father won't negotiate for peace, Gabriel will be taken, or killed. What will that do for the morale of your fighters?"

Captain Peters stared intently at her a long while. "This sounds like the ploy of someone trying to save the life of a man she cares about. Any truth to that?"

All the leaders were now scrutinizing her closely, looking for a lie. "Yes," she said without reservation. "I care for Gabriel. And if we get past all this, I suspect that will grow. But I want you to understand something, all of you. If I felt nothing for Gabriel, even if I held him in contempt, I wouldn't want this kind of civil infighting. It's bad for the empire."

"You're saying you'd be doing all this anyway," Donovan summarized. "You know what? I believe you."

The others held their judgment a few moments more, but conceded the same.

Faythe felt a huge wave of relief. And immediately acknowledged the irony of feeling relief for the commitment of unprecedented forces to war.

"Thank you," she said, shaking every leader's hand. "I did invite your colleagues from east Yorkeland, the Borderland, and elsewhere. But I knew it was unlikely they'd arrive in time. I'll trust you to share this message with them as best you can. I don't want to risk compromising you or the effort with channel communication."

In matter-of-fact fashion, each nodded and descended the stair, leaving her in silence again.

Maybe ten minutes after they had gone, another set of footsteps came up the stairs. Faythe turned, expecting to see one of the other militia leaders, arriving late. Instead, she saw her mother, Arabelle.

"Really, Faythe, plotting treason with rebels? I thought we had raised you better."

Faythe shook her head. "How did you know—"

"Why is it you and your brother constantly underestimate me? Have I not ruled at your father's side for nearly thirty years?" Arabelle stepped to the east-facing balustrade and looked toward the sun.

"But—"

You've been coming here to *think* since you were eight years old. What sort of mother would I be not to have the place monitored?" She pointed to a couple of tiny drones wedged into cracks and crannies across the face of the building. "And Peters is right, what you're doing is treason," her mother said with no real indictment in her voice.

Faythe let out a long breath. "Well, I won't change my mind."

"I know that, too," her mother said, the hint of a smile on her lips.

"I could argue that I'm working to assure peace," Faythe stated dryly. "The only difference is I'm focusing on domestic issues rather than foreign."

"And I'm sure your father would accept that excuse without debate." Arabelle's sarcasm was light but certain.

Faythe sighed and turned to her mother. "I've spent all my time working in the interest of the empire in lands far from here. Securing trade agreements, treaties, favorable terms. All that's been good. But this is different. I feel like I'm starting over, but with the right goal now. To repair the empire internally. Build a future for all our people, not just the trade class." She paused, wondering. "Are you going to turn me in?"

Arabelle held Faythe's gaze long enough to give her pause, then said simply, "No. I agree with your logic, and purpose. And, I also don't believe it's going to escalate that far."

Faythe shook her head. "War, you mean?"

"You and your father are a lot alike," Arabelle said. "Both driven. Both smart. And both moved by the intangibles real music can offer. It's just been a while for Nafaryus. Since before he bore that name, even. But I think he will remember. He won't want to be pushed into it. He'll shut down if he feels forced. But, I believe you and Gabriel can remind him."

Faythe had never heard her mother talk about her father that way.

"It won't happen overnight," Arabelle quickly added. "There's real risk you may fail. And even if you succeed, the empire won't change over to some new thing tomorrow. But a reminder. That's a seed worth planting and cultivating. And I'm going to help you do it. So, no, I won't be turning you in." She looked down at the ruins of the cathedral. "Maybe it's good we start here," she said. "I feel like we could use a few good prayers in all this."

Faythe looked at her mother as if she were seeing her for the first time. "You pray?"

"So do you," her mother said with a wry smile. "After all, when you get right down to it, music is a prayer. One we say when words just aren't enough."

CHAPTER 25

—◉—

It was late morning when Gabriel entered the Passage Hotel just off the Ravenskill square. Dignitaries from all across the south of the Great Northern Empire had begun to arrive for some kind of peace summit. A runner had been sent to fetch him. The visiting politicians had requested an introduction to "the singer." Standing in a close circle to one side of the lobby were two women and two men, like orbiting satellites a dozen attendants frittered nearby, seeming ready for a task to complete. The runner led Gabriel past this layer of servants to the dour group talking quietly amongst themselves.

"May I present, Gabriel of Ravenskill," the runner said, bowing slightly at the waist.

Conversation stopped, and the four dignitaries turned to face him.

Gabriel put out his hand. "Governor Reesh of New Pavonya. It's an honor to have you here in Ravenskill."

Reesh gave him a look of surprise and some appreciation, but asked a question. "You knew we were coming?"

"No," he answered.

"The runner gave you our names," she followed.

"Yes, but I know your name and face and reputation." Gabriel pointed to the Ravenskill Militia patch on his upper sleeve.

Stephan Owen, Governor of New Maineland nodded to the obvious. "Military leaders study the political landscape of their enemy. You're no different. But we're not here on behalf of the emperor."

"A peace summit," Gabriel said. "That what the runner called it."

"That's what Faythe called it," the Provost of Victory Island, Issac Denal, said, joining in. "There'll be real talks at some point, I'm sure. But today, we're mostly a deterrent."

Gabriel understood immediately. "She thinks the empire will reconsider destroying Ravenskill if there are ranking empire officials here, especially if you're here in the name of peaceful resolutions."

She's crazy smart, Gabriel thought, and smiled.

"I appreciate the risk you're taking by being here." Gabriel made sure to look them each in the eye. "The situation is volatile. We're trying to avert a military strike."

Reesh nodded as if all that was obvious and not worth talking about. "Why is the emperor afraid of you? Let me rephrase: Is there something in your music we *should* be afraid of?"

Gabriel offered a sad smile. "The fact that you ask a question like that shows how far off course we really are." He paused, ordering his thoughts. "The government effectively makes slaves of those who don't work directly for the empire. Among the slaves, the emperor is not a loved man. He's right to be wary of anyone he uses this way."

"But about the music?" Reesh insisted.

"The loss of music began to happen initially through complacency—why do something a machine can do?" Gabriel still could not understand this, as much as he knew it was true. "But along the way, the empire realized that sound could be used to produce the opposite effect. Instead of inspiration and comfort, it could suppress ... deaden."

"And your music is the former kind," Denal surmised. "Which is why the emperor fears it. But we've heard it's not just music. That it can … move things. Move people."

Gabriel gave them an ambiguous smile. Better for them to still have questions, especially since he knew their loyalties were to Daryus. Faythe had worked her magic to get them here, but that didn't guarantee anything.

A moment later, almost in unison, the four dignitaries raised various com devices, some wore bands about the wrist, some held pocket-pad com links, Reesh looked ahead as if she wore the in-eye comm lenses. Their faces all seemed to tell the same story.

"What is it?" Gabriel asked.

Reesh surveyed the room, the people, the exits, and finally Gabriel. "An invasion fleet is coming in off both the northeast and southern shores of Endless Isleland. An empire constituent evacuation warning has been issued."

Gabriel dashed to the window, looking north. Nothing in the skies yet, but it wouldn't take them long. Scout drones would come miles ahead of the rest, relaying intelligence, enemy positioning, flushing out early counter attacks.

"Damn," he muttered, the sound echoing flatly back at him off the window glass. "Either Nafaryus lied to Faythe. Or Daryus is playing hero."

He turned to entreat the visiting leaders to help them, and found himself staring at a bank of impulse pistols and not a few swords, though they looked largely ceremonial or perhaps just never used.

"A ruse?" Gabriel glared with disdain at the lot of them. "Did you come with this intent? Or are you suddenly afraid and want leverage against your own army when they come to crush my town?"

Reesh shook her head. "Faythe's a hell of a diplomat, but Daryus will be emperor. Only a fool betrays a future king. This way, we tell them we have you, they place the fleet in a holding pattern, your city is saved, and we demonstrate our loyalty to the empire and its heir."

Gabriel didn't want to reveal his private meeting with Nafaryus, but he needed them to understand. "Faythe and I are meeting Nafaryus tonight to discuss a truce. He's coming to Heaven's Cove. This," he pointed out the window toward the sky that would soon be filled with drones and battle cruisers, "isn't Nafaryus' doing. Unless you believe he'd betray his daughter's trust. I know you support Daryus, but I'd think twice about doing so at the expense of his daughter."

The imperial governors and provosts exchanged doubtful looks.

Gabriel pressed, "Daryus is pushing a military agenda ahead of his father's negotiations. Maybe he doesn't know about the meeting tonight. But even if not, the attack, by Nafaryus' command, was to come *after* today. Not now. This is murder and treason on the prince's part. Do you want your names associated with that?"

Reesh raised her impulse pistol more purposefully. "None of that matters. The story will be that a few of the empire's bravest leaders used statecraft to come to Ravenskill and capture the leader of rebellion after learning that he had no intent of complying with the emperor's demand."

Denal raised his weapon, too. "We'll send them our coordinates. Knowing we have you in custody, they'll provide us a safe path from town."

The stirrings of panic rose in Gabriel's chest. The duplicity. The impending invasion. The lost chance to try and convince Nafaryus.

He focused his thoughts, and gave a single rough shouted note. "No!" Deep and rasping, it tore from him and knocked his would-be captors to the floor with terrific violence. Nearly all lay unconscious, concussed, or dazed. Gabriel sprinted from the hotel into the street, and ran north from town to the north-city post, where he relayed what he knew to the ranking officer, Captain Townsend, the oldest living militiaman in Ravenskill. Several of the militia fighters stationed there followed him north in military landcraft, while a few activated the local comm-network and raced to spread the word, mobilize Ravenskill.

Ten minutes later they rolled up to the shore along the Great Northern Sound. Empire drones and battle cruisers filled the horizon like birds in migration.

"Oh my God," Gabriel whispered. He'd never seen a force this size.

"Gabriel!" Townsend to his left shouted and pointed.

Gabriel shifted focus and saw it. There were new classes of drones coming at them. Some were still spherical, but varying in size and configuration, weapon mounts showing new kinds of artillery and sound dishes. But other drones had no discernible geometric shape. And they varied widely in size and obvious use.

Behind them came more battle cruisers than Gabriel could count, more drones flying in escort all around them.

Ravenskill would be so heavily outnumbered …

"Arhys has gone to the south shore to meet the fleet coming up from the North Sea," Captain Townsend said. "You're in command."

Several around Gabriel fell silent awaiting his orders. This was beyond him. How did he lead a relatively inconsequential resistance force against such power? With a song?

He dug into his pocket and pulled out the neck band Rawls had given him. *It'll throw your voice three miles*, the engineer had said.

But once Gabriel started to use it, how long before the empire adapted, flew out around them and took down Ravenskill while they tried to rush back and defend her.

"Gabriel?" Townsend whispered. "How do you want to deploy?"

Gabriel struggled to answer. He'd failed long ago to save Evangeline. He'd not found real battle song, except recently to bring down a single man, and that was with the memories of the assassin's own killings creating psychic poison and pain in the man. But this …

Townsend put a hand on Gabriel's shoulder. "It doesn't have to be right. It just has to be now." Townsend smiled just enough that Gabriel saw it. The old man was telling him they needed leadership, not salvation.

Gabriel put Jeffer's device around his neck. "Back to the north post," he said.

"Closer to Ravenskill?" Townsend said with clear doubt.

"Two lines. One a half mile north of the northeast post, one starting at her northern walls." Gabriel gave the orders fast. "The lines need to extend all the way around the city. Air weapons manned by your best operators. And get the civilians to safety. Go!"

The command went out as the north shore invasion force advanced quickly toward Ravenskill. Orders were relayed ahead on smallnet frequencies, and land-to-air defenses were set at block intervals in a sweeping circle. When Gabriel got to the outer ring, every rooftop had a man or two with a pulse rifle. They were getting as close as possible to use the empire tech against the drones. Bulwarks had begun to be put up across the roads and streets. Empire ground forces would have a rough time getting through.

Far off, Gabriel could hear the roar of worry. Men and women hollering directions, screaming with fear, some crying, as they sought cover and mobilized for the attack.

Gabriel quickly scanned the area. An old radio tower, hulking and rusted, sat three blocks west. It ascended higher than anything else in Ravenskill. The Empire had installed commlink repeaters at the top. And Ravenskill militia engineers used it for smallnet communications. Neither side would want to see it go down. He assumed they'd avoid destroying it in their invasion. Gabriel turned his land-vehicle that way and sped.

Townsend and a woman named Chloe followed him beyond the fallen gate and climbed behind him up the ancient ruin. Every rung blackened his hands, the rust stabbing his palms like thorns. But he pushed up. He needed to get as high as he could.

Two hundred feet later, he stepped out onto a rusted steel-grate perch near the top that circled the spire. The wind came stronger here. He eased around to face the northeast sky, where the empire fleet had crossed half way toward them.

They were maybe three miles away.

"I hope to God this works," Gabriel whispered.

An eerie silence fell over the radio tower as they waited for the fleet to draw near. High above Ravenskill, looking toward the Great Northern Sound, everything slowed down. Nothing seemed to move or to do so by degree. Even the fleet approaching did so with a slow terrifying grace.

"We'll wait until they're directly overhead," Gabriel ordered.

Chloe's eyes remained trained on the approaching fleet. "What are we going to do?"

"I'm going to see what kind of music they hate," Gabriel quipped. "But they can't know we're here. Trigger an energy cloak as soon as you see the first militia artillery go up at the drones. We'll hide beneath it until as many as possible are in range."

"In range of what?" Townsend eyed Gabriel with optimism.

"I don't know what to call it," Gabriel answered. "But we hope it disrupts drone suppressive sound."

"If you're wrong," Chloe said flatly, "we'll have a long fall to think about another failed rebel technology."

Gabriel heard the frustration in her voice. Too many friends killed in service. Too much hope in prior resistance weaponry. The best defense they had were the audio shields, but they'd only been able to produce a few, and they didn't have a perfect operational history.

"If we're wrong," Gabriel added, "everyone falls."

An explosion rocked the sky, ripping their attention back to the fleet. Forward drones were being hit by a barrage of dogger missiles fired by militia artillery. Two drones began to hurtle earthward. But that made it no easier to count the remaining drones, there were so many. A few more listed, bobbed, right themselves. Then the audio blasts erupted, fired down from audio cones and dishes with crushing force. Tree branches snapped and fell, creating a crackling across the countryside. Buildings crumbled at the edges. The rush of sound whipped the air into violent winds.

"Dearest God," Townsend exclaimed. "They've coupled some kind of force with the sound itself."

Distant cries rose up as militia fighters fell. Rockets continued to ascend, but in diminishing numbers. Another drone dropped hard, crashing into a long flat building, causing an explosion—a new mechanism of the drones to self-destruct when crippled in battle.

The drones then did something Gabriel had never seen. They began to work in tandem. Flying in close proximity, drones paired, and sometimes configured themselves in threes and fours and fives. Together they produced a combined sound working at disharmonies Gabriel had never heard. He could feel them in his chest, even from here. They brought up panic and nausea and confusion. And pain.

"Shields! Now!" he screamed.

Townsend and Chloe each fired up a shield. Not something you could see, but the NOMAC music lessened to almost nothing.

The drones began to move more quickly. Militia fighters now had them in pulse rifle range, and began to fire. The blasts pushed several of the drones out of course, affecting their coordinated attacks, but they soon corrected, and targeted the rooftops with their infernal noise.

Across the northeast, buildings began to collapse and explode beneath the drone onslaught.

And the fleet hasn't even begun to fire.

Then another blast tore through the air. Gabriel and his friends dropped to their knees. Sharing looks, each was bleeding from the nose and corners of their eyes. The audio dampeners every militia fighter wore in their ears weren't working at all. This new music didn't seem to depend nearly as much on being heard.

Townsend put a hand on Gabriel's shoulder. "Whatever you're going to do. Do it soon."

Beneath them, the militia mounted a counter surge. A fresh volley of missiles went up, some with smoke emission, to cloud the sky and reduce drone targeting capabilities. Pulse rifles fired on repeat. Carbine weapons were unloaded in heavy bursts. The ground looked like a rippling ocean with sunlight beaming off the waves—gunfire and weaponry flashed everywhere.

Several drones began to fall. But a few in a sky filled with them? And that's when the fleet began its firefight. Energy pulses began to push the air at incredible speed and force, blurring the world, whipping through terrain like a hurricane. Men and women were picked up off rooftops and the ground and sent flying. Heavy craft that were used to launch missiles and heavy artillery were crushed and toppled. A wave of destruction began to push toward the inner line of defense at the town's edge.

Townsend and Chloe kept the audio shield up, their faces now a bloody mess. Screams of pain reached up the radio tower like distant things. Everything. Everything was being laid low. Trees, buildings, vehicles. The dust of pulverized buildings and churning earth created a thick cloud that rolled toward Ravenskill.

They really are razing the town. Leveling it right to the Goddamn ground!

The first drones passed overhead. They were leaving the radio tower intact, for communication redundancy, no doubt. But the new model drones then began to unleash their devastation.

A high-pitched hum filled the air, joined soon by a sonic note so low it could only really be felt. The combination stirred a sensation inside Gabriel's body. He felt loose. Clouded. Aching from the inside out. And that was through the audio shield. Below and all around them, physical objects—those still intact, and those crumbling from conventional drone and energy weapons—simply began to desolidify. They lost cohesion. It was like watching a sand castle dry and fall, but at an alarming rate.

The terrain became a sea of sand and ash and mulch behind a rolling stormwall that ate everything in its path.

Then Gabriel noticed something more. Here and there, a structure hadn't fallen. It looked like precision avoidance. Why?

He didn't have time to consider it further. The destruction had reached the inner line of defense. The fleet still wasn't all within three miles. Did he wait?

Maybe a few moments more.

A third wave of attack began. A new class of weapon.

"Townsend, come in," a comms device squawked. "Townsend!"

With his free hand, the captain grabbed his communicator. "Go!"

"Something we've never seen." The woman on the other end of the communication was clearly running, heavy rapid footfall and labored breathing. "People. They're … dropping."

"Dropping?"

She moaned through the comms device. "I feel it now, too. It's in my chest. I'm forgetting. I feel strange. I don't feel like … who is this?"

Then it sounded like she fell. A smack and the link went dead.

Chloe cursed. "It's true. The empire has a new audio technology that can rewrite human sound."

Gabriel had heard the rumor. He understood it better than most, given his research and own recent use of his song.

"They've mapped us," Townsend added. "The inside of us. It's not enough that they can pulverize our world. They want to unmake who we are."

"Remake us," Gabriel corrected. "They'll use our bodies like husks. Put us back to work … like drones."

"You don't know that," Townsend argued. "My bet is they just want us to suffer. Either way, we don't have any time left."

The sound-storm rolled over Ravenskill proper, dropping everything. Only now, the people didn't seem to be crushed and torn apart as much as shattered inside. Like their souls were being utterly broken. The sound of them detuned to silence.

Gabriel lowered his head, offering a prayer of last hopes. Then, he stood and looked skyward into the midst of the vast empire fleet.

And thought of a song. A rough one.

A last sound.

CHAPTER 26

—◉—

Nafaryus watched a video feed of the attack on Ravenskill. Something must have happened for Daryus to send the fleet in before it was time. Maybe the meeting with Gabriel had been a ruse after all. Maybe Daryus had sniffed it out. But a quick check showed they'd overcommitted to the attack, exposing them nearly everywhere else.

A lieutenant rushed in. "My lord, rebels have mobilized and are on the move toward Ravenskill. Indications are that they'll come up behind the fleet on both fronts."

"We still outnumber them," Nafaryus replied evenly. "And they're not matching the new weaponry."

"That's not all," the lieutenant said, talking fast. "Reports suggest a tri-part strategy in every province. Rebels have sent a third of their force to support Arhys, another third is mounting offensives against our standing police force. And the last third ... is marching on the capital."

"Here?" Nafaryus said. "That's preposterous."

"Not if they mean to have you divert resources back to protect the palace city."

Nafaryus pressed a button, signaling the immediate release of the manufactured footage showing G.N.E. convoys headed into every rebel region. The footage suggested the new cloaking technology he'd leaked a few days prior. Rebel troops would have to now consider whether or not to continue their movement toward Ravenskill and the capital, since it appeared an empire counter-offensive was being mounted against them all. One they couldn't see coming.

He looked up at the lieutenant. "Make an announcement on all channels that our diplomatic efforts with the Midwest Confederation and Eastern Empire have yielded a military pact that has increased the size our army six fold. Show footage of Faythe in her appearances with their leaders."

The lieutenant rushed off to prepare the communication.

There wasn't time for another trip to Forth Truth. Nafaryus called in his information officer to his command and control console.

"Edit down footage from the Ravenskill attack," he pointed to the feed still showing on one of his screens, "and interweave it with file 'Gabriel.'"

The man's hand flashed across the keys as he worked through software to create a seamless video message of Gabriel's death during the attacks, using the file he'd had created by his propaganda team.

"Push it out as soon as it's done," Nafaryus ordered. "All channels. Run it in cycle with the convoy footage."

"Of course, sir," the information officer said, with a tight smile.

Nafaryus nodded. "Dissuasion. It won't stop the zealots. But it will stop the practical, the ones with families and friends. Send them scurrying back to defend their own."

"What are your orders for fortifying the capital, your Highness?" the man asked. "The remaining force here is token at best."

It was Nafaryus' turn to smile. "A third communiqué. Grab moments from the Ravenskill attack footage that demonstrate the new audio technology. Then show the city perimeter audio dishes. Let them know we can push the same tech in defense of the city."

The information officer masked a quizzical stare, as he simply replied, "Aye, aye, Sir."

"We can," Nafaryus responded to the unasked question. "It will impact some of our own, but we can. And we will, if we need to."

The man's hands hesitated a moment before going back to work.

"And open up a channel to Daryus." Nafaryus waited as the man quickly saw first to the new order.

A moment later, one of the video relays switched to a somewhat hazy view of his son, standing on the shore somewhere, the sky behind him filled with the third battalion.

"It was necessary," Daryus said quickly, "I've been in Ravenskill for the past twenty-four hours. I discovered their intent to make a mockery of your order, and plans to mount an assassination attempt."

"At Heaven's Cove," Nafaryus surmised. "You're saying Gabriel is using Faythe to get to me."

Daryus paused a moment, looking regretful. "I'd rather believe that than the alternative."

Nafaryus shook his head. "Faythe would never betray me. She would never deliver me into the hands of the enemy. Gabriel must be something different than what he appears."

"Of that I'm certain," Daryus agreed. "But much of this is being driven by Arhys. The element of surprise was our best option."

"You still should have told me," Nafaryus said, edging his tone.

"I'm sorry, father." His son sounded sincere, but then Daryus was, in his own right, a practiced statesman. "But there wasn't time. I couldn't risk a debate on the initiative. I had to put the Strength Program into operational maneuvers fast to get ahead of their plans."

This made sense. But there was still something about Daryus that he couldn't trust. He knew his son was lying. Not that it changed anything about the situation, but, perhaps, his son was more devious and worthy of the throne than he had thought. Daryus had always been a blunt instrument. Obsessed with might and strength, but this scheme of his was surprisingly conniving. Maybe he had learned something about ruling after all.

"I will still be at Heaven's Cove as planned. I'll expect the surrender of both Gabriel and Arhys at that time."

"It will be an honor to deliver both," Daryus said. "The northern invasion force has already made groundfall. We're going in from the south momentarily. Arhys is bringing half his militia to meet us. It will be over soon."

Nafaryus nearly keyed off the display, then stopped. "You're sure they can't best us. If you fail, we'll be in a weakened position when I arrive. I'd be forced to have Faythe negotiate a settlement."

"I won't let that happen," Daryus said, and shut down his comms unit, but not before Nafaryus caught a glimpse of the self-satisfied smirk growing across his son's face.

The control room remained quiet for a long while, save the busy hands of his information officer seeing to Nafaryus' other orders. Something didn't feel right. Arhys wouldn't engage in full scale civil war without some belief he could win. Perhaps that had everything to do with Gabriel. But redundant planning had saved Nafaryus more than once.

This time, he opened the commline himself, using an access code only he knew. He waited patiently. A few moments later, Regent Grace Storal's stern elderly face flickered onto the screen. This link was strong, giving the lines in her face had the look of fissures.

"You look healthy," Nafaryus began. "That bodes well for the Eastern Empire."

"I look old," she replied, then cut straight to it. "There's military activity in your world. Is this an advisory call, or do you need help."

Nafaryus liked Grace. No compunctions. "Both," he said. "And to keep it simple, I have new audio technology I'm willing to share—to a point—in exchange for the immediate deployment of your nearest battalion into G.N.E. I'll account for provisions."

"And what's my compensation for each man that falls?" she asked bluntly.

"I've already stated what I will share, but," he quickly added, "this is primarily a show of force and support, not actual combat."

Grace stared through the screen at him, her old eyes as sharp as ever, and hinting at the beauty she'd been fifty years ago. "I wouldn't do it for you alone. I want you to know that. You're a selfish bastard. And your son's worse. But for Faythe. I'll do it for her, since I can see her brokering you some peace internally. She's the one who ought to get the crown, you know."

The screen went blank, Grace signing off without a goodbye.

Nafaryus didn't dwell on the woman's commentary, and immediately repeated the call with the MidWest Confederation. An easier conversation.

He may not need any of this. But he'd be damned if he'd get caught without military support if it all went to hell. He led the empire. He'd earned the right. And he meant to keep it. Different from his promised payment for the support; he'd never give them the actual technology. The breakthrough meant expansion soon.

A slow smile came to him at the thought of using sovereign allies today who might be provincial governors under his rule tomorrow.

The last thing he did before leaving the communication offices was place a call to a very old friend.

CHAPTER 27

———●———

Stepping onto the bridge of the aerial command cruiser, Daryus gave the order for full assault.

"Sir, what about the north shore invasion fleet?" his first officer, Owens, asked. "They made landfall several minutes ago. They're already pushing into the town."

Daryus allowed time for a thoughtful pause. "Full assault," he repeated. It meant nothing should be left alive. Nothing.

The new tech would do its work. But he needed to be sure there were no gaps. That, and he now he wanted to make a statement. Crush everything.

"But sir, we're showing signals of Empire leaders in the center of Ravenskill." The officer consulted his terminal. "Distress signals."

"Do we know who?"

The officer paged through a set of information, and looked back with worry tight in his face. "All the southern province governors."

Daryus shut his eyes, forcing himself to remain calm. They were his strongest supporters. What the hell were they doing in Ravenskill today, of all days!

"Outcome if we delay?" Daryus asked. But that was just for the logs. He'd already decided. Because he knew the outcome if they delayed. He'd modeled hostage scenarios, which were essentially the same. Still, the record must show he'd been *thoughtful*.

"If we modified the approach to eliminate only those people we've audio-mapped, we could send a recon team to pull them out," the man said.

"Leaving roughly twenty-nine percent of the population untouched. Most of those are militia fighters." Daryus folded his arms across his chest. "And the town would remain intact."

"Correct, sir," the officer confirmed. "And some few would likely escape ahead of the new drone sound library. The alarm was sounded in Ravenskill several minutes ago."

He took a heavy breath, as one should when making a hard decision. "No. Full assault. Everything … everyone goes down. We'll memorialize our fallen colleagues who, no doubt, were here in service of the Empire, once we've put down the rebellion once and for all."

Daryus had no idea why his key political allies were in Ravenskill. But he'd bet Faythe had something to do with it.

For now, he let it go. The advance drones were beginning their crushing assault on the ground, working in from the coast. Sound blasts were tearing ranches and homes and fields to shreds, pushing a wave of dust and debris, and whipping ponds and lakes into water spouts. The battle cruisers added to the devastation with pulse bursts at two-second intervals. Endless Isleland from the shore inward fell under a wave of destructive sound and energy.

His own cruiser had moved a mile inland, when anti-aircraft missiles began to rocket into the sky. A few drones took direct hits and began to list.

"Those three are compromised," he said. "Send them on impact trajectories where the rocket launchers are most tightly clustered. Activate ignition upon impact."

The hit drones dove at a fast slant toward the militia front, where the rebels fought up from the cover of broad oaks and a number of mobile defense shields—acoustic-resistant steel.

A moment later, they hit the earth and exploded in a fire both hot and chemical, taking several dozen militia fighters with them.

"Broaden the line," Daryus commanded. "They don't have enough to fight across more than half a mile. We'll take out those we can in the center. The rest will swing wide and go on to Ravenskill."

Drones began fanning out left and right all across the sky. They flew at different altitudes. Some went high—those with narrow attack options, controlled pulse tech, and the new-audio signature tech that worked outside the audible spectrum. While others flew low, those with the brute force attacks that pounded indiscriminately. The remainder flew ahead, between, and behind, for recon, signal relay, and to communicate coordinates for targeted strikes.

"The new drones haven't misfired or malfunctioned once," his first officer commented.

"Didn't anticipate they would," Daryus replied. "I've been testing them in Quebec State skirmishes for three years."

His First-in-Command worked hard to mask his shock. Battle tech use in other nations was a command only the Emperor could give. But Daryus never asked permission. He'd only shared data under the guise of his own simulation models with his father's audio and battle engineers.

Just before the fleet got beyond the range of the ground militia's counter-assault, several concussive explosions rocked the skyline ahead. From the ground, plumes of dirt and debris shot skyward. They came from somewhere near the Ravenskill Militia bunker. And, at the head of each stream of dirt, leaves, and shattered wood, was a drone.

"What in the hell?' Daryus leaned forward, as if doing so could make sense of what he was seeing.

"Decommissioned class," his officer said. "We haven't used those in years."

The drones began to rush toward them. They'd obviously been reprogrammed.

"Connect with them. Initiate self-destruction!" Daryus shouted.

"They predate destruction protocols." The officer still seemed to be trying, rapidly keying commands through his terminal. "I can't establish a link."

"Nevermind. Full focus on the enemy drones. Blow them out of the sky." Daryus watched, waiting for his fleet's might to turn their extensive numbers against the handful of drones.

Pulse fire and audio waves shifted, pushing in concert at the old drones. But in a bright orange-yellow flare, the enemy drones pushed their own concerted audio signal out in a protective shield, filling the sky with a cacophony of angry sound that seemed to compact space. Daryus could hear it through the hull of his cruiser.

"They've modified it somehow," Daryus said. "They weren't able to replicate the drones, but they affected their sound library."

"How do you know—"

"Because they would have brought the fight to us long ago if they could manufacture drones themselves." Daryus reasoned impatiently. "At the very least there'd be more than five here now to push us back. They're severely outmanned."

As he said it, the old drones seemed to develop dozens of circular openings. Dark circles stared out in every direction like ominous eyes.

Before Daryus could call for a new tech counter, the old drones exploded in a stunning fiery display. And from the conflagration around each erupting drone shot dozens of small rockets, angling fast with blue-stream trailers toward the drone and cruiser fleet.

"Shields!" he shouted.

His First Officer hit a general command button, taking immediate control of the fleet, and pushed out an audio wall to meet the racing missiles.

But the signal created by the old drones came ahead of their rockets, clearing a path, and muting the audio shields just enough that their payloads struck home.

All across the monitor panels, screens went dark. The sky erupted again in reds and oranges and yellows. Black and grey smoke billowed outward in expanding clouds. Imperial drones began to free fall. Not all, but maybe half. And more than a few cruisers began to list heavily.

The sky stood choked in flames and smoke. The attack had been a one-time tactic, something Arhys had likely been planning for years. But it had been effective.

And in the wake of it, the militia ground attack re-commenced. Carbine weapons began to bark, as the sky filled again with artillery shells.

"Enough!" he yelled. "Push all audio maps down in a sweeping canvas. Anyone there whose signal we've collected. I want them sloughing off to nothing!"

The high-altitude drones shot forward, formed a line, and began a flight path out and over several square miles at full flight speed. The frequency spectrum monitor lit up like the sky just had, as the sound-maps of Ravenskill citizens and militia fighters were dropped violently down to disrupt their bodies, tearing them apart like a glass shattering beneath the onslaught of an extreme pitch.

"Bring up the surveillance audio," Daryus commanded.

The speakers came to life with the distant chatter of men and women coordinating their counterstrikes. Then, a moment later, screams.

The audio maps were finding their owners. And violently so.

During their visit to Ravenskill a few days ago, they hadn't been able to scan everyone. But they'd gotten many of them. And those they had, were feeling it now.

Enemy air missiles launched with less frequency. Carbine weapons, too. The sky calmed.

"Renew ground bursts," Daryus ordered. Destroy everything between here and Ravenskill. And when we get there, we'll leave just so much dust."

The fleet came back into formation and began again to surge. The flanks had gotten ahead of them, so that they moved across Endless Isleland like a large crescent moon.

Behind them a concussive blast rattled the trailer cruisers, including Daryus's command ship. Several drones were sending damage reports.

Daryus pulled up a new view. "God damn it!" Rebel support factions had brought their measly navy to the fight. But those old frigates could hurl artillery shells, and a damn long ways at that. He couldn't ignore them.

"Second battalion stays on course," he shouted. "Start razing Ravenskill. I'll take third battalion and the standard tech drone fleet and eliminate the rear threat. We'll catch up. Go!"

The fight ahead continued, but second battalion, with the new drones, would put down the remaining militia fighters easily enough. Daryus pivoted the third battalion around and rushed back toward the coast.

Maybe a dozen ocean battleships and destroyers filled the sea a half mile off-shore. Immense barrels across all their decks fired in alternating rhythms. Sonic booms came just after explosions disintegrated forward drones and rattled others. The sound of naval artillery was a fearsome one, but not of itself harmful. But their shells … some were fragmentation mortars, others explosives. Some shot incredibly nimble missiles.

And they didn't let up. It looked like they intended to empty their armament stores. A last stand maybe. The firing went on and on.

Daryus's third battalion took some heavy damage. Audio shields did nothing against these great guns.

"Send the concussive drones out wide and behind them." Daryus commanded. "Bring the suppressive audio drones in low, just above the water. Get their guns aiming away from the cruisers."

Orders were relayed quickly, and maneuvers shifted the shape of the fleet.

"All impulse weapons on continuous fire," he ordered. "Try to breech their hulls."

As the drones took new attack formations, the fleet spread out and angled higher, energy pulses dropping like seismic waves. But the force wasn't penetrating the ship steel. And the deck guns rose and began launching their shells and projectiles skyward. Blasts shook the cruisers. Another began to list.

"Focus the attacks!" Daryus shouted. "Try to warp the barrels. Hodges, Flinn, Sallona, fire rhythmic bursts into the ocean on their shore-side. Co-ordinate. Let's get the water swelling so bad they can't hold aim."

Suppressive audio began to hammer the naval guns. Rebel fighters saw more than one barrel bend just enough to render them inoperable. Storage containers were opened by the rebels and manual air-missile launchers were quickly dispersed across the decks and renewing the insurgent attack.

But not for long.

"Once the deck guns are down, sweep the ship topsides of everyone." Daryus pointed savagely. "Lay them out!"

The ships also began to rock, the concerted bursts from his three strongest cruisers creating sea-storm size waves that frustrated rebel efforts as their ships rode the heaving ocean.

"Sir, the rebels are shifting focus," his First Officer called. "It's an abdication tactic. They know they're losing."

"Where?"

Before the officer could answer, Daryus's command cruiser shook with a violent strike. Alarms began to wail. They would lose flight capabilities in less than a minute.

"Remaining operational deck guns," the officer yelled, jumping up from his terminal and heading for the door. "They saw us at the center. Assumed we carried command. Rockets came too—"

The man disappeared down the exit corridor.

"God. Damn!" Daryus hit the console with his fist. He triggered the evacuation button, and rushed to his own private escape craft.

Dropping into the flight seat, he dispensed with the harnesses, and ejected. The cruiser began to explode and fall just behind him. He saw only one life craft darting away from the wreckage. That meant a good hundred men and women were either burning or likely to be evaporated when the cruiser struck the water and self-destructed.

He put it out of his mind, and slipped fast to the nearest cruiser, docked, and started for the bridge.

"This is Commander Daryus," he said into his commlink. "I'm now on Cruiser Alashian. I'm assuming command. Send twelve drones on impact paths with the rebel vessels. Give them full cover. I'll be on the bridge deck in two— ”

The commlink went dead.

Daryus sprinted. As he went, the lights along the corridor floor seams turned yellow. *Retreat.*

He got to the deck, where the ship's officers were staring out the window. The second battalion was rocketing past them high overhead, moving out toward the sea. Away from Endless Isleland.

“What's going on!” Daryus demanded.

The ranking officer, Seelia Danmount, didn't turn when she said, “Something's happened with the north invasion force. We got one partial transmission before it stopped.”

“From who?” Daryus went to the command terminal, and tried to bring the links back online.

“The Emperor,” she said, sounding distant, as she continued to watch the second battalion racing away from the island. “He called for us to retreat. Every craft and drone that can still function.”

That's when Daryus understood the look in their eyes. These military men and women had never considered the possibility they could lose to the rebels. Service had always been safe. Clean. From the decks of these advanced crafts with their weapon arrays, it was academic.

Now, Nafaryus had ordered them to retreat. Daryus could deny it if he wanted to, but the truth of it remained: This was real war. The rebels wouldn't be the only ones dying at scale. And it wouldn't only be the drones and forward grunts that fell.

The tide had turned somehow on the northern front. And his father was pulling back to preserve what was left of his forces.

The cruiser began to ascend, fast, shooting southwest with the rest of second and third battalion.

Daryus had only one thought. *Another failure.*

CHAPTER 28

H ell was erupting on Endless Island, and Faythe had no intention of waiting until Ruthers could get her a flight window. For all she knew Gabriel was already dead. The video feeds had shown him clearly enough at the top of a signal tower. Then the feeds ended. Went blank.

With her most trusted two guards, she stepped onto the Imperial Dock. The waters of the North Bay were calm, and in an imperial watercraft she could be at Ravenskill in a few hours. Well ahead of their rendezvous with her father at Heaven's Cove, and maybe she could stop this preposterous fighting. Daryus had to be to blame.

"Ravenskill," she said to the captain of the boat.

"My lady?" the man said with obvious reluctance.

She nodded firmly. "Where the fight is, yes. And as fast as this thing can move."

"Aye, aye," he replied.

Her guards stepped down before and after her, per protocol, and exchanged proper identification with the boat personnel.

She got below into the communication center of the fastboat, and fired up the feeds again. Still nothing from Ravenskill, though other channels were working fine.

A response request message showed on her private screen. She keyed it up. Midwest Confederation and Eastern Empire communiques. Odd. She hit the call channel, and waited. A few moments later, Regent Grace Storal's face emerged on her screen.

"You're father's an ass," the regent said first.

"And you're a shrew," Faythe responded. "Did you call me to exchange immutable truths?"

The woman laughed, the sound dry and rough. "Nafaryus has promised to share new audio technology with the Eastern Empire in exchange for the services of one of our full battalions."

Faythe stared into the monitor a bit dumbstruck. "And you said?"

"You know we keep a full contingent on our side of the Borderland." Grace didn't blink at all. "They're moving into G.N.E. space as we speak. For show, your father says. Apparently your brother isn't first rate at resource management."

"So, you've taken the alliance I brokered and made it a war pact." Faythe got her feet back under her. "Bad business, Grace. And you know it. Are you that desperate for weapons tech."

"Who isn't?" she said as if stating more truth.

Faythe thought a moment. "Then you're an expansionist. And I read you wrong. That's my failure."

"Don't play your politics with me, Faythe. That's not why I signed the accord. It was honesty that got you your deal." The woman tapped the screen as if tapping Faythe. "Try again."

Faythe nodded. "I'm trying to broker peace internally. Stop the infighting. My father's agreed to meet the spiritual leader of the rebel militia. I believe we can come to an agreement."

"With your father," Grace said, incredulous. "Not likely."

"I'd rather run at those odds than have you help us escalate this to full war where the odds are everyone loses." Faythe tapped the screen back.

"Except me," Grace said. "G.N.E. may find itself in need of new leadership in the aftermath—"

"If military leaders fall, I will take the throne," Faythe shot back. "And you may trust that a few weapons will be the least of your problems if you try to move on us."

The old woman cackled. "By damn, that's good to hear."

"Recall them," Faythe said. "Whatever technology was promised isn't likely to come in full, unless you know something about my father that I don't. And more than that, we don't need arms escalation right now."

"But I *do* need to protect my people," Grace countered. "I may not be an expansionist, but your father and brother surely are."

"I won't let that happen," Faythe said. "I give you my word."

The woman studied Faythe's face a long while. "All right. I'll bring them home. When this is through, you come on back down here. We'll find an acceptable way for you to repay me."

The screen flickered off.

Faythe quickly sent a call in to the King of the Midwest Confederation. An automated response told her that Thomas Smith, the king, was answering Nafaryus' call, and that he wouldn't be dissuaded. He was simply doing Faythe the courtesy of letting her know in advance, given her strong work with his nation on export and import functions.

Bad news. The Midwest had the strongest fighting units known across the former Americas. The people there fought with pride and loyalty and with honest objectives in mind. They were strong, physically. Emotionally. Very different from the coastal empires, where whims swept through the culture like the tides.

Nafaryus would have his great army. Half of it anyway.

She had to get to Ravenskill and stop this.

Half way out into the great bay, the engines suddenly shut down. The momentum shift threw her forward a bit.

One of her guards knocked and entered. "We're not under attack. Technical malfunction of some kind."

The bank of communication monitors went down, too.

She hurried from the room to get topside. On deck, the captain shrugged his shoulders. "Never seen this happen. Can't even call in for help."

Faythe forced herself to take a steadying breath. She couldn't drift here as in a doldrum. Not now.

On the northeast horizon, another vessel appeared, moving swiftly in their direction. Her guards ushered her back beneath the battle canopy, and took position in front of her. The captain deployed his crew to range weapons.

"Hold your fire until you hear my call," the captain hollered. Then he turned to Faythe, "We'll do everything needed to protect you, my lady."

"You should go below deck," her senior guard said. "It's not safe up here."

"If its rebels, I want to speak with them," Faythe replied.

"And if it's pirates?" he asked.

"Then I want to speak with them," she said, giving him a wry smile.

"Worst detail I was ever given," he said, returning the smile.

"And you're the worst guard ever assigned to me." She put a hand on his forearm. "And thanks for that."

The vessel closed fast. Mounted all across her bow and sides were weapons of varying range. The telltale armaments, though … sound dishes.

A few moments on, the Imperial attack craft pulled up alongside them, both boats rocking in the waves of its approach.

Onto the deck emerged a familiar face. Lieutenant Ruthers. "Just couldn't wait for me to get you that flight window, could you?"

"How did you know—"

"All imperial craft have monitoring and shut down software," Ruthers replied. "I'm responsible for all imperial docks. Even antiquated ones like the one at the bay."

"You shut off power to the boat," Faythe said.

"Everything is grounded." Ruthers directed a crossing bridge to be set out. "Engagement called off. Some comms are down. You need to get back to the palace now."

Faythe crossed to the other vessel.

"Take it back in, captain," Ruthers ordered the other boat, then turned to Faythe.

"I'll drive to Ravenskill, if I have to," Faythe said, losing her composure. "I have an overland vehicle. I'll avoid roads. You have no jurisdiction over vehicles with tracks and wheels."

Ruthers sighed. "Is there a man at the other end of this lunacy?"

"Men are always involved in lunacy," Faythe said cryptically.

Truth was, she did want to get to Gabriel. Rationally, she told herself they'd just met. But on a deeper level, she knew something genuine was there between them. After an army of politicians courting her favor, coming at her with their hollow talk and vanity, she wasn't about to give up on Gabriel.

Ruthers uttered her caustic laugh. "It's like one of those old books. The love kind."

Faythe stepped close to the lieutenant. "My charge is diplomacy. That includes the empire. I will have my own motivations. But make no mistake, I would try to put peace back in place no matter who's involved."

Ruther's looked back, unimpressed. "That include your father? Your brother?"

Stepping closer still, so that the short woman would feel her breath when she spoke, Faythe said. "Especially them."

Ruthers didn't move, staring back. "You might be the only diplomat I've ever respected enough not to shoot. All right. Back we go. I'll keep my promise. You try and exercise the patience of a diplomat."

"In the meantime, people are dying on Endless Isleland," Faythe argued.

"Not only there," the woman said, signaling the boat driver to go. "Fighting has erupted in every province. Rebels are taking it to the standing police force. And those not fighting there," she turned to look at Faythe when she said, "are marching on the capital. Your little flight may turn out to be more of an evacuation than anything else."

Faythe had just an hour ago been watching the video feeds from Ravenskill. "Not with the technology my father has. It just means more rebels and civilians will die."

Ruthers stared back. "It's war. People die."

As much as she wanted to stop all the fighting and dying, Faythe found herself praying that one of those people wasn't Gabriel.

CHAPTER 29

T he Imperial Fleet filled the sky. Drones old and new. Battle cruisers flying at varying altitudes. It looked like the End Wars Gabriel had read about. This was an annihilation force. How many had died already in the sound-storm rolling over Ravenskill? Even if it stopped now, they'd be years rebuilding what had been leveled. Weeks burying the dead, for those not torn apart to nothing.

All of it swelled inside him. The suffering. The loss. The unfairness. His own anger. And it all began to form a sound deep down inside him. He couldn't hold it inside. Didn't want to. Looking heavenward into the midst of the great fleet, he let it out. A terrible sound rose up and out. A bray of shouted anger, part song, part fury, ascended the sky. Bright and resonant, it filled space, growing larger and louder, reaching distances he never could have imagined.

And as he focused the song of him, something beautiful, something terrible, happened.

Drones were pushing their suppressive and destructive audio earthward. Some had a new kind of sonic blast that seemed able to target individual, rendering them instantly like scarecrows—lifeless and limp. The collective sound of the drone attacks came like a dreadful symphony. Unmusical. And yet belonging together in their cacophony.

Against it, rose Gabriel's shouted song. And after a few moments, it all changed. The drone attack, Gabriel's counter.

They reached an unlikely balance point.

They canceled each other out.

Across the broad sky, between the drones firing down their audio death and Gabriel's angry voice, between heaven and earth, the world went silent.

Gabriel nearly paused, wondering if he'd lost his voice with the force and intensity of his song. But he remembered Jeffer's words, *three steps past the old noise cancelling tech.* This band, it threw the sound, but it amplified it, changed it. Brought it into a synchronized harmony with the drone sounds.

But Jeffer had said it was modeled after the standard drone audio library. There were new sounds in the sky today.

Gabriel instinctively knew his own music had grown. He'd focused his attack on the fleet as a broad whole. He'd taken in the several forms and drone music and fashioned an angry reply to answer them all. The band around his neck gave that sound larger life.

And from it all, the visible world became silent as the grave. It looked like a dream. Drones and cruisers moving slowly against the backdrop of clouds and sky, the world below frozen in fear and disbelief.

Next to him Townsend and Chloe were trying to communicate, with each other and over their commlinks. Their faces pinched in frustration. They couldn't hear each other. And their devices had gone silent, too. Usable frequencies had been disrupted. Gabriel's song had taken up all the space. Disallowed the transference of signals.

The silence was a sweeping, impenetrable thing.

And it stretched on. And on. As Gabriel sang the heart of him. Every last bit of anger and retribution and defense he could conceive. A rough sound.

He wasn't sure how long he'd been singing, when the cruisers adapted, and pushed forward, opening up impulse attacks. Something Gabriel's song hadn't factored.

The silence began to break with the sound of rushing energy and impacted Ravenskill buildings, and people.

Gabriel evolved his song, going deeper with his sense of the physical forms of the flying machines. And deeper with the silence. He meant to put his song inside them, the same way they were doing with their new audio library and Ravenskill townspeople. And he meant to quiet everything.

The weapon around his neck gave his song reach, as it modulated down, became richer, more guttural. And more focused still. He now felt it instead of hearing it. And words weren't a part of the song. Not preplanned words. He let out whatever came to mind to give the sound the right meaning.

And the hulls of the cruisers began to tear. Engines exploded. Several started to plummet earthward.

Gabriel sang on, pushing harder, but remaining focused on this new sound. Other cruisers shook violently, as if caught in a hurricane, but rocked from the inside out. A few exploded altogether, filling the silent sky with fire and smoke.

After several minutes, he couldn't sustain it, and fell to his knees beside Townsend and Chloe. Their eyes held questions. He could only shake his head that he didn't know.

The sound of war rushed back in. Drone attacks with their awful, varied sounds fell upon Ravenskill again. Impulse weapons tore up buildings and people alike. Several turned focus on the radio tower now, no longer caring, it seemed, about destroying their signal repeaters. Gabriel was silencing signal anyway.

"Come on!" Chloe shouted.

She grabbed Gabriel's hand and began pulling him down the stairs. Townsend came behind. They rushed, as the old tower began to take impulse blasts.

Townsend continued to fire up the sound shield at their rear, keeping them mostly free of the drone noise. But the tower groaned and listed. Some of the girders started to buckle.

"Hurry!" Chloe moved at a reckless pace, yanking Gabriel down the stairs.

"You've got to do something," Townsend said. "Or we'll never make it to the ground."

Gabriel took a deep breath, and shot a burst of song up the tower, letting the sound of it carry in the steel itself, like a conductor, out and up into the sky. The sound bit at the hulls of the nearest cruisers and drones, shaking them, and momentarily disrupting their attack. Several drones that didn't explode shifted away, moving in erratic patterns as their internal workings fried and shorted.

Gabriel, Chloe, and Townsend used those moments to hasten faster still. Twice Chloe fell, taking Gabriel with her. Townsend was more surefooted, and kept the shield up as he negotiated the steps.

Then the attack resumed, and the tower began to thrum with the impulse blasts. Rust flaked from the tower, dropping like brown-red snow all around them. Some of the girders began to fall, as well, clanging off the tower as they rang like insane chimes as they dropped in deadly jangling paths toward them.

"Again," Townsend shouted.

Gabriel heaved two breaths and repeated the burst of song. Again the cruisers shook in the sky, giving them precious moments to descend.

They repeated the cycle, and were twenty feet from the ground when the tower began to crumble entirely.

"Jump!" Chloe said, and leapt over the side of the stair railing.

Gabriel didn't hesitate, doing the same. Townsend came just after him, still holding the audio shield gun at their rear.

They hit hard, and rolled. Chloe looked to have hurt her ankle, but stood, grabbed his hand, and began hobbling toward an open area south of the tower. Townsend never missed a step. The old man was every bit the soldier he'd been thirty years ago.

The tower began to fall. Girders came off at an increasing rate, much of it went over like a giant redwood felled in the woods. The screech and groan were ear-splitting, as rust filled the air like specs of empires lost.

But they got clear.

Before any of them could speak, Chloe jabbed Gabriel with a hypodermic. "Adrenaline," she said. "You need it more than I do. Get the song of yours back up there. Now!"

A surge moved through him, and he didn't need to be asked again. He stood, threw back his head and let out the song. This time, he coupled it more purposefully with the destructive tone needed to bring down the metal machines.

And silence filled the sky.

Several of the cruisers began to burst again, even as the eerie calm reclaimed the heavens. Drones, too, began to fall. Not all of them. But many.

"Holy Gods," Townsend whispered beside Gabriel.

"That's what we've been waiting for," Chloe replied. She slapped Gabriel's leg in thanks and celebration.

Gabriel's throat was beginning to tire. To burn. He couldn't do this for much longer. He had to stop. Gulp air. Swallow. When he did, several drones vectored toward them, diving with alarming speed, pushing their noise ahead of them. Townsend kept the sound shield active, but the collective force of the drone sound libraries were beating down on them, and Gabriel dropped to his knees. His ears began to ring hard.

Townsend tried covering his ears over the plugs. Chloe did the same. They wouldn't be able to outrun this. The drones were on suicide assignment. Explode on impact and take them out in a conflagration of fire and twisted metal.

Gabriel shook his head. After all they'd done, he couldn't let it end like this. Even if they exploded now, the fallout would hit them at insane speeds with shredded metal. They'd be flayed alive. But what could he do?

From his knees, he took as much air as he could, imagined the sound of stillness. Adding it to the silence he'd so quickly become acquainted with. He put his hands around the band on his neck, stared into the hurtling drones and their acoustic nightmare, and let out a new sound. This one didn't ascend in rough tones, but in a bright sustained bray that left his mouth, and passed from volume and force to silence and stillness.

The hurtling drones came to fast stop just yards above. They stood frozen in the air, like overlarge child toys. No sound. No movement. Hanging there. Defying gravity. But of no threat.

The song of it reached higher, and across the sky everything stopped, like bugs in amber. It looked like a dire painting of war, stuck in time.

It was like standing in that painting, surrounded by it all, as quiet as a museum and as motionless as it becomes at midnight.

But he couldn't sustain this song forever. The sounds were growing rapidly inside him. His understanding increasing exponentially with each new use. And the collar gave it all reach. But he still needed breath and stamina, and he was God-awful tired. His throat ached and throbbed. His entire body, even with the adrenaline, seemed ready to shut down.

If he let go, though, they would die.

With his last bit of breath, he reversed the song, pushed with everything he had, and sent the drones hurtling back the way they had come.

A wave of pressure pushed up from the clearing and promulgated skyward and outward, knocking every craft back like a shockwave from an antiquated bomb, and all still in this terrible silence.

When he could sing no more, he collapsed into Townsend. They three of them watched as the empire fleet slowly righted themselves in the sky, stabilizing against gravity. Drones and cruisers hung suspended for a few moments, as if gauging their next move.

Then, the sky began to open up, as the war machines turned and flew northwest, away from Ravenskill, and in the direction of the capital.

"Well, I'll be damned," Townsend muttered.

Gabriel had no idea how Arhys had fared on the southern front, but he managed a weary smile that they'd turned this side of it back.

He shut his eyes, and tried desperately to catch his breath through his raw and aching throat and chest.

CHAPTER 30

—◉—

Arhys knelt on the ground, watching the Imperial Fleet retreat across the sky to the southwest. His arms were tired. One leg felt like a muscle had torn. But they'd won. Somehow, they'd won. The battle, if not the war. But Xander was still missing,

"Gather the dead," he ordered from his knees. "Lay them out and cover them. Bring all available medics to treat the wounded. Initiate recon. I want any intact Imperial tech that fell. Go."

His officers moved at his command, slower, some hobbling. As recovery efforts got underway a small convoy rushed into their midst—a couple of landcraft bearing the Eastgate insignia—a constellation of white stars on a field of blue.

A short man with a shaven head bustled into camp with almost comically taller subordinates chasing to keep up. He came straight to Arhys.

"I'm Captain Darron Sularo," the man introduced, jabbing a small but muscular hand at Arhys.

"Arhys—"

"I know who you are," Sularo said back. "How can we help?"

Arhys surveyed his entourage of officers. "You already did. Your rear attack saved our ass."

Sularo smiled, and took time to light a cigar and puff it into full smoke. "Good one with the puns, are you? Well, good. Hate a leader who takes himself too seriously."

It was Arhys turn to smile. "You don't know me very well."

"Enough chit chat," Sularo chided. "We got your initial call. And we were steaming your direction, when a second call came in."

Arhys waited.

"Princess Faythe, no less," Sularo said with a laugh. "Can you beat that? The big Nef's daughter, going traitor. I drank a toast to that lass then and there." He drew a long breath of smoke and puffed it in a way that said only real men smoked cigars.

"She's not her father," Arhys confirmed.

"Still, we almost turned around at the last moment." Sularo turned a half circle, checking out the recovery ops for a moment. "Message came in that the Empire was sending a sizeable ground force into Eastgate."

Arhys considered the timing of it. "Maybe. But it sounds like a scare tactic to keep you away from here."

"Well of course it's a scare tactic," Sularo said with impatience. "The thing is whether it's true or not. But it was all physics, really. We were nearly here, and knew we could do more good today on your flank than steaming back to arrive late at an Eastgate party that might never get thrown."

Arhys simply nodded, and began to rub his aching leg muscle.

"Bigger issue facing us is the movements of our neighbors." Sularo hunkered down close to Arhys, his cigar smoldering between them. "You catch any of that yet?"

"I've been a bit busy," Arhys replied. "And I really don't have time for—"

"Eastern Empire and the Midwest Confederation are both marching our way," Sularo pushed on. He pulled the cigar out and licked his lips. "Eastern ninnies got into the Borderlands already. Though, there's word that they may be turning back. Could have something to do with our little victory, I don't know. But the Midwest hayseeds are moving fast. Seems those corn-growers have a new aerial tech. Their advance fleet will be here by morning."

Arhys tried to process what he was hearing. "The Emperor made a hasty pact to increase the size of his opposition force."

"Ayeah," Sularo said.

"And he must have recalled what remained of his own fleet. Regear for a more potent offensive." Arhys tried to stand, and found the pain excruciating now. He remained down. "We won't ever beat an allied force. I've used up my best defenses. And you won't outlast many aerial assaults."

A slow grin spread on Sularo's face. He popped the cigar back in his mouth with a kind of glee Arhys hadn't seen in a long while.

"You haven't heard anything about the northern invasion, have you?" Sularo very visibly scratched his genitals.

"I expect a status report any moment." Arhys looked up, and in fact his information officer was running at full speed toward them.

Sularo followed Arhys gaze to the woman racing toward them. "I'd love to be the one to tell you, but I think it should come from one of your own."

Lieutenant Angela Carrow came to a quick stop, her dark skin glistening with sweat. She must have run from the rear comms center. She gasped a few breaths and spoke around her own grin as she pointed toward the last of the Imperial fleet moving away.

"The northern front," she said, and sucked another breath. "Smallnet went dead for several minutes, but then it came back on and lit up with messages from the northern front. Heavy casualties. Massive destruction."

Arhys failed to see why this would bring grins to military officers—his or other provinces.

Angela must have recognized his confusion. She shook her head. "It was bleak. New Imperial tech. Rolling destruction. But Gabriel stopped it. He went up the old signal tower and did something."

Arhys heart began to pound. "He sang? He found a way to use the music against them?"

Angela's brow pinched. "That's the odd part. Reports say he was singing, but everything went completely silent. All Imperial sound attacks were rendered useless, inaudible."

The irony of that brought a rare grin to Arhys face. "Fighting noise with silence. God damn."

"That's not all," Angela added. "Several Imperial governors were in Ravenskill at the time of the attack. They were killed. Intelligence suggests they were Prince Daryus' political allies."

Sularo clapped Arhys on the shoulder. "Defeated the Empire, brought our Gabriel's power to the enemy, and took out the dark child's firmest supporters. Not a bad day's work."

The smile on Arhys' face faded. Xander. Now, more than ever before, Daryus would be eager to kill the boy if Arhys didn't comply. The prince had been humiliated in his attack of Ravenskill.

Arhys nodded thanks to Angela, and put a hand on her wrist. "Can you confirm anything regarding new Imperial alliances?"

The woman frowned. "Yes. The belief is it will quadruple the size of the Empire's forces. And add new war tech we haven't developed the expertise to combat." She gave him a firm, reassuring look. "But we have Gabriel. Something's awoken in him. I have to believe the Emperor will think twice before sending another annihilation force. It should buy us time to consolidate efforts." She looked up at Sularo. "That thing stinks," she blurted, waving away cigar smoke.

The captain made no apology. "Get used to it sweetheart, if you want to consolidate efforts with us."

She turned back to Arhys. "A unified rebel force isn't insignificant. We need to do more there." She stopped, a new, more honest expression taking hold of her face. "But I'm not sure any of that will matter without Gabriel. I don't mean to sound defeatist. But our strength is raids. Small, targeted attacks. We don't have the resources, even in alliance, to fight a sustained war at scale. Not without tech the Empire can't or hasn't yet been able to adapt to."

Arhys was nodding, but inside his conscience burned. He conjured Evangeline's face. He could see the look in her eyes when he'd promised to make sure Xander had a good life. A free one.

Sularo snapped his fingers to get Arhys' attention. "You have the look of a man who feels too small for the things being asked of him."

Angela stepped toward the small man to defend her commander. Arhys put out a hand to stop her.

Sularo only laughed. "That'd be the kindliest touch of a woman this Napoleon has had in a dog's age. Let her come."

With some effort and a great deal of pain, Arhys stood. "We're all too small for this," he answered. "I don't like the idea of all out civil war. It means more innocent people will die. But don't mistake my hate for death for fear." He put out a hand. "Thank you for your help. I'd suggest you get your navy healthy again fast."

Sularo clapped Arhys on the shoulder again. "Damn tootin'. That's what I like to hear. I'll be in touch. And you, miss," he said, "if you ever need another post, I'd take you in a heartbeat on my ship. No hanky panky. Unless that's your thing."

This was Sularo being genuine. And Angela, to her credit, knew it. She saluted Sularo and went back to her post.

Sularo bustled back to his vehicle, and the convoy beat a fast path back to the shore. Arhys snapped open a field pain kit, and took two of the heavy dose pills. He signaled for his own truck to be brought. He checked his two weapons—an impulse pistol and an old heavy gauge revolver, reloaded, called for his senior team.

"This isn't over," he said. "I have some business tonight. Mobilize all militia to first treat the critically wounded. Then establish places of safety. Use the bunker to capacity, even for civilians. Once that's done, see to the dead. Warren, get going on rebuilding plans. That will give the people confidence, and something to do soon enough."

"What if they come back?" Warren questioned.

"Not tonight, they won't." Arhys motioned his driver out, and climbed behind the wheel. "I'll be in the command room before first light. I'll want status reports from everyone."

Arhys saluted and hit the accelerator. He took the old roads past Port of the Wake, heading toward Heaven's Cove. He meant to be there before dark, and get a lay of the land.

((O))

By the light of a nearly full moon, Arhys limped into the old amphitheater at Heaven's Cove. The pain meds had knocked back the ache in his leg, but his knee had gotten stiff and hard to use. He surveyed the area.

No one here.

This outdoor theater had long been abandoned. A hundred years at least. But it had sprung up in the decades after the End Wars as a way to try and salvage the arts of the distant past, create a tie to humanity that somehow testified to the finer parts of mankind and connected them across the near annihilation of the human race. It still held a kind of beauty. The way ruins do. Telling of the past. Showing wear but still enduring. The ghosts of story and passion had seemed to get into the very stone. No one was here, but it didn't feel vacant.

This was where Daryus had said to meet him. Arhys hoped losing today's battles hadn't made the prince spiteful enough to renege on their agreement.

He checked his weapons again. A habit. And sat on the first stone row of the theater, staring at an empty stage. Sometime in the next hour, he'd trade the only advantage the resistance had ever had to the empire in exchange for his son.

And not only his son, but his son's future. His freedom. A good life.

There'd always be war. Arhys had begun to believe that. He wasn't sure even Gabriel could stem that tide. And Arhys was a warrior. He'd die of it someday, he was sure. But Xander? That shouldn't be his fate.

"But he's also my brother," Arhys whispered into the cool night. "Gabriel isn't just a tool of war. He'd my brother."

Even whispered, the words carried in the acoustics of the old theater.

"God damn," he said, and dropped his head into his hands. "I can't make this decision."

But he already had. He'd told Daryus to meet him here. Gabriel was already on his way, per the arrangement with Faythe and Nafaryus.

Then a thought. *There's still time.*

Arhys lifted his head and looked around. He began to run scenarios in his head. Scenarios where he killed Daryus, saved his son and Gabriel, and gave Xander the better life he'd promised by either defeating the Empire or forcing them to a truce. And they had the princess on their side now. And rebel leaders across G.N.E. ready and willing to cooperate in a more coordinated resistance.

There were risks. Could he rescue Xander, however Daryus played that out? Could Gabriel keep doing what he'd done, and stay ahead of the Empire's ability to adapt? Could the rebels stay honest and not bicker among themselves? Could they stand against foreign armies, too?

Arhys struggled with every question for the better part of an hour until the simple answer distilled on his mind like dew on a morning field: He had to try.

He could hear Gabriel's voice in his head. His brother had told him he would stand by him no matter what. And he'd kept his word. Today he'd found his voice in a way Arhys had always hoped. The use of it had sent the Empire running. How could he now not keep his own word to Gabriel, to his people, to himself. The answer was, he could. He could do all that and save Xander, too. Or, at least, he could try. In the end there was no other choice.

There'd be no exchange. He'd die trying to get his son back while preventing Gabriel from being taken by the Empire. He'd fought the prince and the Emperor all his life. He wasn't going to stop now.

The largest risk threatened to seize him up. *Xander could die.*

Arhys pushed that out of his mind. He would be watchful. He'd maneuver the best he could to keep his son safe. That was the priority. It may come down to timing, some impressive lying, his aim—

"Good evening," came a voice from the west end of the theater. "I have to admit. I was a little concerned you wouldn't show. Even with it being your son and all."

Arhys turned to see Daryus enter the amphitheater from the right side of the stage. With an obvious sense of self-importance, the prince came to the center and stared down at Arhys where he sat. Near where Daryus had emerged, partly behind a pillar, Arhys caught a glimpse of Xander, tied and sitting on the stone flooring.

Arhys didn't try to stand yet. He'd save movement on his leg until it was necessary. "I'm surprised *you're* here," Arhys replied. "Not a good showing today."

Daryus' smile briefly faltered. "Oh, that. I'll admit of a few surprises from your filthy fighting teams. But the data we gathered will make next time the last. Not to mention support from other nations, of which I'm sure you're aware."

"Bullies are only tough when their cronies are around." Arhys scanned the theater left to right, and behind him, too. "So, where are your drones? Or security detail? I know you didn't come alone."

Daryus made no reply to that. "Where is Gabriel?"

"Untie my son," Arhys demanded. He wanted his boy to be able to run when the time came. "I won't let you take Gabriel until I have Xander."

"I suppose," Daryus said conversationally, beginning to walk the stage like a thoughtful player, "that if I simply wait, Gabriel will arrive as planned, quite separate from our agreement."

Panic crept into Arhys' heart. Daryus had learned about the private meeting with Nafaryus. "Doesn't matter. I can alert him. Send him away."

"Really," Daryus said with mocking skepticism. "I think your brother wants peace. I think he and my sister are going to try and broker a treaty.

I think he's coming to attempt it, and taking him will be an easy matter, without your help. So, maybe I take them both. Gabriel and Xander. As payment for what you did today."

Forgetting his bad leg, Arhys stood. "I was thinking the same thing."

Daryus laughed, and shook his head. "You still have no idea what you're dealing with. Ah, well, that's the profile of the zealot: belief in the impossible."

"Gabriel won't be going with you," Arhys said, limping toward the stage. "And my son is staying, too. If you're smart, you'll leave while you can. And I'll meet you on the battlefield soon enough."

Daryus stopped pacing, looked around at the neoclassical amphitheater. "Wonderful irony, actually. The tragedy of your life, playing out here. It's like an old Greek story of hubris, isn't it. And your son has to watch it happen, all bound up in his little ropes."

Arhys shot a look at his son, who was struggling against his bonds, and actually looked like he'd gotten a hand free. Looking back at Daryus, he raised his old revolver.

"How quaint," Daryus remarked. "Is this the best you have, or is it some kind of sentimentality for the old days."

"It's because it will tear a hole in you," Arhys said, nearing the stage.

"I see. Well, before you do, can I tell you about what I've been doing the last few years. Maybe it will help you in your fight against my father and me."

Arhys aimed the gun. "Are you free, Xander?"

Xander stood, his ropes falling away. "Yes, dad."

Daryus gave the boy an unconcerned glance. "Resourceful boy. He'll make a fine addition to the imperial ranks, if he doesn't die."

The words were grating in Arhys mind. He could see Evangeline, even now, lying on a barren spot of cracked earth after giving Xander life. He could hear himself promising her to keep him safe and give him a better life.

Arhys focused again on the prince. "You're right about one thing. Some good irony here. A new tragedy where a boy dies and disappoints his father. Only, that boy is you."

He pulled the trigger of his gun, and an immense report filled the amphitheater, as a flash of fire erupted from the barrel.

But something happened. Or didn't happen. Daryus didn't drop. *Did I miss?*

Daryus smiled, and took two steps toward the edge of the stage. There, he reached out and gently took hold of something glinting dully in the moonlight.

"I do have to admit," the prince said, holding up the bullet for closer examination, "there *is* a raw kind of beauty in the old weapons."

Shaking his head Arhys fired again. With the same result. "Some new technology. You brought your God damned NOMACS."

The prince tossed the bullet aside with casual disdain. "Part of something I call the Strength Program. It's a compression technology. Interesting too. It has the effect of inhibiting physical mass from approaching a target—a drone or cruiser—but allowing egress. To be honest, I'm quite pleased with its performance against your gun. We've tested it, but not like this. Good data to have."

Arhys unloaded the rest of his shells, the gun blaring in the theater, flashing against the dark of night. And each round came to a standstill in air as if caught in some kind of invisible gel. They hung in front of the prince's head and chest like still flies.

This time, Daryus simply stepped to the side, as if from behind a curtain. "You see what I mean now, I assume. The irrational behavior of a zealot. Belief in the impossible." Two small drones hovered into view above and to the left and right of the amphitheater stage. The moon caught on their surfaces, illuminating dish arrays and other weapons.

Arhys did understand. But he wasn't giving up without a fight. Unhurried, he reloaded his gun.

"And stupid," Daryus added. "Or maybe just desperate. All right then, reload."

Arhys finished. He looked again at Xander. "I love you," he said, the words carrying in the tuned acoustics of the theater. He wanted to say it now. No telling what would happen next.

"Touching," Daryus said.

Arhys aimed again at the prince. Shot once, then quickly pivoted and fired two rounds at the NOMAC on the left. Their focus on protecting Daryus left them exposed. At least for a moment. His aim was true on the first. The heavy load from the gun ripped the drone's dish apart. Arhys swiveled to get the second, but the NOMAC shifted fast, causing him to miss.

"Not stupid, after all," Daryus said, clapping slowly. "Allow me, now, the opportunity of sharing another element of the Strength Program."

Arhys muscles painfully tightened. His gut and chest compressed and he vomited as he fell to his knees.

"You see, I have an audio map of you, and I can use that to play a unique kind of song. Your song. But," Daryus descended the steps to stand over Arhys, "out of tune, if you will. It deconstructs you from the inside. Frequencies, you understand."

Arhys' whole body burned. He had the feeling that he might explode, that he'd become fragile, less substantive. Blood began to run from his mouth and nose and eyes. He caught a red-blurred glimpse of Xander coming across the stage. Was his son's face a mask of horror? It was hard to tell.

"This, my friend," Daryus said, hunkering down. "Is what so many of your people felt today while you and I played along the south shore. And this is what they will all feel soon. I'll be sure they know, too, that they're dying inside because of you."

Arhys couldn't speak. His lungs had collapsed. He could feel his insides letting go, somehow. Losing cohesion. He began to shiver and convulse.

He gave a long look to Xander, regret filling him as his son stared back from just behind the prince with a mix of sadness and fear. *I'm sorry, Xander. I'm sorry, Evangeline.* He tried to reach a hand up toward his son. A last gesture. But his body wouldn't obey.

Darkness came into his eyes. His teeth cracked. Bones inside him shattered, sending splinters into his flesh from the inside out. His skull split in several places.

I didn't betray them, was his last thought.

((O))

Daryus stared down at the lifeless body of his military enemy. It had been unsatisfyingly easy. But he still smiled over the body.

"After your win today," Daryus whispered to the corpse, "I decided you had to die tonight. Demoralize your militia. Besides, no one shows me up. Not you. Not Faythe. Not anyone."

The death had been recorded. "Broadcast it now, everywhere," he said, ordering the drone to send the video file out over every channel.

Next was Gabriel. The savior of the people would be here soon. "I'm going to kill your brother, too," he told the dead militia leader. "Do what I should have been allowed to do three days ago. Take the hope away from your rebellion for good. I suspect my father will be just as pleased with me delivering a dead messiah as a live one. His own propaganda has already told the world Gabriel is dead. So, really, I'm just making good on my father's commitments." He chuckled to himself at that.

Then the sound of quick movement, and the boy dashed past him, sweeping up his father's gun. Like a smaller version of the dead leader, he aimed at Daryus and took two steps back, creating a little space.

"Like father, like son, then." Daryus shook his head. "That's what they used to say. Which means, little Xander, that you're now going to die, too. How does that sound? You can be with your ineffectual father, your pitiful mother, and soon enough your wrong-minded uncle."

Xander raised the gun. Daryus invoked the new compression tech with a look to the drone. But the boy did as his father had. He shot once, then whipped around and unloaded at the drone.

The first shot hit the drone, but missed the dish. The second ripped the dish apart, spinning the drone like a ball.

Daryus' compression shields were gone. A stab of worry ripped through him, as Xander turned and began pulling the trigger at him. But the gun only clicked, out of shells.

Daryus smiled. "Pity. That showed real courage. But it will go unrewarded." He pulled his knife and leapt at the boy.

Xander threw the gun full force into Daryus' face. It glanced off his forehead, tearing a deep cut. Blood began to run into his eyes. Then the kid raced into the darkness beyond the amphitheater, disappearing into the night. Daryus might have chased him, but he couldn't miss Gabriel when he came. That was the true prize. And at that very moment, the sound of running footsteps grew louder in the distance.

Daryus rushed into the deepest shadows of the side stage, positioning himself behind a pillar with a clear view of the theater. A moment later, a dark hooded form rushed in, sliding on their knees to Arhys' side. Weeping rose in hollow echoes.

Slowly, Daryus skulked from the shadows, creeping nearer Gabriel who mourned over his dead brother.

The night air was chill. Daryus noted it. It touched his skin, increasing the thrill of finally putting down the empire's only real threat. Beneath the stars at Heaven's Cove, where Faythe had convinced her father to come and sue for peace, Daryus would reclaim power. No one would be able to argue against his place in the Empire.

Impatient to feel his knife sink into this pitiful savior's flesh, and knowing he couldn't afford to face the singer and his strange gift, he took two fast steps and drove his knife into Gabriel's back. He pushed hard, sinking the steel to the hilt. Oh, how satisfying this death was. The yield of flesh to his weapon. Taking this life by hand. Having power to destroy a messiah!

The form slumped forward and rolled off Arhys' body, flopping face up to the heavens.

By the light of the moon, he saw it. Saw her. His sister. Faythe.

Dearest Gods!

He hated her, but as a brother hates. Not to murder. Not this. How?

He dropped down, checking for a pulse. She looked up at him, life still in her eyes. "Daryus?"

"Faythe, why? What are you doing here now? You were to come with father and mother?"

She gave him a stern look. "You thought I was Gabriel. That's why you did it."

"I'll get you to the palace," he said. "You'll be all right."

He lifted her and got maybe ten steps before the pain pinching her face grew insufferable. "I can't," she said. "Please, put me down."

Daryus did as she asked. "Rest a moment. But you don't have a choice. You'll die otherwise."

"I heard the gun." She licked her lips, swallowed against a froth rising on her tongue. "Father is coming. We have to convince him to stop the war. I have to stay."

She was becoming incoherent.

"The war will never stop as long as the people have Gabriel," Daryus argued.

Faythe game him a patient look, even through her pain. "We should all want peace," she replied. "Fathers and sons … and sisters should all have the same kinds of chances, no matter where they're from. I thought you believed that."

Daryus stared at her a long time, the old feelings bubbling up. "It doesn't matter what I believe. The world is what the world is. And I will be emperor. I'm not going to let idealists upset the balance of things. Everyone loses that way."

And far down inside him, though he hadn't planned it, and would never have done so, Faythe dying … wasn't a bad thing for him. He felt real regret. And it surprised him. After living in her shadow for so long, it surprised him. But he couldn't ignore the difference it would make if she weren't around.

As soon as that thought crystallized in his mind, his hatred for Gabriel began to escalate. Because after it was all said and done, he did love Faythe. He hated her, too. That brother's kind of hate, of jealousy and pettiness. But not the real or mortal kind of hate. She was family. And that thought got inside him. He may have just killed a member of his own family. It taught him something about humanity he hadn't understood before. And that human part of him was able to know a different kind of anger. A righteous anger, if he had to name it.

He wanted to kill Gabriel now so badly he could taste it. For all the reasons he had before. And now because it had all made him his sister's murderer! Because the truth was, she was fading. Nothing could save her. There just wasn't time.

In the distance, footsteps approached, coming up a walkway to the theater. Once again, he hid, this time quickly typing a command into his comms device for an array of new tech drones to converge here. He'd commissioned them to escort his father from the northern coast into the theater. But he would need them himself, now.

A few moments later, Gabriel walked into the theater, saw the prone bodies, and rushed to them, falling to his knees as Faythe had just minutes ago.

This time, Daryus would wait for the drones to arrive. From the shadows, his indignation burned inside him, and he reveled in watching Gabriel's grief.

CHAPTER 31

───────○───────

Arhys lay still, eyes open, vacant, staring heavenward.

"Dearest God, no," Gabriel pled.

He felt for his brother's pulse. Nothing. He tried chest compressions to stimulate his heart back into rhythm. But his body felt pliable, as though the bones were gone. He tried driving air into his lungs with his own mouth, but there was stoppage, as if his brother's lungs had been destroyed or were no longer there.

"I was late," he whispered over his brother's body. "I'm sorry. I'm so sorry."

The sobs came up from his gut, throbbing in his throat. After all they'd been through. After coming this far in their struggle, it came to this. His brother dead because he came to secure the area for Gabriel's meeting and plan to talk peace. Maybe Arhys had been right. Maybe peace was a fool's belief.

Then a thought occurred to him. His music. Maybe he could sing something for Arhys in a way he hadn't been able to for Evangeline. He tried to summon sound. Anything. But his throat ached and throbbed from the day's fight. A few notes sputtered like dry husks rubbed together.

Anger began to burn alongside his grief. He shook his head and bit back the frustration. He seethed through clenched teeth, "I will avenge you." It hurt even to speak.

"Gabriel?" came a soft, weak voice.

His attention snapped to the second body maybe a dozen paces beyond Arhys. *No.*

He stood and stepped quickly around his brother, rushing to Faythe. She lay prone, a runnel of blood from one corner of her mouth.

"What happened?" he asked. "Never mind, we're getting you to a medic."

She shook her head in a slight way. "There's no time for that—"

"We have to try," he argued, preparing to lift her.

"Listen to me," she said. "I don't have much time. You need to be here when my father arrives. You need to finish what we started. He'll listen. I know he will."

Gabriel had a painful flash of Evangeline laying on the ground eight years ago, with him at her side, helpless.

Faythe took something from the inner pocket of her cloak. "It plays music," she explained. "Song two-thirty-seven. Maybe you can weave it into what you sing to my father. I think it might strike a chord with him." Her body convulsed twice. She gasped, caught her breath. "He and his father wrote it," she finished.

Any other time, the revelation would have left him speechless. Right now, Gabriel's insides felt like a twisted knot. Moment to moment he wanted to cry, run, fight, scream.

"A long time ago, his own father shared music with him," she explained. "He's only forgotten. Memory might bring some gentleness."

"I'm not feeling gentle," Gabriel said. "This isn't how it was supposed to go."

She smiled. "I care for you, too." She grimaced, arching her back a moment. When she settled back, she looked up at him. "It was brief, but it meant something."

Hot tears started again in the corners of his eyes. "It did. And I think it would have meant something for a long, long time."

Her smile returned on trembling lips, her body starting to shut down. "Are you telling me you love me?"

"That's the only word that makes sense." He took her hand.

"Good," she said. "I'd hate to be the only one."

Faythe's beautiful smile, her razor sharp mind, her kind heart, all in a moment, they were going still. The vibrant woman she'd been was simply ceasing to be. Her breathing had begun to slow. The silence that followed, the heavy silence, came crushing down on Gabriel.

He'd never known a worse feeling than having to watch someone he cared about pass away.

His heart began to race. He didn't know what to do with the force of feelings that surged inside him. Loss of the opportunity to love this woman. The absence of her goodness in a desperate and dangerous world. His brother's death. The war that he couldn't fight without him. Hundreds of thousands of people who looked to him for leadership and salvation from the tyranny of the empire.

It all descended on him like a thousand yolks he could not bear.

Those who could have helped him lay dead and dying all around him.

The love of family. Gone.

The chance of a life with Faythe. Gone.

His chest began to heave. His lungs and mind grew hot and loud. And before he knew what he was doing, he threw his head back, and all the anger, the loss, the frustration, everything shot out in a guttural scream.

The terrible sound filled the amphitheater, and echoed skyward off the inflexible stone.

It went on for long moments, a visceral bray, the heart of him, going up and out.

Part agony. Part something more. Something of his gift. The darker part of it.

The sound filled up space. And time. Compacted it all.

Finally, he had no more breath. The scream fell off. He slumped back onto his heels, his shoulders slouched forward nearly to the ground.

He was spent. Physically. Spiritually. Nothing was left.

Placing Faythe's hand back at her side, he had one last thought. Maybe a few notes of farewell. Part of the lullaby he'd crafted for Evangeline's elegy. But when he went to give those few notes life, his voice failed.

The deep ache and pain felt like glass splinters in his throat.

Not even a farewell song.

He forced himself not to cry, the tightness of it too much to bear for his damaged voice.

He could only sit there, waiting for Faythe to die. For the emperor to come. Gabriel touched Faythe's music player. Whatever song two-thirty-seven was didn't matter anymore. He couldn't sing it anyway.

Sometime later, someone rushed into the amphitheater behind him. He turned enough to see Xander fall and crumple over Arhys' body. The boy sobbed, his cries muffled with his face against his father's chest.

Gabriel had thought the suffering couldn't get worse. Nowhere lower to go. But then, an older grief showed up, that sound of a child grieving for a dead parent. He'd heard it before. Ravenskill men and women dying in battle, and Gabriel delivering the news, trying to offer comfort. And sometimes consoling a parent who'd lost a son or daughter.

The death.

The lost chances of time with loved ones.

It continued to stack all around him. He was no savior. He was no leader. He was no warrior.

If there was a hell, it was surely like this.

Heaven's Cove, this old theater, had seen tragedy play out again. Under a spray of stars in the dark of midnight the aging stone became the only witness to so many different ends, all part of an unfortunate story.

The blackest of ironies, this was. And Gabriel, frankly, didn't want any more of it. With any luck, Nafaryus would simply kill him.

How long was it? A minute? Ten? An hour? Gabriel had no way of telling how long he'd slouched there, numb and adrift, when Daryus wandered out from the somewhere in the depths of the theater stage. Above him, eight NOMACS came into view, spreading out in a circular formation around the perimeter of the theater. These were the newer, smaller drones. These were the new tech models.

Gabriel didn't bother to brace. He just waited for the prince to end him. But Daryus staggered a bit. He descended the short stairs and came up on the other side of Faythe, maybe five paces off.

The prince held his ears, blood on his fingers. Gabriel knew intuitively that something had happened to Daryus when Gabriel had screamed. Something in hearing the sound of it had gotten inside the prince. Destroyed his capacity to hear anything.

Daryus wobbled and made a clumsy effort to get to one knee. His wide eyes caught the moon, showing Gabriel the depth of hatred the man had for him. The prince raised a comm device. Gabriel assumed he'd give a NOMAC command to destroy him. Maybe the same way they'd killed Arhys.

With that thought—Arhys suffering beneath these new Goddamned NOMACS technology, some infernal music, no less—the numbness broke.

Daryus keyed something on his device. Gabriel rolled onto his back, gathering what strength he had to sing his new song. The silent kind.

But he'd forgotten his voice was gone. The effort brought a rash of stabbing pains in his throat and chest. He began to cough up blood.

And a moment later, a pressure started inside his body. Something was finding the sound of him, and exciting it to a dangerous level.

This is what it feels like ...

"Stop!" came a deep command.

Daryus didn't seem to hear it, and the pressure in Gabriel mounted.

The owner of the voice spoke again. "Jack, shut down new tech weapons universally."

The mounting pain inside Gabriel suddenly ceased. He heaved a long breath, the feel of cold air down his throat sending more shards of pain into his neck and chest and mouth. But the pressure immediately subsided, and the blinding pain began to recede, his eyes clearing and showing him the night sky above the theater.

"Oh my God," cried a woman. Then came rushing feet.

Gabriel turned to see Queen Arabelle race past Daryus and fall beside Faythe. "What happened?" she asked with quiet authority.

"He killed her," Daryus lied.

Arabelle felt her daughter's chest. "She's still breathing. It's faint, but she's still alive. Nafaryus, hurry!"

The emperor was already running, several Imperial guards behind him, and a man the Emperor's age. Nafaryus dropped to his knees beside his wife, and put his fingers on his daughter's neck. "Her heart is slow. We won't get her to a medic in time."

"We're Goddamned well going to try," Arabelle said.

Nafaryus put a hand over his wife's. "Make her feel at ease." There was a softness in the emperor's voice Gabriel had never heard.

"Let me end this," Daryus said, his voice louder than needed. He grabbed his head on one side as he did so. Talking seemed to aggravate his ears. Softer, he added, "There's no reason to keep him around. Killing him will put an end to the rebellion once and for all. And for God's sake, he did this to Faythe."

Nafaryus sat back, looked up at his son, stood. "No. I may not like this savior of the people. But he didn't hurt Faythe."

Daryus followed his father's lips intently, watching him form the words. "You weren't here," he argued. His raised voice brought his face into a pinch of obvious pain. He paused, regaining his composure. "I give you my word."

Nafaryus simply pointed up to the drones. "Surveillance says otherwise."

Daryus shut his eyes against the condemning evidence. "A mistake. And I'm truly sorry, father. I thought she was Gabriel--"

"Who I was coming to meet with, to discuss peace," Nafaryus said. "Get out of my sight."

Daryus turned defiantly to his father. "Don't tell me you meant to bargain with the rebels. What's happened to Faythe has made you soft in this moment. But don't give in to that, father. It's tragic. But the empire has to remain strong. We don't negotiate with insurgents. We still have half the fleet. I saw the call for foreign support; they're on their way. We can put down this rebellion."

Nafaryus walked slowly up to his son. "Get. Out. Of. My. Sight."

Daryus got carefully to his feet and stumbled back to the stage behind them.

The emperor knelt once more beside his daughter. "I should have seen," he said with a tone of regret. "A man is stubborn and full of pride until those things steal away what he cherishes most. That's a shame I'll have to live with. No apology is enough." Silent tears welled in the man's eyes.

"I won't leave you," Arabelle said to her unconscious daughter. "I'm right here. And do you want to know a secret," she whispered—the sound carrying in the theater acoustics, "I'm a praying woman. Not a fashion of the court. But who gives a damn for that. I'm going to pray now. And give this to grace. If you can hear me, don't give up. I'm not."

The queen bowed her head and began to very quietly offer some kind of prayer. Gabriel couldn't make it out, but it held a kind of comfort for him all the same.

Nafaryus then came to Gabriel, gently dropping to one knee beside him. "The people's messiah," he said with a new tone, understanding inside it. "I've seen it," the emperor said. "I've seen what your song can do. It's more than what I knew as a boy. It's more than good feelings. There's a power in it, isn't there? It can move people, change them."

Gabriel looked up at the man. "Like the NOMACS," he offered in a guttural ruined voice.

"No," Nafaryus said. "Altogether different from that." He put a hand on Gabriel's chest. "You have no reason to trust or believe me, but I tell you that the man kneeling here is not the same as the one that left the palace a few hours ago."

Gabriel believed him. He'd seen what loss looked like and could do to a father. It stripped away self-importance and the long list of priorities. It made things simple and clear. Usually too late. And that was the dark irony of it. It was a hard won clarity. But it couldn't be faked.

"She's remarkable," Gabriel managed. "You should be proud."

Nafaryus nodded. Smiled. "Like no father anywhere."

"What now?" Gabriel's voice, even whispering, hurt like hell.

"The empire will be different. That I can promise you." He looked back at Faythe. "She'd do a better job of it than I would, though. If I could trade places with her, I would. But since that's not a possibility, we can't lose her."

Gabriel knew what was coming, and shut his eyes against the request.

"Help her," Nafaryus asked. "There's something in your song. Something that can help her. It has to. I ask as a father. But I also ask because we all need her to help make the changes ahead of us." He gave a fretful smile. "And from what I see, you may want her here a while more, yourself."

Gabriel could see just one thing. Evangeline. On a dry field in the far southwest of the Borderlands, she lay, dead. And he knelt at her side, wailing up, the ground cracking like a lakebed parched and dead and fissured for a thousand years. He'd tried to help her. Heal her. And he'd failed. His music. His gift. It hadn't brought back family. It hadn't brought Arhys' wife and Xander's mother back to them.

In that utter moment, he'd failed.

He might know his gift better now. But the weight of this moment pressed down harder. And he'd spent his voice. First on the tower. Then again here, in a violent cry that shattered his ability to sing.

He opened his eyes and sighed as he caught Nafaryus's hopeful gaze. "I can't. I would if I could, but my voice is gone." Even the words came in a husk, as if he'd been breathing smoke and coughing a week gone by. "I wouldn't know what to sing. Or how, really. But I'd try. I try everything—"

"You have to try," Nafaryus pleaded. "Please."

Gabriel tried to sing a single note. His voice couldn't produce the sound. It came out like husks of corn rubbing in the wind.

Nafaryus sat back, his face instantly heavy, the lines deeper, his eyes lost and distant.

Gabriel began to cry silent tears. *What good is this gift,* he thought.

Perhaps it was the ghosts of entertainments past. The songs of plays that had gotten into the stones of this place now ringing forward in time. Perhaps as failure gripped him, his mind unwound, spinning away to better places, anyplace but here. Perhaps they were memories of things he'd read, crowds singing together at celebrations in the time before the End Wars.

Whatever the truth, he heard it. Unmistakably, Gabriel heard singing. Lots of voices. A chorus, low and sometimes awkward, but gradually growing stronger, both in nearness and confidence. In some ways, the unpracticed sound of it made it better. More true. It slowly began to fill his mind. And he embraced it as a dream or fantasy or lunacy that shielded his mind from the horrors around him.

But soon enough, the reality of it became clear enough. He was hearing this in the real world. The sound of it off the theater sound was unmistakable, the flat echoes, the way it drifted on the night air.

He turned, looking past Xander and Arhys, as into the theater from the east came Himney, followed by dozens, then hundreds of Ravenskill citizens and militia fighters. They filed in, filling the theater, stepping lightly, but singing. Not boisterously, not now, but together, in a beautiful unison. Octaves from male and female voices. Higher notes from children, some on their own, some holding the hands of their parents.

It had the quality of a reverent fight song. Measured. Expectant. It encouraged. It bolstered. So many off-tune singers, but giving it their very best, undaunted by their inability.

Nafaryus looked up, confused, a moment's fear passing to something like respect in his face. Daryus looked baffled, as if seeing a thousand people singing but not hearing them appeared the oddest thing to his eyes.

Arabelle looked up, too, momentarily suspending her prayer. Something in her face spoke of gratitude but also seemed unsurprised—like a look of faith proved sure.

Xander, too, looked up. Spying Himney, the boy dashed into the man's arms. The bakery owner ambled over to Gabriel, one arm holding Xander close as he came.

"Hardly a time to be lying down," Himney observed with a smile.

Gabriel shook his head. "I've nothing left."

"Well, I had a feeling about that. Care to hear it?" Himney hugged Xander in close. "You lie right there while I explain—"

"Himney," Nafaryus blurted. "I told you to be here early. You might have prevented this." A hint of the emperor's ire crept into his voice.

Gabriel stared up at Himney. "You know him?"

"An old friend," Nafaryus answered. "And my senior mole in Ravenskill."

A new kind of horror flooded through Gabriel. "Himney?"

"Now, settle yourself," the baker said. "Yes, there are a few misdirections I've offered as to my past. And yes, our king here and I have a long history. And yes, he absolutely thinks I'm his spy in Ravenskill."

Nafaryus's eyes narrowed. "*Thinks* you're a spy?"

"Ayeah," said Himney. "I guess now's the right time to tell you I've been playing you double. I gave you information that I felt could actually help the people gain an advantage. To be honest, I'm glad it's over. Baking is a good deal more gratifying that spying."

A surprising laugh came from Nafaryus. "No wonder we could never get the upper hand against such a small, ill-equipped force."

"Partly," Himney offered. "Most of that is a credit to Arhys, God rest his soul."

Gabriel nodded to that. None of this changed anything, though. Gabriel was done. For now. Maybe for good. "My voice is gone. I can't feel or touch whatever gift I had."

"Nonsense," Himney said. "Because here's the thing. You've been singing to us and for us for years, right? In crowds. In battle. After battle. Before

battle. In celebrations. In remembrances. When emperors come to town."
He pointed at Nafaryus. "And my favorite: When you come to my bakery for
warm rolls. More than once you favored me with this tune or that."

Gabriel said nothing, unsure what any of this could mean.

"Don't you hear it," Himney said. "Listen. All around you. These people
you've been singing for all your life, they're singing tonight for you. A little
something of your gift got inside them."

Himney paused comically putting his hand to his ear as if listening
intently. "Now, merchant Corey sounds pretty off to me. Mother Jenzen a
little light in volume. Farmer Slotter must have throat damage. And the kids,
well, they sound like angels, even though they mostly just blurt out random
notes." He hunkered down, bringing Xander with him. "But none of that
matters a good God damn. Know why? Because it's got nothing to do with
the notes. It's got everything to do with the feeling. They're giving back, my
boy. They're singing it all back into you."

Gabriel looked around at the theater. He knew nearly every face. They
smiled at him as they sang. He stared back at Himney. "It doesn't work like
that."

"I'm taking back your savior credentials," Himney jibed, and laughed at
his own joke. "Of course it works like that. We're not great. But we can get
loud. And if I don't miss my guess, when this crew sings how much you've
meant to them at the tops of their lungs, something inside you is going to
swell. Heal, maybe. Do you understand?"

Gabriel caught a far glimpse of meaning, but it was obviously too slow
for Himney.

"Ah, my boy, music is a gift. You gave it to us. Now we're giving it back.
Life doesn't mean a tinker's damn without it. We learned that from you."
He patted Gabriel's cheek like a father would. "You've gone through a hell
of a lot just lately. And so you've lost a bit of hope. Forgotten a tad of what
makes you unique. But that's not permanent. And we're here to rush it along.
Because we need you. And frankly, my boy, you need it, too."

Himney surveyed the theater floor and laughed. "Hells, we all need it. My old friend," he looked at Nafaryus, "you need a song right now more than anyone. Except maybe your daughter there." Himney's face got serious fast. "Gabriel, that lass needs you, too. I saw the light in your eyes when you spoke of her, so I know you'd like to make a good song to help her. And I know plenty about who she is and what she stands for. We all need her." He stood up, patted Xander on the head.

"So," Himney boomed with his barrel chest, "I'm going to whip this crowd into a song-frenzy. It may pain you a bit to hear it, given our lack of expertise, but you're going to love the enthusiasm."

Himney spun, took Xander's right hand, raised it, and swept a pointed hand around at the theater of would-be singers. Then he thrust his pointed finger heavenward, indicating volume. The song they'd been singing shot to a roar. Some voices were out of tune. Some could only shout the words of a simple song Gabriel had never heard. But many made a fine job of it.

And Himney was right. The enthusiasm was infectious. The theater resounded with the music. If Gabriel were any judge, they got better by the moment, too. But even that didn't matter. Their song got inside him. It stirred his heart. He suddenly felt like he had actually made a difference. That his small contributions were the thing. Not any grand battle or weaponizing of his music. It was leading the heart to the correct decision. It was choosing the right when you came to a path that divides.

Something did swell inside him. Desire of a type and force like he'd never felt. It moved through him, erasing the pain in his throat, erasing any lingering doubts. Maybe, living up to the expectations he'd thought everyone had of him had never been glory and victory on a battlefield. Maybe it was as simple as sitting with a father when he was grieving for his dead child, and doing everything in his power to bear that pain with him.

The chorus of voices got stronger. Gabriel sat up, and gave Himney a long look of thanks. The man shook his head as though it were just another warm roll.

Gabriel reached out and put a hand on Nafaryus' shoulder, and gave him a smile of reassurance. He didn't know if his song could do anything for Faythe. But by hell, he was going to try. Even if what came out sounded like the rub of road grit on the sole of a boot.

He crossed to Faythe, where Arabelle had sat attendant to her daughter. She looked at Gabriel with a small smile.

"What?" he said.

"They're singing song two-thirty-seven," she replied. "Himney must have taught them. Isn't he just the best baker you know?"

Gabriel looked down at Faythe. "I don't know if this will work."

"I think," said Arabelle, "that trying is what's important. Also," she added, "I've said a prayer. So, I like our chances." She reached out and took his hand.

Gabriel touched the music player Faythe had given him. Listened a long moment to the song rising up from the theater, and started to sing.

He didn't know what to expect. The sound of gravel. Extreme pain. But none of that came. Weak at first, but quickly growing stronger, he added his voice to all the rest. He didn't hold back, either. This was no lullaby. This was no plea. This was a fight song. This was a command to take back life. He sang with all the energy inside him. His voice boomed over Faythe.

And when he thought he'd reached a new level of force and meaning, he went further. He invited all the images of cracked earth and all the words of immoral leaders and took them in and used them to fuel his song. He thought of Evangeline, and his failure there. He thought of dead friends. He thought of Arhys. But he also thought of a sky filled with death machines brought to silence and stillness by a song. And, at last, he thought of Faythe, the earnestness of her heart, the powerful intelligence inside her. He envisioned the future with her that he'd secretly harbored. And he gave that voice, too.

And before he saw Faythe, he saw Arabelle's face light up, her eyes fill with tears. Gabriel looked down to find Faythe staring up, a smile on her face seemed to say that she knew he could do this. That he would.

He bent and folded his arms around her.

And around him, the song went on unabated, loud and long and reaching heavenward.

CHAPTER 32

—◦—

E ight years.

Eight years of regret and living with the memory of failing Evangeline finally eased in Gabriel's mind. Xander's lifetime.

But Xander now stood nearby, an orphan. Still holding Faythe, Gabriel looked over at his brother's son, who Himney held close. His face, among all the rest, held none of the hope or happiness from the song, or from Faythe's revival.

Gabriel motioned for Xander. Himney walked the boy to them, where Xander sat, watching him with a flat expression.

"You meant more to your parents than anything ever did," Gabriel said. "And your father meant everything to me. So, if it's all right with you, we'll bury him together. We'll speak the best words we know over his grave. And then, you'll live with me, and I'll do my best to be as good a man as your father was. How's that sound?"

Xander's eyes softened. Tears came. Then he grabbed Gabriel and hugged the hell out of him. Nothing ever felt so good. Because nothing makes you feel needed like the firm embrace of someone who needs to be held. Gabriel hugged Xander back, hard.

"And if things go the way I imagine they might," Faythe said beside them, "I may impose on you two fine young men to add a third to the party."

Gabriel smiled at her over the top of Xander's head. He very much hoped that, too.

Himney put a hand on each of them. "Love is often wasted on the young, mincing about so. You both are too damned polite. You're a family now. Oh, sure, get to know each other better. But that's all just formalities, isn't it? These three days have been like three years in getting down to the brass of who you really are. Don't waste that with reservation and rationale. Go fall in love, already!"

"Yes, sir, Mr. baker-spy," Gabriel replied.

That brought another deep rolling Himney laugh. "I have to admit, it had its moments."

Gabriel then whispered in Xander's ear. "Your father only ever wanted you to be free. And happy. That's what he promised your mother. Now that's my promise, too."

Xander never looked up, only kept on holding him tight.

Nafaryus leaned in, and kissed Faythe's forehead. "I'm a fool. I shut my father out. Left music behind. And nearly lost you by doing it all again. I won't make the same mistake twice."

Jack ambled up. "You're looking well, Faythe."

She laughed. "They were singing it," she said. "Song two-thirty-seven."

"Ayeah." Jack squatted next to Nafaryus. "They sounded rather better than its composers, if I'm any judge."

Arabelle mocked a scolding expression for Jack, then placed a finger on her husband's chin. "Do you remember it?"

Nafaryus nodded. "Dad and I wrote it." He looked up at Himney. "Awfully manipulative to have it sung to me here tonight."

"Everything I learned about manipulation ... well, you know." Himney gave a burst of laughter.

Understanding then lit in Nafaryus's face, and he turned to Jack. "You not only gave her the music device, you pointed out my song? You're as double as Himney here."

"That's debatable," Jack said while nodding.

Nafaryus looked back at Faythe. "I thank you both for your duplicity. Jack," he then said, a bit more command in his voice again, "disable all drone sound weapon libraries. Leave open only communication channels and relays."

Jack immediately withdrew a device from his pocket, punched several keys. "Done."

Then the emperor extended a hand to Gabriel. "Consider this a truce. Tomorrow, imperial forces will help to begin rebuilding what's been destroyed. The sick and wounded will be cared for by our best medics. And honor will be paid to all those who've fallen in service."

Gabriel reached across Faythe, who still lay between them, and shook Nafaryus's hand. "I wish my brother had been here to see this."

Himney chimed in. "I have a feeling he was."

Faythe looked up at the baker-spy. "You believe in an afterlife?"

"I'll fight the man who doesn't," Himney put back. "Too much beauty all around for it to be random. Besides, you going to think music and Gabriel here are a product of caprice? No damn way. I'll never be one to listen to my head over my heart. Life wouldn't be worth a tinker's damn that way."

Jack cleared his throat with dramatic flair. "As a man who spends all his time with science and data and logic and rational thought ... I couldn't agree more." With a bit more seriousness in his voice, he said, "We wouldn't have been in this whole mess if we'd struck a better balance."

Gabriel turned and gave a long look at his brother. So much good was on the cusp of beginning. But Arhys was still dead.

Nafaryus must have seen Gabriel pause to mourn Arhys, because he got up and went to Daryus. "What you've done … you have to be accountable for it. You'll have to be tried in the courts."

A snarl of anger twisted Daryus' lips, as he watched his father speak. "You're telling me I'm going to prison," he said, as if interpreting the message, as if not understanding every word with his deafened ears.

"I did to you what I did to my father," Nafaryus admitted. "I take some blame in all this. And I will stand by you through it all. You'll pay your penance, and with some luck, down the road, there'll be better days for you."

Daryus didn't seem to be tracking it all. Nafaryus issued a command for one of the drones to convert his words to text on Daryus's device. His son read it, and caught his father in a long stare, a strange look in his eyes, as if he were experiencing something unfamiliar.

Nafaryus asked a couple of the guards to help Daryus to his cruiser. Arabelle gave Faythe a kiss on the cheek, and joined her son to bear him company.

With that, Gabriel's shoulders relaxed, he breathed deeper. The air tasted sweeter. "It's over. The fighting. The slavery. It's all over."

"Not quite," Nafaryus interjected. "We have a lot of work to do to restore music to the empire. I have an entire hall filled with instruments. I apparently have people who still know something about music," he gathered looks from Jack, Faythe, and Gabriel, "so you three will immediately begin a restitution program. I want new schools in every city and town in the empire. And in every one, I want qualified instructors teaching music. For the adults, start night classes."

A bright feeling swept through Gabriel. "And music broadcast through the drones." He held up Faythe's music player. "We can start with these. Replace the NOMAC sounds."

"Great idea," Nafaryus agreed. "But not only that. You may consider yourself my court composer. New song, every week."

"There should be concerts," Himney added. "Traveling players until each town has their own. And warm rolls, for free, funded by the empire, for every concert-goer."

Gabriel liked all the ideas flying around. "Sounds like you know a little something about writing songs," he said to Nafaryus.

"That was a long time ago. And not much even then."

It seemed revolution had another gentler side, as Gabriel offered, "I can teach you."

AFTERWORD

───────◯───────

RICHIE CANNATA

I f you have ever heard or seen Dream Theater perform, then you can attest to how articulate and intense they are as musicians. The band's music, musicianship, and album production are second to no one in our industry. That's why, as a studio owner and professional musician myself for many years, I feel I was blessed to have them record several albums with us at *Cove City Sound Studios* here in their homeland of Long Island, NY, including *Train Of Though*, *A Dramatic Turn Of Events* and the self titled *Dream Theater*. Their most recent album recorded at Cove, *The Astonishing*, was the embodiment of all they do so well and much, much more.

The two hours plus, double CD was both written and recorded here at the studio in beautiful Glen Cove with guitarist John Petrucci taking on the heavy lifting as producer of this amazing project as well as author of the original story and album's lyrics. The music was co-written by John and keyboardist Jordan Rudess over the course of several months with bassist John Myung and drummer Mike Mangini eventually adding their brilliant playing and interpretation, and singer James LaBrie expertly voicing each of the album's seven distinctly different characters. Since 2003 I've had the honor of welcoming these talented musicians in to my studio and watching them create a lot of great music here. However, this time they were taking things to an entirely new level, and *The Astonishing* was to be extraordinary.

The creative experience for Dream Theater initially unfolded with them finding their comfort zone with us in order to be able to compose and arrange the music here at Cove City. The studio became their veritable 'home away from home,' where it took the belief and hard work of a very strong nucleus of people to make it all happen, including engineer and mixer Rich Chycki, guitar tech and studio coordinator Maddi, assistant engineer Jimmy T., studio manager John Arbuckle and the rest of the Cove City staff who would stay the course for 5 months, 7 days a week, to satisfy the needs of the band, management, and record label in order to make this album the tremendous success that it would eventually become.

The equipment housed at Cove, as well as the studio space itself, also played an important role in creating the right environment for the guys. The album was recorded on our 8068 Neve console in our huge live room, with play back on our SSL console inside of our control room. The combination of our classic vintage outboard gear and updated and modern digital gear enabled Rich to capture every one DT's 82 inputs during basic tracking and overdub sessions. The band used every inch of our studio during their stay at Cove. John Petrucci used the quiet privacy of Studio C to work on lyrics while John Myung found our upstairs lounge to be the perfect practice sanctuary where he would of course play every minute he could, which is normal for him. Jordan decided to track all of his keyboard parts in the control room and so a massive keyboard rig was set up, taking up all of the available space at times, but that yielded the most amazing sounds and performances. Both John and John tracked in the control room while their amps were mic'd up in soundproof booths in order to maximize isolation. Man, most days it looked like a NAMM showcase booth in the studio no matter which room you stepped into! Mike's drum kit was just incredible and sounded amazing in the big live room and I really enjoyed smoking cigars with him while on respites in between tracking. What a blast we had!

The guys basically lived at Cove City Sound Studios during this time and were here through a couple of seasonal changes, which in the Northeast meant going from shoveling snow just to be able to park their cars, to celebrating spring time by eating cannoli's and enjoying an espresso outside at St. Rocco's bakery. The best! Glen Cove is really such an amazing place with beautiful Long Island 'Gold Coast' mansions, a culturally rich Italian-American influence, and lots of incredible restaurants. We brought in so much great food each night to keep everyone fueled up and happy in the studio, and truly had such a great time. JP's chocolate cake analogy (that he coined while recording *Dream Theater*) where he compared a slice of rich, multi-layer chocolate cake to his equally as delectable multi-layer guitar sound in order to be able to visualize what he was going for sonically, was one of my favorite moments. There is a framed picture of the famous 'cake slice' hanging in the control room for proof!

The fun wasn't all analogies, though. Throughout the recording, Rich did things to make everyone laugh. Often, these were small off-the-wall side productions. One was called "Bad Larry." If you ever see the DVD of The Astonishing, the menu music is "Bad Larry." It's an old swing thing done for fun. I played the saxophone on that one.

Living just minutes away from the studio, I was really able to enjoy what was transpiring inside those walls with my friends, who were not only working hard, but genuinely having a great time while making great music. And *The Astonishing* is, in my opinion, a zenith point for the band melodically and rhythmically. It's an amazing piece of music, that in many ways plays like a motion picture. And to be frank, I think that comes, at least in part, from what I like best about Dream Theater, which is that there is no smoke and mirrors. No substance abuse. It's pure talent. God-given ability. They don't distort the playing with any substance. It's intense practice, followed by intense performance and production. No fluff. And while it may sound odd, it was refreshing that the studio kitchen was filled with vegetables, fruits, coffees, etc., vs. what is often used as refreshment. I've been around a long time, and it just doesn't get any better than these guys in the music industry.

We went at it eight-twelve hours a day, seven days a week. Sometimes the whole band was there, playing together. Sometimes individual players laying down tracks. I have to tell you, there were times when JP sat in the control room just shredding. It's mind-blowing when he's trying out a new sound. And just to give you another tidbit on their dedication as players, I don't believe I ever saw John Myung with his hands not on his fretboard, even when eating dinner.

My relationships with the guys have grown stronger with each project recorded at Cove over the years, and this is something I will treasure forever.

I strongly believe that anything really great does not come quick and easy. Everyone on the Dream Theater team poured their blood and sweat into making this masterpiece a reality and seeing things through from inception to delivery. It was truly a team effort where everyone stepped up his or her game. Time was never wasted during the process with band members ready and hungry to do their part, whether preparing separately or working together as a unit. The process was uniquely DT as they analytically created musical passages for the educated ears and discerning tastes of their dedicated fans all around the world eagerly waiting to appreciate the album. Each member's personality worked harmoniously with the others throughout this creation, allowing it to become the best it could possibly be. And the strengths of each individual added to the collective energy, rather than becoming a distraction, and really helped drive this project home.

The Astonishing is a piece of musical history for everyone to enjoy for many years to come. Thank you to Dream Theater for letting me and all of us at Cove be a part of this special musical and spiritual experience. It was an honor.

Richie Cannata
Original Billy Joel Band
The Lords of 52nd Street
Cove City Sound Studios

SONG
TWO-THIRTY-SEVEN

A SHORT STORY BY
PETER ORULLIAN **&** JOHN PETRUCCI

Deep in the Hall of Lost things, Edward sat beside a window warm with summer sun. High up in the palace, beyond several wings of empty and forgotten halls, silence had wrapped this place up tight—the perfect graveyard for music instruments that hadn't known a player's hand for generations. None, that was, save Edward's and his father's.

He placed the music player in the windowsill and clicked it on. It was a one-of-a kind artifact, as far as he knew. Something from a time gone by, before the End Wars, when music was freely available. His father, the emperor, had given him the player a few years back. But the device wasn't only a player, it could record, too. The recording function was his aim today.

He carefully took up his beaten guitar—an item he had to leave here whenever he left, since music was forbidden—and rested it in his lap. He took a deep breath, shut his eyes, and imagined the first few notes.

Without rushing, he gently began to strum the old strings. The soft hushing sound of it reached up into the vaulted ceilings like a prayer. Maybe it was, at that—he needed the song to help him change his father's mind.

He deliberately shifted his left hand as he kept simple time, brushing the nylon strings with his right thumb. He'd memorized finger positions from a water-stained chart left in one of the instrument cases. And a few other chords he'd figured out on his own. The sound of his simple song filled the hall with another kind of warmth besides the sunlight, a warmth of familiarity he couldn't explain. With it, he played the song the best he could, because the tune was, after all, a gift.

The music reverberated all around him, giving him the same kind of confidence and sense of peace all the old songs on the player did. But maybe *more* than confidence. *Definitely* more. Creating a song felt like saying something in a way his words were incapable of doing. It touched someplace deeper, was more than communication.

As he lost focus, his fingers missed and he strummed a bad chord, ruining the performance. He stopped, frustrated, and sighed into the last echoes of his final notes. Maybe music was too hard. Or maybe he just wasn't naturally given to it. There weren't instructors or other musicians around to teach him or measure himself against. But he wouldn't give his father a song with sour sounds, talent or not, especially since it was a tune they were composing together.

He hit a button on his player, erasing the recording, and set himself to play it again. This time, after starting the recorder, he looked out the window—*you know this song*, he told himself—and started to play again as he stared away, out over Lake Halcyon and toward the Broad Plaine. He let his mind fly before him, trusting his endless practicing.

And amidst the company of tarnished brass horns and violins and dusty pianos, he settled into it, and began to sing with his untrained voice a simple but important melody and lyric.

He smiled more than once, knowing his father would find this gift unique, something to sit still for, to appreciate. And maybe with it, Edward could convince his father to let him shed his second name, his court name, given him the year before: *Nafaryus*.

The thought of his intent, and of the insidious royal name he now bore, brought emotion that thickened his voice. He choked back the tears, but this attempt at the song was now also ruined as his voice quavered in its delivery.

He shut off the player and sat in the grave-like silence a long while. He understood court names. He knew their purpose—to inspire certain attitudes and responses from those he was meant to rule. But how had the man who'd given him that name—*Nafaryus*—been the same man who slipped him the music player and whispered:

I think it's time you and I had a secret. Something to bond over. It will require a trust between us. But it will also be something we can share, just you and I.

It hadn't been long after that, that they'd begun their own amateur attempts at writing a song together. Just here and there across the years. Nothing serious, just an extension of sharing the secret of music.

"When did music become taboo?" he asked himself. He actually wasn't sure if it was a law, or if society has simply ceded music to the machines, making its pursuit unseemly.

Edward knocked the guitar with the palm of his hand, sending a muted echo out around him. He was no master musician, but it didn't take much to feel the effects of song. Actual music wasn't something that inspired fear. Quite the opposite, really. Music emboldened the soul. If there really was a law against it, that would be why. Emboldened citizens were hard to keep in line.

All of which brought him back to his dilemma: He didn't know how he'd be "Nafaryus" while keeping hold of real music. The paradox of it twisted inside him.

For years since his father had given him the player, they'd exchanged private grins over the gift. And more than once they'd gotten themselves to the Hall of Lost Things to listen together, sometimes working on their song. Those were his best memories: listening to music jounce along the tubes and strings of the instruments, talking about the songs, sharing the thoughts they inspired, writing a phrase or two. Just he and his father.

But those moments had become infrequent in recent years, partly because Edward was taking more responsibility in the court.

"For a dead kingdom," he intoned into the silence of the Hall of Lost Things. "Who wants to rule a people numbed by drone music, or who hate you simply because of who you are."

Mostly, he hated it because it took his father away so often.

But not today. Edward's only request for his fourteenth birthday was an hour's time alone with his dad. To play him their song. And maybe convince him to rethink the court name he'd given Edward.

So, he set his feet, queued up the recorder, and began to play once again. This time he went at it with more energy. Not hard or angry, but with intensity. He felt both present and far away as he played. He could feel his skin begin to sweat with his effort, and it felt good. When he sang, it was without reservation.

To his own ears, the Hall of Lost Things had never sounded so wonderful. It was a right church of music.

The song was over before he knew it, and he turned off the recorder. He'd done it. He'd finished their song. And he'd captured it as a gift—part of that special secret—for his father. A peaceful satisfaction settled inside him, rather unlike anything he'd ever felt before. He imagined it must be how musicians felt when they'd delivered a satisfying performance.

Checking his personal comm. device he saw that the hour had nearly arrived. It had taken him longer than he'd planned to record the song. He snatched up the player, plunked down the guitar, and raced from the Hall of Lost Things.

Once past the empty and abandoned palace wings, he rushed in and out of palace servants and officers moving about the halls in their routines. A few gave him sidelong glances of disapproval as he raced toward his own room where his father was supposed to meet him.

A regular palace party would still be held that evening. But the gift he'd requested of his father was an hour of the man's time. He dashed into his room, out of breath, but grinning already, eager to share what he'd done.

The room lay empty.

No matter, his father was notoriously late. Edward used the time to straighten up a bit, and queue up the song on his music player. He wanted everything just so.

Along about half past the hour, an alert sounded at his comm. panel. His spirits sank. He knew what this would be.

When he keyed up the monitor, his father's face flickered into view. "I'm sorry, son. Negotiations with the rebels has run long. I can't be back to the palace tonight. But I've suspended talks this half hour for us."

"Over the comm.," Edward said.

"Not ideal," said his father. "But better than nothing."

Edward nodded non-committally.

"This is the life we lead," came his father's voice. "Me, your mother, and soon you. The responsibility doesn't suspend itself for special occasions."

"Hard to be emperor and a dad." Edward said it flatly, but he meant to hurt his father a bit with it.

The face on his monitor didn't move for quite some time. The silence that stretched between them was heavy, like they were growing apart by the moment. And he knew his father could just as easily call him on it; Edward had felt the draw of power. He wasn't the same as he was the day his father had given him the music player, either. In some ways, his only connection to who they'd both been was the song. The stupid, silly, beautiful little song.

But he didn't flinch. He stared at the man on the screen. He'd only wanted an hour.

Then, his father's face softened. "It's been months since we've spent any time together. And I'm sorry. I'll do better. I give you my word."

With that, Edward, for a moment, saw clearly into the past, recapturing a bit of who he and his father had been, their friendship. The life ahead, of being emperor, of rebels and politics and armies and responsibility, it all faded. He wouldn't have to be Nafaryus. He could be the one who shared secrets with his dad about music and spent time beside sunny windows.

"I got you something," he finally said.

"But it's *your* birth—"

"I wanted to," Edward cut in. "It partly belongs to you, anyway." He grinned secretively.

"All right, then, let's have it," said his father, crossing his arms imperially on his side of the screen, pretending at pomp.

Edward reached to start the recording, song two-thirty-seven. Their song. But somehow just playing the recording didn't seem right. He stopped. "Dad, can you wait for ten minutes. Hold this channel. I'll be right back. "But—"

Edward didn't wait. He raced from his room, all the way back to the Hall of Lost Things. His lungs burned from the effort, but he didn't linger to rest. He grabbed the old guitar and rushed back, drawing even more ireful stares from the palace staff as he returned.

He slammed back into his room and locked the door, coming back to face the monitor, where his father had kept his place.

Seeing the guitar in Edward's hand, his father's lopsided grin crept into his face. "I should have been there."

"Yeah, you should have," Edward returned, smiling. "Now, just listen."

Edward took several long breaths to steady himself. When his breathing was normal again, he began. He recalled the feeling of playing with intensity, and made the guitar hum!

He missed a few chords, and his voice cracked twice. But all told, he thought he'd never played better. His room resonated with the sound. And the message, to his own ears, came forcefully in the words, but equally in the notes and rhythms and resonances.

When he'd strummed the last chord, he let it ring out, staring down at his hands. When all was silence again, he looked up. His father's face held a look he'd never seen. It was the look of a man who realizes the absences in his life. There, too, on his face, beside the regret, was pride. And love.

"Edward," said his father, his voice faltering. "My God, Edward. What you've done with our song. I could never ..."

Edward smiled. He'd never known his father to be at a loss for words.

Then his dad's eyes grew tearful. "It's just what we do. I didn't think long upon it ... I had no idea the name would hurt ... I'm coming home right now. You stay put. I'll be there by dinner."

The comm. panel flickered off, and Edward sat in the sudden silence feeling that familiar warmth again. The song had worked. He wouldn't have to be Nafaryus after all. And it looked like he'd get more time with his dad in the bargain.

He lay back on his bed, counting the minutes to dinner.

((O))

Half an hour before his more formal birthday celebration, Edward made his way to his mother's chambers to clue her in on his conversation with the emperor. She hated to be blindsided by news. He found her half-dressed in her evening gown, sitting before her mirror, a thousand-league stare in her eyes. A handkerchief she clenched in one hand.

Her eyes came up, seeing his reflection in the mirror behind her. At the sight of him, tears came, as though they'd been close to the surface, or maybe it was a freshet of grief come again.

They shared a long, heavy stare.

"Mom?"

After another long moment to compose herself, she whispered, "Edward, your father's landship was ambushed by rebels as soon as he boarded for home ..."

"Mom?" the weight of grief began to pull him down, aching in his gut and chest. It felt like madness.

She shook her head, and buried her face in her kerchief.

((O))

Later that night, by the light of a waxing moon, Edward sat again near the window in the Hall of Lost Things. He didn't speak. He certainly didn't make music. He just sat like one more neglected instrument, and cried for his father.

Sometime later, he tucked the old guitar back into the racks with all the rest, and hid the music player out of sight and in a difficult place to reach. Not that he'd be reaching for it.

He put it all away. It was too painful to hold or look at or listen to. He shut it all up.

Then, when the silences had taken full hold upon him, he left the Hall of Lost Things to take up the name given him by his father.

By any living God, they'd know his name.

GENESIS OF THE ASTONISHING

NOTES & ART

In this section we've aggregated some of John Petrucci's hand-written notes, as well as a few sheets from David Campbell's score. We've also included some early art renderings of characters, locations, and the NOMACS. These served as formative materials in delivering the story, music, and visuals that brought The Astonishing to life.

Structural Considerations

ACT 1
- overture:
  - instrumental
  - big & dramatic
  - introduces many main themes

- 2nd Song:
  - main or secondary character introduced

- 3rd or 4th Song: * set up Conflict *
  - ensemble

* Songs shift moods throughout *
  - can start gentle, build and return many times
  - go from sad to hopeful
  - go from large & proud to sensitive
  - change in song style

- need a main male or female lead ballad around 5th song

* constantly bring in melodic themes which will carry through story *

* introduce main characters early on *

* create accompaniment pattern
to repeat as motif throughout album *

ACT 1

1- Overture: instrumental, huge
                main themes
- illustrate both desperation and hope
- ominous dystopian mood
- big & hopeful
- Scary Nafaryus theme
- N.Macs nose/music

2- Song by Atticus (narrator) (Gabriels theme)
   fast and uplifting
   sets up story and background (history)
   introduces Gabriel (have a theme)
- introduce music from song 7 (with narrative)

3- Gabriel Song
   hopeful and strong   * accompaniment
                      theme first
   turns doubtful and questioning purpose appears
   sensitive
- plant seed for song 14 (sad, eerie)

4- Atticus backstory
   introduces "X" and Evangeline
   states Atticus' purpose & motivation
- plant seed for music used in song 12

5- Nafaryus Song (Dark $\frac{12}{8}$ vibe)
   dark, fast & powerful
   introduces family (Fayth, Dargus, Arabelle)
   illustrates envy & threatened feeling

* accompaniement major themes

6- Main Gabriel "hit"
 - gets interupted by Nafargus
 - resumes full song
 - very catchy & melodic
* before resuming, discovery of Faythe *
* at end, state connection to her *
7- Main Faythe ballad: (use music referenced in song)
 melodic, memorable (main subline melody #1
 her back story, her 'secret'
 changes musical moods
 - Show her innocence and hope but
 also lonliness and isolation
 like Gabriel (relates to him)

— Heavy oompa
(8- Dark, ominous Nafargus' threat to
→ people, 3 days
 - Arabelle noticing store between
 Gabriel and Faythe
 - Faythe obsessed with seeing Gabriel again

 9- Ensemble, big, strong, powerful
 Atticus army not backing down
 morphs in and out of Gabriel doubting
 - Use rising melody — plant 'Brother' seed
 10 Faythes plan to go to Ravenskill
 Arabelles understanding — hopeful
 dark twist as we introduce Darqus'
 plans for capture of Gabriel

Orchestral Score

Dream Theater

"The Astonishing"

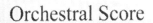

Music by John Petrucci & Jordan Rudess

Lyrics by John Petrucci

Orchestra and Choirs Arranged by David Campbell

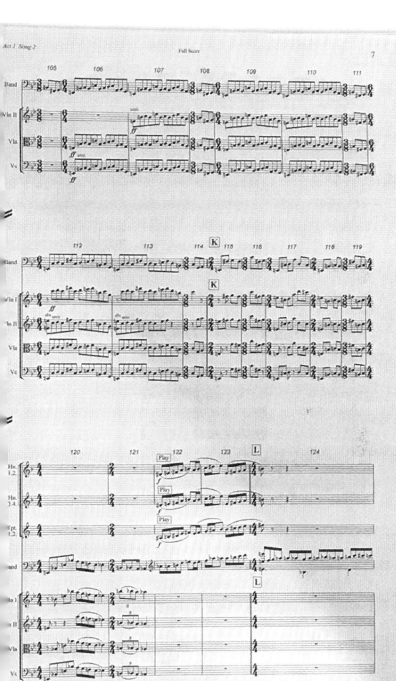

ACT 1 SONG 3

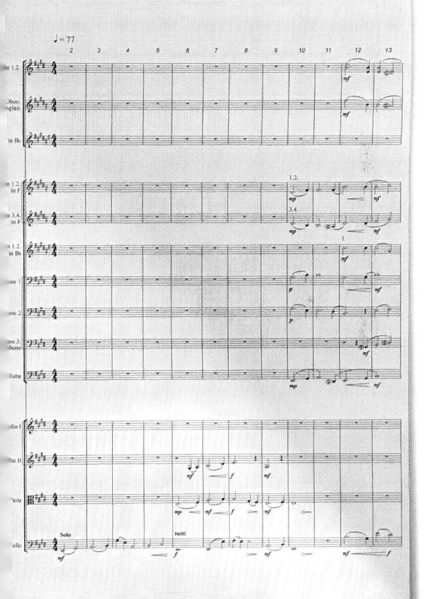

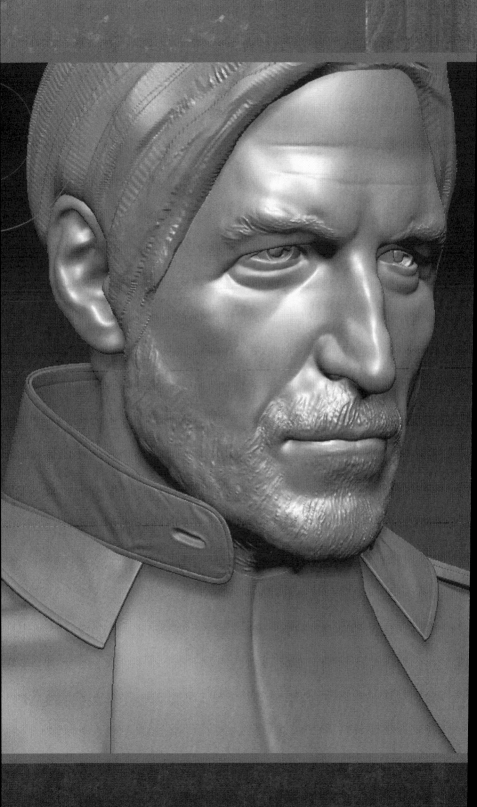

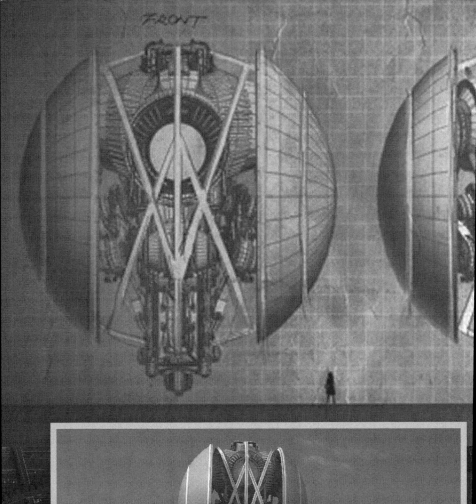

FRONT

front

no logo

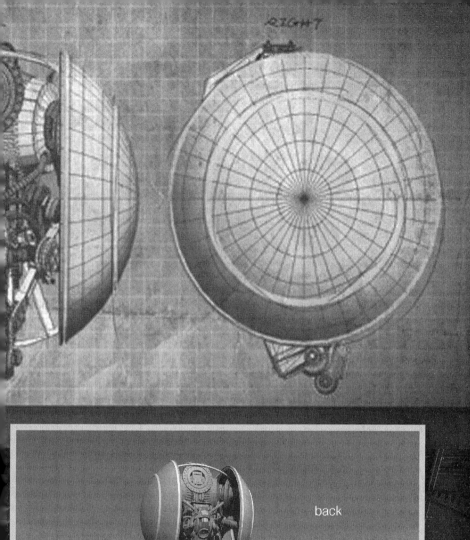

RIGHT

back

top

INTERVIEWS WITH

DREAM·THEATER

JOHN PETRUCCI

—◉—

PETER ORULLIAN

◎ *What aspect of* The Astonishing *story are you most proud of?*

The thing I'm most proud of is that it joins together a lot of some of my favorite movie genres, storytelling genres, and TV genres, but it centers around music and centers around how music is so important not only in my life but in the lives of the members of Dream Theater and so many people around the world. I'm proud of the central concept, where music is the focal point and having the story based around the concept: What would happen if music disappeared, if people weren't able to have that creative and emotional outlet? What would happen to the world? And in the case of the story things go very badly.

◎ *Which characters stories move you the most? And has that changed from conception to this point in time?*

It has shifted a bunch and after reading the novel it was even shifting more because you have given so much more depth to the characters, and back story. It made me kind of shift back and forth. When I was originally writing the story, of course, the idea that there would be this musical savior,

Gabriel, immediately made me focus on him. As I started to write it and see the importance of some of the other characters and how they developed through the story, Arhys really stood out. He's just this guy who is conflicted, wants to do the right thing, and suffered major loss in his life. He has this tremendous responsibility in raising his son and towards the people that he's protecting as a military commander. And he struggles a lot. All the characters struggle at some point, but his story ends so tragically, and he had to sacrifice so much, it gives me a special connection and empathy for his character.

◎ *Does that character affinity influence songs that you might personally gravitate to more? The interesting part of that question might be that there's a story element in terms of what the song is doing to advance the narrative. But then there's a whole separate thing, which is just musically which songs do you really love to play?*

Not necessarily. Some of my favorite songs are from characters like Nafaryus that focus on him, like "Three Days." Musically we were able to explore some different styles, some comical elements, some of the heavier songs. And on the flip side, the songs that are the most emotional for me to play and listen to a lot of times are the ones coming from Gabriel and Faythe. Because I think with those two characters there's this real depth and there's this real connection that they have. And they're songs, for me, that lend themselves to heartfelt story telling, songs like "Chosen" or "The Answer" or "Act of Faythe." Those songs are more introspective. A lot of those are songs where we're trying to tell a character's story through music and we had to have these moments where you're getting a glimpse into how they're thinking and feeling. So that introspection creates more emotional songwriting opportunities.

◎ *What was the most challenging aspect of writing* The Astonishing?

The whole scope of it. My idea was really to create this world that encompassed more than just the Dream Theater album. I wanted the story to be rich enough, good enough, have the characters be strong enough to write an entire live show around. That was the initial idea. If I had it my way, it would have been better to actually present the show first, before the album was even out. It would be the type of thing where you can buy the album at the show. Because it was written more to be a live performance experience to tell a story. So the challenge was to try and make all those different elements, and continuing here with the novel. And seeing all of that to fruition, starting with the original story, trying to lay it out, come up with characters, write it, write the music along with Jordan, recording this massive over two hour long album, having these incredible arrangements from David Campbell and all that music being recorded around the world—orchestras and choirs—creating this incredible mix that Rich did with this ridiculous abundance of tracks we had, and then turning that into a live show as far as the production was concerned and the animation elements (which took a year, getting the company Lucien out of Montreal to create everything we wanted to create), and then everything else that surrounded it and came from it, the video game . . . So it was this whole Astonishing world that I saw three years prior. And so, the short answer was getting all of that to actually become a reality.

When I think about how long this took from inception to reality, and how many hours and all the work and all of the intense songwriting, and layout out the story, and coming up with the themes, and I could go on and on, the amount of work was more, the amount of effort was more, than was ever put into any Dream Theater album to date.

○ *Obviously you're personally invested in all the material you've written for Dream Theater. Is there something any more satisfying or gratifying about the type of show that you've done with* The Astonishing—*not that the others aren't great—but in presenting material that really delivers a narrative. How is that experience different?*

For sure. There was something deeply satisfying about presenting the show in a way that met or exceeded the expectations that I had, that Jordan had when we talked about what the show should actually look like. I remember when we were looking at production companies online and looking at things like projection mapping, and seeing these budgets that production would come up with, and then getting to that point to making the characters come to life with animation, and how the set would actually technically work with the LED towers, and how it would be transported and set up every night. Then there were the kinds of venues we wanted to play, you know, playing three nights in a place that would normally house operas and musicals or really just unique and iconic venues, like the Frankfurt Opera House, or three night stays in Paris or Amsterdam. That was a big deal. Being onstage, hearing the intro, walking out there, and being in it . . . I always envisioned that the stage and environment and venue would transform into the world of *The Astonishing* live, that you'd be immersed in it. That was one of the most incredible and satisfying feelings as a performer, especially after working out all the glitches and technical issues that go along with trying to put on a show like that. You have no idea. I could not have been more proud standing on that stage. Especially at the end when the credits are rolling and the orchestral music was playing . . . it felt triumphant, it really did.

◎ *In your development of music motifs for the characters in* **The Astonishing,** *did you also use certain keys or modes, or did you rather apply and modify the motifs as needed for the song and situation?*

I would say not really keys, but modes yes, but not in a way that was over-thought. As a musician, I knew which tonality or mode would evoke the mood I was going for. It becomes more instinctual as far as using modes in writing, because you know as soon as you play a certain kind of scale it's going to evoke a certain vibe and emotion, and you just go to those things naturally. It's kind of like if you're painting, and you want something to look a certain way or evoke a certain kind of emotional response, you know what color to go to that does that. Same thing with writing and using music theory and modes, it's not an over-thought process. It's an instinctual process. It comes from years of playing, and having a musical education and background, but it turns into something that's very instinctual when you try and do that. That was something that was very fun, because we were writing very specifically. We'd take a paragraph or two from the story and write a song. And so we knew exactly which characters, what was happening, the vibe, was it dark or light, scary or foreboding, triumphant or glorious or sad, and we immediately just went to those things we knew would help us pull those out. So, it was a very fun writing experience.

○ *You've written other concept albums, and certainly done storytelling in individual songs on albums. Is this the first time that the story came first, and you wrote the music back to the story? Or have you taken that approach before?*

This was definitely, I would say, the first time that technique was explored to this extent. A little bit on Scenes from a Memory, where we'd be like, 'Okay, we need the ending song.' It wasn't specific, though, because we didn't have the story first. We wrote the music first. And so, the story was being written and the lyrics were being written as we went and it kind of came together. So that was more like, 'Musically we're at the end, so we need the grand finale.' This was really super specific song-writing about that was done about characters or scenes that were taking place in the story. So, yeah, this is the first time this method of song-writing was explored to this extent, without a doubt. Even in the other storytelling kind of songs that Dream Theater has done in the past—"Killing Hand," "Count of Tuscany"—all that music was written first, coming up with a topic after music was written. This was completely a whole different approach. This was like scoring music to a story that's written.

○ *Will you ever do another concept album?*

The work that was put into this, and the extent of taking the idea of a concept album to the extent that we did really scratched the itch as far as concept albums. Even everything that was done marketing-wise, the entire campaign leading up to the record with the two sides, and the characters, and the reveals, our deluxe box set, the NOMACS . . . this was taken further than we have ever taking anything as far as a concept album. So that itch has been scratched for now. It doesn't mean that somewhere down the line there might not be a conceptual album of some sort. But writing something to this extent is not something that I see happening again in the near future.

◎ *Many of the Dream Theater fans have expressed the desire to have the next Dream Theater album to be really heavy because there were a lot of songs on* The Astonishing *where you were trying to evoke more fragile emotions. Do you guys have the itch to do something specific? Or will you go back to producing whatever just comes more naturally, and you're not sure exactly what that is?*

Well, we do have an idea to do something specific. And we do have concepts and desires that we're all on the same page about. I wouldn't say that they're reactions to anything. But they are as a result of having gone somewhere in so much depth and detail that now that we've done these incredibly dense arrangements and orchestrations that were so symphonic, and we did a number of ballads, that we're ready to do something new. We don't plan on doing that on the next album, since we've done that already to such a full extent. The next one we feel like we can go back to being more traditional—whatever that means as far as Dream Theater is concerned, since all our albums are all different—but more traditional as far as being a prog metal band. Everyone's on the same page as far as that's concerned.

If there are any concerns or speculation about *The Astonishing* representing the new direction of Dream Theater, that's just not the case. *The Astonishing* is one hundred percent written stylistically around the concept of the story and the characters and this specific purpose. So, that's kind of cool. And what it does for us is give us a nice refreshing and optimistic look at the next thing, which is what I love about doing this. Every time we put out an album, we tour, we have a great time. Then we take a little time off to get that urge again to get in there and be creative. It's a new opportunity to do something different, to do something cool. To try and top the last thing we did. It's so exciting. I love that constant renewal that happens with being able to do this. It's not like you're stuck in this weird Ground Hog's Day where you have to constantly do the same thing.

○ *Is there anything about the training you had early on at places like Berklee that is paying dividends for you now?*

Yeah, constantly. The knowledge musically as far as theory, as far as harmonic theory and training, chord theory and training, and improvisation and all that stuff, it's stayed with me all these years. And it was a great jumping off point. Because really, I only went to Berklee for one year. But what I learned, and how I learned how to continue to learn and pull knowledge in, and be hungry, and ask questions, and research, and dive in . . . that had a profound effect on me. And it's something that I still do. And I'm still in that mode of wanting to learn, and being inquisitive as to what other guys are doing, and how they're getting certain sounds, or exploring certain styles of playing a little more because I really don't have a handle on them, or a certain improvisational library of ideas more because it's something I could develop. I'm still in that mode of musical knowledge absorption frame of mind.

○ *Are we going to see another solo album anytime soon?*

Yeah. Plans right now are that I have two G3 tours coming up, US and Europe. So, timing is tricky. But I have the material. And I'll be playing new material on those tours. And eventually when I'm able to breathe and get myself into a studio, I will record another solo album. It's definitely something I want to do, and is long overdue in terms of conventional standards of album follow-ups. But Dream Theater definitely consumes, in a good way, most of my professional and creative time. That's just the way it is.

○ *In your opinion, how much does practice play a part in a musician's proficiency versus raw talent?*

You know, practice is more developing the craft. And there's a balance in any scenario where there's an art and there's a creative element, whether it's being a chef or musician or athlete, or artist or dancer or choreographer. Where there's an expressive element, there's no doubt that there are people on this planet that are just gifted in those areas, and they're lucky enough to have found it and connected with it at an early stage in their life, where they realize it's what they're meant to do. But even when that exists, you can talk to anybody in any of these fields, and the amount of hours that it takes to hone in and perfect and nurture the craft of any of those arts is countless. So, it's also unavoidable. You can't just have a certain talent and then not work at it at all and expect that it will be what it's fully meant to be. That's just not the way it works. That's not the way life works.

○ *Do you have a favorite key or mode to play in?*

You know, as far as the modes, the basic major scale modes, Lydian is one that has this epic sound whenever you go into it. So, it's one of my favorites. But it really depends on the application. The guitar camp I did this summer, I conducted an entire master class on modes, and the moods that they evoke, and how to use them and when. It's really interesting. But it really depends on the application.

○ *Because* The Astonishing *shares so many similarities with musical theater, are there particular shows you've seen that you've liked a lot?*

To me, when I was thinking about this kind of story where there are multiple character development arcs and dramatic turns, I thought of Les Mis, I thought of Jesus Christ Superstar. Obviously, things like Book of Mormon or Spamalot aren't going to have a lot of influence on this. But the style where there are a lot of characters and trajectories and drama and intensity are the ones I thought about more.

○ *If you were doing* The Astonishing *today, but had all the knowledge of the last few years, is there anything you'd do differently?*

The number one thing is what we talked about. In a perfect world, it would be to present it as a show as its debut. That's how it would be released. You'd go to the show, and the album would be on sale at the show, so you can have a memory of what you saw. I think that would have really effective, and incredible.

◉ *Is there a song that's particularly challenging to play? Not that you can't, but that you've got to be on your game?*

Songs in set two, where it got tricky and takes a lot of focus, because there are a lot of time signature things and syncopation things going on in the last few songs. Songs like "The Walking Shadow" and "My Last Farewell." That section was some of the more challenging music to put together and make it turn out the way we wanted, because it was creepy, and twisty, and dark, and sinister, and we wanted to create confusion. That was hard to master for the live version. It took a lot of focus to do every night. Eventually we got used to it. But initially it took a lot to put that together and get everyone on the same page.

◉ *You've talked to me about your kids, and how they're now going out into the world in their own ways. Did being a father inform* The Astonishing *in any particular way other than in a more general sense?*

For sure. There's no doubt that all the experience I've had revealed itself or helped guide how I wrote certain characters or feel about certain things that were happening. One hundred percent. Going back to Arhys, and the whole idea about how he is so committed to raising his son Xander and giving him a better life, that's something that as a father you can really identify with and connect to in a very emotional way. And even the deeper aspects of Nafaryus and Arabelle and how they were trying to manage this whole thing with their children and their feelings towards questioning what they were doing. That comes from being a parent, and having this concern that you want to make sure that when you're gone that they'll be able to navigate their lives in a way that is successful and positive. I definitely infused that into those characters and the storytelling, and that's the only thing that can genuinely come from being a father.

○ *There's a real element of faith in the story. Obviously, at the most transparent level, you have a character bearing the name. But is there anything deeper to that relative to you as a person that informed the storytelling?*

Definitely. Who I am as a person, and my values, my upbringing, my religion being Catholic. All that stuff, not in a preachy way, and I'm always careful about this, but never in a way that's screams this is a Christian rock themed story. I've never written that way, because that type of things is not the way I want to write music. It's not the musical path I want to take. But those sorts of mysteries, and those ideas, are somewhat obvious in this case. Things like calling Gabriel a savior, and the whole idea that he's conflicted with having this incredible gift, and it is almost seen as a burden where he asks, 'Why me?' Then there's the betrayal of his brother, and the role of Nafaryus. A lot of that stuff is influenced by the Passion Story. But again it's taking the symbolism of it, not the underlying message or peachiness. It's the symbolism and influence of that, like Jesus Christ Superstar.

To me, the symbolism in the Passion Story is so powerful that I definitely drew from those themes. You can definitely see the Jesus story narrative in a lot of this. But it wasn't meant to be a Chronicle of Narnia thing, where I'm trying to have a hidden thing, where characters are supposed to be analogous to anyone, in particular. It's just more of taking them as an influence in the same way they would find their ways into Star Wars, like archetypes.

JORDAN RUDESS

─────●─────

PETER ORULLIAN

◎ *What aspect of* The Astonishing *story strikes you the most? Or moves you the most?*

I love the idea that music can force all of this. This is something that John and I spoken of as ideas as we got into the whole thing. So that's something that really resonated with me. I think it's something that was a great path to go down for the band, being who we are. It was fun to also create the sound of the NOMACs, the anti-music, that in my mind was really cool as well. So, I'm thinking of doing an album of all NOMACS, ya know? (Laughs)

NOMAC music! (Laughs)

Video club, you know? New York City.

It could even be the New Years ball that drops in Times Square!

There you go. Totally! NOMACS head or something. But that's the beautiful thing about it. You have this great character, Gabriel, who represents this beauty and magic of music, organic, really human spirit of music. This story has so many different aspects to it. I don't know how you see it as a writer, but to me I just feel like there's so many different things going on in this story. There's really a lot happening. And so the overall theme just sticks with me.

That's actually one of the questions I have. It's an interesting thing because I know you, and I know that you are a technologist in many regards. You work on that cutting edge where technology is helping music to go new places in terms of how it can be created. And you and I have spoken about that before. So it's an interesting question for you, because on the one hand you're on the bleeding edge of that, and part of the story seems to instead champion this idea of music as a human expression. And so I'm really interested in your thoughts around that because I know you as a player, too. You do these great videos all the time on Facebook where you're using some new piece of technology I've never seen. These tools are so foreign. You know, they look foreign to me.

Right, right, I get that. Well, a lot of the interest I have in technology is this idea that the technology is able to respond on a high level to the human being. What I mean by that is that you know these tools that I use, an example being like the Seaboard. It's an evolutionary product in regards to the keyboard. But the whole thing about it is that it's even more responsive than a keyboard synthesizer ever was to your touch. So although it's very high tech, it's so different. The reality, and the reason I like it, is because everything I do with fingers, every motion I do, every direction I travel or pressure that I apply becomes recognized and part of the musical experience. So that is a great use of technological advancement and that's really interesting to me because the more resolution of expression we get with technology the more human it becomes or can sound, because it becomes smoother and more analogue in a way.

The problem I see with technology is not technology itself. It's allowing the technology to become separate from the human experience. It's like when the human being hands it over to a tool and that piece of technology lets say is all of a sudden acting on its own. In *The Astonishing* you have these NOMAC characters. They've totally taken over music and people are no longer in charge of it. That's an extreme example, but let's sit at a drum machine and just let it go and do its thing and it's cold and stiff, there's not much to it. But as soon as you apply yourself to the machine as a human being and work with it to get things out of it that become more appealing, more in tune with who we are and our nature, then all of a sudden the technology kind of works for us. It's all about the human being. So I feel it's the relationship that's important.

○   *Is there a particular song that you gravitate to? And if so, has that changed over time?*

There's so many songs that it's hard to have a favorite one. Although, I guess there may be those that I kind of lean toward for sure. I think of one my very favorite songs that I sometimes point out is "A Life Left Behind," because it's a real mixture of the progressive side and it's very melodic and it's kind of large. And it's also a song was fun the way it came about. All the music was written by John and I, but this particular one had a real interesting balance.

The way it came together makes me smile to think about because there's this guitar riff at the beginning John wrote, this guitar pattern. I said, 'Oh great. That's the line.' I said, 'Now you go take a walk and I'll write something to go with it, to go over it.' So I wrote something with something almost like a Yes vibe with words that went over it that kind of fit. And it didn't matter to me whatever way he ended up playing rhythmically, because I got the words where I wanted them. Next that happened is this funny thing which is very Dream Theater. John asked, "How are you hearing it?" (Laughs) I just said, "This is where I thought it would be cool with words." He's said, "Well, I don't know what you're doing, but it's cool."

And then Mike Mangini was finding everybody's little idea, and making it work. And so that was the whole first part that was really cool. But then, of course, the meat of the song, John shows to us at sound check. And then I came to reading his script, and playing around with the whole chorus. It's a really nice one.

○   *What was the most challenging part of writing* **The Astonishing***?*

The challenging part was the scope of it all. And I guess it would be similar to what you have to do by taking everything you're given and making sense of it all in the book and finding even more to it and putting it all together. For us we had to assemble all these ideas, John with his story wanted to make something that really worked as a story that was cohesive. But then how do you write music to it and have something that is consecutive and really supporting the story, reflecting the story. We wanted to have recurring themes and motifs, and overtures, and entr'actes. So it wasn't so much coming up with musical ideas. I can sit at the piano all day and just play stuff. Some of it maybe good, some of it maybe not. At least I can throw out whatever. But to find the ideas that really fit at the right time, to use motifs and work with them in interesting ways. Like if there's a theme we wanted to bring back and would then have to re-harmonize, like the brother theme. Sometimes I'd take a walk and get out of the studio if I hit a wall. Things like that were harder.

⊙ *What was the most gratifying part of writing* The Astonishing?

It was great to be able to expand my output for Dream Theater a little bit different and a little bit more than what it's been in the past. It was more open to my bringing in styles that normally wouldn't fly. This was something that I could write like a film score, introducing romantic themes. And here it was working into a Dream Theater record, much to the dismay of metal fans. (Laughs) They had dart boards up for me, all the Dream Theater metal fans. Hey, here on the record for you, I have to say that some of the melodies, the Disney-esque melodies… I'm not responsible for all that. I take credit for writing a lot of music, and some of it is maybe schmaltzy, but some of the really sweet things, that's not necessarily from me.

⊙ *I've read a lot of the commentary about this not being a Dream Theater record. But one of the things that is consistent about Dream Theater is that you take chances and try new things. So in that way it's not divergent at all, is it?*

What's divergent is going so far away from the constant more metal energy. Every album we do is a little different. But this one had a lot of dynamics, and soft parts. A lot of ballads, a lot of stop and go. So it demands a certain attention span, a certain patience, especially if you're used to Dream Theater and its harder edge. It's asking a lot to stop so much and have so many mellow parts. I get that. I really understand that.

We get what we put out there. We spent so many years developing a certain kind of audience because we delivered the kind of material we did. And then we change it up a lot, which I think is wonderful and great and *The Astonishing* is probably my favorite Dream Theater album of all of them. But I get how people feel about it. It's like Radiohead when they changed their style and all of the sudden they're doing songs. Next thing you know, they're like some electronic group.

◎ *Is there a particular performance that is memorable for you?*

The first show in London was memorable because the expectations were so high and there was so much work to get it together. And it was memorable getting everything together. But also the Radio City Music Hall show is memorable. It was a sold out show. Doing *The Astonishing* in New York City was pretty cool.

◎ *Is there any difference for you in performing a record that tells a story with characters that go through change, versus what you've done so much of, which is playing hits from your catalogue?*

For me especially it's different because I start and stop so many songs in this album, and set the mood for so many things. So it's very demanding. There are not a lot of breaks. You have to constantly be on. The story goes on, one thing connects to the other. Especially the way it's all synchronized together. There's no chance to space out. That makes it a very different experience for me than anything we've ever done before. It's tiring. At the end of the night, you feel like it's time to unwind.

○ *Were there certain keys or modes that you used for certain characters?*

There are motifs that relate to the different characters for sure. And we tried to pick music that reflected the energy of the character. Like with the Nafaryus character you've got the tri-tones. And that definitely makes for a certain sound and feeling. So when it comes to Faythe you're in a lovely major theme. My background has theater and Broadway to it in the sense that I've played so many of those songs, and my wife is a producer in the theater business. So it was fun jumping into that world.

○ *With* The Astonishing *was the lyric and vocal melody writing the same as it is with other Dream Theater albums?*

Yes. But with *The Astonishing* John knew for each song which characters were being portrayed, and so he knew the right melodies and lyrics. Some of the melodies were written ahead of time because the nature of melody is so important to this music. So we often had melodies but not lyrics.

○ *You guys have done songs on some albums that do a little bit of storytelling like "The Count of Tuscany." When you write those kind of songs, where the lyrics are coming after the music is done, does the story you're trying to tell in the context of a single song suggest changes to the music, or do you usually find ways to fit the story to what you've already put down musically?*

With *The Astonishing* we were very much supporting the story with the music. With something like "The Count of Tuscany" the story would be constructed to the music, following the swell of the music to see what works.

○ *How has your time at Julliard helped you as a touring musician and song-writer both in Dream Theater and your other projects?*

First, my piano instruction was from some of the highest linage in that world. My teacher was an assistant to Rosina Lhévinne, who is probably the most famous piano teacher of the last hundred years. So what I learned there as far as my approach to the instrument and the way I play the instrument is the foundation for everything that I do. What that means basically is that I've developed a technique that enables me to take my musical ideas and get them through my fingers. If I have an idea, fast, slow, whatever, it can come out as I hear it in my head.

○ *Do you have a perspective on how much musicianship is inborn verses how much you can spend time practicing and training to develop?*

I believe there are a lot of people out there, especially in the classical world, where you'd see them play and acknowledge that they're great pianists and they might not even have that much musical talent. It's just the sheer amount of work to coordinate what's on the page and get their fingers to make it happen. A pianist like that might not even be able to recognize music intervals or have a rhythmic sensibility. So I think those things just come natural to a person. Are you rhythmical? Do you feel rhythm? Do you have a sense of pitch? So it's definitely a combination. Someone who is lucky enough to have natural ability and also be trained is a good thing.

○ *What advice would you have for an aspiring keyboard player?*

Get out of the business while you still can!

○ *What other sorts of art do you enjoy?*

Over the last few years I've been really into working with visuals. And luckily I am in the IOS world with my company and everything. And so I play around with all the tools.

○ *Over the course of your career have there been any technological break-throughs that have been pivotal or groundbreaking that you think helped shape your playing or the music that you can create?*

I've been very involved with the advancement of the technology. And one of the main interests that I've had is being able to use a fretless technique in addition to diatonic notes. On a piano, everything is defined. Play a note, you're on, you're off. There's no in between. And I am passionate about playing the piano. However, it's a whole opening to be able to play between the notes, to be able to decide.

When I got a Minimoog, it was all about learning how to bend pitch with the pitch wheel. But then it became more about having my finger on the pulse of the note. I want to be in charge of everything that happens with my finger on the note. So I started this company called Wizdom Music, and developed an app called MorphWiz which was really about that. It was opening up that possibility where you could play along a surface and bend from one note to another or you could lock in pitches so it's more piano-like and freely go between those; but also express notes along the vertical access, so as you play a note you can milk that note and have different things affect the timbre.

And that led me to explore a lot of different people developing technology. Things like the Haken Continuum was one that I worked on a bunch and developed some ideas with. And most recently the Roli Seaboard which I mentioned before. This seaboard is an interesting evolution of the piano keyboard, and the idea of that is it also allows you to express on the vertical access and bend pitch and also play diatonic pitches very much like a piano, while having a bit of a piano form factor. So I was fairly involved in bringing that instrument out into the world as well. These days I'm doing similar things like GeoShred, which is my latest app that brings it to another level.

○ *Do you have a desire or vision for a way technology can go to another level, where the technology hasn't been invented yet or they can't support the idea or place you want to go with the music?*

I wish we could go forward in time and see what is going to happen with the ideas we are playing with now, because things aren't quite there yet for what I imagine. I just started getting into virtual reality and augmented reality, wondering how my app MorphWiz could be brought into that world where it becomes a three dimensional experience.

○ *Is there a particular musical that you love and that's been inspiring?*

A bunch of them. Recently one that was pivotal in the Broadway world, and an important statement musically, was Spring Awakening. I thought the music to that was really good and different.

○ *Do you have a favorite key that you just love?*

D minor. It's the saddest of all keys. (Laughs) If I want to be happy I'll play in G.

○ *Where do you look for inspiration as a musician?*

Drugs, generally. (Laughs) When I have time and I'm relaxed and I don't have a million things on my mind, I can sit at the piano and feel inspired. Playing the piano is the same and maybe easier than talking. For me to just sit down and play something you've never heard before is as easy as this conversation. It's just expressing where I'm at, at the moment and its phrases.

○ *If you could do* The Astonishing *again, what would you do different?*

I'd give them an "all metal" album. (Laughs) I wouldn't play keyboard. I'd just play an eight string guitar myself and wear some kind of Viking outfit.

○ *What musicians have been influential to you?*

In the keyboard world I always say Keith Emerson was a real hero of mine, and unfortunately he's no longer on the planet and that's very sad. But that whole movement of progressive music beyond my training at Julliard—and I loved a lot of the music I studied there, like Chopin, Debussey, whatever—the prog was the most inspirational to me spiritually, musically. It really meant more to me than anything else. And I'm talking about bands like Yes, Genesis, Gentle Giant, King Crimson, and Emerson Lake and Palmer and that whole school.

○ *Is there a particular song in* The Astonishing *that's challenging to play?*

There's a part in "Three Days" that's really hard. I don't know why I wrote it. But with pencil and paper, I was figuring something out, and when I was done I went, "Holy shit, this is hard!" On tour, I would forget to practice it so it would get to a place where it started to fall apart. So, I would say to my tech, "remind me of that," and then I'd sit and nail it down; practice with him slowly; practice what I wanted it to feel like when I'm on stage. That's one of the biggest lessons I could offer to any young player, especially if they're going to be doing live performance. Don't' just write the part, but also imagine what you want it to feel like when you're in the heat of the moment. Otherwise the nerves take over and your body tenses and it's not pretty.

○ *When you're just putting something into your music player or sitting down to play, where do your preferences lie?*

I generally go for more mellow music. I'm a fairly mellow guy. I like writing all kinds of music. I write metal music and classical music, I enjoy it all. And I can put myself in those frames of mind. But when I sit at the piano, the first thing I'm going to want to do is heal myself with the music. It's personal. I want songs that just feel good and it will center me. That's how I use music on my own. So if I just sit down at the piano, it's going to be pretty mellow at first. And also if I'm going to listen to music, it's going to be stuff that's resonant to me. Whether it's listening to Steven Wilson's music or Sigur Rós or Boards of Canada or the Beatles. I'm not generally going to put on a Slayer album to feel good. Not for me. Everybody's different.

○ *You have this passion and ability and interest in technology adoption, but you also have this very real ability to infuse your playing with humanity. So is it fair to say that as the technology evolves you are more able to express your humanity?*

Yes as the technology moves forward it's getting more possible for me to express myself. I'll always be able to sit at a piano, and that to me is very complete. But if I sit at an instrument that has some of these features that we're talking about like responding to every aspect of my touch in a very organic fine resolution sort of way, then yeah, its becoming closer to allowing me to do things that I was never able to do before.

○   *Are there any particular pieces in Dream Theater, on your own, or in the other groups you're a part of that are real standouts, where when you're done, the experience of it feels like you landed what you meant in a way you rarely do?*

I think a really important piece for me in this more recent chapter of my life is The Explorations for Keyboard and Orchestra. I think it was a really important statement. It felt really good to do. I liked the results. For anyone who really wanted to know who I am as a musician, they could get a lot out of hearing that, a lot of information. It really encapsulated so many stylistic ideas, things that I care about and wanted to say all in one.

JAMES LABRIE

—◉—

PETER ORULLIAN

◉ *I'm interested to know, with* The Astonishing, *is there anything about the story that strikes or moves you? I know it's different for everybody when they think about story and what resonates or hits them. But for you, is there anything in particular that moves you.*

Well I think that one interesting fact, and there are several, but the one that I thought was cool that John made a part of the story is losing that connection with the human element which is what creates music. And so the whole story is based on the idea that we've lost touch with things that resonate with us; things that make us human beings; things that unite us. And so that in itself is a very powerful aspect of the story for me. But the interesting twist that John put on it is the very person that is an advocate of not allowing music to come from humans is the very person who grew up loving and having to hide it himself, and that's Lord Nafaryus. So I think it's cool as the story goes on and it comes to a close, we find that Nafaryus—very similar to his daughter, Faythe—is secretly in love with music. And so then, if anything, he should've been the easiest one to persuade to get rid of the NOMACS and unite as a whole. Not just in a social sense, but in a human sense. So I think that is one aspect of the story that really moves me.

◎ *Just in terms of performance are there any of the songs that you have seemed to gravitate to? And has that changed over time?*

Yea, actually there is one that has remained true the whole time through and that's Ravenskill. And interestingly enough, that's one where I'm representing a female character and a male character. So you have Arhys and Faythe confronting one another, and it's for Faythe to be able to connect with Gabriel in the sense that she wants to let him know that she might find a way that she can prevent her father from wanting to eradicate Ravenskill and Gabriel, and particularly what Gabriel represents. Gabriel's a beacon of hope for the people. So that song moves me in a couple ways because it's a very monumental moment in the storyline, but at the same time I think it's a very powerful dynamic as a singer because I'm trying to be convey feminine subtlety on one hand, while portraying something more aggressive on the other—Arhys protective posture toward his brother. So I think that that song, even when I was thinking of how I was going to approach it as a vocalist before going into the studio, was something that really took a lot of focus and a lot of my attention.

Whereas, I have to be honest, a lot of the album is kind of... and this is a hard thing for me to put into words so that I don't come off sounding like (laughing) cocky or arrogant or anything like that, but for the most part I've got to tell you it was almost like reading over your notes in the morning before going into work and addressing your company. That's how it was for me. I would listen to the song that I was going to sing that day, because, you know I was going in pretty much every day and I would kind of review my notes as to how I wanted to approach this song and create that voice. So especially for this song I knew that there was going to be the two characters face-to-face, and so this was a very important part of the album where the two were interacting but in a more confrontational sense. But at the same time, I wanted to get across how emotionally bound they were for what they represented.

But I mean, since then, you know, songs like "The Road to Revolution" and "*The Astonishing*" that we wrote where, for instance, you have Arhys in the spiritual world communicating with his brother, Gabriel, and saying you must go on. You must be the example to my son. And then everyone else coming out and realizing what it is they truly represent and almost discovering themselves. So I found that with those songs, John really hit the mark lyrically. And the music, you know, it speaks for itself. I think the music is phenomenal throughout and I can't imagine anything else, you know anything being added to it or anything being taken from it. But those songs… they're just gorgeous to me. You know, it's the best way for me to describe it because they really do bring closure to the movements. And that was very exciting to sing because I'm touching upon everyone. Everyone has a piece. Everyone has something to say.

◎ *So you talked about some of the characters. Were there any of the characters that you personally identified with? The assumption someone might make is it's Gabriel because he's the voice. But I know you're also a father and there's this whole dynamic with Arhys and his son which is very moving. So I'm wondering if there's a little piece of each of those that you were able to touch upon or if there's one that felt more like you that you were able to invest more personally in?*

Yeah, you know, it's funny you say that. There was Arhys and Xander, but the character that I sided with more and the character that I understood implicitly, as far as like trying to guide me, was Nafaryus. I really just felt that this guy, what he presented to people was a façade. It really wasn't himself. It was this guy putting on this big tough exterior. But I could tell there were a lot of emotions and a lot of frustrations that lived within this man. Because I think as you go through the story you realize that he's got a lot of pent up feelings that he suppressed for so long.

And so I really sided with that because what I've always done, Peter, I've always read into the lyrics. Whether it's lyrics that I've written or lyrics from someone else, it's something that I feel is the job of any vocalist. You have to make it a part of who and what you are as a human being. And you have to be able to convey it through your own interpretation so that it becomes believable. And for whatever reason, when I was reading through the story or even reading the actual lyrics, I kind of made an initial connection with Nafaryus because I just felt like, *I get this guy. I get what he's going through.* And it was really easy for me to know immediately the voice that I had to create for this character.

In fact, when we started recording the album I remember saying to Rich, I said, "You know, I'd been thinking, let's just start at the beginning and just go song to song. But I can't do that because I first and foremost have to create a template for each singer. So where should I start, you know?" And even though I wanted to go right at the "Gift of Music" and start there and start going along with the narrator and all that stuff, I wanted to first and foremost focus on Lord Nafaryus. That song, you know? And just making it. And I did. I focused on the first part of it and then that's when I flipped to other songs to create Faythe and the narrator and Arhys and so forth and so on. But he was, for sure, the first guy that I related to.

○ *You actually mentioned one of the things I wanted to talk a little bit about. One of the things I heard, even on my first listen, was this differentiation in the voices. Which, I assume, would have been a challenge. There's a Broadway show called Jekyll and Hyde where the lead character has to play and sing both parts. I remember listening to that and the first time I heard it, it was actually hard to distinguish in some songs that it was the same vocalist. So when I was listening to you, in some songs having to switch point of view, it was impressive. And so one of the things I wanted to ask you was how you approached differentiating the voices.*

Yeah, I think first and foremost I had to start with my understanding of each of the characters as people. And then being able to really internalize what they were saying to me. And how can I bring that to myself so that when I'm singing it my interpretation becomes sincere and believable, right? And so, there are moments where I'm flipping back and forth between characters, or I'm telling something different within one character and it has to be understood. So I think the biggest support or guide for me was just really understanding what was being said. You know, what was trying to be communicated, and what is the message here?

I felt like I'd be successful as long as I had an absolute understanding of what was trying to be said, or what that person was going through emotionally. Because the whole ride was all about this emotional spectrum. And the emotions would flip flop at times, and whether it was within one character or whether it was the interaction and the misunderstanding between characters, that was something that I fully had to be able to embrace. And if I didn't, then I knew that I was just going to be singing through these songs like a machine or always worrying, 'Does that sound good?' Or, 'Docs my voice sound good?' And it couldn't really be about those things. It had to be about: Did I hit the mark? And I guess, once again, I've always trusted it: My initial reaction to something.

I need to be able to believe myself first before I believe anyone else. And even though I had a sound board there, and Rich, and he and I have worked together for 30 years, I still felt that I had to be convinced first and foremost before anyone else. Like he could've been telling me, "No that was an awesome change! I didn't expect you to go there!" And he did say those things. But I remember just thinking, I've got to be able to sing this, and when I say, 'Hang on a second, can I hear that back,' it had to be immediate. There had to be no if's, and's, or but's. That's basically how I was able to tackle this, even though it was very solemn at times. Let's face it, Peter, it's like you said, you have one voice to work with. So even though you want to be able to have the listener be able to completely identify with each character when I do that transition—and it has to be somewhat seamless so that it is like another singer coming in—it is very subtle, right? Because you are using one organic instrument and you can only go so far. So, I think a lot of it was conveyed through the emotion.

○ *Is there a particular song that is challenging athletically to sing in this concept album, or is this one less about vocal athletics?*

Oh no, there are definitely vocal athletics in here. There's no doubt about it. I mean, "Three Days" I find is very vocally athletic because it's very dynamic. You have the more comfortable range and voice, and then you're screeching all of a sudden. And it's also about delivering something that feels powerful. And as I mentioned, "Ravenskill" is a challenging song vocally, first because it can get rangy and go into a higher register, but also about maintaining the characters within it.

I'd say that "A Moment of Betrayal" can be very challenging vocally. And "The Path that Divides." And "The Walking Shadow" can be really intense. Even some of the more balladesque songs come with a challenge, like "Act of Faith," where I have to really be that tender, very light voice. So, yes, there are athletic sides to it. I'm hoping that this does go to the theatre. I would really be curious to see other vocalists doing this; both male and female, and see how they'd portray each particular character vocally. I'm really going to be very very curious to hear it, you know?

◎ *You have such a long career, and you've done so many albums where it's episodic, meaning the songs aren't related. And now you do something like* The Astonishing, *which is working to tell a deeper story. Is the experience as a vocalist of doing a whole night where you have this story arc any different—not better or worse—but different for you as a vocalist verses singing the typical concert?*

Yeah, there's definitely a difference, even more so with this album, *The Astonishing*, just because I was representing seven characters. And so it's not only for me as a vocalist to go out live and go, 'Okay, I've got to be vocally be on." I've got to warm up, and bring my voice back to that level, and make sure that I'm focused. This is like bringing myself up to a level vocally that I know I'm going to be able to, so to speak, knock it out of the park. But at the same time, being able to realize moment-to-moment that I'm moving in and out of character voice. And you know things eventually become muscle memory and your body takes over and you just naturally go there.

So, this was even more challenging to be able to replicate the album each and every night and do the characters justice even more so than when we did *Scenes from a Memory*, which was another conceptual album. But with that, even though there were characters, it was more separated from me, because one song would more than likely be the voice of one person. It wasn't this interaction within songs. So this was definitely more, I would say, challenging in that sense than anything else. Like you said, we are going to go out and do our 25th anniversary of *Images and Words*. That's just more or less about being true to each song, and that's been pretty much the case on any given tour. When you're singing that particular song, you want to be in the right voice for that song and that moment. You know, it's not like representing characters. It's representing that particular song and what I did for that song.

○ *Where do you look for inspiration as an artist and musician? Is there anything that kind of inspires you and keeps you motivated?*

Any given musician and any given band you look at their albums, and it's like a time capsule, right? I mean it shows you where they were collectively as people. What was influencing them and what was moving them and what they were going through as human beings. You know, we ride a very dynamic existence here, don't we? You know we can very high one day and we can be very low another day just by what is going on in our lives. And I think for me my inspiration is what I just said. Everyday living; everyday interaction with people and loved ones, acquaintances and/or business, you know.

And then the other side of that is your observation and seeing people and seeing how they communicate with one another; seeing what they have to say about something; even like a phrase or a line that comes from somebody that makes you think differently and that could be my inspiration. Watching the news, I think, is very inspirational to me. Reading books is very inspirational to me. So it's taking all that collectively and it eventually becomes who you are in that particular moment in time. And I think that inspires you or directs you as to where you want to go with an album. Whether it be with Dream Theater or other music that I create. It's what I'm feeling or what I've been touched upon recently within the last six months, year or a couple of years. So that's basically my tuning fork.

And then the other side of that, too, is as a vocalist I'm always looking at how I can grow. Because I think any singer should always be growing; you should always be learning. You become wiser. You become more enlightened. You become closer to your instrument. And you find easier and better ways to express that and be able to utilize that gift, I guess. And so to me I think that's a challenge, but it's a challenge that I want and it's exciting. And with this album was a new way to try and grow as a vocalist. And I was like, bring it on!

⊙ *That's great, and really insightful. Related to that, I know that you've done some formal vocal training. And so my question for you is how much of a vocalist's success do you think is raw talent and ability as a musician—like God-given— verses application and diligence and practice?*

I'm glad you asked that because you know my answer's going to differ from any other vocalist. I'm sure they all feel different about that, but I truly feel, Peter, that ninety percent of what I am today and what I've always had was with me from the age of five-years-old. So as far as you're saying, "raw talent?" I think it's ninety percent. I think the other ten percent, as invaluable as it is, is just things that can bring more awareness and wisdom toward what it is you want to accomplish as a singer.

And yes I've done formal training here and there throughout the years. But to be completely honest with you, as much as I understand that and as much as I appreciate that, when I'm behind a microphone in a studio or behind the microphone live it's really me being who I am as a singer. It's me being just a human being that is tapping into what's been given to me and really just throwing it out there. So if I don't feel good one night and I'm sick, I'm really at the mercy of my instrument being organic. I can prepare myself through my warm ups and with everything that I've been taught. But at the end of the day, it's what my body wants to give me. And at the end of the day, most of the time, it's me just going out there and utilizing what's been given to me from birth. It really is and I have so many singers coming to me when I'm on the road and they're asking, "Can you ...?" as if I'm going to give them a two minute synopsis of how it is to be a great vocalist. It's just not that easy.

Here's my best advice for any singer. Experiment. Learn about yourself. Yes, you're going to realize your limitations, but don't look at that as that's it, that's as far as I can go. I don't believe that. I think that it's up to the individual if you really really wanted to be committed to becoming a great singer, then experiment all the time as a singer. Be singing in the washroom. Sing where you feel acoustically like "Oh this sounds fucking great!" Because that's what you want. That's inspiration. You want to be in an environment that makes you sound great, where you can really appreciate the acoustics of your voice and then expand on it. And the more you do that the more you're going to be able to say, "Oh my God. I just did something there. That's really cool. I just felt something there and not only did I feel it and it felt great but it sounded great." And that to me is the best advice.

I can tell you what you're going to do to warm up. I can tell you what you're going to do when you cool down. But ultimately just freaking get in there and start using your voice and see where you can go with it, and that's when you're going to discover all these little facets of yourself vocally that make you unique. That's what's going to make anyone that ever hears you or me identify with us and like us. And that's it.

○ *Yea that's good advice. All right let me break the monotony a little bit and ask you something slightly frivolous. Is there a music-related film that you like? I love films like Amadeus and Mr. Holland's Opus. Is there one that's your go to feel good film that's got music as part of its theme?*

Hmmm. Well, I'll tell you what, I just kind of surreptitiously came upon this movie, and I just saw the DVD. This is when we went to the store and would buy DVD's. It was called: Children of Dune. And I don't know if you ever saw that one, but the composer is Brian Tyler. And I remember watching the movie and the movie was well done. It was very well done, actually. It was the sequel to Dune, I believe. In any case, the soundtrack is absolutely phenomenal. It really supports the story and the visuals. And I remember I actually posted it on my Facebook or my website years ago. Then, after I posted it, this guy comes on my website and says, "James here is my personal email if you feel like emailing me one day I would love it." And it was Brian Tyler. And so I did. I emailed him and said, "Hey Brian, I really appreciate you coming in and saying that because he went on to tell me he loved Dream Theater and my solo work. He said he couldn't believe that I was a fan of the movie and was absolutely floored by the songs and compositions.

◎ *If you could have a conversation with any one musician living or dead who would it be, and what would you ask them? I'm thinking all the way back Mozart, or could be someone who's a contemporary of yours that you admire.*

Yeah, I don't have to think too hard about that. It would be Freddy. If he could sit here in the living room with me and we could just chat, you know. So, first of all he was the consummate front man, a phenomenal musician, incredible voice, and I'd just like to sit down and talk to him and ask him about *his* inspiration. And I think, if you read into his lyrics you see the music that supports what it is that he was talking about. And that's not to take away from Brian or Roger or John. These guys were all integral to making Queen who it was. But to sit down with Freddy. That's the guy that I want to meet, because I'd also see those human flaws, none of us are infallible, and that to me is what makes us who we are. And especially someone like him who was so expressive and so connected with being an amazing musician and amazing singer.

Live he was this guy who was so extraverted. But then this shy and meek and introverted guy offstage. It seemed he could flick a switch and become this larger than life person on stage. And he was huge in the studio, too. Then when I see him in interviews he seemed kind of shy. That's somebody that I want to understand more. Or, maybe not, you know? There's always that too, right? You sit down with one of your heroes, and then you don't care for them anymore. Maybe you wish you'd never done it. But I can't see that being the case with Freddy, or at least I hope it wouldn't be.

○   *How would you describe your vocal development? Like in the early days with Winter Rose all the way through to* The Astonishing. *Has your approach changed or has that remained a fairly consistent thing? Or have you seen growth in ways you hadn't anticipated as a vocalist?*

We were touching on how I feel that ninety percent of it has to be there to begin with, and that the ten percent is very essential to making you understand your instrument better and take care of it. But I don't know, I think that the early days and leading right up into joining Dream Theater and even doing The Images and Words tour a lot of it was just what had been given to me and just me staying true to myself as a singer. But I think, and this goes other places, that my vocal development was interrupted because my vocal injury, which I know you understand as you were a big supporter of mine through that. You understood that many years ago. But it was interrupted in the sense that when I had my vocal rupture, I was completely at a loss. And then I went into a very dark place as a person.

So it was really hard for me to believe in myself anymore as a singer and as a person that had so much confidence and so much belief. It was really a weird moment for me in my life and I think there were some years there where it was very destructive to me. First the injury prevented me from moving on and developing further. And I remember just prior to the injury being in a place where I felt my voice getting stronger and stronger and thinking the next time I'm just going to try and do some frickin' insane things. And I remember this reality came upon me that was shattering. First and foremost as a singer it was just devastating, that I had to somehow figure how I was going to get through this unfortunate situation to a point where I could believe in myself again and actually get the voice to cooperate with me because there was some good eight years where my voice was just so unpredictable; so fragile that I didn't know if I was going to be in a position to keep doing it.

So then when I got over that hump, which wouldn't have been until… Oh my God, man, like maybe Black Cloud Silver Linings? You know, I had a good moment there. Probably when we did Train of Thought and that whole tour was a kind of shining moment. I remember the voice, for whatever reason, came back on line and it was just really strong and I was very dedicated to it. And I was able to go and do that tour and I'm sure that if I listened to 90% of the shows on any given leg, that the voice was absolutely frickin on fire.

And then I went down into a slump again? And it was really bizarre. But luckily by Black Clouds I was able to get back to remembering who I am. I started to develop myself as a singer again and dedicate a lot of time to it and started to try to, once again, explore my voice. And I think that really came through on A Dramatic Turn of Events. And I feel like I'm on an upswing I hope to be able to continue doing that. And even if you listen from 2010 and on, like with my solo albums, Static Impulse and Impermanent Resonance. The same thing is going on with those, as well. But I think I was able to step back and reflect on what I was going through and try to put it into a perspective that could once again be positive. So it was kind of a tumultuous ride for me.

○ *Have you had to develop or think about certain vocal preservation techniques? Because you do ask a lot of yourself.*

(Laughs) I'm glad you see that, Peter. Once again, you see it. Yeah, the preservation is that I need to warm up very slowly. It's like waking up a giant. You know, you don't just smack him in the face and say come on. You have to wake him up very slowly and give him a cup of tea or something. For me, that is probably the most important—the way that I warm up before any given performance. And also the way that I cool down—so that I'm bringing it from a singing position back into a speaking position. Because if I don't do that, then there's vocal fatigue that will ensue.

And the other part is, now more than before I sit down with the guys when we're constructing a set list—which we didn't used to do together, because Mike made all the set list so there wasn't always a lot of communication there. It used to be just, "Well, here's the set list." And so what I've done ever since we released A Dramatic Turn of Events is I've worked with

John so he and the band know where I want to start. And if you track it, you can see I'm gradually escalating the intensity and range so that I'm allowing myself even more time to open up. By the time I'm doing the second step, and if there's anything that's ridiculous, my voice is already opened up and it's ready. So that's enabled me to be able to consistently go out and perform the way I want to.

Of course, if I'm sick, I'm screwed? Many vocalists will want to change the melody when they're sick. When a vocalist is sick, there needs to be compromise.

I've also gotten better about liquids, water. I'm constantly sipping slightly cooler than hot water with a teaspoon of honey from my thermos. That's essential. I'm also much more careful about the foods that I eat, concentrating more on fruits and vegetables. I make sure that I get a lot of potassium, take my vitamins, do intense power walking of three miles a day with interval changes so I'm up and down and sweating. Great cardio is also essential to any singer, to have that power and that reserve to be able to project.

Because I'll tell you something, Peter, when I had that vocal injury, what I lost—which I'd always had and it was there at any given moment of the day—was the high falsetto stuff, particularly the screeching stuff. Now I have to warm up to that, whereas before you and I could be walking down the street and you'd say "Give me an F sharp." And I'd just do it without thinking, because it was just naturally there. And then I after the injury I noticed I couldn't do it off-the-cuff anymore, because it basically sounded like shit when I tried. That was very frustrating because that had just always just naturally been there. I had to rethink that approach as well.

So, all these things really lend themselves to me once again being able to grow and be as consistent as a human being can be. And any singer out there will have an appreciation for what another singer has to do because they've lived it. They've had to do it. They've had to be at the mercy of this organic instrument saying one day, 'I'm your best friend,' and the next day saying, 'I don't really care about you.' (Laughs) What are you going to do? You know?

So, we all go through it. We've all had to experience it. And that's the part where you walk on stage and you go, 'Shit! Why did I decide to become a singer? Oh I know why. Because I love it.' Even if you don't love it at that exact moment.

○ *One of my questions is what are you most proud of? And it would be easy for you to choose a moment of perfect vocal performance, but it occurs to me as I listen to you that working through several years where you're in a dark place with the unpredictable and staying determined might also be something you're pretty proud of.*

Yeah, I mean, absolutely. Thank you. I look back on that. Now I can reflect on that and I go, 'Wow.' You see that once again if you look at anything that goes on in the world on any given day you see people that are living or have been living in absolute horrible conditions. And then you ask yourself: What the hell makes them go on? What is it? What are they fricking digging down into that enables them to continue? And I'm able to have a little sense of that. I'm nowhere near living in the misery that some people have to endure everyday in this world. But I can reflect now and look back on those years and I do ask myself, 'How did I do it?'

Part of that answer is that I absolutely love music. I love being a part of it. I love creating it. And I love being a singer. It's been my number one love along with my family all my life. So I think that's part of it; I never wanted to let that go because I couldn't imagine life without music. And the other part is just that human spirit, you know? Where do we get that strength? Is it something that is existential, or is it something that is just within us?

I'm glad I am where I am today. And thank God that I had band mates that were supportive. Because they knew. They knew I was going through shit. They knew I was compromised as a singer, from where I'd been at one point. And they were supportive. They were what band mates should be, to a point where I even questioned myself. I had to ask myself if I would have been as supportive as they were in their shoes. I can now honestly say that yes, I would because that's the kind of person I am. I don't have a mean streak in me. I'm not insensitive. And so I can see myself saying, 'Hey man, I know what you're going through. Just give us what you've got and don't hurt yourself.' It's been an incredible ride no doubt about it.

○ *Obviously you must have a certain affinity for progressive rock; progressive metal. And I've heard your solo stuff which is, I think, excellent. But I'm also wondering where some of your other musical preferences lie. I remember talking to you one time and you said you dig guys like Nat King Cole and other vocalists. I'm wondering, on your way to the supermarket, what's going to be in your CD player?*

A band that I just got into recently is: Nothing of Thieves. I think the singer has a very cool voice. It's more alternative pop, I guess. You know, there's Haken, which is a progressive band from the UK and they've done some shows with us. I think they're phenomenal. Just a frickin' amazing band. So that's something else. You know, Switchfoot, which I think is an incredible band. I think John, the singer, is my favorite lyricist in the world. He's a phenomenal lyricist, and their music is just great. Great melodies, great hooks. They're more like a pop rock kind of band, so that's something that I would be listening to. You know, I've always loved One Republic. I think Ryan is just phenomenally talented. So there's that. I think the new Kansas album with the new singer was great. I was blown away. I thought it was amazing. Bastille, I like some things about them. But you know, I tend to want to listen to more alternative kinds of pop rock music these days. You know, that's a few of the artists that I have an appreciation for that I would be listening to these days.

○ *So you talked about always wanting to explore and try new things. What would you like to try? I know you did a project where you worked with some classical vocalists, which was very cool. Is there something else that if you got the opportunity you'd love to try? Maybe a different genre or different forum?*

I did this rock opera last year with Arjen Lucassen called The Theater Equation. And I had a phenomenal time doing that. It was with a great cast of singers and people, which is number one on my list. It's the kind of person you are. And I would love to one day—it's funny, you mentioned it earlier—to do a theatre production like Jekyll and Hyde. Like Le Mis. I would love to do that, or even doing some of the more poppish theater like Phantom of the Opera, for example. That's something that I think I would love to be able to dedicate myself to doing for a six month contract, where that's what I do six days a week. That's who I am. And really being able to discover myself in that capacity as a singer and as a person and as an actor, as well. And being able to really convincingly do those parts vocally and as an actor well. And I've talked about it for years, but the window of opportunity to do so is just so not available. It doesn't avail itself to me. And you know as we speak here, Peter, I've been in touch with Matt Gillory. He and I are already starting to work on another solo album. I say solo album but it's really a Gillory/Labrie project, because that's what it's always been since I've been working with him, which is unbelievable in itself, since is 1998. So it's incredible that I've been able to do what I've been doing. And eventually sometime in 2018 we'll be doing another D.T. album. But I also hope with this next solo album, and were really trying to strategically line it up, is to be able to go on tour. And the musicianship in that band is phenomenal, as well. So to be able to bring these guys back on tour…. Because I did it in 2005 with them, but I haven't been able to that since so it's long overdue; gotta do it.

◎   *John and Frank were putting together a pitch for Broadway, and I asked him if I could help because I've done some stuff like that. I don't know what's going to come of it. I think it would be great. If it did, would you want to actually be in the Broadway production of* The Astonishing*?*

I said to John and Jordan, obviously it'd only make sense that I'd show up at some point and sing one of the characters one night, right? So it'd be like a cameo, and they said absolutely, you have to. It's funny you're saying this because then I try to imagine that? Is it something that maybe I'd want to dedicate myself to for say three months. But I don't know if that would translate well, because I think it'd be okay for me to do it for one week where I'd play, say, Lord Nafaryus. I think maybe that would be cool. But to actually become a part of that production for an extended period of time, I think that it might take the wind out of the sails for what it represents on Broadway. I really do. And I think it would be better for someone to hear another singer represent whatever it is that they're going to be.

○ *I hope at some point your schedule lines up with all your other projects where you get the chance to do a Broadway production like that.*

Oh, I hope so. I really do. Absolutely. And you know, I've spoken with my manager. I told him that if and when I want to really be serious about, we need to dive in with both feet. He told me we'd make the right calls and get in touch with the right people. I mean Jordan is in the band and his wife is a big part of theater. I'd probably just have to say, "Danielle, I'm ready. Let's go," and she'd make something happen.

○ *Okay, well I'll keep my fingers crossed on that. And you already answered my last question. I was going to ask what's next for you. But it sounds like you've got another solo project with matt and then another DT album. So, it sounds like you've got your next few years figured out. Are there any other projects percolating that you can talk about, or is that going to be what you're doing for the next two or three years?*

Well, I already sang on The Historian, on the new Arjen Lucassen ablum that will be coming out soon. And it is another conceptual album on his part. I think he's phenomenally talented, and he's such a great person. And he got several other amazing singers on the project. So that is something that I did and that is coming out.

Really my main focus right now is obviously the touring with Dream Theater. And then to really get the ball rolling on the next solo album, because I'd like to be recording those tracks by late spring if possible.

JOHN MYUNG

—O—

PETER ORULLIAN

○ *What aspect of* The Astonishing *are you most proud of?*

Just getting through the challenge of taking in all the music written by Jordan and John P and then being in recording form, the recording process was a definite challenge.

○ *Which of the characters stories moves you the most?*

The most moving part of the story is not any one particular character, but more the concept in how music can bring people together.

○ *Is there a particular song that you gravitate to? And has that changed over time?*

No, for me I see it as one grand song with many movements.

○ *Which character do you most identify with?*

The real thing I identify with is again the positive message in the story, not any one particular character.

○ *What was the most challenging aspect of writing* The Astonishing*?*

John P wrote *the Astonishing* so the challenge for me was more of interpreting what John and Jordan wanted to do on this album.

○ *What was the most gratifying aspect of writing* The Astonishing*?*

It wasn't so much the writing since that was Jordan and John, for me it was more of getting an understanding of what was going on musically which became clearer as the drums tracks were being recorded, it was a gratifying experience once all the bass was recorded.

○ *Is there a specific performance of* The Astonishing *that was particularly memorable? Where and Why?*

The show at Radio City Music Hall in New York City was a memorable night, a very fitting place for the show. The venue setting was important and played a role in the overall delivery of this album.

○ *Is the experience of telling a story throughout a full night concert any more satisfying than other types of shows? Or maybe just how is it different?*

It's all relative for me. It took the same amount of time and energy that is normally allotted for a DT show. As long as everyone had a great night that is what lends itself to it being a great experience.

○ *What advice would you have for aspiring songwriters?*

Keep an open mind to life and live. It is a process of taking what you've gathered and making it present day.

○ *How much does practice play a part in a musician's proficiency vs. raw talent?*

Practice is a big part. It's the experience with an instrument that is ultimately needed. No real substitute for that.

○ *Is there anything you'd do differently relative to* The Astonishing, *if you were to do it again?*

I think there is always something, if we had all the time in the world to do so, but there is a practical side to it all.

○ *Where do you look for inspiration as a musician?*

I look for energy, that feeling that tells me this is good so record it now before it's lost. Inspiration for me is something that happens while I'm doing more so than thinking. Another time it happens is when I first pickup the instrument at the start of a new day.

○ *What other forms of art do you enjoy? Engage in?*

Music takes most of my time. It's where my focus is. It would be cool to have time put aside to take in great art in places like Vatican City, Maybe take some philosophy and art courses if I had the extra time.

○ *Over the course of your career, are there any technological breakthroughs that were pivotal or groundbreaking that you think really shaped your playing or the music you can create?*

Computer technology has played a big role in the way we can create and record music as a band. This album is a good example of that.

○ *What's your favorite musical?*
The Wall by Pink Floyd.

○ *What's your favorite music-related movie?*
The Song Remains the Same by Led Zeppelin

○ *Which musicians have been most influential in your development?*
For me it's more of what a particular band did musically: Rush, Yes, and Iron Maiden started it all for me. They gave me the bug for music. It's why I picked up a bass guitar.

○ *What's the most challenging song on* The Astonishing *to play? Why?*

The whole piece is a challenge, everything from the heavy unison riffing to the most delicate and subtle of parts. It all requires concentration and feel.

○ *When you're not playing in Dream Theater, where do your musical preferences lie? In terms of composition?*

I record music with The Jelly Jam. I love working with Ty Tabor and Rod Morgenstein. They are part of my extended musical family.

○ *How do you balance your interest and adoption of technology with your very real ability to infuse your playing with human expression?*

Technology is just a tool, just like my bass guitar is a tool. It's about the experience you accumulate with an instrument and the music one translates to that instrument.

○ *Of all the music you've composed, are there any standouts which make you particularly proud? Or that you just connect with more than others?*

Every album means something different to me. They represent different periods in my life. Each album is its own unique time stamp.

○ *What your favorite concert you've ever been to?*

It's probably the last Rush concert I went to, which was Rush on their Time Machine Tour.

○ *Three albums on a desert island, which ones do you take?*
Rush "Fly by Night"
The Beatles "White Album"
Massive Attack "100th Window"

○ *Favorite Christmas carol?*
"O Come All Ye Faithful" done by Sarah McLachlan.

○ *What's next for you outside your DT work?*

I'd like to get some quality time spent at home, play some golf, and work on new musical ideas.

ᛗIᛕE ᛗᚨᚾᏀINI

PETER ORULLIAN

◎ *What aspect of* The Astonishing *are you most proud of?*

I think I'm most proud of being able to improvise the recording of the drums as I had no idea what the intended result of the songs was to be other than basic (guitar and piano only) outlines that John and Jordan made. I had no idea what vocals, beats or anything else should or would be. But maybe I'm not so much proud as relieved that so much of what I improvised actually worked out and that John was pleased with my work, knowing that my understanding of it was minimal.

◎ *Is there a particular song that you gravitate to?*

The song I gravitate to is "The Walking Shadow" because it is a "metal" sounding track, and I got to use some of my higher level skills for the drumming in that song. I gravitate to what is fun for me to play.

◎ *Is there a specific performance of* The Astonishing *that was particularly memorable? If so, where and why?*

I cannot think of one that was different enough from another as my main focus is quite literally short-sighted. Live, I have to keep time perfectly to video time code, and it is a huge responsibility with a lot of pressure. So I was deeply focused on counting beats, bar numbers, and time signatures while looking at what I was hitting most of the time and trying not to make one mistake in three hours, or the show would have seized and shut down in its tracks. Honestly, I don't remember much past my 8 inch tom-tom.

○ *Is the experience of telling a story throughout a full night concert any more satisfying than other types of shows?*

Not for me, no, as I am not telling the story so to speak, but playing the parts that are a piece of the overall presentation. I just want both the audience and myself to like what I am playing in any show. We are first and foremost a band that people come to see perform. They come because they want to watch us play, so that is my primary job and interest. If what is being said is absorbed differently by the audience, then I'm happy as long as they're happy.

○ *If not more satisfying, is there any way in which presenting a story through music is different?*

For me it really isn't different in that each show becomes one giant song for me anyway. My concern is creating the rhythmic foundation so that the other band members can place their notes on mine. That's my job.

○ *Did you select specific patterns or approach for particular characters?*

By default, no, as I was not asked to be part of the creation, development, or art work for any characters. I truly believe that my sense of humor is so outlandish and wild, that I may have corrupted what John wanted anyway. I can't imagine the names I would've come up with, or the wild looks.

○ *What advice would you have for aspiring songwriters?*

That depends on the job one has to do for sure. If you're hired, do what you're asked. If it is for joy and personal fun, then write music that you like to listen to and play.

○ *How much does practice play a part in a musician's proficiency vs. raw talent?*

As talent is really just a seed, practice plays THE role in making the talent become real. More practice hones the talent and the playing becomes ever more proficient.

○ *Is there anything you'd do differently relative to* **The Astonishing,** *if you were to do it again?*

There are so many variables that make up a "situation" where one small thing can alter or change some of, or everything else. I'd have to know what my role was first in that situation and at what time in order to even think of the choices I'd have, and what I'd do differently. If my role was the same, there's nothing I could do differently anyway but just improvise drum parts, which means that they would be different here and there.

○ *Where do you look for inspiration as a musician?*

I look to being grateful for my gifts as a musician, number one. I didn't choose being born, nor from who or when, so I feel kind of in debt for how blessed I am. My inspiration is really about showing up to my maker having done something productive with the gifts I was given.

○ *What other forms of art do you enjoy? Engage in?*

Every now and then, I browse through various artists pages on social media, but I am not an art buff with traditional art. I like Dali-esque, digitally made pictures. I honestly look at Creation as the best art. The universe and even simple trees blow my mind because I know how no creature of the Earth could create that and how the Golden Ratio is inherent in nature and see that as art. Another kind of made up art I like is how TV shows interpret what deep space looks like, or how they try to depict what happened in nature without really having anything but fragments of the truth. After all, we have to remember those science shows are using digitally made interpretations of what they think, or want something to look like. The digital technology is just unbelievably striking and fun to view.

◎ *Over the course of your career, are there any technological breakthroughs that were pivotal or groundbreaking that you think really shaped your playing or the music you can create?*

The main technological breakthrough for me was the record player than could slow down an LP record to 16 speed. That shaped almost everything I think of, like, play and want to play because it changed the meanings of "truth" and "perception" to me. In other words, hearing parts slowed down showed me the truth of what was being played such that my perception, or perception in general, has become a scary thing that may have nothing to do with the real, only one truth of anything. Not interpretation and not perception, but one truth: where do the notes fall, at what velocity are they played and what is the tone of each hit.

◎ *What's your favorite musical?*

I don't have a favorite although I do like a few songs from Jesus Christ Superstar and would therefore have to rate that at the top. They aren't my style as the music is too light for my taste to enjoy them on that level, but I'll attend them if a family member or friend is performing in them. I really enjoy seeing them perform doing what I could not possibly do ever!

◎ *What's your favorite music-related movie?*

The Song Remains the Same by Led Zeppelin is my favorite. I love when John Paul Jones says, "We're going on tuuuahh." I use that line every time I leave my house. I love the English accent!

◎ *Which musicians have been most influential in your development?*

The most influential musicians in my development were all drummers. From age 2 to 20, I learned all I could from the catalogs of: Ringo Starr, Bobby Colomby, Danny Seraphine, Buddy Rich, John Bonham, Neil Peart, and Terry Bozzio. There are now at least 100 other drummers that influence my constant development that are all special and all do 'their' thing better than I ever could. That inspires me and I love supporting fellow drummers. There are also musicians like Itzhak Perlman and a long list of guitarists/soloists that have made me think differently in how I set up my drums to accompany their parts when I play. In other words, I need my melodic tom toms to be staggered in an Apex shape rather than descending pitches from right to left, or left to right like a traditional drum set is limited to. The apex shape from small to large diameters allows me to play in ascending or descending pitch order without crossing my arms. I had never seen or heard if this before it came to mind to try it.

◎ *What's the most challenging song on* The Astonishing *to play and why?*

I suppose you could pick any of the slower, more dynamically quiet and spacious songs as being the most difficult to play because I really had no idea what their final content would be with regard to vocals, solos and many other instruments. I don't inherently play slowly and spacious with lighter beats when I sit down to express myself on drums. I have to really try to just do a job in hitting things to form a kind of rhythmic grid for the other players. I had to do that in school band. I tried really hard to do it well on *The Astonishing*. It was a challenge in a big way. In the end, the challenge was playing the "right thing." That's tough when I had no idea what the music was beyond scratch guitar and piano demos.

◎ *When you're not playing in Dream Theater, where do your musical preferences lie? In terms of composition?*

My preferences lie in an energetic and repetitive, short song oriented environment. I compose heavy rock/metal riffs in a loop oriented environment too. For example, I'll base my songs on an initial 2 to 4 bar riff, or by constructing an original loop made of samples of some kind. Something different or just energetic has to keep my interest. It could be a type of riff I haven't heard before, or a cool use of parts of my drums, or just something that makes me want to smash drums or play wild geometric shapes with my patterns.

◎ *How do you balance your interest and adoption of technology with your very real ability to infuse your playing with human expression?*

Technology is most valuable in terms of saving a lot of time. It helps me compose drum parts by not having to "know" a whole song. It also allows me to express myself on instruments that I have not practiced playing.

◎ *Of all the music you've composed, are there any standouts which make you particularly proud? Or that you just connect with more than others?*

I don't as of yet have any stand out compositions.

◎ *What was your favorite concert you've ever been to?*

My favorite concert was the most meaningful one, which was also my first. It was Rush on their Hemispheres tour.

◎ *Three albums on a desert island, which ones do you take?*

In order of appearance in my life:

Led Zeppelin IV

Rush: A Farewell to Kings.

Black Sabbath: The Mob Rules

◎ *Favorite Christmas carol?*

My favorite Christmas carol is Silent Night.

◎ *What's next for you outside your DT work?*

I'm not sure if touring with John Petrucci on the G3 tour qualifies as "outside" Dream Theater work, but after the Images, Words and More tour, that is what is next at this point. My working on my solo album has been happening and continues to. I am trying to secure a singer, then I'll be able to finish it.

SONG LYRICS

FROM DREAM THEATER'S
THE ASTONISHING

FADE IN:

EXT. NEW MAINELAND (ABOVE EMPEROR'S PALACE) - DAY

NOMACS
Instrumental

DYSTOPIAN OVERTURE

Instrumental

THE GIFT OF MUSIC

EXT. RAVENSKILL TOWN SQUARE - DAY

NARRATOR
Far in the distant future
Beyond the pages of our time
Cold-blooded wicked tyrants
Threaten the freedom of mankind

Corruption, lust and greed
Define the new nobility
Changing the course of history

Across the vast North Empire
Most people struggle to survive
Living a meek existence
While their secluded leader thrives

ARHYS
We are living day to day
Forced to bear the lion's share
People just don't have the time for music anymore
And no one seems to care

My friends I've seen the chosen one
Our quest for freedom has begun
He will be the answer to our prayers

There walks a God among us
Who's seen the writing on the wall
He is the revolution
He'll be the one to save us all

My brother Gabriel is all the hope we need
Shining like a beacon in the night
Shepherd of Ravenskill

A reason to believe

Music is the gift he brings
The songbird stops to listen when he sings

THE ANSWER

EXT. RAVENSKILL PARK - DAY

GABRIEL
I don't pretend to have the answer
Never said I held the key
But somehow they see a light inside of me
Am I not the man who I was meant to be?

As the people gather round me
I never felt so all alone
Is this the chance to be someone?
My moment in the sun
Why am I afraid of facing the unknown?

They are finding faith in me and they believe I'm the one to set
them free

A BETTER LIFE

INT. RAVENSKILL REBEL COMMAND - NIGHT

<u>ARHYS</u>
As fearless leader of the Ravenskill militia
The blood of warriors
Flows throughout my veins

My brother's gift remains my secret ammunition
It is our hope, our pride
A catalyst for change

Still the fires of revolution burn within my eyes
On this perilous road to freedom
He's our one and only guide

For many years I've seen our people starve and suffer
How many more will die
Before we stand and fight

They ask me Arhys,
"Could things be any tougher?"
The answer's no surprise,

"Yes, you bet your life!"

Now the fires of revolution won't burn for evermore
I see liberty in our future
And it's one worth fighting for

We all long for a better life
Like a dream that can't be denied
This is the moment
Now is the time
Freedom if we live or if we die

I shall give him a better life
I swore this vow to my dying wife
Sure she would not survive

Peacefully
She slipped away
The meaning in my life
Was born that day

And so I found the strength to carry on with this crusade
It is my fate

Evangeline
You lived a life of misery and pain
Evangeline
I'll never let your memory die in vain

Evangeline
My heavy heart still bleeds
I dedicate my life to set him free
And I will carry on to plant the seeds
I promise in the name of our new son
This battle won't be over until it's won

LORD NAFARYUS

INT. EMPEROR'S PALACE - NIGHT

NARRATOR
How the rumors are spreading like vines
Of a man who has been glorified
News finds its way
To The Empire one day
Where the envious ruler resides

NAFARYUS

THE ASTONISHING

Should I fall for the stories I hear?
Is he really a threat I should fear?
Such a foolish young man
Doesn't seem to understand
So let me be perfectly clear

He may have them inspired
Eating out of his hand
But he'll never be ruler of this land

For myself I must see
What the hype is about
I admit I'm intrigued

I've heard the whispering of revolution
I know the aim of your plan
You think insurgency is your solution
And put your faith in one man

NARRATOR
His decision is made
So his journey begins
Off to the edge of the realm
To meet the savior

In the coming days
They'll announce his grace
And he'll ask to be amazed

As a symbol of power and might
It will make for a breathtaking sight
In a massive display
With his family and guards by his side

NAFARYUS
Arabelle who means the world to me
Our loyal son, my heir, your future king

And Faythe I treasure more than all the diamonds in my crown
It isn't hard to see
I couldn't be more proud

Into the far off reaches of the land
To witness this great spectacle first hand
Is Gabriel the God he claims to be?
I guess we'll see
Yes we shall see

A SAVIOR IN THE SQUARE

EXT. RAVENSKILL TOWN SQUARE - DAY

NAFARYUS
We have come to hear him sing
To see this gift your savior brings

NARRATOR
A crowd has grown
And all are mesmerized
But silence quickly falls
As Lord Nafaryus arrives

NAFARYUS
Please don't stop on my account
Show us what we've heard so much about

ARHYS
In peace
We gather here today

DARYUS
Don't make him ask again
Do as my father says

THE **ASTONISHING**

GABRIEL
Brother, worry not today
I will share my music
And they will soon be on their way
They only know the noise machines
So I'll treat them all to sonic ecstasy

Never in my dreams could I deserve
To ever see a vision quite like her
Then unexpectedly
I'm taken by surprise
An angel just appeared before my eyes

WHEN YOUR TIME HAS COME

EXT. RAVENSKILL TOWN SQUARE - DAY

GABRIEL
When your time has come
And you're looking toward the light
All that really matters
Is what you leave behind

So let your heart be free
Keep your spirit burning bright
Set down the stones you carry
Take the weight off your mind

When you're facing the path that divides
Know that I will be there by your side
Find your strength in the sound of my voice
And you'll know
Which choice is right

In this fleeting life
We can sometimes lose our way

But night is always darkest
Just before the new day

When you're facing the path that divides
Know that I will be there by your side
Find your strength in the sound of my voice
And you'll know
Which choice is right

FAYTHE

This very moment
Was always meant to be
I never noticed
But all at once I see

On the worst of days when I felt most alone
With no one to share the secret that I hide
I grew numb to all the emptiness inside
But now I've found my home

ACT OF FAYTHE

EXT. RAVENSKILL TOWN SQUARE - DAY

FAYTHE

I never knew they spent their days in rags
While I enjoy the life they'll never have
Yet deep within their eyes
Hope still survives
And they don't seem to think this world's so bad

Even as they gather in the square
They know a better life exists out there
With unity and pride
Faith stays alive

ᴛʜᴇ ASTONISHING

How can I pretend that I don't care?

I have always felt alone
Living like a stranger inside of my own home
Maybe now's the time to greet the winds of change
Could my destiny
Be right in front of me?

As a child behind the palace walls
Often times I'd search its secret halls
And hoping I would find
A treasure cast aside
I came upon the greatest gift of all

My music player
My private paradise
My music player
A refuge I must hide

Been lost at sea forever
Adrift and far away
Now finally for the first time
I know I found my way

THREE DAYS

EXT. RAVENSKILL TOWN SQUARE - DAY

NAFARYUS
The admiration
The applause and the cheers
I am impressed
You've brought us all to tears

To think I didn't notice
The way you looked at her

Now step down from your throne
And let me bring you back to earth

Need I remind you?
I am the ruler here
Don't overlook that fact

Swearing allegiance
To anyone but me
No, I won't put up with that

Hide and protect him
Send him away
I'll never play this game

Stand by your savior
One thing remains
I'll find him just the same

IMPERIAL GUARDS
Brace yourself
Bow down to Nafaryus

Pray for help
Kneel before Nafaryus

NAFARYUS
He'll surrender on his own
If not, there'll be hell to pay
I'll tear down this city stone by stone
You only have three days

Send home the rebels
Call off the fight
In no uncertain terms

Should you refuse me
Fear for your lives

THE ASTONISHING

Ravenskill shall burn

<u>IMPERIAL GUARDS</u>
Brace yourself
Bow down to Nafaryus

Pray for help
Kneel before Nafaryus

<u>NARRATOR</u>
With this frightening decree
Nafaryus departs
They're left to weigh the gravity
Of his threatening remarks

Judgment day will soon arrive
In only three days time
Will Gabriel get out of this alive?
This remains the question on their minds

THE HOVERING SOJOURN

EXT. RAVENSKILL - DAY

<u>NOMACS</u>
Instrumental

BROTHER, CAN YOU HEAR ME?

EXT. RAVENSKILL REBEL COMMAND - DAY

<u>ARHYS & REBEL MILITIA</u>
Brother can you hear me?
Your life is in my hands
I will not surrender

Never yield to his demands
If we stand together
We will never fall
Brother we're the answer to your call

Brother can you hear me?
You must not be afraid
I will march beside you
Have no fear
Be strong
Be brave
We sing the song of freedom
Our voices will resound
Brother we will never let you down

GABRIEL

On the road to revolution
We're bound to make mistakes
There's a price that we must pay
For every choice we make

Freedom is a reason
To stand up or give in
But someone has to lose
And someone has to win

Brother can you hear me?
I am not afraid
I will not forsake you
I'll be strong and I'll be brave
I sing the song of freedom
My courage knows no bounds
Brother now I stand on solid ground
Brother I will never let you down
Never let you down

A LIFE LEFT BEHIND

INT. EMPEROR'S PALACE - NIGHT

FAYTHE
I never knew
Someone was out there
A long way from nowhere
Who could open my eyes?

All of this time
While I was sleeping
The world changed around me
Now I've never felt more alive

I'm waking up
From a life left behind
To see what lies ahead
I'm waking up

ARABELLE
Fate found a way
To bring them together
Once and forever
And won't let them go

Nothing I say
Can keep her from leaving
Her life has new meaning
I lost her a long time ago

FAYTHE
I'm waking up
From a life left behind
To see what lies ahead
I'm waking up

I'm waking up
Now that yesterday's gone
Won't close my eyes again
I'm waking up

I'll plan to return well disguised
Make sure that I'm not recognized
Tomorrow a new sun will rise

And somehow I'll find you

Nothing will stand in my way
Soon I will see you again

I'm waking up
From a life left behind
To see what lies ahead
I'm waking up

I'm waking up
Now that yesterday's gone
I will never look back
I'm waking up

ARABELLE

You'll be her shadow as she moves my son
But she can never know you're there
She is alone and rebel guards are everywhere

DARYUS

I'll keep her safe from all danger
Won't let her out of my sight

Did I fail to mention my honest intentions?
This is the chance I deserve
Heed my words justice will be served

THE ASTONISHING

RAVENSKILL

EXT. RAVENSKILL - DAY

NARRATOR
Morning breaks beyond the night
And she's a world away
Through crowded streets
This quiet hooded stranger makes her way

FAYTHE
Please, excuse me
Sir can you help me?
Where can I find this man?

TOWNSPERSON
Sorry, can't speak
Someone is waiting

FAYTHE
Yes, I understand

NARRATOR
As her will
Starts to fade
And all but disappears

Like a ghost
Suddenly a boy is standing there
And all is clear

FAYTHE
I'm your friend
Trust me don't be scared
I am looking for your father and I promise
I can help
Now take my hand

SONG LYRICS

We haven't time to spare

NARRATOR
Hopeful and innocent
Sensing no danger
He sees humanity
Behind the stranger's eyes

Her true identity
Will be revealed when she sheds her disguise

EXT. REBEL TRAINING CAMP - DAY

FAYTHE
My intentions are faithful
There's a chance we can still end this game
I'd be forever grateful
To see him once again

ARHYS
You dare to stand
Before my eyes
You're one of them
Why would I trust you?

FAYTHE
It's not like that
I can't go back
Hope fades away
With each passing second

Lost in this moment
Is where I want to stay
This can't be broken
We need to find a way
Gabriel

I would wait a lifetime

Just to see your face
But all we have is one more day

<u>GABRIEL</u>

I remember your father was moved by my song
I know when he's sees we're united that he'll understand
We will walk this road together
We will face this hand in hand
With music and love on our side we can't lose this fight
Tomorrow our dream comes alive

CHOSEN

INT. GABRIEL'S HIDEOUT - NIGHT

<u>GABRIEL</u>

Her words ring true
Her message clear
How can he hear
Through all the noise and dissonance?

I've seen a sign
That he can change
If given just a chance

Against all hope
We found a way
And it is all because she trusts in me

Why have a gift
You can't embrace
When all you need is faith

And there's a reason now I see
The reason I've been chosen
She sees the light inside of me

A reason to believe

But I can't climb this mountain without you
No I can't face this on my own
With you by my side we will open his eyes
And the truth will deliver us home

And there's a reason now I see
The path that he has chosen
He fears the light inside of me

In the absence of song
He's forgotten right from wrong
Our voices will release him
He's refused to listen far too long

I'm convinced beyond a doubt
There can be no other way
He just has to hear me out
There's so much I need to say

But I can't climb this mountain without you
No I can't face this on my own
With you by my side we will open his eyes
And the truth will deliver us home

A TEMPTING OFFER

EXT. RAVENSKILL - NIGHT

<u>DARYUS</u>
Trustful boy
Unaware who's watching
Open the door
I am right behind you

INT. HOME OF ARHYS AND X - NIGHT

DARYUS
Don't resist me child
There's no use in fighting
We'll be here a while
Do you recognize me?

Look into my eyes
I'm the face of freedom
When Daddy does arrive
He's in for a surprise

ARHYS
How dare you step inside my home!

DARYUS
His life is in my hands

ARHYS
You monster leave my son alone!

DARYUS
You do know who I am
Your love for him is strong

ARHYS
He's just a boy
He's done no wrong
This fight's not his to lose
I have everything you want

DARYUS
Your next decision
Will decide his fate
So listen to the words I have to say

Give up the chosen one

And you will guarantee your son
Lives the life you never had

Wealth and prosperity
Beyond what you have ever seen
And best of all Xander will be free

He'll never want again
It's such an easy choice
Just think about your son

And I won't have to stand
In Faythe's dark shadow anymore
I am through with being pushed aside
Tired of fighting for my father's pride

Take the evening to decide

DIGITAL DISCORD

EXT. NEW MAINELAND (ABOVE EMPEROR'S PALACE) - NIGHT

<u>NOMACS</u>
Instrumental

THE X ASPECT

INT. HOME OF ARHYS AND X - NIGHT

<u>ARHYS</u>
Betray my blood
To save my son
A hopeless choice to make

But who am I

If not the one
Who's meant to keep him safe?

Is trust and loyalty still justified
If I deny him of a better life?

Gabriel
Has always been
The strength I call upon

But nothing breaks
A father's will
To do what must be done

Should I turn my back on him?
Abandon all our plans for revolution?
Will hope and freedom die by morning light?

Evangeline
I swore to you
To love and guide our son

Destiny
Has shown his face
And now the time has come

Desperation blinds me
And through these bloodstained eyes I see the light
A better life is worth this sacrifice

A NEW BEGINNING

INT. EMPEROR'S PALACE - DAY

FAYTHE
Father I implore you
Don't believe a word

He is not the enemy
That is just absurd

You may see his talent
As some kind of threat
But I knew we were meant to be
From the day we met

Give us both a chance
For a new beginning
Nothing would mean more to me

He is just a man
Can't you show him mercy?
Sympathy and strength go hand in hand

NAFARYUS
This man's a fraud and a hoax
He'll only shatter your hopes
Saddest of all is to watch how you fall
For this person who you hardly know

FAYTHE
Ignorant and stubborn
You have no respect
Not just for your flesh and blood
But all who you protect

Listen without judgment
Keep an open mind
If you can not see the truth
You're the one who's blind

We don't stand a chance
That is his opinion
Mother can you talk to him?

ARABELLE

Try to understand
How they must be feeling
Misery's to know what might have been

NAFARYUS
Why would I ever concede
To listen to this fool? How can you be so naive?
You must be living in a world of make believe
Do you really think this charlatan is who he claims to be?

ARABELLE
Not long ago there was a time and place
You too possessed the same desires as Faythe

You knew how it felt to feel invisible
Music calmed your soul just like a drug
Remember Bug?

FAYTHE
Father is it true
Bug was always you?
Finally I can reveal
How music makes me feel

Now you understand
Why I was hiding
This changes everything

NAFARYUS
I will grant the chance
For a new beginning
In the end the final word rests with me

THE ROAD TO REVOLUTION

INT. GABRIEL'S HIDEOUT - DAY

SONG LYRICS

FAYTHE
He only sees what he desires to see
It took a while but finally he agreed
Though everything may not turn out as planned
If love's a risk
It's worth the chance

GABRIEL
I know where there is faith there's always hope
We'll meet beneath the stars at Heaven's Cove
Where ghosts of yesterday
Once filled the lighted stage
Taking our first step down a new road

EXT. RAVENSKILL - DAY

DARYUS
Arhys time is running out
What will your decision be?
If you still have any doubt
Think about Evangeline

INT. HOME OF ARHYS AND X - DAY

ARHYS
On the road to revolution
Our salvation's never free
There's a price for liberation when you stand for your beliefs

When the man in the mirror
Takes a long hard look at me
Will the person staring back, be the man I want to be?

INT. EMPEROR'S PALACE - DAY

NAFARYUS
Change my mind?
A waste of time

For soon he will be mine

<u>ENSEMBLE</u>
Open eyes
Help me see which choice is right

○

ACT 2
2285 ENTR'ACTE

Instrumental

MOMENT OF BETRAYAL

INT. HOME OF ARHYS AND X - DAY

<u>GABRIEL</u>
Brace yourself my brother
I have breaking news
The Noise Machines lie still tonight
There's no time to lose

No more threats of bloodshed
No more pain and fear
Ravenskill will brave the storm
Our victory is near

You are acting very strange
Nervous and on edge
I will be a voice for change
Brother give me strength

ARHYS

Burning rose
Secrets sold
Moment of betrayal

Kiss of death
Blood revenge
Moment of betrayal

I have sworn to live and die
By the warrior's code
Never leave a man behind
May God redeem my soul

I will give you what you need
My brother for my son
Guilt and shame will burden me
Until my days are done

Meet me tonight where the stars touch the sky
He'll be alone there with nowhere to hide

Burning rose
Secrets sold
Moment of betrayal

Kiss of death
Blood revenge
Moment of betrayal

He will be defenseless
I'll look on
Say I put up a fight
There will be no witness
They will call you a hero tonight

Burning rose
Secrets sold

THE ASTONISHING

Moment of betrayal

Kiss of death
Blood revenge
Moment of betrayal

Threats and Lies
Changing sides
Moment of betrayal

Risking all
Saviors fall
Moment of betrayal

HEAVEN'S COVE

EXT. HEAVEN'S COVE AMPHITHEATER - NIGHT

NARRATOR
Under the glow of the midnight moon
Where the stars touch the sky
Stand the long forgotten remains of a time gone by

Heaven's Cove was a wondrous site
Once a beautiful place
Now an empty shell like a memory that time erased

As the pivotal moment draws closer
Every shadow and whisper ignite
Music will rise like a phoenix from the ashes on this night

BEGIN AGAIN

INT. EMPEROR'S PALACE - DAY

SONG LYRICS

FAYTHE
I gave up hope
Was dead inside
Stayed lost within a world I chose to hide

Then I found my faith in him
And now I can
Begin again

I once believed
Our fate was sealed
But now at last the truth has been revealed

In an instant life could change
And now and then
Begin again

I know that I am meant for something more
That life beyond these walls
Has greater things in store

When I heard his voice I realized
I'd never be the same
Instantly I knew my life had changed

I dream of peace
Above all else
To share a world where we could be ourselves

We must learn to rise above the past
Before we can at last
Begin again

THE PATH THAT DIVIDES

EXT. HEAVEN'S COVE AMPHITHEATER - NIGHT

THE ASTONISHING

NARRATOR
The evening stars shine brightly
Over Heaven's Cove
As night descends in silence
The fated scene unfolds
Consumed with trepidation
Arhys hears his brother's voice

GABRIEL'S VOICE
As you're facing the path that divides
I will always be here by your side

ARHYS
I feel my pulse begin to race
Beads of sweat drip down my face
I have made a grave mistake
What have I done?
My blood for my son?

It's not too late
I won't betray him

DARYUS
I knew the day had come
And you could be tempted
To give up the chosen one
And finally end this
Do anything for your son
A terminal weakness
But now you're as good as done

ARHYS
I didn't have a choice
And I was defenseless
I didn't believe his voice
And fighting was senseless
But now I can see the truth

I've come to my senses
I shouldn't have trusted you

NARRATOR

Arhys was never aware
His son had followed him there
Confused and deathly afraid
X watched his hero be brave

ARHYS

On the path that divides
You were there by my side
There will be no betrayal tonight

I found courage and strength
In the words you once you sang
Tore the truth from the lies
On the path that divides

DARYUS

You dare defy your prince?
Well you just threw your life away
Along with Xander's dreams
You chose the wrong man to betray

NARRATOR

Two hungry warriors
Clash in the shadows of the night
But there's a cost with every fight
And Arhys' fight for hope
Cost him his very life

MACHINE CHATTER

EXT. HEAVEN'S COVE AMPHITHEATER - NIGHT

THE ASTONISHING

NOMACS
Instrumental

THE WALKING SHADOW

EXT. HEAVEN'S COVE AMPHITHEATER - NIGHT

XANDER
What have you done?
You murderer
My father's dead
Your day will come

DARYUS
Don't hold your breath
The night's still young
Confront your death

Like father, like son

Who's this I see?
Approaching me
The Chosen One

NARRATOR
Drawing closer pace by pace
The walking shadow hides its face
Never aware of the looming attack
Like stepping right into a trap

As his weapon
Finds its victim
Mortified, he's shocked to find the shadow is Faythe

MY LAST FAREWELL

EXT. HEAVEN'S COVE AMPHITHEATER - NIGHT

GABRIEL

Angels above
Have you deceived my eyes?
Be still my love
I won't leave your side

All my life
I have walked alone
Now I've found my home in you
Only I'm too late

Have I wandered into someone's nightmare?
This is more than any heart can bare

You stole my brother's life
How many more have to die
Before you will open your eyes?

Don't leave me now
Hold on for one more breath
Stay strong somehow
This can't be the end

All your life
You have walked alone
Now I am your home
So take my hand and don't let go

Crushing pain and crippling grief
Nothing like I've ever felt
God above and souls beneath
Hear my last farewell

LOSING FRYTHE

EXT. HEAVEN'S COVE AMPHITHEATER - NIGHT

THE ASTONISHING

NAFARYUS
My foolish pride
My selfish heart
Lost in the dark
Blinded by my arrogance

And now you beg for one last breath
And I'm the one to blame

There's a reason now I see
The reason you have chosen
To find the light inside of me
If only I believed

ARABELLE
Here I am
Don't be afraid
I will never let you slip away

Look my way
You must be brave
Find the strength to live for one more day

I will keep from losing Faythe
I will ask for grace
And hope will find a way

NARRATOR
Like a candle's dying flame
With forgiving eyes
She starts to drift away

NAFARYUS
Gabriel my son
I see the tide is turning
Can the chosen one
Keep her fire burning?

SONG LYRICS

I would trade my life
Just for one last moment

Use your gift I beg
May life begin again?
May life begin again?

WHISPERS ON THE WIND

EXT. HEAVEN'S COVE AMPHITHEATER - NIGHT

<u>GABRIEL</u>
If I still had something left
I'd surely use my gift
To give her one more breath
To see her smile again
And yet my gift is gone
Along with all her dreams
It vanished with a scream
My fragile voice has all but disappeared
I've nothing left to give
The words I wish I'd said
Just whispers on the wind
And now all hope is dead

HYMN OF A THOUSAND VOICES

EXT. HEAVEN'S COVE AMPHITHEATER - NIGHT

<u>NARRATOR</u>
Out of the shadows
One by one they came
To shed their light upon his moment of doubt and pain

THE ASTONISHING

A thousand voices
Rang out through the night
A symphony of mercy for their savior
Too tired to fight

And as the chorus grew
A thousand hearts beat true
Then like a glowing beacon in the dark
Hope came shining through

Amazingly the savior found his voice
And all together they rejoiced...

<u>GABRIEL AND TOWNSPEOPLE</u>
Glorious sound
Guide her tonight
Out of the darkness
Into the light

Merciful song
Set her soul free
Unbind the chains of endless sleep

Choirs on high
Grant her new life
Make me a vessel of thy boundless grace
Music has shown her the way
She lives today!

OUR NEW WORLD

EXT. RAVENSKILL - DAY

<u>GABRIEL</u>
Like your father once said
Life is not what you're given

It is how you decide to live
On the path you have chosen

So together we'll build a new world
A better world
We'll build a new world
Our new world

FAYTHE

I know you're scared and alone
But we will face this together
Through the innocence in your eyes
They will live on forever

In their memory we'll build a new world
A better world
We'll build a new world
Our new world

GABRIEL, FAYTHE AND X

We'll build a new world
A better world
We'll build a new world
Our new world

We'll build a new world
A wondrous world
We'll build a new world
A bold new world

POWER DOWN

EXT. RAVENSKILL - DAY

NOMACS

Instrumental

ASTONISHING

EXT. RAVENSKILL - DAY

ARHYS' SPIRIT
Brother can you hear me
His life is in your hands
He is just a child and still too young to understand
Show him love and courage
That freedom knows no bounds
Tell him he could never let me down

XANDER
Father
I will make you proud
Rest in peace

GABRIEL
I always had the answer
All this time I held the key
And now that I see
The reason to believe
I can be the man who I am meant to be

FAYTHE
Because of you I live again
Now I can be a voice for change
And help to build a world that's fair and true
So they can live the life they never knew

NAFARYUS
On the road to revolution
There are lessons to be learned

All the things you thought that mattered
Are lost at every turn

When the light of my existence
Was slipping through my hands
Pride and ignorance receded
To reveal a humbled man

ARABELLE
My prince, my son
You got lost along the way
In light of this new burden that you face
You are forgiven on this day

ENSEMBLE
People, can you hear us?
Peace has been restored
The silence has been broken
Music reigns for evermore
We sing a song of freedom
Together we are bound
People, we shall never hold you down
We will build our world on common ground
And we'll live once more
Eternally
In harmony
Our lives will be
Astonishing
Again

FADE OUT.

THE END

SONG-BY-SONG BREAKDOWN

FROM DREAM THEATER'S
THE ASTONISHING

BY

JOHN PETRUCCI

As part of the run-up to the release of The Astonishing, Dream Theater released information online about the story. Here we've published some of those materials which were shared by the band to give context for the story as it existed at the time, and as the album itself delivered it. As noted elsewhere, John gave Peter free reign to deepen character motivations, flesh out the world, and add new people and places to broaden and enrich the story.

ACT 1

1 - DESCENT OF THE NOMACS

In the year 2285, The NOMACS (Noise Machines) appear over the Emperor's palace on New Maineland. A small 'army' of the dronelike machines is seen with one main NOMAC hovering in the foreground scanning the city in a display of control and supremacy. NOMACS were initially conceived by people in their quest to create the world's most perfect music but instead, turned into something much more insidious. Born out of the vacuum created as a result of the suffocation of human expression along with exponential advances in technology over time, they stand as the only semblance of entertainment remaining in the world. NOMACS music is now the only music anyone knows or listens to, and the only music that still exists. The very soul of what was once real music is now lost in a digital quagmire of emotionless sonic madness.

2 - DYSTOPIAN OVERTURE

An instrumental overture that contains all of the major reoccurring musical themes used throughout the album. Themes are associated with specific story settings and character appearances. This piece sets the mood for ACT 1 and introduces us to the newly redefined landscape of the former American Northeast now known as The Great Northern Empire Of The Americas.

3 - THE GIFT OF MUSIC

Over the course of nearly three hundred years, ever dwindling natural resources coupled with the excessive abuse of presidential power and extreme government-wide corruption has lead to the return of a feudal society throughout the country.

This is not necessarily the gleaming, space-exploring future we've grown accustomed to imagine yet instead a dystopian world to come which in many ways resembles more of a time and place back in mankind's harsh history. The margin between rich and poor has widened to a point beyond recovery where ruthless dictators once again rule over vast empires. Along with their families and nobility, they now possess all of the land, wealth, power and control over whatever spoils remain on Earth.

Meanwhile, the general population lives in scattered townships across the region struggling to exist amidst a climate of extreme economic and social oppression. The resulting dichotomy between the magnificence and splendor of the big cities and the modesty and simplicity of the decaying rural villages contributes greatly to the division between classes. In this dramatically redefined landscape, what was formerly known as the Northeast region of the United States is now a new super kingdom called G.N.E.A. or The Great Northern Empire Of The Americas. It is in this new land where we find the ominous Lord Nafaryus thriving in his tyrannical role as Emperor and Head of the Realm. From the comfort of his opulent palatial residence on metropolitan New Maineland, he is able to keep a watchful eye on all that transpires throughout the Empire.

Since working class families are now consumed with the day-to-day challenges of survival, forced to bear the lion's share of taxes needed to support the Empire, any dedication, investment or interest in the arts has all but been abandoned.

People just don't have the time or the desire to participate in any of the creative forms of human expression that art, dance and especially music have to offer anymore. And, why should they? Life may closely resemble that of more ancient times in most ways, but now, the only music to be heard is electronically manufactured and performed by the NOMACS.

This brings us to the village of Ravenskill; a small, somewhat isolated town on Endless Isleland located far from the Emperor's palace and the frantic pace of metropolitan living. Ravenskill is a close knit community who's inhabitants enjoy a renewed sense of family due to the simplicity of current times, yet who struggle and toil under the harshness of life's reality under Nafaryus' rule. It is here where we find our unsuspecting hero Gabriel, increasingly being looked upon as 'The Chosen One' who will liberate the people and lead them in a victorious revolution against Lord Nafaryus and his advocates. He is seen as a shining beacon of light in this seemingly dark and hopeless situation because of a very unique and magical talent that has been neither heard nor nurtured in many, many years…the divine gift of music.

Gabriel was born and blessed with the natural ability to sing and to make music on a level that is simply… astonishing.

Mindlessly programmed to withstand the cold and passionless cacophony of the NOMACS, people are transfixed by Gabriel and transported back to a time where true art created by human beings was celebrated and consumed as the ultimate nourishment for the soul. It is mesmerizing to all who hear him perform and the sound of his voice is as cathartic to those around him as the most advanced medicines available. So much so that the spirit of hope and enlightenment has overtaken and inspired not only this small township, but also many others in the region. As word spreads of this newly discovered savior, plans for an uprising are brewing and people everywhere are talking about Gabriel's magical power.

4 – THE ANSWER

Ever so humble and not exactly viewing himself as a natural born leader, all of the attention showered upon him and the tremendous expectations placed on him have made Gabriel very uncomfortable and confused. While blessed with a captivating charm and presence, Gabriel is often puzzled by his uniqueness and largely seen by folks as a bit of an enigma. Although adored by many, he questions his purpose in life and the meaning of his gift ultimately leaving him to feel very alone and isolated. He spends most of his time by himself and is conflicted…why was he The Chosen One? This was not something he asked for but it is obviously something that was meant to happen to him. He embodies the very essence of promise and hope that the inhabitants of Ravenskill cling to and it is he whom they wholly place their belief in. They see something extraordinary in Gabriel and are depending on him to rescue them from hardship and oppression and deliver them their freedom. As he ponders his role in all of this, he yearns for meaning in his life and searches for a path to his destiny, which…he will soon find.

5 - A BETTER LIFE

It is Gabriel's older brother Arhys who is his biggest supporter. As Commander of the Ravenskill Rebel Militia, it is his strong belief in Gabriel that fuels the fires of revolution in his eyes. He sees Gabriel as a catalyst for change and the people's one and only appointed guide on the road to freedom. He is convinced it is Gabriel's destiny. Arhys also has another reason to want to be free of this life of adversity…his eight year old son Xander whom he affectionately calls 'X'. His love for Xander and longing for a better life and secure future for him is what keeps him motivated and willing to push forward with the crusade through these increasingly difficult times. As a single father he carries the memory of X's mother and his only love, Evangeline, with a heavy heart and with deep dedication.

Knowing that she would not survive the birth of their son and recounting the life of misery and misfortune she endured, he promises her on her deathbed that he will see to a better future for X and devote the rest of his life to their son's safety, prosperity and ultimately, his freedom. Arhys proceeds to further educate the townspeople of Gabriel's powers and plant the seeds for an uprising amongst them.

6 - LORD NAFARYUS

Like vines racing across the landscape, news quickly travels throughout the region and talk of Gabriel's increasing popularity and the mysterious gift he possesses eventually reaches Lord Nafaryus himself. The ruler, both intrigued as well as envious of the apparent influence Gabriel has over the people decides to pay the residents of Ravenskill a visit. Concerned, he want's to see what all the hype is about and whether or not Gabriel truly presents a threat to the Empire. He is also aware of the rumblings of a revolution beginning to surface throughout G.N.E.A. and in order to quell any foolish talk of mass rebellion, is prepared to make an example of Gabriel if necessary. Along with his exquisite wife Empress Arabelle, his loyal son Crown Prince Daryus and his daughter, the beautiful Princess Faythe whom he treasures more than life itself, they embark upon their journey to the far-off reaches of The Realm in order to witness first hand what has become known as 'Gabriel's Gift'.

Traveling across Eden's Way and over the Emperor's Bridge to Brother's Crossing, they'll ultimately arrive in Ravenskill where they will undoubtedly get to meet this mysterious savior face to face.

7 - A SAVIOR IN THE SQUARE

In Ravenskill a large crowd has assembled in the town square, as it often does, around Gabriel whom we find playing an old, beatup relic of an acoustic guitar and singing an uplifting song ironically about believing in who you are and knowing that when your time has come, you will answer the call as it is your destiny. Not only are Arhys, X and all in attendance amazed by the remarkably strange and magnificent instrument he is playing (as they are not used to music coming from anything but machines) but at the same time their souls are lifted up and wonderfully transported by his angelic voice to the point of aural ecstasy. Gabriel's divinely inspired music has a mystical way of penetrating even the most guarded individuals and transcends all generations while reawakening the dormant feelings of passion, power and self worth in anyone who hears it. It is at that moment that Nafaryus and his entourage arrive in the square, startling and alarming the townspeople. Gabriel stops singing and a thick silence falls upon the gathering.

Everyone is very aware that they are in the presence of the Emperor and the Imperial Family and the danger associated with that very scenario. Flanked by his guards, Nafaryus addresses Gabriel saying, "So, this is Gabriel The Astonishing." "Please, do not stop on my account." "Continue as you were."

Arhys responds to him, "We are gathered here in peace my Lord and want no trouble" to which Nafaryus replies, "We are only here to witness for ourselves what we have all heard so much about." "Gabriel's remarkable gift."

After an uncomfortable pause, Prince Daryus looks at Gabriel and with a threatening tone says, "Do as my father says…savior!"

Gabriel knows he has no choice and as he starts to lay his fingers on the guitar, he spots Princess Faythe standing next to the Empress and is absolutely mesmerized.

She is…astonishing.

8 - WHEN YOUR TIME HAS COME

Gabriel commences playing and starts to sing the words of a deeply moving song. At first sheepishly and then with confidence and passion he sings the lines…

When you're facing the path that divides
Know that I will be there by your side
Find your strength in the sound of my voice
And you'll know
Which choice is right

In an instant, the words strike a very deep chord within Faythe and as if awoken from a spell, the Princess' eyes lock with Gabriel's. Like a lightening bolt from the heavens and without hesitation, they immediately know that they are meant to be together and that this encounter was no accident. It is clear that somehow this moment marked the first step on the path to each other's destiny. Up until now there had only been one thing that she truly connected with which comforted her and gave her hope on the days when she felt most alone. It happened to come from a secret she'd been hiding for many years...

9 - ACT OF FAYTHE

A vision of delightfulness with a look both enchantingly provocative and innocently demure at the same time, he has never before laid eyes upon anyone quite like her and her inescapable beauty pierces his soul. Gabriel however has not quite captured the princess' attention yet as she is distracted by the scope of her surroundings and completely in awe of the number of people peacefully gathered in the square that afternoon. She is moved by the sense of togetherness and community being displayed before them, all amidst dreadful and practically unbearable living conditions. As a sheltered princess accustomed to the excesses of her palatial life, she is certainly not used to seeing any of this. Her heart immediately goes out to them and she is touched by their collective innocence and flickering sense of hope that a better life does exist somewhere out there.

Although possessing her father's tenacity and stubbornness, she is very much not aligned with his way of thinking or harsh methods of ruling. In many ways she, like Gabriel, shares the same feelings of isolation often feeling like an outsider in her own home. She is alone, shielded from the bleak world by an over protective father, and longing for a purpose. And also like Gabriel, yearning for meaning in her life and searching for the path to her own destiny.

As a young girl growing up on New Maineland, she was a very curious child and used to keep herself entertained by going on adventures throughout the palace. One day while on one of these journeys she stumbled upon the Great Hall of Artifacts buried deep within it's underground corridors. It is here that she found something remarkable; an antique digital music player very common during decades past but now deemed obsolete. It was filled with thousands of songs from all sorts of talented artists from a distant time when music was still created and performed by humans. It had a strange engraving on the back that simply said, "To BUG". She didn't know what it meant but that never mattered to her. She carried it with her wherever she went, always being careful to conceal it from those around her, especially her father. Relishing any private opportunity she could get to escape the realities of her cold and shielded imperial life, with her ear phones careful hidden beneath her hair and her hood, she'd lose herself in the beautiful sounds of long ago. Still as a young woman, there is not a day that goes by without her stealing a moment to listen to her prized secret device, the magical vessel that carries her spirit throughout the endless adventures of her imagination. Hearing Gabriel play the guitar and sing with an almost indescribable air of grace and beauty that day is the first time she ever feels such an overwhelming sense of safety and belonging outside of her private rendezvous with her music player.

18 - THREE DAYS

When the song is finished, the crowd erupts in glorious applause and even Nafaryus, notably moved by Gabriel's song is momentarily caught up in the contagious atmosphere of elation surrounding him. He is quickly brought back to reality however when he notices how Gabriel and the Princess are gazing at each other and immediately shouts out, "Enough!"

Empress Arabelle also catches the two locked in an infatuating stare and a quick glance from Faythe to her mother ensures that she knows the Empress is aware. Sensing that things are quickly about to go very wrong, Arhys has Gabriel obscured from view by his soldiers and swiftly whisked away and out of Nafaryus' sight.

Lord Nafaryus will not tolerate the adoration and allegiance of his people to anyone other than himself and his jealousy of Gabriel's power over them as well as his insecurities about the future of The Empire makes him feel the need to demonstrate his superiority. He immediately sees Gabriel as a threat to The Realm. The Emperor very smugly addresses Arhys and the townspeople saying that they can hide and protect Gabriel all they want but that he will not stoop to their level and take part of some sort of foolish cat and mouse game in order to find their 'Savior'. He ensures them that 'Gabriel The Astonishing' will come to him willingly and surrender himself in person to his highness or suffer dire consequences. Nafaryus then declares that Gabriel has three days to give himself up and guarantee the disbanding and surrender of the Rebel Militia and cease of all talk of revolution. Staring maliciously at X who is attempting to cower behind his father's back, he continues to state that if 'The Savior' refuses to comply within that time, he will return with his forces, and he will hunt Gabriel down destroying every home one by one and killing every inhabitant until he is captured. And with that terrifying decree, Lord Nafaryus and his entourage depart Ravenskill leaving the stunned villagers to process the gravity of their newfound situation. As they head back to the palace, Princess Faythe is consumed with the vision of Gabriel and their obviously magnetic connection.

Still intoxicated by his music, she is obsessed with the overwhelming notion that she must see him again.

11 - THE HOVERING SOJOURN

NOMACS Instrumental

12 - BROTHER, CAN YOU HEAR ME?

Back in Ravenskill Gabriel has gone into hiding and is being protected by Arhys' men. Commander Arhys is convinced that his civilian army combined with the bordering rebel forces in the region is strong enough to protect the town and that there should be no talk of Gabriel's surrender under any circumstances. Gabriel however is severely traumatized by all of this and is questioning the possession of his so called 'gift' now, more than ever. His surrender will clearly mark the end of any possible chance of peace and freedom for his people and will also most likely ensure his own demise. How can he abandon all that they've worked for, all that they stand for and all they have sacrificed for? On the other hand, how can he be so selfish as to make his own life worth more than all of the innocent inhabitants of his town? In the midst of all of this, he cannot shake the vision of Princess Faythe from his memory. He is completely absorbed with the thought of her and entranced by her inescapable beauty. Gabriel has come to a major crossroads in his life and knows that a turning point is imminent.

13 - A LIFE LEFT BEHIND

After returning home to the palace, Princess Faythe realizes that her desire to see Gabriel again is not waning and that she is desperate to be with him no matter what the cost. It is simply something that she can most certainly feel yet cannot explain. She knows instinctually that fate has brought them together and that they both have a higher purpose to fulfill by their union so she makes a plan to return to Ravenskill the next morning. As to not alert the rebels or alarm the locals who may recognize her and think her a threat, she decides it is best to conceal her true identity while traveling outside of the palace.

Empress Arabelle, ever in tune with the princess' intentions sees that she is planning this trip and confronts her about it.

After seeing the spark of joy and passion in her daughter's eyes as she talks about her feelings for Gabriel; eyes that have been cold and empty for so long, now ablaze with excitement and hope, she knows that the right thing to do is to let her go. She could not possibly deprive Faythe of pursuing her true love. Always the protective mother, the Empress has Prince Daryus secretly follow his sister in order to ensure her safety. Daryus willingly complies but has evil intentions of his own which he is all too eager to carry out.

14 - RAVENSKILL

Upon arriving in Ravenskill on the morning of the second day, the disguised princess asks if anyone knows where she could find Arhys knowing that no one will voluntarily offer up Gabriel's whereabouts and will certainly think of anyone asking as suspicious. Frustrated and exhausted, not really getting anywhere due to high levels of anxiety and vigilance amongst the townspeople, she eventually catches a break. She sees a young boy playing in front of a fountain and recognizes him as Arhys' son Xander. Faythe's gentle nature and sensitively alluring eyes win over the boy's trust almost instantly. She convinces him that she has a way that she can help his father as well as Gabriel if she can just speak to him. Of course, all the while her brother Daryus has been watching her from afar and is now equally equipped with the information required to set his plan in motion.

X innocently leads the princess to the military camp where Arhys is preparing the rebel forces. Faythe takes the Commander aside and very bravely reveals her true identity to him. At first he is immediately tempted to arrest her and hold her as leverage against Nafaryus but she assures him that her intentions are true and that she has a way to end the conflict and restore peace but that she will only share it with Gabriel.

Reluctantly, Arhys eventually agrees and leads her to where Gabriel is being hidden. Upon seeing each other they embrace and promise never to be separated again. First though, the conflict with Lord Nafaryus needs to be resolved before the three days expire. She tells Gabriel that she is certain she can convince her father to spare him as well as all of Ravenskill and that she has seen a gentle and forgiving side of him before that need only be reignited. Although there is not much time left, she is convinced that through their unity her father will see a way to restore peace to the land and give up his preposterous witchhunt.

The Princess's words resonate with Gabriel and he remembers how his song in the square temporarily moved Nafaryus the day before. Gabriel is convinced that the absence of art and music and the incessant drivel being spewed out by the NOMACS has caused a sort of emotional hibernation amongst Lord Nafaryus and his supporters, ultimately leading to the deadening of his soul and the lack of any compassion in his heart. If Gabriel could just meet with the Emperor and Empress, he knows that through the power of his magical gift of music, especially with their daughter by his side, he could reawaken their spirits and bring harmony back to The Realm. Nafaryus need only agree to ignore the NOMACS for a moment and just listen. Excited to share this encouraging plan with her father, she returns to the palace to speak to him and convince him to meet with Gabriel.

15 - CHOSEN

The Princess's words resonate with Gabriel and he remembers how his song in the square temporarily moved Nafaryus the day before. Gabriel is convinced that the absence of art and music and the incessant drivel being spewed out by the NOMACS has caused a sort of emotional hibernation amongst Lord Nafaryus and his supporters, ultimately leading to the deadening of his soul and the lack of any compassion in his heart. If Gabriel could just meet with the Emperor and Empress, he knows that through the power of his magical gift of music, especially with their daughter by his side, he could reawaken their spirits and bring harmony back to The Realm. Nafaryus need only agree to ignore the NOMACS for a moment and just listen. Excited to share this encouraging plan with her father, she returns to the palace to speak to him and convince him to meet with Gabriel.

16 - A TEMPTING OFFER

Meanwhile, still in Ravenskill, Prince Daryus follows Xander on his way home that evening. As X is about to enter his house, Daryus overpowers him and forces his way inside where the devious prince holds the boy hostage and waits for his father to return. Arhys eventually comes home only to find that Daryus has broken in and is now holding X's life in his hands. Recognizing his son's captor to be Prince Daryus and keeping X's safety in mind, he immediately withdraws any efforts to apprehend the prince and instead asks him what he wants. Daryus makes him an offer that will put Arhys in an extremely complicated and life altering position...If Arhys delivers Gabriel to him, Prince Daryus will in return guarantee the safety, protection and prosperity of Xander for the rest of his life. He will enjoy all of the riches The Empire has to offer, the best education and a privileged life equal to that of Nafaryus' own son. He will be in want of nothing for the rest of his life. As he sees it, the choice is easy because either way, they will capture Gabriel in the end. This way, he will be his son's hero. Why is this so important to Daryus? He has lived in the shadow of his father's outward love and adoration of Faythe his entire life. He has been unfairly pushed aside and expected to just 'be a man', 'suck it up' and relinquish any need of parental approval or praise. He could never quite measure up to the Emperor's expectations and is deeply jealous of his father's favoritism shown towards the princess. Daryus sees the successful capture of Gabriel as his opportunity to win over his father's respect and gain the admiration he deserves.

17 – DIGITAL DISCORD

NOMACS Instrumental

18 – THE X ASPECT

Daryus remains in Ravenskill for the evening and gives Arhys the rest of the night to consider his offer telling him that he expects an answer by morning or the deal is off. Obviously Arhys has a seemingly insurmountable decision to make. How can he possibly turn his back on his own brother? How can he betray the trust of his soldiers and his fellow people altogether abandoning the plans for revolution they have been working so tirelessly on for years now? Then he remembers the promise he made to Evangeline before she breathed her last breath; to see to the protection and livelihood of their son and to the dedication of his life to X's eventual freedom. After a mostly sleepless night, he concludes that he has no choice and with Xander's best interests in mind, contacts Prince Daryus agreeing to the terms of his offer. He vows to divulge the time and location to Daryus later that day, where the exchange of Gabriel's freedom for the sake of X's future will take place.

19 – A NEW BEGINNING

That morning Princess Faythe isn't having quite the same luck convincing her father to meet with Gabriel and the unwelcome news of her being in love with 'the enemy' further compounds his unwillingness to cooperate. Nafaryus finds the notion of a meeting both absurd and fruitless since by the start of the next day, his forces will be bearing down upon Ravenskill with all their wrath and fury if her boyfriend, 'The Savior' does not surrender himself as the impostor he truly is. Princess Faythe pleas with him that they only ask for a chance to be listened to without judgment and if the Emperor is not convinced upon the conclusion of Gabriel's message, then he will agree to surrender himself fully and with honor as per Nafaryus' wishes. Perceiving any negotiation as a sign of weakness however, Nafaryus shows no intention of even considering what he views to be his daughter's foolish desires. Faythe is frustrated by her father's ignorance, thick headedness and absence of compassion for the people of his Empire as well as his lack of respect for her feelings. It is then that Empress Arabelle expresses that she's seen enough of this stubbornness between the two of them and enlightens him to the fact that if he doesn't agree to this meeting, his daughter will never forgive him and that he will lose her forever.

"I remember a time when you too possessed Faythe's romantic innocence and passion for life's unexplored mysteries...BUG." says Arabelle to her husband.

It is then that Faythe realizes that the word "BUG" inscribed on the back of her music player was referring to her father and that it once belonged to him!

It had been given to him as a gift by his own father who shared the same secret affinity for music made by humans as Faythe eventually would. As a very young boy, Nafaryus was always zipping in and out of the palace halls and buzzing around his father's feet trying to get the busy Emperor's attention (hence the nickname 'BUG'). The rare times when he wasn't consumed with balancing the many affairs of The Realm, his father would privately submit to the therapeutic bliss of his own secretly kept digital music player, often times inviting young Nafaryus to indulge in these undisclosed soul-soothing escapes. His gift of the music player to his son was his way of letting

Nafaryus know that they would always have that special connection no matter how complicated life may eventually get. As time passed however, Nafaryus grew into adulthood and his father the Emperor grew old and tired. The allure of the imminent passing of the crown to the ambitious prince and all of the power and control associated with it far out-shadowed the indulgences of some silly music player. In the course of time his father fell ill, eventually passing away and with the rise of the NOMACS drowning out his memory, the music player was discarded by the newly crowned Emperor Nafaryus and ultimately forgotten. Until…now.

For the first time Princess Faythe reveals the secret music player she'd been both relishing and concealing almost her entire life to the Emperor saying, "See father, you also once enjoyed the beauty of real music and not just the garbage of those dreadful NOMACS."

"Where did you get that child?" Shouts Nafaryus to which Faythe responds, "Never mind that." "I am not a child anymore father, I am a woman who doesn't want to be told what to do or who I can or cannot see anymore!" "Now please reach inside your soul and show me that you are not just the heartless dictator you have come to be known as."

Not able to contest the wisdom of neither his wife nor his daughter, Nafaryus concedes, knowing that if he persists, he risks losing the princess forever and so agrees to the meeting.

If Gabriel truly is 'The Chosen One' and can sway him as his beloved daughter says he can, then he will cease all plans of attack on Ravenskill and award him his freedom. If not, then he will accept Gabriel's surrender as promised, at which point it will be sure that she will never see him again.

28 – THE ROAD TO REVOLUTION

Elated, Princess Faythe immediately shares the news with Gabriel who is still in hiding back at Ravenskill. He tells her that he knows of the perfect neutral location for this summit and that the only way this is ensured to work is if the meeting takes place that evening, under the dance of the stars and the glow of the midnight moon at a once magnificent but since abandoned amphitheater on the edge of town called Heaven's Cove. It is against the dramatic backdrop of a place where music once poured from the lighted stage where Gabriel will best be able to showcase his miraculous musical gift and is sure that once enlightened, there is no way the Emperor will be able to follow through with his plans. As a symbolic gesture of peace Faythe agrees to sing together along with Gabriel so that when her father hears the purity and innocence of love and unity in their combined voices, the fate of their future will be sealed. Aware there is always the chance that the outcome of tonight's events may not turn out as they both desire, Gabriel and Faythe decide it best to meet at Heaven's Cove ahead of time in order to relish what may possibly be their final moments alone together and to rehearse for their performance that evening. Faythe shares the location with her father and later that day Nafaryus and Arabelle begin to make their way to the amphitheater at Heaven's Cove on Endless Isleland, the Emperor outwardly pessimistic and with guards in tow prepared for what he predicts will be Gabriel's surrender.

ACT 2

1 - 2285 ENTR'ACTE

An instrumental which recaps the musical themes used thus far.

It is meant to reacquaint the listener with the music and set the mood for Act 2.

2 - MOMENT OF BETRAYAL

Gabriel immediately tells Arhys the news about his meeting with Nafaryus at the abandoned amphitheater and his plans to rehearse with the

Princess beforehand. He is convinced that this is the opportunity he's been waiting for…a chance to use his gift as a conduit of peace and the means for preventing any further bloodshed of their people and the destruction of Ravenskill.

Gabriel is of course unaware of the plans of betrayal made between his brother and Prince Daryus and he notices that Arhys is acting strange and seems uncharacteristically nervous and uncomfortable. He suspects that it is the safety of his younger brother and the looming threat of attack on their village that he must be concerned about. Regardless, Gabriel leaves to prepare for the big night and Arhys, upon now receiving the information necessary to entrap his brother, contacts Daryus and tells him that he will deliver Gabriel to him that night at Heaven's Cove. Still struggling with his conscience, and not fully trusting the prince's intentions, he tells Daryus that he is secretly meeting his brother there to discuss the final plans for the uprising but does not reveal the information about Gabriel's intended encounter with Lord Nafaryus or his plans to rehearse with the princess. He assures the prince that with only the three of them there, Gabriel will have no chance and that he promises to stand by and let his brother be captured. Afterwards he will tell everyone that he put up a fight to protect him, but to no avail. The prince will be able to present the captured 'Savior' to his father and finally for once, be seen as the hero.

3 - HEAVEN'S COVE

As the pivotal moment approaches on the evening of the third day, the night sky above Heaven's Cove is dark and still with the only light provided being that found in-between the shadows created by the decaying structure under the pale glow of the moonlit sky.

4 - BEGIN AGAIN

Faythe realizes that her life has now taken a new turn and that through her destined relationship with Gabriel, she has been given the opportunity to start anew. She feels that there must be more to life than what she has come to know and that she is somehow meant to fulfill a higher purpose. She dreams of a peaceful world where everyone is given a chance to prosper and where all citizens could be free to follow their desires and express their creativity. She is resolved to use the power of her royal status to champion the changes necessary to realize this vision, and to be the voice of the people as they journey towards justice and equality.

5 - THE PATH THAT DIVIDES

Arhys nervously awaits Prince Daryus and Gabriel at the barren amphitheater for the moment of betrayal that will ultimately lead to his brother's capture. He is completely unaware however that X followed him there and is hiding behind a tree watching with curiously as his father awaits the Prince. Miraculously though, Arhys bravely decides that alas there will be no betrayal tonight…As Prince Daryus comes into view eager to reap the rewards of his crafty plan, Arhys recognizes the same malicious look in his eyes that his father Nafaryus had in the square as he leered at Xander and threatened the people of Ravenskill. It is at that moment that Arhys summons a well of courage and integrity deep within his soul and recalling the message in the words of the song sung by Gabriel in the square only a few days ago…

When you're facing the path that divides
Know that I will be there by your side
Find your strength in the sound of my voice
And you'll know

He declares to Daryus that Gabriel is his blood and he would rather die than betray his brother or his people to which the prince resounds, "Then, tonight you die!"

A fight ensues and although Xander can only make out the twisted shapes in the shadows as the struggle goes on, it is apparent after a final grunt from his father that Daryus has stolen Arhys' last breath and with that he was gone.

6 - MACHINE CHATTER

NOMACS Instrumental

7 - THE WALKING SHADOW

X comes running out of the dark crying and clinging to his father's lifeless body startling Daryus who was unaware that he was present. The prince would have ended the young boy's life right then and there but is suddenly distracted by a dark figure approaching him through the theater's corridor. "Of course!" "It has to be Gabriel arriving for the meeting with his brother," he mutters to himself. He's thinking that now not only will he be the one to capture The Savior, but also to deliver the dead Commander of the Rebel Militia in the same night! As the cloaked figure quickly approaches, Prince Daryus, hiding in the shadows, prepares to attack. When the figure is just about upon him he leaps out of the darkness and unleashes a seemingly deadly strike sure enough to take Gabriel down permanently. However, as if in slow motion, just as his weapon is about to make contact, he comes face to face with the figure and looking into its eyes realizes that it is not Gabriel. It is his sister, Princess Faythe who was on her way into the amphitheater to meet with him! Faythe was unaware of any imminent danger since she was listening to her music player, earphones hidden beneath her hair and hood as usual.

8 - MY LAST FAREWELL

Unfortunately, it is too late. His weapon meets its target and her limp body falls to the ground leaving Daryus standing there utterly in shock and completely horrified over what he has just done. Only seconds too late, Gabriel arrives to see the stunned prince perched over his cherished Faythe who is lying on the ground and left gasping for her final breaths. He stumbles towards her in disbelief almost simultaneously noticing his brother Arhys lying lifeless only feet away with X crying over his father's dead body. At that moment the overwhelming, soul crushing feeling of grief and pain become more than any man could be expected to handle and while covering X's ears, Gabriel unleashes a blood curdling scream straight from the darkest depths of the abyss at a level unsustainable to the human ear.

Faythe is unaffected due to the protection of her earphones but Daryus is not so lucky. The scream shatters the prince's eardrums causing irreversible nerve damage and rendering him hearing-less. He is now doomed to live inside of his own soundless prison with the rest of his lifetime left to lament in a barren wasteland of silence over his despicable actions.

9 - LOSING FAYTHE

At this point Lord Nafaryus and the Empress only a short distance away having heard Gabriel's outcry and wondering who or what could produce such a sound, begin to descend upon the amphitheater along with the Emperor's guards. They cannot believe their eyes when they arrive to see the gruesome scene that just took place…their only daughter, Lord Nafaryus' angelic jewel of his crown, the Princess of G.N.E.A., lying motionless in Gabriel's arms. Their son the prince, blood stained and still clutching at his head, hands over his ears. They both run over to the princess sobbing and pleading God not to take their precious daughter from them. During this time, also curious as to the loud sound that came out of the night and the commotion coming from the usually silent Heaven's Cove, residents from the surrounding area start to gather around Gabriel and Faythe. One, two, three at a time until the entire amphitheater is filled with people both bewildered and traumatized by the events unfolding under the moonlight that night. Lord Nafaryus takes his daughter's body from Gabriel and stroking her hair begins to confess his regrets to her. Through burning tears and a weary voice he apologizes for his stubborn pride and his foolish ego.

He concedes that this is entirely his fault and that none of this would have happened if he weren't so envious of Gabriel and the powers he possesses. She smiles at him as she starts to fade away offering forgiveness with her eyes but her flame is flickering so very faintly at this point and will quickly be extinguished for good. Suddenly, Nafaryus has an epiphany...If Gabriel truly is The Savior as it has been said, then the miraculous healing power of his gift could be used to save the princess' life!

18 - WHISPERS ON THE WIND

He humbly pleads with Gabriel to sing. Sing until the heaven's open up and the grace of God shines down upon his daughter and releases her from the clutches of death. But Gabriel cannot sing. The scream which he bellowed forth upon seeing his dead brother and the fallen princess, the scream which deafened Prince Daryus and alerted everyone in the region of this terrible nightmare they all were experiencing, had rendered his voice useless. He wanted to sing. He tried but was only capable of producing a few scratchy whispers.

11 - HYMN OF A THOUSAND VOICES

All seemed hopeless and futile at that moment but just as Gabriel had predicted that everyone would know what to do when they are called upon, a choir of voices begins to rise from the people gathered in the amphitheater under the moonlight and together they answer the call. They had listened to Gabriel's message and truly taken it to heart and now it was they who were providing the hope and strength needed for him in this grim and seemingly desperate situation. They were the collective beacons of light in the darkness guiding him through the night. As their singing voices grow louder and louder, it is discovered that they themselves are the true revolution. They have given Gabriel the strength and belief he needed to be able to find his voice.

And he does indeed! Music flies out of his vocal chords like beaming rays of light from the sun and it sounds like a chorus of a thousand angels. Nafaryus was right. The beautiful Princess Faythe does, as it happens, open her eyes and is freed from the chains of eternal sleep. At this moment, Gabriel finally knows why he has been given this remarkable gift and why he truly is The Chosen One…Gabriel The Astonishing.

12 - OUR NEW WORLD

Everyone rejoices but there is one very sad and unresolved piece to this complicated puzzle…Gabriel has lost his brother and Xander his father. X is now alone in the world without the loving guidance of his father to protect and nurture him. But this story has always been about fulfilling one's destiny…

It is now clear that together as a new family, Gabriel and Faythe shall be the ones to raise X, and he will not be left to walk through this harsh world alone. Arhys' death was not in vain. He kept his promise to Evangeline of their son one day being a free man and enjoying a prosperous life.

13 - POWER DOWN

Eternally grateful, Lord Nafaryus immediately puts an end to the crusade against Gabriel and the people of Ravenskill and orders his guards to silence the NOMACS for good.

14 - ASTONISHING

The Emperor has listened to the collective voice of his people and promises to govern The Realm as a fair and just leader.

Together with the insightful guidance of his beloved Empress Arabelle, they will lift the restrictions holding back his people and promote free will so that all inhabitants of G.N.E.A. will be given the opportunity to seek a better life for themselves and their families. Aware of the new struggles that Prince Daryus will now face, Gabriel and the Princess agree to offer him their full forgiveness and accept him into their newly united family. He is pardoned by Lord Nafaryus for his crimes who also vows his commitment to the care and protection of his son who will need his father's help as he navigates the hardships of his new handicap. Prince Daryus finally has the love and attention he so desperately yearned for from his father.

Peace has at last been restored to The Empire and the people now pledge their allegiance to a new way of life; A better life where art and creative individualism are celebrated and the astonishing power of music made by humans is treasured and enjoyed by all once again, and so it shall be forever.

FINAL SYNOPSIS

BY
JOHN PETRUCCI

As John has shared, he formalized the story in his own mind and wrote it down as a way of rallying the band to the project and focusing their song-writing efforts. This synopsis was John's final document in articulating the story which would inform the album and the release in general. As noted previously, John gave Peter free reign to deepen character motivations, flesh out the world, and add new people and places to broaden and enrich the story.

Our story takes place in the year 2285…

O ver the course of nearly three hundred years, ever dwindling natural resources coupled with the excessive abuse of presidential power and extreme government-wide corruption has lead to the return of a feudal society throughout the country. This is not necessarily the gleaming, space-exploring future we've grown accustomed to imagine yet instead a dystopian world to come which in many ways resembles more of a time and place back in mankind's harsh history. The margin between rich and poor has widened to a point beyond recovery where ruthless dictators once again rule over vast empires. Along with their families and nobility, they now possess all of the land, wealth, power and control over whatever spoils remain on Earth. Meanwhile, the general population lives in scattered townships across the region struggling to exist amidst a climate of extreme economic and social oppression. The resulting dichotomy between the magnificence and splendor of the big cities and the modesty and simplicity of the decaying rural villages contributes greatly to the division between classes. In this dramatically redefined landscape, what was formerly known as the Northeast region of the United States is now a new super kingdom called G.N.E.A. or The Great Northern Empire Of The Americas. It is in this new land where we find the ominous Lord Nafaryus thriving in his tyrannical role as Emperor and Head of The Realm. From the comfort of his opulent palatial residence on metropolitan New Maineland, he is able to keep a watchful eye on all that transpires throughout the Empire.

Since working class families are now consumed with the day-to-day challenges of survival, forced to bear the lion's share of taxes needed to support the Empire, any dedication, investment or interest in the arts has all but been abandoned. People just don't have the time or the desire to participate in any of the creative forms of human expression that art, dance and especially music have to offer anymore. And, why should they? Life may closely resemble that of more ancient times in most ways, but now, the only music to be heard is electronically manufactured and performed by the Noise Machines better known as NOMACS. They were initially conceived by people in their quest to create the world's most perfect music but instead, turned into something much more insidious. Born out of the vacuum created as a result of the suffocation of human expression along with exponential advances in technology over time, they stand as the only semblance of entertainment remaining in the world. NOMACS music is now the only music anyone knows or listens to, and the only music that still exists. The very soul of what was once real music is now lost in a digital quagmire of emotionless sonic madness.

This brings us to the village of Ravenskill; a small, somewhat isolated town on Endless Isleland located far from the Emperor's palace and the frantic pace of metropolitan living. Ravenskill is a close knit community who's inhabitants enjoy a renewed sense of family due to the simplicity of current times, yet who struggle and toil under the harshness of life's reality under Emperor Nafaryus' rule. It is here where we find our unsuspecting hero Gabriel, increasingly being looked upon as 'The Chosen One' who will liberate the people and lead them in a victorious revolution against Nafaryus and his advocates. He is seen as a shining beacon of light in this seemingly dark and hopeless situation because of a very unique and magical talent that has been neither heard nor nurtured in many, many years…the divine gift of music.

Gabriel was born and blessed with the natural ability to sing and to make music on a level that is simply…astonishing.

Mindlessly programmed to withstand the cold and passionless cacophony of the NOMACS, people are transfixed by Gabriel and transported back to a time where true art created by human beings was celebrated and consumed as the ultimate nourishment for the soul. It is mesmerizing to all who hear him perform and the sound of his voice is as cathartic to those around him as the most advanced medicines available.

So much so that the spirit of hope and enlightenment has overtaken and inspired not only this small township, but also many others in the region. As word spreads of this newly discovered savior, plans for an uprising are brewing and people everywhere are talking about Gabriel's magical power.

Ever so humble and not exactly viewing himself as a natural born leader, all of the attention showered upon him and the tremendous expectations placed on him have made Gabriel very uncomfortable and confused. While blessed with a captivating charm and presence, Gabriel is often puzzled by his uniqueness and largely seen by folks as a bit of an enigma. Although adored by many, he questions his purpose in life and the meaning of his gift ultimately leaving him to feel very alone and isolated. He spends most of his time by himself and is conflicted...why was he The Chosen One? This was not something he asked for but it is obviously something that was meant to happen to him. He embodies the very essence of promise and hope that the inhabitants of Ravenskill cling to and it is he whom they wholly place their belief in. They see something extraordinary in Gabriel and are depending on him to rescue them from hardship and oppression and deliver them their freedom. As he ponders his role in all of this, he yearns for meaning in his life and searches for a path to his destiny, which...he will soon find.

It is Gabriel's older brother Arhys who is his biggest supporter. As Commander of the Ravenskill Rebel Militia, it is his strong belief in Gabriel that fuels the fires of revolution in his eyes. He sees Gabriel as a catalyst for change and the people's one and only appointed guide on the road to freedom. He is convinced it is Gabriel's destiny.

Arhys also has another reason to want to be free of this life of adversity... his eight year old son Xander whom he affectionately calls 'X'. His love for Xander and longing for a better life and secure future for him is what keeps him motivated and willing to push forward with the crusade through these increasingly difficult times. As a single father he carries the memory of X's mother and his only love, Evangeline, with a heavy heart and with deep dedication. Knowing that she would not survive the birth of their son and recounting the life of misery and misfortune she endured, he promises her on her deathbed that he will see to a better future for X and devote the rest of his life to their son's safety, prosperity and ultimately, his freedom. Arhys proceeds to further educate the townspeople of Gabriel's powers and plant the seeds for an uprising amongst them.

Like vines racing across the landscape, news quickly travels throughout the region and talk of Gabriel's increasing popularity and the mysterious gift he possesses eventually reaches Lord Nafaryus himself. The ruler, both intrigued as well as envious of the apparent influence Gabriel has over the people decides to pay the residents of Ravenskill a visit. Concerned, he want's to see what all the hype is about and whether or not Gabriel truly presents a threat to the Empire. He is also aware of the rumblings of a revolution beginning to surface throughout G.N.E.A. and in order to quell any foolish talk of mass rebellion, is prepared to make an example of Gabriel if necessary. Along with his exquisite wife Empress Arabelle, his loyal son Crown Prince Daryus and his daughter, the beautiful Princess Faythe whom he treasures more than life itself, they embark upon their journey to the far-off reaches of The Realm in order to witness first hand what has become known as 'Gabriel's Gift'. Traveling across Eden's Way and over the Emperor's Bridge to Brother's Crossing, they'll ultimately arrive in Ravenskill where they will undoubtedly get to meet this mysterious savior face to face.

In Ravenskill a large crowd has assembled in the town square, as it often does, around Gabriel whom we find playing an old, beat-up relic of an acoustic guitar and singing an uplifting song ironically about believing in who you are and knowing that when your time has come, you will answer the call as it is your destiny. Not only are Arhys, X and all in attendance amazed by the remarkably strange and magnificent instrument he is playing (as they are not used to music coming from anything but machines) but at the same time their souls are lifted up and wonderfully transported by his angelic voice to the point of aural ecstasy. Gabriel's divinely inspired music has a mystical way of penetrating even the most guarded individuals and transcends all generations while reawakening the dormant feelings of passion, power and self worth in anyone who hears it. It is at that moment that Nafaryus and his entourage arrive in the square, startling and alarming the townspeople. Gabriel stops singing and a thick silence falls upon the gathering. Everyone is very aware that they are in the presence of the Emperor and the Imperial Family and the danger associated with that very scenario.

Flanked by his guards, Nafaryus addresses Gabriel saying, "So, this is Gabriel The Astonishing." "Please, do not stop on my account." "Continue as you were."

Arhys responds to him, "We are gathered here in peace my Lord and want no trouble" to which Nafaryus replies, "We are only here to witness for ourselves what we have all heard so much about." "Gabriel's remarkable gift."

After an uncomfortable pause, Prince Daryus looks at Gabriel and with a threatening tone says, "Do as my father says...savior!"

Gabriel knows he has no choice and as he starts to lay his fingers on the guitar, he spots Princess Faythe standing next to the Empress and is absolutely mesmerized.

She is...astonishing.

A vision of delightfulness with a look both enchantingly provocative and innocently demure at the same time, he has never before laid eyes upon anyone quite like her and her inescapable beauty pierces his soul. Gabriel however has not quite captured the princess' attention yet as she is distracted by the scope of her surroundings and completely in awe of the number of people peacefully gathered in the square that afternoon. She is moved by the sense of togetherness and community being displayed before them, all amidst dreadful and practically unbearable living conditions. As a sheltered princess accustomed to the excesses of her palatial life, she is certainly used to seeing any of this. Her heart immediately goes out to them and she is touched by their collective innocence and flickering sense of hope that a better life does exist somewhere out there. Although possessing her father's tenacity and stubbornness, she is very much not aligned with his way of thinking or harsh methods of ruling. In many ways she, like Gabriel, shares the same feelings of isolation often feeling like an outsider in her own home. She is alone, shielded from the bleak world by an over protective father, and longing for a purpose. And also like Gabriel, yearning for meaning in her life and searching for the path to her own destiny.

Gabriel commences playing and starts to sing the words of a deeply moving song. At first sheepishly and then with confidence and passion he sings the lines...

> *When you're facing the path that divides Know that I will*
> *be there by your side*
> *Find your strength in the sound of my voice*
> *And you'll know*
> *Which choice is right*

In an instant, the words strike a very deep chord within Faythe and as if awoken from a spell, the Princess' eyes lock with Gabriel's. Like a lightening bolt from the heavens and without hesitation, they immediately know that they are meant to be together and that this encounter was no accident. It is clear that somehow this moment marked the first step on the path to each other's destiny. Up until now there had only been one thing that she truly connected with which comforted her and gave her hope on the days when she felt most alone. It happened to come from a secret she'd been hiding for years...

As a girl growing up on New Maineland, she was a very curious young woman herself entertained by going on adventures throughout the land. While on one of these journeys she stumbled upon the

Great Hall of Artifacts buried deep within it's underground corridors. It is here that she found something remarkable; an antique digital music player very common during decades past but now deemed obsolete. It was filled with thousands of songs from all sorts of talented artists from a distant time when music was still created and performed by humans. It had a strange engraving on the back that simply said, "To BUG". She didn't know what it meant but that never mattered to her. She carried it with her wherever she went, always being careful to conceal it from those around her, especially her father. Relishing any private opportunity she could get to escape the realities of her cold and shielded imperial life, with her ear phones careful hidden beneath her hair and her hood, she'd lose herself in the beautiful sounds of long ago. Still as a young woman, there is not a day that goes by without her stealing a moment to listen to her prized secret device, the magical vessel that carries her spirit throughout the endless adventures of her imagination. Hearing Gabriel play the guitar and sing with an almost indescribable air of grace and beauty that day is the first time she ever feels such an overwhelming sense of safety and belonging outside of her private rendezvous with her music player.

When the song is finished, the crowd erupts in glorious applause and even Nafaryus, notably moved by Gabriel's song is momentarily caught up in the contagious atmosphere of elation surrounding him. He is quickly brought back to reality however when he notices how Gabriel and the Princess are gazing at each other and immediately shouts out, "Enough!"

Empress Arabelle also catches the two locked in an infatuating stare and a quick glance from Faythe to her mother ensures that she knows the Empress is aware. Sensing that things are quickly about to go very wrong, Arhys has Gabriel obscured from view by his soldiers and swiftly whisked away and out of Nafaryus' sight.

Lord Nafaryus will not tolerate the adoration and allegiance of his people to anyone other than himself and his jealousy of Gabriel's power over the as well as his insecurities about the future of The Empire makes him the need to demonstrate his superiority. He immediately sees Gabriel as a threat to The Realm. The Emperor very smugly addresses Arhys and the townspeople saying that they can hide and protect Gabriel all they want but that he will not stoop to their level and take part of some sort of foolish cat and mouse game in order to find their 'Savior'. He ensures them that 'Gabriel The Astonishing' will come to him willingly and surrender himself in person to his highness or suffer dire consequences. Nafaryus then declares that Gabriel has three days to give himself up and guarantee the disbanding and surrender of the Rebel Militia and cease of all talk of revolution. Staring maliciously at X who is attempting to cower behind his father's back, he continues to state that if 'The Savior' refuses to comply within that time, he will return with his forces, and he will hunt Gabriel down destroying every home one by one and killing every inhabitant until he is captured. And with that terrifying decree, Lord Nafaryus and his entourage depart Ravenskill leaving the stunned villagers to process the gravity of their newfound situation. As they head back to the palace, Princess Faythe is consumed with the vision of Gabriel and their obviously magnetic connection. Still intoxicated by his music, she is obsessed with the overwhelming notion that she must see him again.

Back in Ravenskill Gabriel has gone into hiding and is being protected by Arhys' men. Commander Arhys is convinced that his civilian army combined with the bordering rebel forces in the region is strong enough to protect the town and that there should be no talk of Gabriel's surrender under any circumstances. Gabriel however is severely traumatized by all of this and is questioning the possession of his so called 'gift' now, more than ever. His surrender will clearly mark the end of any possible chance of peace and freedom his people and will also most likely ensure his own demise. How can he that they've worked for, all that they stand for and all they have the other hand, how can he be so selfish as to make his all of the innocent inhabitants of his town? In the cannot shake the vision of Princess Faythe from his memory. He is completely absorbed with the thought of her and entranced by her inescapable beauty. Gabriel has come to a major crossroads in his life and knows that a turning point is imminent.

After returning home to the palace, Princess Faythe realizes that her desire to see Gabriel again is not waning and that she is desperate to be with him no matter what the cost. It is simply something that she can most certainly feel yet cannot explain. She knows instinctually that fate has brought them together and that they both have a higher purpose to fulfill by their union so she makes a plan to return to Ravenskill the next morning. As to not alert the rebels or alarm the locals who may recognize her and think her a threat, she decides it is best to conceal her true identity while traveling outside of the palace. Empress Arabelle, ever in tune with the princess' intentions sees that she is planning this trip and confronts her about it. After seeing the spark of joy and passion in her daughter's eyes as she talks about her feelings for Gabriel; eyes that have been cold and empty for so long, now ablaze with excitement and hope, she knows that the right thing to do is to let her go. She could not possibly deprive Faythe of pursuing her true love. Always the protective mother, the Empress has Prince Daryus secretly follow his sister in order to ensure her safety. Daryus willingly complies but has evil intentions of his own which he is all too eager to carry out.

Upon arriving in Ravenskill on the morning of the second day, the disguised princess asks if anyone knows where she could find Arhys knowing that no one will voluntarily offer up Gabriel's whereabouts and will certainly think of anyone asking as suspicious. Frustrated and exhausted, not really getting anywhere due to high levels of anxiety and vigilance amongst the townspeople, she eventually catches a break. She sees a young boy playing in front of a fountain and recognizes him as Arhys' son Xander. Faythe's gentle nature and sensitively alluring eyes win over the boy's trust almost instantly. She convinces him that she has a way that she can help his father as well as Gabriel if she can just speak to him. Of course, all the while her brother Daryus has been watching her from afar and is now equally equipped with the information required to set his plan in motion.

X innocently leads the princess to the military camp where Arhys is preparing the rebel forces. Faythe takes the Commander aside and very bravely reveals her true identity to him. At first he is immediately tempted to arrest her and hold her as leverage against Nafaryus but she assures him that her intentions are true and that she has a way to end the conflict and restore peace but that she will only share it with Gabriel.

Reluctantly, Arhys eventually agrees and leads her to where Gabriel is being hidden.

Upon seeing each other they embrace and promise never to be separated again. First though, the conflict with Lord Nafaryus needs to be resolved before the three days expire. She tells Gabriel that she is certain she can convince her father to spare him as well as all of Ravenskill and that she has seen a gentle and forgiving side of him before that need only be reignited. Although there is not much time left, she is convinced that through their unity her father will see a way to restore peace to the land and give up his preposterous witch-hunt.

The Princess's words resonate with Gabriel and he remembers how his song in the square temporarily moved Nafaryus the day before. Gabriel is convinced that the absence of art and music and the incessant drivel being spewed out by the NOMACS has caused a sort of emotional hibernation amongst Lord Nafaryus and his supporters, ultimately leading to the deadening of his soul and the lack of any compassion in his heart. If Gabriel could just meet with the Emperor and Empress, he knows that through the power of his magical gift of music, especially with their daughter by his side, he could reawaken their spirits and bring harmony back to The Realm. Nafaryus need only agree to ignore the NOMACS for a moment and just listen. Excited to share this encouraging plan with her father, she returns to the palace to speak to him and convince him to meet with Gabriel.

Meanwhile, still in Ravenskill, Prince Daryus follows Xander on his way home that evening. As X is about to enter his house, Daryus overpowers him and forces his way inside where the devious prince holds the boy hostage and waits for his father to return. Arhys eventually comes home only to find that Daryus has broken in and is now holding X's life in his hands. Recognizing his son's captor to be Prince Daryus and keeping X's safety in mind, he immediately withdraws any efforts to apprehend the prince and instead asks him what he wants. Daryus makes him an offer that will put Arhys in an extremely complicated and life altering position…If Arhys delivers Gabriel to him, Prince Daryus will in return guarantee the safety, protection and prosperity of Xander for the rest of his life. He will enjoy all of the riches The Empire has to offer, the best education and a privileged life equal to that of Nafaryus' own son. He will be in want of nothing for the rest of his life. As he sees it, the choice is easy because either way, they will capture Gabriel in the end. This way, he will be his son's hero. Why is this so important to Daryus? He has lived in the shadow of his father's outward love and adoration of Faythe his entire life. He has been unfairly pushed aside and expected to just 'be a man', 'suck it up' and relinquish any need of parental approval or praise. He could never quite measure up to the Emperor's expectations and is deeply jealous of his father's favoritism shown towards the princess. Daryus sees the successful capture of Gabriel as his opportunity to win over his father's respect and gain the admiration he deserves.

Daryus remains in Ravenskill for the evening and gives Arhys the rest of the night to consider his offer telling him that he expects an answer by morning or the deal is off.

Obviously Arhys has a seemingly insurmountable decision to make. How can he possibly turn his back on his own brother? How can he betray the trust of his soldiers and his fellow people altogether abandoning the plans for revolution they have been working so tirelessly on for years now? Then he remembers the promise he made to Evangeline before she breathed her last breath; to see to the protection and livelihood of their son and to the dedication of his life to X's eventual freedom. After a mostly sleepless night, he concludes that he has no choice and with Xander's best interests in mind, contacts Prince Daryus agreeing to the terms of his offer. He vows to divulge the time and location to Daryus later that day, where the exchange of Gabriel's freedom for the sake of X's future will take place.

That morning Princess Faythe isn't having quite the same luck convincing her father to meet with Gabriel and the unwelcome news of her being in love with 'the enemy' further compounds his unwillingness to cooperate. Nafaryus finds the notion of a meeting both absurd and fruitless since by the start of the next day, his forces will be bearing down upon Ravenskill with all their wrath and fury if her boyfriend, 'The Savior' does not surrender himself as the impostor he truly is. Princess Faythe pleas with him that they only ask for a chance to be listened to without judgment and if the Emperor is not convinced upon the conclusion of Gabriel's message, then he will agree to surrender himself fully and with honor as per Nafaryus' wishes. Perceiving any negotiation as a sign of weakness however, Nafaryus shows no intention of even considering what he views to be his daughter's foolish desires. Faythe is frustrated by her father's ignorance, thick headedness and absence of compassion for the people of his Empire as well as his lack of respect for her feelings. It is then that Empress Arabelle expresses that she's seen enough of this stubbornness between the two of them and enlightens him to the fact that if he doesn't agree to this meeting, his daughter will never forgive him and that he will lose her forever.

"I remember a time when you too possessed Faythe's romantic innocence and passion for life's unexplored mysteries...BUG." says Arabelle to her husband.

It is then that Faythe realizes that the word "BUG" inscribed on the back of her music player was referring to her father and that it once belonged to him!

It had been given to him as a gift by his own father who shared the same secret affinity for music made by humans as Faythe eventually would. As a very young boy, Nafaryus was always zipping in and out of the palace halls and buzzing around his father's feet trying to get the busy Emperor's attention (hence the nickname 'BUG'). The rare times when he wasn't consumed with balancing the many affairs of The Realm, his father would privately submit to the therapeutic bliss of his own secretly kept digital music player, often times inviting young Nafaryus to indulge in these undisclosed soulsoothing escapes. His gift of the music player to his son was his way of letting Nafaryus know that they would always have that special connection no matter how complicated life may eventually get. As time passed however, Nafaryus grew into adulthood and his father the Emperor grew old and tired. The allure of the imminent passing of the crown to the ambitious prince and all of the power and control associated with it far outshadowed the indulgences of some silly music player. In the course of time his father fell ill, eventually passing away and with the rise of the NOMACS drowning out his memory, the music player was discarded by the newly crowned Emperor Nafaryus and ultimately forgotten. Until…now.

For the first time Princess Faythe reveals the secret music player she'd been both relishing and concealing almost her entire life to the Emperor saying, "See father, you also once enjoyed the beauty of real music and not just the garbage of those dreadful NOMACS."

"Where did you get that child?" Shouts Nafaryus to which Faythe responds, "Never mind that." "I am not a child anymore father, I am a woman who doesn't want to be told what to do or who I can or cannot see anymore!" "Now please reach inside your soul and show me that you are not just the heartless dictator you have come to be known as."

Not able to contest the wisdom of neither his wife nor his daughter, Nafaryus concedes, knowing that if he persists, he risks losing the princess forever and so agrees to the meeting. If Gabriel truly is 'The Chosen One' and can sway him as his beloved daughter says he can, then he will cease all plans of attack on Ravenskill and award him his freedom. If not, then he will accept Gabriel's surrender as promised, at which point it will be sure that she will never see him again.

Elated, Princess Faythe immediately shares the news with Gabriel who is still in hiding back at Ravenskill. He tells her that he knows of the perfect neutral location for this summit and that the only way this is ensured to work is if the meeting takes place that evening, under the dance of the stars and the glow of the midnight moon at a once magnificent but since abandoned amphitheater on the edge of town called Heaven's Cove. It is against the dramatic backdrop of a place where music once poured from the lighted stage where Gabriel will best be able to showcase his miraculous musical gift and is sure that once enlightened, there is no way the Emperor will be able to follow through with his plans. As a symbolic gesture of peace Faythe agrees to sing together along with Gabriel so that when her father hears the purity and innocence of love and unity in their combined voices, the fate of their future will be sealed. Aware there is always the chance that the outcome of tonight's events may not turn out as they both desire, Gabriel and Faythe decide it best to meet at Heaven's Cove ahead of time in order to relish what may possibly be their final moments alone together and to rehearse for their performance that evening. Faythe shares the location with her father and later that day Nafaryus and Arabelle begin to make their way to the amphitheater at Heaven's Cove on Endless Isleland, the Emperor outwardly pessimistic and with guards in tow prepared for what he predicts will be Gabriel's surrender.

Gabriel immediately tells Arhys the news about his meeting with Nafaryus at the abandoned amphitheater and his plans to rehearse with the Princess beforehand. He is convinced that this is the opportunity he's been waiting for...a chance to use his gift as a conduit of peace and the means for preventing any further bloodshed of their people and the destruction of Ravenskill. Gabriel is of course unaware of the plans of betrayal made between his brother and Prince Daryus and he notices that Arhys is acting strange and seems uncharacteristically nervous and uncomfortable. He suspects that it is the safety of his younger brother and the looming threat of attack on their village that he must be concerned about. Regardless, Gabriel leaves to prepare for the big night and Arhys, upon now receiving the information necessary to entrap his brother, contacts Daryus and tells him that he will deliver Gabriel to him that night at Heaven's Cove. Still struggling with his conscience, and not fully trusting the prince's intentions, he tells Daryus that he is secretly meeting his brother there to discuss the final plans for the uprising but does not reveal the information about Gabriel's intended encounter with Lord Nafaryus or his plans to rehearse with the princess. He assures the prince that with only the three of them there, Gabriel will have no chance and that he promises to stand by and let his brother be captured. Afterwards he will tell everyone that he put up a fight to protect him, but to no avail. The prince will be able to present the captured 'Savior' to his father and finally for once, be seen as the hero.

As the pivotal moment approaches on the evening of the third day, the night sky above Heaven's Cove is dark and still with the only light provided being that found inbetween the shadows created by the decaying structure under the pale glow of the moonlit sky. Arhys nervously awaits Prince Daryus and Gabriel at the barren amphitheater for the moment of betrayal that will ultimately lead to his brother's capture.

He is completely unaware however that X followed him there and is hiding behind a tree watching with curiously as his father awaits the Prince. Miraculously though, Arhys bravely decides that alas there will be no betrayal tonight...As Prince Daryus comes into view eager to reap the rewards of his crafty plan, Arhys recognizes the same malicious look in his eyes that his father Nafaryus had in the square as he leered at Xander and threatened the people of Ravenskill. It is at that moment that Arhys summons a well of courage and integrity deep within his soul and recalling the message in the words of the song sung by Gabriel in the square only a few days ago...

When you're facing the path that divides
Know that I will be there by your side
Find your strength in the sound of my voice
And you'll know
Which choice is right

He declares to Daryus that Gabriel is his blood and he would rather die than betray his brother or his people to which the prince resounds, "Then, tonight you die!"

A fight ensues and although Xander can only make out the twisted shapes in the shadows as the struggle goes on, it is apparent after a final grunt from his father that Daryus has stolen Arhys' last breath and with that he was gone. X comes running out of the dark crying and clinging to his father's lifeless body startling Daryus who was unaware that he was present. The prince would have ended the young boy's life right then and there but is suddenly distracted by a dark figure approaching him through the theater's corridor. "Of course!" "It has to be Gabriel arriving for the meeting with his brother," he mutters to himself. He's thinking that now not only will he be the one to capture The Savior, but also to deliver the dead Commander of the Rebel Militia in the same night! As the cloaked figure quickly approaches, Prince Daryus, hiding in the shadows, prepares to attack. When the figure is just about upon him he leaps out of the darkness and unleashes a seemingly deadly strike sure enough to take Gabriel down permanently. However, as if in slow motion, just as his weapon is about to make contact, he comes face to face with the figure and looking into its eyes realizes that it is not Gabriel. It is his sister, Princess Faythe who was on her way into the amphitheater to meet with him! Faythe was unaware of any imminent danger since she was listening to her music player, earphones hidden beneath her hair and hood as usual.

Unfortunately, it is too late. His weapon meets its target and her limp body falls to the ground leaving Daryus standing there utterly in shock and completely horrified over what he has just done. Only seconds too late, Gabriel arrives to see the stunned prince perched over his cherished Faythe who is lying on the ground and left gasping for her final breaths. He stumbles towards her in disbelief almost simultaneously noticing his brother Arhys lying lifeless only feet away with X crying over his father's dead body. At that moment the overwhelming, soul crushing feeling of grief and pain become more than any man could be expected to handle and while covering X's ears, Gabriel unleashes a blood curdling scream straight from the darkest depths of the abyss at a level unsustainable to the human ear. Faythe is unaffected due to the protection of her earphones but Daryus is not so lucky. The scream shatters the prince's eardrums causing irreversible nerve damage and rendering him hearing-less. He is now doomed to live inside of his own soundless prison with the rest of his lifetime left to lament in a barren wasteland of silence over his despicable actions.

At this point Lord Nafaryus and the Empress only a short distance away having heard Gabriel's outcry and wondering who or what could produce such a sound, begin to descend upon the amphitheater along with the Emperor's guards. They cannot believe their eyes when they arrive to see the gruesome scene that just took place… their only daughter, Lord Nafaryus' angelic jewel of his crown, the Princess of G.N.E.A., lying motionless in Gabriel's arms. Their son the prince, blood stained and still clutching at his head, hands over his ears. They both run over to the princess sobbing and pleading God not to take their precious daughter from them. During this time, also curious as to the loud sound that came out of the night and the commotion coming from the usually silent Heaven's Cove, residents from the surrounding area start to gather around Gabriel and Faythe. One, two, three at a time until the entire amphitheater is filled with people both bewildered and traumatized by the events unfolding under the moonlight that night. Lord Nafaryus takes his daughter's body from Gabriel and stroking her hair begins to confess his regrets to her. Through burning tears and a weary voice he apologizes for his stubborn pride and his foolish ego. He concedes that this is entirely his fault and that none of this would have happened if he weren't so envious of Gabriel and the powers he possesses. She smiles at him as she starts to fade away offering forgiveness with her eyes but her flame is flickering so very faintly at this point and will quickly be extinguished for good. Suddenly, Nafaryus has an epiphany…If Gabriel truly is The Savior as it has been said, then the miraculous healing power of his gift could be used to save the princess' life!

He humbly pleads with Gabriel to sing. Sing until the heaven's open up and the grace of God shines down upon his daughter and releases her from the clutches of death. But Gabriel cannot sing. The scream which he bellowed forth upon seeing his dead brother and the fallen princess, the scream which deafened Prince Daryus and alerted everyone in the region of this terrible nightmare they all were experiencing, had rendered his voice useless. He wanted to sing. He tried but was only capable of producing a few scratchy whispers. All seemed hopeless and futile at that moment but just as Gabriel had predicted that everyone would know what to do when they are called upon, a choir of voices begins to rise from the people gathered in the amphitheater under the moonlight and together they answer the call. They had listened to Gabriel's message and truly taken it to heart and now it was they who were providing the hope and strength needed for him in this grim and seemingly desperate situation. They were the collective beacons of light in the darkness guiding him through the night. As their singing voices grow louder and louder, it is discovered that they themselves are the true revolution. They have given Gabriel the strength and belief he needed to be able to find his voice. And he does indeed! Music flies out of his vocal chords like beaming rays of light from the sun and it sounds like a chorus of a thousand angels. Nafaryus was right.

The beautiful Princess Faythe does, as it happens, open her eyes and is freed from the chains of eternal sleep. At this moment, Gabriel finally knows why he has been given this remarkable gift and why he truly is The Chosen One...Gabriel The Astonishing.

Everyone rejoices but there is one very sad and unresolved piece to this complicated puzzle...Gabriel has lost his brother and Xander his father. X is now alone in the world without the loving guidance of his father to protect and nurture him. But this story has always been about fulfilling one's destiny...

It is now clear that together as a new family, Gabriel and Faythe shall be the ones to raise X, and he will not be left to walk through this harsh world alone. Arhys' death was not in vain. He kept his promise to Evangeline of their son one day being a free man and enjoying a prosperous life.

Eternally grateful, Lord Nafaryus immediately puts an end to the crusade against Gabriel and the people of Ravenskill and orders his guards to silence the NOMACS for good. He has listened to the collective voice of his people and promises to govern The Realm as a fair and just leader. Together with the insightful guidance of his beloved Empress Arabelle, they will lift the restrictions holding back his people and promote free will so that all inhabitants of G.N.E.A. will be given the opportunity to seek a better life for themselves and their families. Aware of the new struggles that Prince Daryus will now face, Gabriel and the Princess agree to offer him their full forgiveness and accept him into their newly united family. He is pardoned by Lord Nafaryus for his crimes who also vows his commitment to the care and protection of his son who will need his father's help as he navigates the hardships of his new handicap. Prince Daryus finally has the love and attention he so desperately yearned for from his father.

Peace has at last been restored to The Empire and the people now pledge their allegiance to a new way of life; A better life where art and creative individualism are celebrated and the astonishing power of music made by humans is treasured and enjoyed by all once again, and so it shall be forever.

Made in the USA
Middletown, DE
06 April 2019